GRIEVE

Joshua Humphreys was born in Melbourne in 1985. He was
miseducated at La Trobe University where he read Modern
and Ancient History. He spent two years writing and
performing in comedy plays and doing stand-up before
deciding he should be writing novels. So he has spent the last
few years gallivanting around Europe and Southeast Asia. In
2015 he published his first novel, *Waxed Exceeding Mighty*. For
six weeks he smuggled copies of it into London bookstores
and exhorted his readers to steal them. In 2016 he dressed up
as a mermaid and published *Exquisite Hours*. That novel sold
out six print-runs in seven weeks and allowed him to gallivant
with especial vigour. In April of that year, Humphreys
travelled through the former Yugoslavia in search of a magical
sword. He was arrested in Serbia for bedding a shepherdess
and subjected to 48 hours of onion torture. He suffers still
from an irrationally specific fear of Serbian onions. He
introduced adult colouring books to the pencil-despising
mountain people of north-eastern Albania and in Kosovo ate
yoghurt with three heads of state and a goat who owned a
tractor. He did not find the magical sword. In June he went to
Southeast Asia, where he defeated three heads of state
(different ones to the ones he ate yoghurt with) in a
tournament of Laotian arm-wrestling, winning thereby the
title of 'King of The White Elephants.' In late July he travelled
to the Holy Land, where he is said to have beheaded a camel
with one blow of his sword. Not a magical sword. A regular
one. Obviously. In Jordan he met Michael Jordan, and in
Saudi Arabia picked snowberries with Frank Saudi-Arabia and
after working for a time as a Yemeni leopard salesman he was
expelled from the region when he was discovered attempting
to sell jaguars disguised as leopards. He soon had to check
himself into hummus rehab. In August he returned with his
uncle, Mel Gibson, to The Orient. In Burma he and his uncle,
Mel Gibson, learned from a jungle hermit how to make
magical undershirts, and they sell them now, he and his
uncle—Mel Gibson—to extremely stitious Filipino politicians.
When he and Mel Gibson, who is his uncle, tried their hands
at the Vietnamese fish-based martial art of Ca Bong,
Humphreys' uncle, Mel Gibson, was so displeased at being hit

in the belly with a mackerel that they, Joshua and his uncle, Mel Gibson, parted ways. Returning to Europe in September, Humphreys worked for a fortnight as barista to the pope. He was fired for making a lewd joke when His Eminence complained that his cappuccino had too much head. He was convicted in Holland of attempting to read a bedtime story to Mick Jagger and in Malta was tarred and feathered for disrespecting a locally revered squid. For most of October his best friend was a treasure-hunting squirrel called Alexandrina. His hair is not his own; he wears a toupee made of goblins' beards that's said to ward off the bull crap of moon-hugging yoga instructors. Then it was his birthday. He was the chief inspiration for Dustin Hoffman's character in Rain Man. He taught Jack Nicholson how to falcon and has twice worked as Daniel Day Lewis' dialect coach. Draaaaaaaaaiiiinaaaage. His efforts have been integral to the conservation of the Californian Stink Badger. He is the 'other brother' to whom Beyoncé refers in Single Ladies. He is very happily banned from France. And despite his own frequent assertions he is neither the rightful King of Thailand nor the long-lost Doge of Venice. He is currently writing with his uncle, Mel Gibson, an opera based on his gallivanting. He divides his year between Vietnam, Italy, and Melbourne. He would divide it between his heirs, but he has none. *Grieve* IS his ~~eleventy-first~~ third novel.

JOSHUA HUMPHREYS

GRIEVE

a comedy novel

INGROWN BALLOONS

MELBOVRNE   VENICE   BANGKOK

ISBN: 978-1-544-77627-9

Grieve first published by Ingrown Balloons in 2017.
It was written in Siem Reap, London, Melbourne, and Bangkok.
It was licked, smote, shod, inseminated and spread upon toast
—entirely contrary to the above legal warning—in Tajikistan.
Stupid disobedient Tajiks.

Ingrown Balloons supports the European Goblin Fund, the leading
European charity for goblins. All our titles are printed on goblin-free
paper, with little else in mind but the safety and integrity of goblins.
Our paper procurement policy adheres strictly to the
United Nations Declaration of Goblin Rights and can be found at
www.ingrownballoons.com/goblinsareourfuture

Cover artwork by Samuel Humphreys

SAMUELHUMPHREYS.COM

JOSHVAHVMPHREYS.COM

NOTE TO THE ENGLISH EDITION

In 1867 the manuscript of *GRIEVE* was discovered in a cave in Scotland by the renowned Japanese swordsmith, Tiramisu. Awed by the work's nobility, Tiramisu translated it into his own tongue— later into his own language—as *Konushima Grieve: an ancient epic poem in six books*. For decades the book was revered in Japan as a treasury of martial virtue.

After the Second World War, American scholars endeavoured to publish it in its original, only to find the English manuscript had been lost in a noodle fire. With very little accuracy it was translated back from the Japanese and published in 1974 in Los Angeles as *GLIEVE: an of long ago righteousmess poems to the six book*.

GLIEVE somehow found its way into the comedy clubs of West Hollywood, where it quickly gained a reputation as hirarious. Steve Martin called it the funniest book he ever led, Robin Williams kept always a copy in his suit jacket, saying the book never failed to make him raugh out roud.

Larry David, an enthusiastic admirer of the work, funded the research necessary to return it to its original form.

150 years after its discovery it is here published as *GRIEVE*.

It is quite banned in the suburbs which it disparages.

It is very banned in Russia.

C O N T E N T S

I want a hero; an uncommon want.

BYRON

I am different from other men my age. All they want to do is to live happily and die old. I would be willing to live in torture, die tomorrow, if for one day I could be truly great.

PATTON

Mortals falter. Kings act.
And the mortal who acts?
Well that motherfucker becomes king.

POWERS

GRIEVE

THAILAND
CONQVERED

Chapter One

STVPOR MVNDI

1

Few are the occasions for which one takes delight in rising before dawn.

In that unlifted darkness—the not-quite-black and not-quite-grey—cicadas screeched from the infinite trunks of the giant trach trees. A single road cut straight upon the sand of the jungle was to a distant point given by hovering yellow lamplight. A low mist, escaped from the leaf litter, hung still in the clearing between roadside and forest, where soon thieving baboons would with waiting thumbs assemble.

An old woman pedalled gaily on—in silence until she hit a pothole and the bell on her bicycle dinged. Soon she was overtaken by the buzzing of a motorbike drawing a wooden cart, a boy on its edge weighing down with his feet a tarpaulin. A family of five gripped tightly to one another as they whirred past on a scooter. At last the fermata of the insects was met and drowned out by the hurtling of a minivan.

Following though losing ground, a neon-green tuk-tuk conveyed a quartet of Parisians, the children of which had not for days spoken in a congenial voice to the parents. A purple blaze of trailer was overtaken by a red; another van almost slipped its wheels off the asphalt as it overtook both—and in a wooden carriage lined with strips of blue there came slowly up, their faces in their hands and baseball caps at their crowns, three young Australians. Between them two and a half hours' sleep, they had left their fourth, Mark, as a cubist angel on the floor of their hotel bathroom—his limbs at right angles, his halo an orangey-salmony splatter of his national cuisine regurgitated. One of them between his palms growled from his throat: 'Urghhhhh my fucking God.'

Another said, 'What the actual fuck?' as their driver slowed to pull into the queue that had already formed; brought them to an abrupt halt quite further back on the road than he was used to.

'Urghhhhh,' came as three pained groans from behind him.

'We wait OK.'

Shortly they were second-last in the queue; then third as it amassed behind them—soon not even halfway along a still succession of couples long-married and fresh, unseparated of age by alike resentment; of vans of Chinese as sober and indifferent as the day they were soberly and indifferently conceived; of groups of girls on less sleep and more tequila than they.

A short way towards the front of the unmoving procession a pair of Missourans, all night violently feuding over text messages she had found in his phone, had a torch shone at their faces by a man in a powder blue mandarin collar. He spoke to the driver in their own tongue, who gave a warily descending, 'Oooo.' He said, 'Today no visit,' and lowered his torch and walked on to direct his beam at the mullets of a deranged family of Muscovites.

The young man leaned forward and said tersely (he was already made anxious by the realisation that his girlfriend was a mess of hysterical suspicion and insidious snoopery), 'What'd he say?'

'Are they serious?' the young woman snapped, seething at the prospect of spending the rest of her six-week trip, which began yesterday, with a boy who was just like the rest of them and still in touch with that slut from Cancun.

'Oh no,' said the tuk-tuk driver, who did not at all like to bear bad news. 'He say today no visit. Or we maybe can wait.'

'For how long?' said the young woman. 'I want to see the sunrise. We're here to see the sunrise.'

'All right,' said the young man, crossing to the bench closer to the driver.

'Don't All Right me. We're here to see the sunrise. We only *came* to see the sunrise.'

'Will you calm down?'

Her eyebrows soared as her chin sunk. 'You want *me* to calm down? … Ha!' she blurted.

'Meng, did he say how long we have to wait?'

'He say maybe four hour.'

'Four hours!' said the young woman. 'That's just *great,* we'll miss the sunrise!'

'But I think today cannot visit.'

'I don't understand, why can't we visit?'

'Hmmm,' said Meng, pondering.

'Why can't we visit?' said the young woman.

'Calm. Down.'

'Fuck. You. … Meng! Why can't we visit?'

From a long-abandoned path in the forest there emerged a horse.

18

It heaved its shadow of a rider up the dusty bank and clopped slowly along the road's centre, amid then past the established confusion and rising docility of the trail of hopeless tourists.

The heavens turned navy blue over the still-dark earth, the trunks of the trees now at the same ashen shade as their foliage. The rider, a silhouette in dwindling night, sat erect in his saddle with unmoving eyes, his head raised slightly as he passed above the grounded beams of vehicle headlight.

Overhead became a gentle mauve and the ticket inspectors who had formed a line beyond which no tourist would that morning pass were soon able to see in the early light the rider's helmet, its two silver stars, his high black boots glinting in stirrups. His horse was watched with gaping mouth and dumbfounded brow from beneath wooden canopy and through minivan window. As he neared the front of the queue the inspectors beheld in the dawn the rider's beige jodhpurs baggy at the thighs, the seven ribbons at his chest, his riding crop in tan gloves at the reins, his revolvers in shoulder holsters. At last the dull green of his shirt and the shimmering black of his mount's coat rose from the darkness and the inspectors parted as they beheld—two of them for the first time—the proudly weathered face of Hector S. Grieve.

He passed over them a stern glance which quickly turned to an exultant grin. The gently smiling pink which began to speckle the horizon to the east and the temperature, tolerable at so early an hour, both belied the cruelty of the coming day—for of the few occasions for which Hector Grieve took delight in rising before dawn, his favourite by far was bloodshed.

Beyond the floating haze on the waters of a moat, wild lunettes of trach and sugar palm formed a kind of battlement before which Grieve with an undetectable twist of his hips turned Selathoa, his fading black Waler. The smell of charcoal dripped sweetly upon the air; birds whooped in the forest and water-bugs whirred cheerfully below. Hector closed his eyes and raised his face to the sky; opened them to sugar and coconut palms black against the sky.

As he turned north, five budding lotus towers rose distant between the water and the swirling white in the east. Overhead, crimson burned through a tangerine aurora as hooves ascended between two stone lions—the thieving of one of whose heads had twenty years ago been ordered by the French—and the colossal seven-headed snakes which guarded in all directions the causeway.

Long steps descended to the leaden blue of the moat and its lily pads. Bats showed no sign of disturbance as around the sashed Vishnu of their gate the horse and its rider clopped. Then, down onto the dry fields which lay before Angkor Wat.

The ancient path was sentried by sugar palms and faceless nagas. Worn sandstone passed underhoof between flaming libraries and the pools and their bathing monks. Crickets everywhere heralded the coming of the day's warmth as the rose-pink danced around the almond towers at the base of a baby-blue firmament.

Palm shadows stretched long at Selathoa's muzzle. With each step the lotus buds rose further in triumph from the earth. Ahead the outlines of six horses and their six riders loomed high in waiting. The mare gave no hesitation as she ascended the steep wooden steps which rose to the gate of The Age Of Kali—in which the Brahmins are prophesied to be ignorant and the times of darkness, the people enslaved not by other men but by passions that are their own—and Hector Grieve beheld in towering faded colour the five stone peaks of Mount Meru.

He rose slowly between faceless lichen-covered lions (which he with some effort and immoderate casualties had recovered tied down on a boat for Pakse). And there, arrayed before him in perfect formation, their rifles slung at their backs, were the young men of the King Voar Regiment. Perpendicular to them and at a more perfect attention, with a golden aiguillette on his shoulder, was the man known to Grieve by a likeness of charm and hair as Elvis.

Selathoa lowered her muzzle and tapped a single hoofpoint twice on the stone as she was brought to a halt.

Long silence as the tack came to rest.

Grieve looked into the eyes of the men facing him. Creases ran as converging rivers to the white and sparkling aquamarine of his own. He cast a squint to the sun, risen as smelted gold. Its heat was already searing—sweat soaked at his elbows and his sun-blonded eyebrows and at the small of his back. He inhaled deeply through his nose and exhaled long and loud. The steel strip in the butt of his ivory-handled revolver glinted. He tucked his riding crop under his arm and took in the vastness of the building—the two tallest palms at its distant corners, its galleries of spiny laterite black as though dripping with oil. Before this, The City Of The King Of The Angels—that which once counted a hundred and twenty kings under tribute and put into the field an army of five million men, whose wealth was built upon the sapphire feathers of the halcyon kingfisher, a temple indebted for its splendour to the greatness of the Leper King and at whose centre lay the Hall Of A Thousand Gods: its once-gilded towers the work of zealous giants or said even to have built themselves—Hector Grieve's voice sounded small and hollow.

'That the ancient ideals of manhood should not be emulated, is the opinion of the coward who cannot live up to them. This we know. That virtue should not be striven for, is the excuse of those who are not worthy of the striving. Every man has a duty to guard the past, the present, the future of his country. You were born in a place whose name literally means Thailand Conquered. Siem Reap. Born were you, for this day.

'There *are* mightier foes than the Thais. Soldiers whose renown make their defeat the more glorious achievement. But there is no greater delight than the revanquishing of an enemy eternal.

'Today should have been a pre-dawn raid. But we know the Thais are lazy mango-sucking sonsabitches who couldn't organise an orgy in one of their own whorehouses. Eventually they'll come with machines of war, riding beasts of tomorrow to steal your yesterday. We meet them with the highest perfections of nature. We ride paragons of a kingdom more noble even than our own. Until you, the Waler was famous for having pulled off the last successful cavalry charge in history. That history, of mankind's holiest places defended by great men, recommences with you. Nine centuries look down upon you. We fought and drowned when the Cham sailed up the Tonle Sap, we fought and won when Jayavarman the Seventh sent the yellow thieves back to the depraved peninsula whence they came. We were *here* when Chao Sam Phraya sacked Angkor Thom and we laid down our lives for our king then as well. The warrior soul does not perish—for here we stand. By practising the noblest profession of which mankind has ever conceived, you shall live forever—on earth, as in Valhalla.

'They expect us to wait. They expect a siege. But all wars are offensive wars. We attack. We're going to cut the bastards off before they can even see the object of their pagan greed. Through your valour the grass will become our army, through your genius for war we outnumber them by thousands. We're going to cut out their living guts and use them to reshoe our horses; festoon our bedchambers with their blood; the fury of our tempest will scatter the sons of Siam!

'Today we go to preserve our heritage. Today to heighten our glory. With heritage and glory, no man's life may be called small.

When talent is paired with resolve triumph is inevitable. The end, is glorious; the striving cannot but be worth it.

'Do not take counsel of your fears. God favours the brave. Victory is to the audacious.

'Chahik si chahiks. Men of men. Let's ride.'

Grieve pulled hard at the reins and turned Selathoa about. She descended to the searing fields of yellow grass and along the avenue of spiny palms Hector kicked her to a canter.

Flanked by the dusty green of the low jungle the King Voar regiment thundered at a gallop back across the grey stone of the causeway, between the stagnant marigold of the moat and a brutally azure sky.

2

Through the dry forest on the hillside which rose to the ruined pyramid of Phnom Bakheng, Hector Grieve looked down over the silent battleground on which Operation Honeysuckle was to take place. Of flat and open fields dotted with tall bushes and lone sugar palms, it was in late November luscious enough to perfectly serve his order of battle. Two kilometres west of Angkor Wat he saw through binoculars three of his men waiting in the scorching sun, watching as mounted sentinels to the northwest. He turned his shoulders to the right, and the forested horizon. Still nothing.

'Time?' he said to Elvis.

He was putting his jacket down on a crumbling stone wall. 'Eight o'clock, sir.'

'Two hours,' said Grieve. 'Lazy sons o' bitches.'

'Not at all Cambodian.'

'Their tanks'll cook them in this heat,' said Grieve, looking to the long patch of green ground to the west, and to the copse above his men. 'Phnongs,'

'Phnongs indeed, sir.'

Then the dust rose.

High in the distance three plumes billowed to form a beige cloud. 'Three,' said Grieve. 'M-41s.'

'Just as you said, sir.'

'Here we go.' His men were already trotting.

The three riders spread out their advance, seemingly to take on each a tank. When the machines reached the trees whose passing was their signal to attack they kicked to a gallop and their horses raced on. Shortly the first soldier broke his line and bolted right.

Somnang 'Groucho' Wales. The name he held at the orphanage; the name bestowed upon him by the regiment, the name he chose for himself upon passing King Voar training—a year-long ordeal of horsemanship, toughness, and elocution. Wales he selected after the exemplary outlaw, Josey. Groucho he was given partly because his disposition was grumpily un-Cambodian, partly because he was once caught painting onto his face in lieu of the facial hair which his people cannot grow, a moustache. His shoulder tattoo—which each successful recruit chose and was given at their induction banquet—was that of the screaming Eastwood poster, upon which when intoxicated beyond his waking brain's capacity the regiment always drew a thick line of greasepaint.

Groucho's horse pounded into the dirt as he outflanked the rumbling easternmost tank, keeping his line until the turret followed him, then the tank itself—the cue for the second rider to break.

Porn 'Risotto' Skywalker. Orphaned as a two-year old and interred by his village, having grown up on his own country's bland incarnation of rice he was in Grieve's mess hall so astounded by what the Italians did with it that within two months of his discovery his uniform would not fit and no horse could under him gallop. Newly chubby, the regiment pounced and the name stuck. Skywalker he selected because his resolution to lose the weight exactly coincided with his first viewing of *The Empire Strikes Back.* Luke's apprenticeship, and in particular his master's dictum, 'Do or do not. There is no try,' had seen him through both his diet and his training; his tattoo was of the exhausted padawan with Yoda in his backpack.

Risotto broke to chase after Groucho and their sprint drew their target precisely as far as was needed. The tank's full speed meant that when it hit the rice field which they had in the night ploughed and waterlogged it flew so far into the mire that its gun stuck, fatally, into the mud. The rear ports pointed skyward. The riders stalked round to wait at its back corners.

'Its arse is in the air,' said Grieve, grinning as he and Elvis looked to one another from their binoculars. 'Like a Kiwi in a leisure centre.'

Its engine was restarted and the tracks ran in reverse as desperately and as loudly as they could. Mud streamed back between the horses. Groucho and Risotto looked calmly to one another as machine guns fired urgently from the ports. They unslung their MP5s and pointed them up at the hatch. It was soon opened. The first Thai, in his black uniform, got it. Groucho, who had served three years longer than Risotto, nodded and the latter walked his mount to the tank's lifted rear and hopped on. In one hand he took two grenades from his belt; pulled their pins and rolled them down the waist of the dead soldier and pushed the body in after them. He jumped back onto his horse and both soldiers drew back and waited to see if the clunk of the explosion would leave them with anyone else to dispatch. Black smoke puffed out of its orifices as the third rider broke left.

Teng 'Pangolin' Tomhanks. Softly spoken at school and always kind to his carers, whether it was his widely set eyes or the curvature of his neck or his insistence on sporting a scaly-looking haircut—and probably a combination of all three—he just looked like a pangolin, that ancient and harmless creature by the world's stupidity endangered. He chose his last name because in training it had been pointed out to him that every one of his favourite movies starred the same actor. He was at first disbelieving. Only after the putting of two televisions side by side and the freeze-framing of two close-ups could Pangolin be convinced that the same man was both Viktor Navorski and Captain Miller. Pleasantly surprised and instantly adoring, his tattoo was of Woody from *Toy Story*, about whose voicing he still had his doubts.

Two Walker Bulldogs rolled loudly on and Pangolin rounded a patch of bushes. He reappeared at the western tank's flank and began to launch grenades at it as he rode. The tank turned to meet him head on and quickly ran into the long strip of pasture that had been soaked in order to slow it down. Pangolin turned about and galloped in retreat at three-quarter pace, turning in his saddle to lob grenades at its left as he fled westwards. As it trudged further from its invading line a tuk-tuk sped from the cover of the copse in which it had been concealed. Its driver sped to draw up beside the steel behemoth.

Oudom 'KFC' Samcolt. The sisters at his orphanage had rescued the very young tuk-tuk driver from that uniquely Cambodian mafia by presenting to Hector Grieve a display of his uncanny driving abilities—pleaded that his skill as a driver would translate to riding prowess—and ambivalently he was accepted. He chose Samcolt because his favourite gun was the 1894 Winchester, which he thought was designed by Samuel Colt. At his induction banquet he mistook an image of Colonel Sanders for a likeness of the inventor and the erroneous tattoo was too good an opportunity for the regiment's wit to ignore. So he became KFC. Though determined in his reasoning, KFC was often mistaken in his nomenclature.

By the modified controls at his thumbtips he launched a rocket from beneath the camouflage of the tuk-tuk's canopy. It hit with a great and accurate clunk the tank's rear. The machine ignored Pangolin and veered left. KFC turned to match its line. The turret began to swing towards him and he fired another rocket with what was once his scooter's horn. On impact the tank's left track momentarily left the ground and its gun was rendered immovable. Then KFC's third rocket hit almost the same spot. The tank jolted to a stop. Black smoke spouted furiously from the cannon's end and a violent stripe of flame blew the hatch off and erupted in diminishing bursts until only a flicker blew in the wind. Soon not a sound could be heard from the new tomb.

'Holy shit!' said Grieve, exhilarated by the ferocity of the blast.

'You ever seen that before?' said Elvis.

'Never,' said Grieve as they moved their binoculars to the final target. 'That's some Normandy shit right there.'

The last tank, unbroken from its line, hurtled on. Between it and the road which led to the devatas in the Hall Of A Thousand Gods there stood nothing but a few towering palm trunks and a patch of high grass.

Leap 'Jerusalem' Dvarapala. Though the amputee uncles of the newest and youngest King Voar could not afford to take care of him, he had spent his weekends away from the orphanage riding—at first on water buffalo, then on an ageing mare which they inherited from another village—out into the fields to help his extended family plow and herd. In training he spent most of his free time studying the lives and campaigns of Godfrey de Bouillon and Guy de Lusignan and the various Tancreds of Hauteville. Free from any defects of vanity and apparently unmockable by the jest of his regiment, they bestowed upon him the nickname, Jerusalem. At graduation he chose Dvarapala, Khmer for 'Defender of Holy Places,' and his left arm was tattooed with the lotus-crowned guardian from the temple of Banteay Kdei with its broadsword pointed between its feet.

As the last tank neared the swathe of high grass Jerusalem gave a loud 'Hya.' His horse lifted its head and kicked its legs up and rose from the ground. He went almost instantly from concealment to a gallop. Jerusalem charged at full speed.

'He is a magnificent soldier,' said Grieve. 'Have a look at him!

Stupor Mundi. The wonder of the fucking world.'

'He'll make a fine captain,' said Elvis.

'I reckon so.'

The cannon raised to firing angle and Jerusalem veered left. As the turret turned to follow him he pulled his horse hard right; he sunk with its front legs as it obeyed. Under unceasing machine gun fire they galloped at forty-five degrees to the tank's line. They passed the steel monster and Jerusalem pulled his horse hard left to come round behind it. He put the reins in one hand and pulled a sticky bomb from his saddlebag. With his teeth he peeled back its wrapper; as he closed in he pulled its fuse. He reached down to plant it on the tank's right track and pulled the reins as hard as he could. The stallion skidded desperately to a halt then reared. The bomb rounded the drive sprocket and exploded. The track pinged and banged apart and the tank creaked to an eerie stop.

Jerusalem pointed his SA80 at the hatch. He could hear behind him the thundering of his regiment racing to join him. He dismounted. With his rifle poised nervously he stepped up onto the armoured behemoth. He heard the hatch being unlocked as he stood over it. Slowly and slightly it was raised. A corner of white cloth emerged—as the door was pushed to upright it revealed itself as a flag. A wooden pole was raised as the King Voars formed an arc at the tank's rear. A hand emerged, then the black-capped head of a Thai soldier, the wrinkles of his face blackened with smoke and dust. He stepped up onto the hull and held an open palm as far from the white flag as it would go.

'Where'd you get a flagpole from?' said Jerusalem.

The surrenderer lowered his head and spoke with some urgency in his own tongue. Jerusalem shook his head in disdainful pity.

'They came willing to surrender,' said Grieve. 'So they failed.'

The Thai lifted his head and raised a single finger then pointed it down to the hatch. Presently there emerged the supplicating hands of a second soldier.

Jerusalem looked his prisoner in the eyes and said, 'You've got a bee on your hat.' He slapped him upside the head and his black cap, with embroidered silver shield over a curved white sword, fell into dust. Jerusalem commandeered it then kicked this first captive from the tank and pulled the second up by the shirt.

KFC and Pangolin took the prisoner's sidearm and handcuffed his wrists to the tuk-tuk. The second lowered his open palms to his back to prepare for restraint. As Jerusalem turned him for cuffing he yelled, 'Grenade!' and kicked the Thai as hard as he could towards the open hatch. He leapt from the hull and before his feet hit the ground the bang of an explosion blew all dust from the tank and sent him face first into the dirt. Three machine guns and one Winchester 1894 opened fire through the cloud of sand and smoke. Bullets clunked and ricocheted into and from the steel armour, cracking and echoing in massive booms out over the battlefield.

3

The tap of a thin cymbal in the darkness.

Its tinking of a slow beat.

A bamboo xylophone skipping and tumbling as a water nymph upon river stones, a small flute flittering sweetly in the clouds above it.

Then a golden crown in a spotlight, flaming towards three golden discs and their three golden towers, a garland of white frangipani dangling at its side. Perfectly still, a wrist and two big eyes and the fullest red lips of a girl's tilted head.

Into the light she stepped, from the gilded lotus brocade of an emerald curtain. Her outcurved fingers and sharply pointed thumb were held as an orchid fixed in the air. The music picked up; she rolled and turned her head upon a golden-embroidered collar. Her silver skirt shimmered at her bent knees as with the beat she put one bare foot in front of the other—lowered the orchid to the other at her stomach and wafted both about her body as hypnotic white smoke.

Soon the music rushed and the stage lights came up. Ten brightly dressed dancers scampered out to kneel behind her. At one beat the bamboo and the cymbals stopped. The lone dancer held her delicate pose. Then an instrument which sounded like a snake-charmer at a bagpipe began to wail. The kneeling girls swayed at the waist. She turned to them and they wafted to their feet. The bamboo and the cymbals came frolicking back and all danced together as Apsaras, delighting nymphs of the clouds and the waters.

In the front corner of the banquet hall a quintet of blind musicians sat cross-legged in pants of blue silk. Beyond the room's iron-framed French doors a white balustrade looked out over the unlit Siem Reap river. Khmer letters in signage of neon red and yellow surrounded a giant blue-lit kapok tree dripping with vine.

Before the old market bridge two high billboards erected by the Cambodian People's Party glowed with the backlit faces of Ear Sohtireak, Governor of Siem Reap Province, and General Hun Monirith, commander in charge of Region Four of the Royal Cambodian Army—between both of whom Hector Grieve was sitting, his white-flecked bronze hair spiking naturally across his high hair line, grinning as he smoked a Cohiba at the head of a table.

Upon the u-shaped arrangement a feast had already been laid. Pol Roger, etna rosso, marsala; pecorino and aged caciocavallo; little bowls of truffle oil and plates of prosciutto nebrodi and canteloupe, tarocco oranges and cannoli; frutte martorane of pomegranate, watermelon, cherries, grapes, figs.

Beside Grieve was Jerusalem, his cheek red from the grazes which sliding across dry soil will give to the face, his shoulder a little sore, the black brim of his captured hat folded to a bend and pushed high and loose upon his head. To Jerusalem's left was Meak Sakona, head of the Department Of Safeguarding And Preservation Of Monuments, and Pangolin and Risotto, gorging. Opposite them—Elvis, Groucho, and KFC.

Each man was eyed in a carefully orchestrated hierarchy by an Apsara as she danced. The girls in less-refined costume smiled at the soldiers in their dinner dress (of red sampot and army green jacket over beige shirt and darker tie) and the flirtation worked its way up to the head nymph who had only to smirk at General Monirith.

Hector Grieve's banquets were for his chief sponsors occasions of prolonged pleasure.

The screeching flute held a single high note as the lights went down. The lesser dancers paraded around to form a line and turned their shapely backs to the tables. They shuffled towards the darkness of the curtain; all but the head Apsara disappeared. Her face too slowly receded into black before the flute whistled its climactic note down to silence.

The men applauded proudly as the room's lights came up. Teak fans whirled fast and silent overhead, potted ferns bowing in their warm wind. Grieve tapped his coupe and rose from the table; the clapping soon subsided. All smiled as they hurried to overfill their glasses.

'Here's to the finest regiment of gentlemanly sonsabitches that an officer could hope for.' He held his glass to the men on his left and to those on his right and all present drank. 'It is my privilege to command you and my privilege to watch you grow into men. And it's my privilege to not only watch you perform the glorious and most ancient duties of a soldier, but to join you in doing so when the battle calls for it. Today, no such call was sounded. I drink to the day when next it will be.' All followed him. 'Each order was carried out in the field not only with perfect precision but with exceptional audacity. I give special mention to Jerusalem, for his bravery and his horsemanship. Take the hat off, Jerusalem. Here.' Hector took the cap from his head and poured foaming Pol Roger into it. He lifted it to Jerusalem's mouth, who turned it sideways and drank from its dripping cloth. The rest of the room drank to him. 'And it is my even greater privilege, indeed my supreme honour, to serve this fine country, with its especially ancient traditions of war, religion, and beauty.' To this all said, 'Choul mouy,' and drank very deeply.

Then Hector Grieve, who had had eight bottles of beer and the better part of a bottle of Pol Roger, slowed in order to be careful with his words. Beside him were his two most crucial allies in Cambodia. Allies, for such as Hector Grieve are apt to incur enemies, and in enemies did Hector Grieve happily abound. Love and money had secured his position of unique favour among Siem Reap's most powerful men: at Governor Ear Sohtireak's feet he had presented his sweetheart.

(Two days before it was to take place, Grieve invited Ear to the first ever banquet that he would give—a feast prepared with no doubt as to the outcome of its prefatory campaign. They with General Monorith drank to celebrate the day Hector set fire to the patch of jungle through which a Chinese-funded caravan was headed for Bayon—their aim, to put on a plane for Shanghai not one but three of its two hundred faces of Lokesvar, embodiment of compassion; drank to celebrate the day he with Elvis and Groucho waited on the banks of the Great Western Lake beside the village that had supplied the raiders with oxen and carts; drank to celebrate the day they rode out to intercept the retreating caravan before it reached the airport and captured from their oxcart perches twelve stone-faceless and smoke-inhaled Tumpoons dressed as Korean tourists.

Hector clapped for the Apsara dancers to return to the room and Ear, after a bottle each of Hankey Bannister and nero d'avola, erupted into a gruff rage when the head dancer bounced into his lap and tickled his earlobe.

The following morning he invited Grieve to tea and apologised for the outburst—gave him his tentative blessing as a protector of his beloved culture—and told him of Bophadevi.

Ear had grown up in the village beside hers, had played with her in the street dirt, had watched her at high school with besotted eyes as she grew into a woman, proposed marriage after months of walking hand-in-hand by the river at dusk—was heartbroken when she told him she had been accepted as a dance student; inconsolable when she rejected him in favour of Phnom Penh and the Cambodian Royal Ballet. The discipline required of her meant that for years Ear got word of Bophadevi only through newspapers. As the ballet recovered from the exterminations of the cultural revolution she became international news as lead Apsara in the company's first tour of Europe. The week of Grieve's inaugural banquet she was bound for the performing centres of North America.

'And you still love her?' said Grieve. Ear gave a forlorn nod.

So Hector flew to San Francisco and attended the ballet and backstage wielded his simplistic but often profound knowledge of the motivations of human action. By the words of a well-meaning though very manipulative love letter translated and handwritten by Elvis he convinced Bophadevi to return to Cambodia.

After debriefing him on the contents of his note, a week later Grieve presented at Governor Ear Sohtireak's feet his sweetheart. She had borne him three children and taught Apsara at the Royal College in Siem Reap.

Thusly, love.)

Hector turned to his right and looked down to Ear and grinned and raised his glass again. 'It is my great privilege to be a mere apostrophe to the hard work of this country's finest administrators. The wealth and stability which the Cambodian People's Party has brought to all of us here, and to the Khmer people, are truly astonishing. We protect the past, Governor Sohtireak builds the present and secures the future. We drink to him. Choul Mouy.' All downed and refilled their champagne.

'And to my very good friend Hun Monirith,' said Grieve, turning to his left—for love *and* money had secured his position of unique favour and at General Monirith's feet he had laid nine bars of gold bullion.

(On his second self-assigned mission as a soldier of fortune Grieve with Elvis—then his only confederate—picked off from the trees with night-vision and sniper rifles a party of villager mercenaries whom he had gotten word were to make an attempt on a frieze of devas at Ta Prohm. Before he had even had a chance to start up his stone saw one of the Cambodians, bleeding from his right lung, was interrogated and told Elvis of the bag of gold waiting as their reward in the hands of a Swiss antiquities dealer in Thailand. They trailered their horses and sped for the border.

Crossing on horseback at dawn, fortuitously they struck upon the clearing wherein the dealer's light plane awaited. They bribed the forest rangers guarding its runway and slashed its tyres. When eventually the dealer realised that his frieze was not forthcoming he was escorted back to his plane by a guard of Siamese rosewood poachers. These barely managed to fumble for their guns as Hector and Elvis broke from the tree line with six-shooters firing.

With a Smith & Wesson No. 3 to his head the Swiss uncuffed the briefcase from his wrist and he and his pilot watched Hector and Elvis discuss the gold's fate and their own.

'We keep it,' said Elvis. 'Think of what we can buy with ten gold bars. New guns. Better horses.'

'We give any indication of wealth and Monirith will think we're profiteering. He'll want in or he'll cut us out.'

'We keep half. We give him half, tell him that was all there was.'

'And how are we going to turn five gold bars into cash without him finding out? You know anyone who can move gold bars in Siem Reap? How much are these things worth?'

'I don't know. And no, I don't know anyone. You're right.'

'We give it all to him. We get trust, we get the full support of the army.'

'And what about them?'

Hector looked to the plane—the pilot in his seat, the Swiss with one foot on the step up to the cockpit. 'We kill them.'

'They're Europeans,' said Elvis. 'International news.'

'Two Europeans found dead in a light plane at the Thai-Cambodian border? Smugglers, no question. Or drug-runners. The Thais won't bat an eyelid.'

'The Cambodians'll cop heat for it, that comes onto us.'

'We let them go then,' said Hector. 'They won't tell anyone. You won't tell anyone will you?'

'Of course not,' said the Swiss. 'Ze gold is not mine. I don't care about eet. Today never happened.'

'He won't tell anyone,' said Grieve, shaking his head and frowning sarcastically. He and Elvis reloaded from the bandoliers at their shoulders.

'So they don't tell anyone, we give all the gold to Monirith, and today never happened, right?'

'Today never apponned,' said Grieve when all twelve chambers were filled. They spun the barrels and flicked them into place and Hector lifted his arm to shoot one and Elvis lifted his to shoot through the windscreen the other.

Early that evening Grieve placed at General Monirith's feet nine gold bars.

Thusly, money.)

All reraised their glasses with Hector.

'By providing the men and the means, and the support by which we operate,' said Grieve, really laying it on, for none of these did the army supply—demanding a hundred percent of all booty taken in Cambodia and repaying him only with his house and the freedom of the city of Siem Reap. 'You do your country and yourself a great honour. We are proud to serve as a branch in your army. I am proud to serve as a general in that army. And we look forward to a long future of together bringing greater glory to the people of Cambodia. Choul Mouy,' and new bottles had to be opened around the table.

'And last but by no means least, to the true protectors of the ancient city of Angkor. To the Department of Safeguarding and Preservation of Monuments, without whose cooperation none of our noble work could be done.'

(It was by the hopelessly corrupt staff of Meak Sakona's Siem Reap headquarters, and the cruel methods by which Mr Sakona manipulated that staff, that Hector Grieve got his scarce operational intelligence. Though he had done Meak no monetary or amorous favour theirs was a thoroughly mutually beneficial relationship. Hector was blind and deaf without the ministry's gossip and the ministry could receive none of their funding without taking credit for the operations carried out by Hector Grieve—allowed to exist outwardly in Siem Reap only as a well-off and benevolent expatriate.)

'Mr Sakona, we thank you. Cambodia thanks you.' All downed another full measure of champagne and Hector at last said, 'Let's eat!'

From the kitchen was wheeled a roasted pig turning slowly upon a spit—coals at its side, a silver tray catching its juices. Grieve had earlier that day bestowed the honour of slaughtering the animal upon Jerusalem, whose rise from the earth to alone charge a tank had impressed the whole regiment. Six years younger than Groucho, Jerusalem had earned the coveted King Voar honour only a week after coming of military age. The regiment conveyed the caged sow to his village and to holy music presented him with the sacrificial dagger. Surrounded by his fellow soldiers he set upon the animal in its pen and opened its throat.

'To the King Voar regiment,' said Grieve, loudly. All stood from their chairs and raised their glasses and drank with each call. 'To the Cambodian People's Party. … To The Royal Cambodian Army. … To the Department of Safeguarding and Preservation of Monuments. … To Siem Reap, Thailand Conquered. … And to Cambodia.'

Each man now took a large swig from a bottle and spat Pol Roger into the centre of the room as though breathing lustral fire. From speakers there sounded loudly a metallic sort of clapping with chirping alarm calls behind it. The captured Thai was led out by a chain at his neck, in high heels and black leotard.

General Monirith growled at him: 'Dance.'

The prisoner stood shyly in the spotlight with his knees together.

'Dance!' insisted the General as Beyoncé's voice called out.

'I no know,' said the Thai.

'Dance to Single Ladies!'

'I no know Single Lady.'

'Everybody knows Single Ladies.'

Reluctantly at first, then with rising enthusiasm as his bashfulness left him—soon with remarkable panache—the captive soldier slapped at his thigh and pointed to his wriggling fingers upon his rotating wrist and bent forward to pound his fists at his feet as he flailed back his head—and he danced to *Single Ladies*.

'Encore!' laughed the crowd as they clapped cigars and champagne bottles together in applause. The prisoner closed his eyes and dropped his head to his heaving chest.

'Encore!' they repeated with threatening vehemence. The Thai shook his drooping head. The song started up again and the clapping ceased. 'Encore,' they most of them insisted. The exhausted captive sighed. Eventually he decided that though he was quite out of breath an encore of *Single Ladies* was much the better option than the probable alternative of execution. So he gave them one.

The Apsara girls returned and giggled into the laps of the men to whom Elvis had assigned them. As the prisoner of war danced on two chefs came out with long knives and cleavers. Waiters brought baskets of bread and bowls of salad. The chefs carved.

Then the men began really to feast, and to chant and to yell, and to revel.

4

Through the entrance hall of Victoria House (so Grieve called his residence, though no Cambodian had ever referred to it as such) the prelude to *The Rhinegold* flowed on loop according to Hector's instructions, for by it did he wish to triumph his way to bed.

His formal boots, identical to his riding except of immaculately polished tan calfskin, echoed over red and yellow marble as he strode through the centre of a blurry star—formed by the frosted yellow of the lanterns, one point overhead, two level with his eyes, all reflected in the shining tiles. It seemed in the haze of the ten bottles of beer and two of Pol Roger—and a half of his special Cambodian whisky—a particularly divine star, and Hector stopped to take it all in. He smiled tranquilly in the golden glow of the home for which he had a rare personal fondness.

He drew aside the mosquito net covering the teak four-poster bed in the guest bedroom and put one knee onto the mattress and whispered, 'Are you awake?'

A single desk lantern lit the room in amber. Christy's arms were wrapped around a pillow. She moaned and said with a tired huskiness, 'That depends. How many men did you kill today?'

'Only you could pick a fight while you're half asleep,' said Hector as he knelt over her.

'Better a fight than a war. I'm just asking a question, you're the murderer.'

'Don't call me that.'

'But you *are* one.'

'Shut up and kiss me.'

She did, on the cheek, and said, 'So how many kids did you orphan?'

'Without orphans,' he whispered, '*you'd* have nothing to do in Cambodia, my hot little dear.'

'I long for the day.' Hector sat on the bed's edge and took off his boots. Christy held tighter the pillow in her arms and rolled further from him. 'You stink.'

'You stink. And what's wrong with being an orphan? You've seen what I do with orphans. If it weren't for me they'd be eating each other's livers in battle.'

'If it weren't for you there wouldn't be any battles for them to be eating livers *in*. You turn them into killing machines.'

'I turn them into men, which is more than I can say for most fathers.'

'You're ridiculous.'

'I've told you not to call me that.'

'I've told you not to wake me up with a hard on when you come home covered in blood. You *are* ridiculous.'

'The world's ridiculous. I'm its only hope.'

'Its only hope is drunk.'

'Its only hope,' said Grieve, putting the front of his thighs to that astounding firmness of behind which almost alone saved Christy's sardonic tongue from expulsion, 'is there.'

Christy moaned and repeated that Hector stank. He kissed her neck and she closed it to him. 'Tell me how many orphans and I might wake up.'

'Enough…' he said, putting his hand at her hip and squeezing, 'to keep people like you away from California.'

'What do you mean, People like me?'

'Hot,' he said, running his bottom lip up the smoothness of her shoulder. 'Sexy,' he said, and pushed her chest firmly into the mattress. 'Joyless,' and he reached in to enclose her breast, 'provincial celebrities like you.' He gripped her panther-black hair at the scalp. 'With a weakness for cute little brown smiles.' He turned her onto her back and into the eyes which he often told her were the most beautiful he had ever seen, and to the face whose unique mix of cute- and lustfulness were raised a hundredfold by evening light, he said, 'And an empty life made less so by parentless children and dangerous men.'

She rolled her head slowly from side to side, whispering every other time that her face was straight on to his: 'Boys. … Ridiculous. … Australian. …' She skipped a pass before finishing the sentence: 'Boys.'

He pushed his face against hers and breathed into her mouth and she let him between her legs.

Covered in sweat they made love, though it was Wednesday, for the seventh time that week.

HOLY SWORD

1

Built as an infirmary by the French in 1931, what was now called by its sole occupant Victoria House overlooked the lawns and white lamp posts of the Royal Gardens of Siem Reap.

Two cream 1931 Citroën C6s, one soft top and one hard, with black running boards and wheel hubs—both at Grieve's disposal—faced one another in the morning sun before the palm-shaded portico which ascended to the dull blonde of the marble-floored entrance hall.

Wooden fans hung at rest above young potted ferns; interwar telephones sat upon new iron pedestals; short-legged water cauldrons floated with arrangements of white spider lily. A stream ran in front of both wings, fed from above by white drainpipes, their spouts moulded as Roman fish, its length swimming with carp and koi and stalked by two pairs of Siamese crocodile. It ran out at both ends to rows of tall and thin jungle trees, their trunks draped with vine, giving the villa a shade of privacy and a little quiet from the surrounding streets.

An antique iron lift serviced slowly and noisily the three floors of the house. Around each storey ran a wide and low verandah arcaded in straw-yellow concrete and littered with teak furniture and pairs of rattan deck chairs. Its niches were dotted with Khmer artefacts, some of them quite priceless, for centuries kept by villages as talismans until bestowed upon Hector Grieve as tokens of gratitude for saving from greater and foreign destruction the edifices of national and spiritual pride from which they had been looted.

From speakers in the hall between the facing ground-floor kitchen and dining room a peaceful Cambodian voice sang softly over her bamboo xylophone. Beyond, the entrance opened out to a vast atrium. Beneath an arch of palm leaves steps descended to the still waters of the ultramarine swimming pool that was the house's serene centrepiece. Surrounded on three sides by wooden decking and white sun umbrellas, the pool was filtered by a cascade trickling over a high slate wall lushly planted for fragrance with frangipani and rumduol.

Back before the steps, an outdoor dining deck overlooked it all. Shaded by high retractable cloth, a long and heavy dining table ran between the French doors of the kitchen and a screen of tall ferns, among which pairs of black and blue butterflies flew vortices in the springtime.

At the end of the table closer to the pool a coffee cup sat in a saucer, two sugar cubes resting in a teaspoon. A small jug of milk was beside a bowl of unsweetened muesli; a glass; a knife, three forks, and a bread plate resting on a wooden placemat. Three English-language newspapers were folded to the left of all this and to its right a notepad and black pen. It was here that Hector Grieve took his breakfast, here that Hector Grieve liked very much to read the journalistic speculations about his achievements, here that after eating he composed epitaphs in blank verse on things he held dear.

At each corner of this floor-fan-cooled space a Cambodian police officer was stationed with his back to the dining table. In silken brown trousers and green collarless shirt, each had a curved and unsheathed sword tucked into the silken scarves tied as belts around his waist.

Hector Grieve emerged from the jungled gardens and paper lanterns of the path which descended from the western wing. He crossed the pool deck to ascend, in his golden-collared yukata of red silk—embroidered all over in blue with the mythical horned beast from which his regiment took its name—to his breakfast.

Though today, most peculiarly, the officers stood also with their backs to a young woman sipping at the last of her iced coffee, Hector sat at his table with neither curious word nor interrupting glance. A sweat-soaked white shirt stuck at the front of the woman's hunched shoulders; a brown fringe dripped with perspiration onto unsmooth skin.

Hector put the two sugar cubes in the coffee cup and placed the pen onto the notepad. As he waited for his Bialetti he looked over *The Phnom Penh Post*—its front page graced with a photograph of the charred Walker Bulldog, the headline: '5 Thais Dead: King Voar Existence Still Denied.' A servant emerged from the dining room with Grieve's coffee and his fruit plate. 'Music, sir?'

'Mmm,' said Grieve in a high tone, as though the request had caught him pleasantly off guard. He looked to the door and said, 'Umm… Beethoven. Sixth.'

He gave the coughed 'Ahem' that was the signal for one of the guards to about turn and taste his coffee. As the man blew at the steaming hot cup three soprano voices began: '*Rheingold! Rheingold! Reines Gold!*' He looked to the dining room. Still they lamented: '*Falsch und feig ist was dort oben sich freut*,' until the servant realised his mistake and rushed to cut the maidens off at the stereo. Hector looked up at the morning's taster. When satisfied that he had survived the drink he took it from him and looked over the front page of *The Cambodia Daily*. It at least had the decency to put his official media portrait on its cover.

The first movement's opening came rolling on and Hector dolloped some yoghurt onto his cantaloupe. He stirred and jabbed with a fork and passed his melon to the morning's taster. He took up the second fork and began his breakfast as he read the second paper's report. It gave tacit support to Operation Honeysuckle though it condemned its bloodshed, which Hector thought minimal considering that all bodies were confined to the tanks in which they had invaded a foreign country. He looked up and stared at the end of the table as though it were, as it should have been, vacant. He folded his arms and stared and briefly squinted an eye. Eventually he brushed with his hands the front of his hair across his head. His plate of bacon, eggs, and raw onion was placed in front of him. He eyed the unfamiliar servant who had conveyed it then grabbed his wrist. Grieve rotated the plate, cut off a corner containing each of its ingredients and handed him the tasting fork. When the servant neither suffocated nor died Hector Grieve sat forward and began composing his own forkfuls.

The glass of the unsettlingly present young woman was refilled by a servant with a hand at his back. Hector leaned away from the table and turned to look upon the guard at his right shoulder, then him at his left. Again he with arms folded stared straight ahead. He clenched his jaw. He dislodged with his tongue a chunk of bacon from between his top left molars. As the third movement began (he had had the second movement removed from his recording for being 'as dull as a meadow of Frenchmen.') he with a finger signalled to the kitchen for another plate. Almost immediately a third and fourth egg were brought with identical accompaniments. It was tasted; he ran his knife through its yolk.

'Mr Grieve,' a feeble and inquisitive voice called from the far end of the table.

Hector slammed down his cutlery.

'Mr Grieve,' repeated the barely feminine voice in a more adamant tone. Hector sliced and jabbed and composed with redoubled tenacity. '*Mr Grieve*,' the young woman shouted, thinking that perhaps she might have gone by lack of volume unheard.

Grieve reslammed his silverware and shouted at his plate: 'General! Grieve. I am General Grieve.'

'General. I'm sorry.'

He retook up his cutlery and put a full rasher of bacon into his mouth. He chewed and nodded with enjoyment and shortly pulled with his fingers a length of too-soft rind from between his lips.

'General Grieve.'

At last he looked at her.

'My name's Carla.'

'I *don't...*' He shook his head. 'Give a Bulgarian rabbit's fuck.'

'I'm here on behalf of Fasolt & Fafner.'

'And who precisely the rapey dolphins… are Fasolt & Fafner?'

'Your family accountants, Hector.'

'*If* you possess the vile contemptuousness to without invitation intrude upon my breakfast then you *will* scrape together the politeness to address me by my proper title. Or are you so Australian? I am General Hector Grieve.'

'Your family accountants, General Grieve.'

'Those balding effeminate hookworms. What do they want?'

'They can no longer extend your line of credit.'

'Impossible. Of course they can.'

'They can't and they won't. Effective the moment I have informed you of the fact.'

'And why the rarely washed testicles not?'

Carla unzipped the folder at her elbow and withdrew from it a single sheet of paper. 'I've taken a flight that has given me quite enough time to look over your spending, General Grieve. … Two crates of Sicilian wine, at nine hundred dollars a crate. A box of Sicilian oranges at three hundred dollars a crate. Three wheels of caciocavallo cheese, at two thousand five hundred dollars a wheel. Two legs of prosciutto nebrodi…'

'Will you stop pronouncing Italian like that? God damn it, you sound like a forklift driver trying to sing opera.'

'…at five hundred dollars a leg.'

'What the fartstorming fuck is your point, shrewperson?'

'And here, I mean… three crates of Pol Roger, at eight hundred dollars a crate.'

'Pol Roger,' said Hector. 'Not Paul Roger, you fucking simpleton. You know I'd almost forgotten about you people? And I was *happy*.'

'Then four thousand dollars in incidental expenses. That's just for one month, and in US dollars. They're even higher in AUD. What could possibly incur incidental expenses of four thousand American dollars, in one month, Hector?'

'General Grieve.'

'You live here for free, I'm led to understand.'

'What do you want again?'

'Mr Grieve, you're broke.'

'Bull-shit,' he chimed with dismissal.

'Mr Grieve,' she said, looking at him with blank sternness, 'you are broke.'

'General Grieve.'

'General Grieve, you are broke.'

'Impossible.'

'The Japanese are no longer buying your book.'

'Good.'

'And Fasolt & Fafner will not be extending your credit any longer. Now we need to know what is incurring incidental *monthly* expenses of five thousand three hundred and sixty-one Australian dollars. If you or we get audited, we need to know what to tell the ATO.'

'What about my father?'

'Broker than you are, Hector.'

'Impossible.'

'I suggest you find a different word, Mr Grieve.'

'General.'

'A word that's a more accurate representation of reality. You're broke. The Japanese are no longer reading your book and your barbaric spending habits have more than bankrupted you.'

'Barbaric? I'll tell you what's barbaric. Your face. The common man. Democracy. Modern medicine, is barbaric. Because it keeps accountants like you alive, when really you should have died in adolescence from a terminal case of being as boring as a busload of Canadians. Did you make an appointment to see me?'

'I spent a week trying to get through to you in order to make one.'

'Goo-ood,' Grieve smiled. 'That *does* mean that I won't see you. Guards!' he snarled and they turned in and surrounded her.

'Can I make an appointment?'

'I take all my appointments by letter. And I don't open my own mail. And none of my servants speak English. Have your request written up in Khmer and once it's been translated and conveyed to me I'll check my diary. Get rid of her.'

A hand was placed at her elbow and she rose and reinserted her sheet of paper into its folder.

'Mr Grieve, you really are being stupid about this,' she said as she was escorted the length of the table.

'Of course I'll have to *buy* a diary first. Then I'm going to fill in the next six months with things I'd rather do than see you. In early February I'll have a festival of day-long enemas. Then I'm going to stroll the slums of Bangalore bare-arsed with Chum under my nuts trying to give the street dogs a fright. In May I think I'll have a course of chemotherapy—that'll be more fun than looking at your face—to cure the cancer I'm going to get from all of April's banging in the fields of gay Chernobyl.'

'Mr Grieve, you mention chemotherapy…'

'Cured, I'll go to New Zealand in June, and chat up the local women. Even that should be less excruciating than listening to you speak.'

'Mr Grieve, you're *very* rude.'

At this Hector Grieve grinned and shook his head. He turned to her and said, grinning even wider, 'War is hell,' and watched the woman's escort disappear into the hall behind him.

He picked up a length of crispy bacon and chomped it in half and threw the rest into his egg yolk. He stared furiously at his breakfast interrupted. Then he looked to the far end of the table. Shortly he put the plate in the palm of his hand and stood up and flung it against the wall of the dining room. With a bang it was shattered and its lukewarm contents thoroughly dispersed.

'Real mature,' said Christy, arrived to breakfast in her silvery blue bathrobe.

Grieve whipped his infuriated face to her. The end of his nose appeared to turn downwards, the corners of his frown to reach almost to his chin; his eyes bulged and the right corner of his right eyebrow shot almost to his hairline. Christy said, 'Jesus,' at just how infuriated it was. He growled and almost snarled. He heaved sharp deep breaths. And shortly he stormed past her face with an erect finger and left her to breakfast alone.

2

Grieve strode out from the porch of Victoria House into the yellow light of blazing heat. The door to the soft-top Citroën was opened by his driver. In badgeless green shirt and khaki tie tucked between his second and third buttons he lifted a boot onto the running board and tapped at the top of the door with a gloved hand.

He was driven beside the slime green of the dribbling Siem Reap river to the Department of Safeguarding and Preservation of Monuments—a compound fenced with high walls of moisture-stained ochre concrete stuck with rusting iron spikes. Cicadas were unceasing in their maddening rattle. Blue and red Cambodian banners overhung from poles beneath a mess of power lines—a decorative perimeter encircling grounds shaded and almost cooled by trees towering and full. The red iron gates were pulled back for his car. Grieve's driver eased around the main stilted building of white weatherboards and came to the stables.

Loung, the regiment's stableman, had already presented himself before the day yard, where were tethered the eight Walers currently maintained at Hector's expense. Loung was, as usual, beaming with pride. The horses of the King Voar regiment were his life's chiefest pleasure. The few hours he each day spent with them he cherished in sunlit opposition to the drudgery of his full-time job—groomsman to the king's Siem Reap stables. The three excuses kept rideable for the enjoyment of the young princesses would, in any horse-loving country, have been called Gluestick, Gelatine, and Frozen Lasagne. The royal daughters of Cambodia called them Donut, Mermaid, and Rainbow. When occasionally they rode the pitiable beasts they did so for a brief time and sadistically. But Grieve's Walers… Grieve's Walers were such animals as to frequently occasion, at the risk of a public beating, the smiling neglect of Loung's royal duties. He stayed with them for as long as possible before he had to walk to the king's stables to prepare the almost-ponies just in case the princesses felt like going for an after-school ride.

'Report,' said Grieve as he reached Loung. He was thrilled beside the muzzle of Comanche—christened by Grieve, as were all his horses, upon importation into Cambodia.

'Not a scratch, sir,' said Loung, who in order to secure the auxiliary role had been required to take Grieve's elocution course. 'Not a single one skin-deep scratch.'

'Good,' said Grieve, stepping into the hay and putting his bare hand at Comanche's bay cheek. He pulled at Black Jack's bridle and hopped the fence to run his hand over the length of Marengo's back. He tapped at Pie-O-My's back leg and inspected her left hoof, then her right. He came to slap Nigger's shoulder and swung himself under his head to stand eye to eye with Augereau. 'How are his knees? Jerusalem put him through quite a bit yesterday.'

'He was tight in the front when I took him out this morning, sir, but I'll swim him later on. He'll be fine.'

'And his coat? No ticks?'

'I've brushed him twice sir, all over. Inspected his coat from back to front. He was covered in burrs but I assure you, sir, even his anus is tick free. Absolutely.'

Grieve turned his chin to Loung while keeping his far eye and his forehead back from him. 'Why did you check its anus?'

'You've got to be thorough, sir. Tick heaven, the anus. Warm. Comfortable.'

'Warm and comfortable?'

'Oh yes, sir!' said Loung with a strange enthusiasm. 'Feel right at home up there they do.'

'Loung?'

'Sir?'

'Don't inspect the horses' anuses.'

'Ani, sir, is the plural of anus.'

'No it isn't. Don't inspect their anuses. And if you absolutely must, for whatever personal reason, don't tell me about it.'

'Of course, sir. … So is it true? What Jerusalem did?'

Grieve moved on to stroke Blue, whom Christy was presently riding. 'It's true.' Then his own beloved Selathoa.

'The regiment's first captain?'

He slapped at her shoulder and brushed a hand over her withers. 'How are we girl?' He put his nose to her cheek and took in fully her familiar scent of chocolate dust. He fed her carrots from his pockets as he stroked her nose. 'There's a good girl.' He said to Loung, 'We shall see,' and left him to take tea on the department's verandah.

Meak Sakona walked out to meet him in white shirt, loose trousers and leather sandals. They reclined beneath two ceiling fans on the dark decking. Meak poured, and then offered a plate of the little coconut macaroons for which he knew Hector had a soft spot.

'How's the head?'

'Mightily sore,' said Meak.

'Monirith had a good time.'

'Still asleep I'm told.'

43

'And the heat?'

'All mine, General. I've been on the phone with Phnom Penh all morning and they said Thailand's going to give them a week of it but then they'll back off. Their king's just died and they'll use this as a distraction against the democracists. The men you killed weren't enlisted soldiers, they were mercenaries who'd bought police uniforms in Surin, so we're all right. They're not happy about the pictures in the papers but they know we'd never fire on a Thai soldier.'

'Oh wouldn't we?' Grieve smiled. '*Good* macaroons today,' and he took another.

'I'll tell Sothea.'

'How is she?'

'Very well. The hospital's getting a new oncology wing. Thanks to you.'

'And the sunrise?'

'A bit blank at the moment. A cousin of one of the secretaries has a whisper of some Frogs for Banteay Srei. But it has not risen yet.'

'Banteay Srei,' reflected Hector. He lifted his jaw and stroked his chin with the backs of his fingers. 'That's good. Open ground. Out of the way of the tourists. Squeeze her for more?'

'I'm looking into a friendship she has with one of the archaeologists at the EFEO.'

'Good, Meak. Good.' Grieve slapped his riding crop at the arm of his chair and was driven to the Terrasse des Elephants to sit at coffee rereading Turenne. Five minutes earlier than usual Elvis arrived by car.

They drank picon bière and ordered aiguillettes de poulet paneés à la poudre d'amande.

'Elvis, is there anywhere where our standing is ahh... temporarily secure?'

'How do you mean, General?'

'Anyone whose sun might be setting?'

'Sir?'

'Anyone we can hold back from?'

'Hold back what from, sir?'

Squinting down from the third-storey balcony at a traffic of mopeds and minivans, through high coconut palms to the fruit shake girls and the grilled meat ladies and the waiting tuk-tuks—at last across to the pink walls and cobalt windows of the Bank Of

Cambodia building which towered above everything, Grieve said, 'Money.'

'Oh. That.'

'Yes. That.'

'Well, the chief of police has that corruption lawsuit in the papers. He needs it more than ever. Apart from that...' Elvis shook his head. 'Is everything all right?'

'What about the monks?'

'The last time we tried to negotiate with them the Maha Nikaya threatened to turn the Young Monks against us. The Great Joyful Proclaimer will have them denounce us as barangs preaching imperialist invasion. We can't have it, we'll be done.'

'Racist pricks. The Ministry of Social Affairs? Come on. They can't still be objecting to the training programs. Our boys have the highest employment rates out there.'

'They know what their orphans are worth, General, and you employ six of us.'

Hector sighed and drank deeply from his beer mug. 'Shit.'

'*Is* everything all right, Hector?'

'Oh yes,' said Grieve, clearly irritated. 'Someone's breathing down my neck about fucking money.'

'We can't take care of them? ... Do they have backing? ... We've done it before.'

Grieve clasped his hands together and put his elbows on the table. He lowered his chin to his thumb and stroked at his bottom lip. Then he stood up and flung his beer mug across the street, smashing a cobalt window. 'I can't go back.' He pointed down at Elvis and the table. 'I'm unhappy there.'

At four his car took him to The Hope For Asian Children orphanage. Elvis met him with Selathoa and Blue and he and Christy rode north to Angkor as the sun lowered in the sky.

Hector and Christy walked the horses through the copper sand beyond the eastern gate of Banteay Kdei, already closed to tourists. Limbless musicians chuckled with one another in their open hut as they packed up their instruments. The women selling scarves and elephant trousers and the men selling paintings all stopped packing up their stalls in order to harass the latecomers. Chickens pecked at the feet of the singhas guarding the Hall of Dancers as insects whirred in the forest. The dropping sun was broiling through the dry leaf and a lone sugar palm. The pair rode before the laterite halls, their spines falling with dusk to darkest black, and entered the splendidly ruinous labyrinth of the temple's inner enclosure.

In their saddles they lowered their heads beneath a collapsing arch and walked the horses along an avenue of purple and ochre and green stone, a topless colonnade of square column, past smiling Apsaras in their greening niches of three-pointed arch and lintels of Kala, Devourer Of All Things; stepped over the roots of the enormous spung tree which crushed the western wall. Grieve showed Christy the niche which contained the guardian gracing Jerusalem's shoulder, then the view from the rear of the complex—the five jade-green towers amid the enormous cream trunks and sprawling mammoth roots of the trees, all of it soaking in the red light of hot dusk.

They ascended the stone platform before Srah Srang, with its sugar palm and stone lions and serpent balustrades. They looked out over the shirtless children playing in long boats in the bog. A smokeless white haze descended on thin islands of faded-green algae. Behind them the sun between the trees became molten orange sunken into a band of ochre, lifting to white and disappearing blue. As they rounded the lake the sun, its brightness unchanged, sat among the colour of ash and first Christy, then Hector, rose to a canter then raced at a gallop by the water's edge, chased by children shrieking barefoot and laughing on rickety bicycles.

They chatted with the kids who normally pestered tourists to buy fridge magnets and warm cans of beer. They screamed and squeaked and reached for Hector's revolvers. He unholstered his ivory-handled Colt Single Action Army.

'Don't give the gun to the kids,' said Christy, slowly pleading.

Hector emptied its cylinder of bullets and grinned and spun it on his finger and flicked around its handle and passed it down to a girl wearing a t-shirt that said, 'I Love My Family.'

All pretended to shoot one another, making 'pkew' sounds with their teeth. It was snatched from child to child as Grieve and Christy rode on.

The shoulders of their horses rose and fell before a vast blanket of rose dust sprinkled in the sky beside a tiny sun. A white zebu strolled through the sluice beneath them with its back to the sunset, reflected all in pink and yellow beneath the forest in argent water. As darkness continued its ascent a boat of children in jeans and soccer jerseys slapped gently onto the muddy shore and began to call for Hector by name. Her shirt unbuttoned to cleavage,

Christy smiled at him from her black saddle. Extensions glued to her eyelashes made her look sublimely exotic. Hector beheld in the evening light that hundredfold raising of her unique mix of cute-and lustfulness.

'You're the most beautiful thing I've ever seen, do you know that?'

'Shut *up*,' she said and kicked the stirrups into Blue's sides to hasten him to a gallop. Hector reholstered his revolver from the lifted hand of one of the boys and gave Christy a quarter of the baray as a head start. He kicked at Selathoa and growled, 'Hya!' He caught her up as they passed silhouette children fishing with bamboo rods in the silvery waters. They quickly came into sight of the hard-top Citroën. Elvis in riding uniform stood waiting to take the horses.

Grieve kept a gloveless hand at Christy's knee as they passed the last of the camera-lugging tourists holding onto the neon insides of their tuk-tuks.

'Tell me something about you I don't know.'

Hector said, 'No.'

'Come on! Tell me about where you're from. Tell me about Melbourne.'

'What about it?'

'Will you ever go back?'

'Not if I can fucking help it.'

'Why not?'

'I'm not happy there. You tell me more about California. Where are you from exactly?'

'Temecula.'

'Oh yes, the place that sounds like a disease. Doctor, I have temecula.'

'Don't you have family?'

'Of course I have family.'

'Tell me about them.'

'Why?' said Grieve, almost growling in opposition to her pestering.

'What do you mean, Why?'

'I've told you before. You know exactly as much about me that is necessary to know.'

'I know exactly as much about *General* Grieve that's necessary for me to know,' she said, saying his name with the deliberate twang and manic roll of the head which she affected when she was being sarcastic. 'What about Hector? What's your mom's name?' He pleaded with her to please stop asking questions. 'Why? Come on, you know my mom's name.'

'That's because I've seen pictures of her, and she's hot.'

'So tell me your goddam mom's name.'

'My mum's name was Anne.'

'Was?'

'Mmm,' said Grieve, grinning momentarily at her.

'I'm sorry.'

'Mm.'

The car turned at Angkor Wat's moat and overhead the sky was as a dawn—returned as light blue with one massive orange and mauve cloud, its width and colossal length given sharply by its edges, glowing red as though heated by fire.

'What about friends?' she said after a time.

'What about them?'

'Do you have any?' she droned, tired of playing teeth-puller to Grieve's biographical mouth.

'Of course I have friends!'

'And what are they like?!'

'They're fun!'

'What kind of fun!?'

'Fun fun! Wild fun. Drinking fun, picking up girls fun!'

'Good!'

'Good! Now what else do you want to goddam know?'

'When was the last time you *saw* any of your friends and family?'

But Grieve's driver was already pulling in at the Charles de Gaulle corner of the royal gardens. Christy sang, *Fun, Fun, Fun,* as she stepped out of the car. Grieve took from its boot two large water pistols and handed her one.

'What's this for?'

'What do you think?'

Hector stepped up into a waiting tuk-tuk. Its driver hit a button and *Bad Moon Rising* started loudly from speakers flush with the canopy.

The riverside was alive with the glurping of frogs and the beeping of car horns—its thin tree trunks coiled with fairy lights, the white French-Khmer lamp posts and their white light, the modern restaurants set quietly back from the street, the town and its bridges neon and short in the distance. Hector casually pumped the handle of his water gun and raised it discreetly to soak the one-way traffic of tuk-tuks conveying tourists to and from their dinner.

He wet a Japanese couple, who after inspecting their chests put their hands in the air and opened their eyes and mouths wide with shock. Hector and Christy laughed and re-enacted their goofy surprise as they were driven on. Then Christy joined, pinging a middle-aged German couple who from their tuk-tuk scowled and waggled a finger and said, 'Nein.'

'They were *so* mad,' said Christy grinning and chuckling and waggling her own finger in derision. They passed before the Christmas lights in the gardens of The Riviera and both opened fire on a wrinkled and golden-haired couple smooching beneath their canopy. They smiled and the male said, 'She bloody wet me,' as they rounded a roundabout.

At a red light Hector thanked the driver and they hopped out of the tuk-tuk. Two Cambodian children on a scooter spied the lowered plastic weapons and smiled and pointed at their driving mother. Hector shook his head with a smile and they nodded theirs and Christy wet them all and they giggled as the light turned green.

They crossed the river and collaborated in raining springwater upon a gaggle of Australian girls, two of whom whined very loudly that now they had to go home and restraighten their hair. Before the covered wooden bridge three legless musicians were poised upon a mat, their traditional combination of bongo, khim, and tro scenting the air with a peacefully ancient calm. Over the water Grieve called to Locust, cross-legged on a mat before silver trays brimming with oily food.

'Locust, this is Christy.'

'What the fuck are they?' she said, instantly panicked. She grabbed Grieve's arm as she looked upon what was being offered.

Locust recited to her his English menu as he pointed to his trays. 'Chilli cockroach. Salted grasshopper. *Very* good. The grilled water bug is cooked in fish sauce. We have deep-fried tarantula, scorpions and lemongrass, and ginger silk worms. For you I think, ginger silk worms.'

'No, not for me! Definitely not for me. Thank you though. Locust?'

'Locust was a King Voar,' said Grieve. 'The men called him Locust because it's the only bug he won't eat. Isn't that right?'

'The locust is a plague animal. What we eat, we are. The last thing I remember my mother telling me.'

'Everything good, soldier? How's the shoulder?'

Christy noticed that while the young man was gesticulating with his left hand his right arm lay still at his side.

'Look…' Locust slowly raised his elbow to forty-five degrees from his body. 'The physio said I'll get it all the way up in a few months.' He put his left hand at his shoulder as he relowered his arm. 'I saw Operation Honeysuckle in the papers.'

'You're not supposed to know its name.'

'I don't know its name, sir. Operation what? Only, Pangolin passed by for a chat.'

'Did he?'

'Mum's the word. Congratulations. It's true what Jerusalem did?'

'It's true.'

'The regiment's first captain?'

'We'll see. You have a good night, Locust.'

'You too, sir. Nice to meet you, Christy.'

'Nice to meet you too,' she said, almost laughing as she shivered and again recoiled from the creatures at her feet.

Hector lowered a palm at his back as they turned to leave. Locust lunged forward to put into it a tarantula.

'You see what you do to these people? Crippled bug salesmen.'

'Locust chose to become a soldier. His brothers all sold bugs, he didn't want to. And he was injured in the line of duty and gets a pension from us four times what he would earn working in a Western hotel.' Hector reached silently behind her and placed the deep-fried spider on her shoulder. She looked up at him and he raised his eyebrows, ready to accept the impending acknowledgment of the undeniable good that he had done the young man. Then his face went blank and he bulged his eyes a little as he looked around to her shoulder. 'What's that?'

'What's what?' she said, trying to look at her back. She turned her head the other way. The instant she saw against the white of her shirt the oily black figure that was to her primordially recognisable as an arachnid, she screamed. She brushed furiously at her shoulder and doubled over and sprinted ahead a few steps. She stamped her feet and spun as she recovered from the outburst. Then she raised the nozzle of her water pistol and smirked and emptied its tank at Grieve's face. He walked calmly towards her and opened his mouth; she moved her aim towards it and he held his arms out from his body then wrapped them around her and pushed his face against hers. She brought her elbows to her chest and put her fingers at his cheeks and they kissed.

50

'Let's do it,' she said.

'Let's do it?'

'I can get all my stuff shipped over. If you're sure.'

'I'm always sure.'

'Then let's do it,' she smiled and nodded. 'On two conditions.'

'*Two*?' he smiled. 'You're going to dictate terms to *me*?'

'Mm hm.'

'Then what are they?'

'You'll call me Sook.'

'Your Asian name?'

'You'll call me Sook, and you'll wear a helmet when you're riding.'

'Like fuck I will. I agree to the first one, Sook. The second's an act of cowardice. Are we doing it?'

'We're doing it!' Christy smiled the largest smile that Hector had yet seen her give and she closed her eyes and raised herself onto her toes and kissed him again. Grieve shot water down the back of her jeans and she shrieked and they laughed against one another's mouths.

3

The courtyard of l'Indochine is at night one of those Southeast Asian edifices, increasingly few in number, which make one feel as though one is walking through an opioid memory.

Beyond two white stone singhas the headlights of a 1937 Citroën greet diners at the open iron gates like eyes above cheeks of polished ivory wheelhub. Lights in the stone-tiled floor lead to a staircase beside a waterfall. Ascending as though to the firmament, its snowy iron balustrade is lit by fairylights burning as orange fireflies in the peacock trees which seclude the restaurant from earthly eyes. Single strings of tiny lights hang from the unlocatable ceiling—sparkling manna sent slowly to fall as consolation.

It was this evening a dreamlike scene shattered for Hector Grieve by the presence of his delectably ejected breakfast guest.

'What the ffff—' said Grieve as he saw her at the foot of the stairs. 'Fuck!? Are you fucking kidding me? How?'

'You're a predictable man, Mr Grieve.'

'Well you're a pterodactyl and a man. So…'

With Christy's hand in his he went up to the restaurant.

'Good evening, General,' said Kolab, the owner and maître d'. 'Your usual table?'

'Kolab, do me a favour.'

'Anything for you, General.'

'There's an Australian thing at the foot of the stairs. A woman maybe. Do *not* let her into the restaurant.'

'Of course, sir.' Kolab spoke in Khmer to two waitresses who escorted Grieve and Christy to the corner of the teak Chinese porch which looked through palm leaves over the street.

'Who's she?' said Christy, nestling into a wicker armchair.

'She's no one. I hate her.'

'You hate her? She can't be no one if you hate her.' Christy read through the wine list. 'What is she, your ex?'

'Ha! She fucking wishes. She's no one, don't worry. Now, tell me again how good this new new life of ours is going to be.'

'Why don't *you* tell me about why you never want to go home?'

'I've told you. I'm unhappy there. Now… our new new life.'

'But why are you unhappy there?'

'Do you promise never to become an uninspiring person?'

'What does that even mean?'

Presently the Australian thing came to be sitting at the table beside theirs.

'This is fucking why. Kolab!' Grieve snapped. 'God damn it, Kolab! I told you not to let her up here.'

'I am very sorry, sir,' he said, and returned immediately to his podium by the landing.

'Kolab!? … What the fuck!?' Hector made with menus a wall between their table and hers.

'Mr Grieve.'

Christy read her own and said, 'Thank God no Sicilian food.'

'Kolab takes care of everything. You don't need a menu.'

'I've never really understood. Why Sicily?'

'Why Sicily? I was there.'

'Mr Grieve.'

'You've been to Sicily?'

'Many times. I was at Himera. The siege of Palermo. I was with Guiscard at Dyrrhachium and took Taormina from the Muslims with Roger the First. And of course, at Gela and the liberation of Messina.'

'What *are* you talking about?'

'I was there,' Hector grinned.

'Gela?'

'The battle of Gela. Operation Husky.'

'What's that?'

'World War Two was the defining moment of my life.'

Still the next table persisted. 'Mr Grieve, we need to talk.'

Hector stared with a clenched jaw out into street, glistening with newly commenced rain. 'Kolab!' he called out to it. 'Kolab, you come here now.' Kolab presented himself. 'Kolab,' Hector pleaded. 'Kindly ask this thing to leave.'

Kolab made to begin shaking his head. 'Sir…'

'Kolab, have I or have I not found two of your daughters husbands?'

'Sir,' sighed Kolab as Carla placed a five-dollar bill in his breast pocket.

Grieve inhaled with shock. 'Kolab!' he exhaled. 'I have *twice* settled disputes with your neighbours that neither the monks nor the elders would settle in your favour. *Have* I not?'

Kolab, clearly fretting, vacillated between the tables. A five-dollar bill was slid into his breast pocket and he looked to the sky and said, 'You have, sir, but…'

'Don't you Sir me. Kolab. I have had you and your wife for dinner at my home. My home! I send politicians, officers, businessmen, to your restaurant, do I not? Ask this pseudo-person to leave.'

'Thank you, Kolab,' said Carla as she inserted a twenty into his breast pocket. He retired immediately and in silence to his podium.

'Why don't you bribe him back, Mr Grieve?'

'General.'

Two waitresses came to Hector's table, one wheeling a wine bucket from which she poured Chablis, one carrying a tray from which she transferred plates of mango salad and grilled meat, a bowl of rice, amok curry.

'You can't afford to eat here, Hector.'

'I don't pay to eat here.'

'Do you wanna sit with us?' said Christy.

'She does not,' Grieve growled.

'She said she needs to talk to you. But you're hiding behind your little fort there.'

'She does *not* need to talk to me. Can you not appreciate that we're trying to have a nice evening?'

'Can *you* not appreciate that you can't afford to have a nice evening here? You are broke.'

'And you are ugly,' he said, exaggerating her biting diction. Then she sneezed. She rubbed her eyes, demonically red—sneezed again. 'What the hell was that?'

She sneezed twice and tipped the contents of her purse onto the table. She rummaged through various pill packets until finding the right one. She chased two of them with a gulp of water and a head toss. 'Have you been riding?'

'What?'

'Horses. I'm allergic to horses. Very, very, allergic to horses. The hair on your clothes. It's giving me hay fever.'

'You should be dead.'

'Hector!' whined Christy.

'God damn modern medicine. Good for nothing but keeping accountants alive. If I'd have known you were allergic I would have brought my saddle up here and smothered you with it.'

'You're so rude.'

Grieve pulled down the wall of menus and grinned and shook his head. 'War is hell.'

Carla discharged another expulsion and immediately said, 'Mr Grieve, your father is dying.'

'We're all dying,' said Hector, shooting her a stern glance.

'Your father has peripheral T-cell lymphoma. Cancer of the blood.'

'You're a cancer of the—' In one movement Hector inhaled through his nose and his eyes became momentarily enraged and shivers rattled his spine. He brought his face back from Carla's table to peer beneath his brow out into the rain. His body slumped.

'It's spread to his bone marrow and he's had a full transplant. He's already spent what remained of his money on treatment but he needs a course of Humilitotyn to stay alive longer than the next six months. Your father's dying, Hector. I'm sorry.'

Grieve sat back in his chair and crossed his arms to push at the butts of his revolvers. For a time he breathed loudly through his nose, exhaling quickly. 'Dad,' he thought, then whispered. For it was in his father's nimbic glow that Hector had travelled to Cambodia in the first place.

Advanced from childhood hero to paragon of bosses, his father sent him to Phnom Penh to see if the family business might assuage his younger son's increasingly embittered temperament. Asked to explore his company's options for setting up a micro-financing institute for drought-stricken farmers, Hector was taken by his father's contact to Sihanoukville, where riding on the beach appealed to him very much more than did the heavily peddled option of visiting in the daytime a red-light district known as The Chicken Farm. He had often galloped horses on sand as a child, his mother keeping three mares in the field behind their Fairhaven beach house. He so visibly enjoyed swimming an unimpressive gelding in the incomparable blue of the Gulf of Thailand that his guide gave him the business card of an affiliate in Siem Reap, where Hector was next headed to do some sightseeing.

Grieve galloped among green fields of young rice and high palm, out to the hills of Phnom Kulen. Dripping with sweat, he found that for the first time in his life he was smiling for no other reason than that he was happy. In the heat which makes the Khmer feel more alive at his chessboard than did ever a European save on the field of battle, Hector stayed a fortnight longer than his father had wished. And it was in those divine weeks that he found himself alone at nightfall in the silent stone galleries of Preah Khan, walking among jade nymphs and amethyst reliefs carved everywhere as overwatching spirits; the bulging golden roots of enormous trees asphyxiating archways and squeezing walls as a slow reclamation of life—there and then that he fell in love with things ancient and dead though still persisting; encircled, overrun, and defeated; ignored.

On what was meant to be his last day of Cambodian sunshine, pacing his hotel's pool in the brown haze of a setting sun, an English-language newspaper was dropped on a lounge barely within reach. Hector flicked his hand until it was dry. On the paper's front page was the story of the theft of half the heads from the bridge of his newly beloved Preah Khan—an Indian-backed decapitation of the warriors pulling Vasuki king of snakes in order to stir up immortality. He found an obvious tactical hole in the account of the bungled recovery of three of the heads from the tanks which had escorted them to the Thai border. He thought he might know something that the Cambodian police did not.

Next day, Grieve talked his way into the Department of Safeguarding and Preservation of Monuments and persuaded its chief administrator—that Meak Sakona whose indolence he would come to despise—that only horses could outmanoeuvre tanks on Cambodian terrain. He was taken to Royal Army headquarters to present the idea to General Monirith. After much embellishment—

indeed the complete invention of his Australian military experience—he was allowed supervised command of a team of buck privates.

At the first rattle of tank track they all of them fled. After the engagement—during which Hector, riding between two Thai tanks, almost succeeded in getting them to fire upon one another—he pleaded with Monirith that he needed his own men. Impressed by the young foreigner's bravery and by his horsemanship—a skill astonishing to Cambodian eyes—the general allowed him to do his own recruiting.

Hector had quickly taken up with an American blonde who was using her gap year to volunteer at an orphanage. Among her charges he found an impertinent young cavalier who had little hope of avoiding the deprivations of the tuk-tuk mafia. His name was Sros, through very quickly Hector began referring to him, by that likeness of charm and hair, as Elvis. Then after the laying of those nine gold bars at General Monirith's feet he began on his Japanese income to import Walers into Cambodia and to work with the multitudinous orphanages of Siem Reap on the recruitment of boys and their drilling into men.

So from William St. Clair who died fighting the Moors in Spain on a quest to take the heart of Robert the Bruce to The Holy Land, to The Great Montrose whose motto was To Conquer Or Bravely Die, from the New South Wales Corps to the 2/9th Cavalry Command Regiment in North Africa, from his father—exemplar of vital goodness and internationally honoured man of action—of Scotch, Swiss, and English blood—to two-star general in the Royal Cambodian Army—now a broke soldier with a dying hero—

Thus had Hector S. Grieve descended.

Seething, he rose with his knuckles on the table. He picked up the bowl of Khmer curry and flung it with some violence at the wall behind him. He strode across the verandah and hurried down the staircase. His driver ran to convey him under the cover of an umbrella to his car.

The downpour beat loudly on the roof, its heavy strikes falling bright yellow in the headlights as the car splashed its way through a traffic of plastic poncho and dirty wake.

Beneath the corrugated iron porch of l'Arc-en-ciel Elvis was entertaining a pair of rhinemaidens over mugs of beer. His dimples sunk deep as he leaned back to rock his chair on its hind legs and smile at making the girls laugh with tales of his uncle Ekkaly.

Grieve hopped from the running board to the bar's terrace. Elvis raised an open arm to him. 'General! Have a seat. This is Alina, and this is Flosshilde.'

Hector looked down at each of them and nodded then said to Elvis, 'It's over.'

'What's over?'

'Walk with me.'

The dimples quite wiped from his face, Elvis said a cheekily regretful goodbye to the girls and stopped at the verandah's edge as Hector walked on. His casual uniform was tailored—with black tie tucked into a grey shirt and thin black belt high at his waist— exactly after Mr Presley's in *G.I. Blues*, though as Grieve was the only King Voar permitted to wear insignia at night it was badge- and patchless.

'Well, come on,' said Grieve.

'It's raining, sir.'

'No shit. What are you, a gremlin? Let's go.'

Elvis pulled his garrison cap low and hunched his shoulders and ran to Grieve's side. They walked the middle of the street, Hector oblivious to the deluge dumping upon him.

'It's over. Give the baboons to the monks at Angkor Wat. You can keep my falcons if you'd like, though I know you don't care for the pursuit. If not, release them in Ratanakiri. Take Vespasian out to that new tiger forest in Mondulkiri. I know they're extinct in the wild, but for a tiger a few hours of ancient freedom is better than a lifetime of captivity. If the men don't want the horses, in a week you offer them to the king, with Selathoa and Blue. If he doesn't want them, you have the men ride them out to Phnom Kulen and you set them free. You do *not* give them to the army.'

'Sir?'

'Just listen. I want a crocodile each placed in the fountains of the Sofitel, Raffles, The Park Hyatt, and Mad Monkey. Do not ask the staff, do it secretly and when they're at their busiest. It'll be hilarious. Don't let Monirith fold the men into the army anywhere below captain. They're all worthy of the rank and they'll make far better officers than his nephews. When I'm gone, empty the Indian Room completely. You remember that fertility idol that Angelina Jolie gave me? Keep it and take it to your sister's place. She's the finest piece of arse I ever had. Not your sister. I never slept with your sister, though she begged me to. Angelina was the finest piece of arse I ever had and I want at least her jade dildo to remember

57

her by. My riding crop and saddle give to the National Museum. My time in Cambodia will go down as historic. I know it. You do *not* give Mongkut's Coronation Umbrella back to Thailand. Give it to Sohtireak. Give him the Cham dragons too, that'll piss the Vietnamese off. The white elephant, I think it's best you destroy. I know I'm not meant to have it and any attempt to sell it will just draw attention. And the shrunken heads... Ah, who gives a fuck. None of it means anything anymore.

'Have the men assemble at 0600 tomorrow. Holy Sword. And meet me at home in an hour with my kit bag and a box of special whisky. Dismissed.'

4

For a time Grieve sat with his ankles crossed on the third floor balustrade of Victoria House. He looked out over the glow of the gardens with a Cohiba and a large Mekong, his seven-and-a-half-inch Colt Single Action Army across his lap, and listened to the crickets.

Eventually he said to himself, in frustration at his own reluctance, 'Ahh fuck this!' He flicked the cigar and pushed the tumbler over the balcony and reholstered the gun

Under a wide and star-flecked sky of darkest blue Christy's body was a long sapphire glimmer as she glided silently along the ultramarine length of the swimming pool's bottom. Lanterns shone yellow in the rumduol above the waterfall; the leaves of the jungled garden glowed white with lanterns.

'Thanks for leaving me at the restaurant,' she said as she crossed her dripping elbows at Hector's feet.

'What was I supposed to do?'

'Act like an adult.' She pinched her nose and ran her fingers back through her hair.

'Sit there and listen to that sucked blister of cheese rind? I don't think so.'

'Well is it true?'

'Is what true?'

'About your dad.'

'I fucking hope not.'

'Can't you call him to find out? Why don't you go home for a while?'

'Home? I told you, I'm unhappy there.'

'But you never told me why. How bad can it be? Why don't you go home for a bit just to check on your dad? When was the last time you saw him?'

'You want me to leave?'

'What?'

'You want *me* out of here. The whole house to yourself? That's what you want?'

'Calm down, it's just a suggestion.'

'Don't tell me to calm down. You want me gone from Siem Reap so you can live it up at my expense, hm?'

'That's not what I was saying,' she twanged, attempting to correct the misconstruance. 'But by the time you get back my stuff'll be here and I can move in properly. We can start our new new life together, like we said.'

'Huge villa all to yourself. You can bring back all the tourists from Angkor What Bar, all the cocaine you can fit in that fake little nose. I don't fucking think so.'

'Fuck you,' said Christy and pushed back from the pool's edge to drift towards the waterfall. 'You know that's not what I meant.'

'Fuck me? Well you know what? If I go, you go. Get the fuck out of the pool.'

'You're an asshole.'

'Yeah and you're a bitch. Get the fuck out of my house.'

'You wish, pickle dick.'

'I'm fucking serious, Christy. Get the fuck out.'

'Come in and pull me out.' Christy submerged her head and kicked off the back wall to again swim the pool underwater.

Grieve stepped over the low glass enclosure of the house's stream and made a huge splash as he snatched his hands down to grab at neck and scaly tail.

When he reappeared at the pool with a Siamese crocodile writhing and chomping in his grip Christy gave a slow and wary warning of, 'Hector,' as she paddled away from him.

He loomed at the water's edge with the animal flat from his stomach. 'I said get the fuck out.'

'Or what?'

'What do you think, Or what?'

'You wouldn't dare.'

The crocodile jolted its body again, its snout snapping left and its tail whipping right. 'Oh wouldn't I?' Hector raised his eyebrows and tossed the thing belly-first into the pool. Christy screamed and splashed urgently for the decking as the reptile swam for her. In one frantic movement she was out of the water and prancing from fright on a sun lounge in her Triangl bikini.

'You fucking asshole!' she screamed.

Grieve grinned as he strode past her, 'Now get the fuck out.'

He marched up the jungled path to the rear of the house. At the stairs he kicked at a loitering peacock. Before he could walk on the bird had lowered its head and was charging him. It jumped to dig its claws into his shin. Grieve said, 'What the fuck?' as it flapped its wide wings about his legs and pecked at his thigh. Instantly he pulled his ivory-handled revolver and shot the bird in its shining blue chest.

Upstairs he unbuckled his shoulder holster and threw it onto the pillows. He pulled three shirts from his closet and laid them on the end of the bed; draped three pairs of hung trousers over them. From his drawers he counted out pairs of socks one at a time. Elvis appeared at the bedroom door with a kit bag.

Grieve took it from him and lifted it onto the bed and unzipped and spread it open.

'Is it really over?'

Grieve tossed the socks into the bag and transferred the trousers. 'How I do hate my destiny.'

5

Hector Grieve sat in full battle dress upon Selathoa at dawn, looking out over the Jayatataka Baray. Its miles of branch-stuck bog reflected in muddied splatters of pink and orange and blue the clouds of a new morning. Above, in the high distance, twists of coral and honey, veined with cyan, curled to the heavens.

The sun soon rose, as Hector knew it would, and Selathoa's hooves clopped across the wooden platform as he turned her about with a pull of her reins.

Through the soft hiss of the arid jungle the tink and hollow hide-taps of a cloistered procession of monks rattled to greet the silvery silence of the day's first light. A single piper began a sweetly wafting dirge as Hector S. Grieve rode Selathoa down the sandy rocks to the moat of Preah Khan, Holy City Of Victory—the first Khmer temple with which he had fallen in love, that triumphant citadel built to honour his father by Jayavarman The Seventh over the battleground on which he defeated the Cham invaders; where now nature and art were engaged everywhere in ferocious battle and in stone was Shiva, destroyer and creator, being destroyed by his creations; where were more guardians of holy places than at any other Cambodian temple; that Holy Sword onto whose roof at dawn Hector Grieve often climbed and there among birdsong contemplated the desuetude of a whole crumbling city covered in turquoise.

He crossed its bridge, between giant balustrades of Vasuki, King of Knakes pulled by a dozen gods and a dozen demons, and remembered upon the looting of their heads all those years ago. He ducked as Selathoa stepped up through the tower of the first gate and stayed low as she rounded the trees which overhung the path. Dry thick vines dangled low from high branches and twisted out and turned upon the ground. He watched hovering dragonflies and chicks scampering into and out of the forest floor as he passed the House of Fire; saw ahead the hoof, pastern, and cannon of his regiment.

To a buzzing and whirring and clicking orchestra of bird and insect—and to that mournful Buddhist flute and its slow samsaric percussion—Hector ascended the mossy steps to the cruciform terrace which lay before the eastern halls of the thousand-year-old city.

At his back the encroaching light was a thick band of violet curving overhead to white and fading high to baby blue. Strokes of cloud dissipated as the sun rose to turn purple in the morning light the flaming archway behind the enlisted men of the King Voar regiment. The short square columns of the galleries and its terraced roofs of decrepit laterite sprawled and descended left and right at their backs. They sat without helmets, Jerusalem in his black war hat, at attention all in their saddles. Elvis was at their centre, his horse a muzzle-length ahead.

Hector stopped Selathoa in the centre of the stone platform and looked to the top of the spung tree whose enormous roots strangled the southern porch. Golden light hit its top and descended slowly as the day came.

Grieve spoke as though into a PA system, halting every few words to let clear an echo that was not there.

'All that is, shall come to an end. ... I've been informed that due to a new and unbearable burden the King Voar regiment must cease all activity in Cambodia. Today does not bring me joy. You are the finest young men that I have ever had the privilege of knowing. I leave you with years, what will be remembered as your finest years, of brilliance behind you—years that will ensure that you conquer any foe, human or immaterial. You have attained an unmatched expertise in the only branch of knowledge worth studying: that of being a gentleman. You have accrued a wealth of experience in the noblest pursuit ever carried out by humanity— you have not only seen, but have repeatedly been victorious in, war, the only place where a man really lives.

'I know, that either in this life or the next, that I'll not only see you again, but will ride with you, in Valhalla as on earth, which surely is where you, and I, shall rest. Though the regiment be dead, its men live on, as forever shall our memory live. In our own minds first, at last in the annals of war and the unassailable history of the greatness of man. It is how we are remembered by succeeding generations that defines the brightness of our legacy. If our memory lives on, who can say that we are dead? To have our deeds recorded, and our work remembered—this… is eternal life.

'I must leave you. It is well for a Khmer to be poor. In your poverty you walk nearer to your Gods. I with money came, and with money tried to hustle the East, but a white man without money just isn't any good. For his worth to now fall below that even of a Hindoo… I'd as soon be dead. I will not live in shame. I leave you.

'But be sure that God provides us always with the masters we need. Though after me, of course, I do realize that a God-king might be hard to come by again.'

His men smiled at familiar memories of General Hector S. Grieve's feigned arrogance. Gently they shook their heads.

'You came to this regiment without a family. I hope that in the men beside you today, assembled for war before The Holy City of Victory, that you have found, as I have, the greatest family a man could hope for. Family is the foundation of sanity and sobriety. It is a man's family that props up his greatness; that humbles his pride; that spurs him on to greater deeds. Remember, that that which is born of valour and honour, teaches valour and honour. Of such were we born, and under such have we as a family lived.

'Audacity, bravery, honour. By these, have I taught you to pursue eminence. Virtue, humility, victory. By these I expect you all to eminence attain. Memory, money, family—galvanized all, by eminence. These, the ancient ideals of manhood.

'In all that you do, remember your training; remember your duty, and be comfortable knowing that the ordeal of combat, in which you have each performed according to the highest standards of arete, alone fits a man for any and every trial through which a wretched and cowardly civilization might put him.

'I leave you all as exemplars of exalted human values. Ours is the oldest honourable profession in the history of mankind. You are in this life either a warrior or a prostitute. Rather live a day as a warrior than a hundred years as a prostitute.

'The end is glorious, the striving cannot but be worth it. When talent is paired with resolve triumph is inevitable.

'Do not take counsel of your fears. God favours the brave. Victory is to the audacious.

'Our Iliads here part. I do not think forever.

'King Voars. Chahik si chahiks. Men of Men.

'Dismissed.'

6

From the radio of the hard top Citroën the opening violas trembled before the marching cellos of Mahler's second symphony. The tyres droned against Highway 6 cleared of traffic. They were joined by the wind, then the rest of the strings, all working up to the Dies Irae of the brass—the symphony given its Cambodian radio debut in tribute to Hector S. Grieve by the Department of Media and Communication.

Police motorbikes led army jeeps which led black sedans with tinted windows. The procession was repeated in reverse behind the two Citroëns, in the first of which Hector Grieve looked disconsolately out the window.

The hanging flowers of the reachapreuk trees swayed in golden bunches in the hot wind over the side lanes of crowd gathered until just outside of town. The people of Siem Reap had flocked to see off a man whose exploits had never been officially acknowledged but whom they all in some capacity revered, even worshipped. Thousands of plaster figurines of the general on Selathoa rode high in the hands of villagers, removed from their household shrines in the hope they might get the chance to gift them as tokens of gratitude for eight years of service.

Grieve sped without wave or smile before the blue and red Cambodian banners and the Buddhist colours flying from the flagpoles of a hundred hotels enormous with fluorescent Korean, Japanese, Chinese signs. Umbrellas tiered as six levels of heaven hung before hotels roofed as temples. Huge concrete cobra fountains spat seven streams of water into new basins. Red dust swirled in the wind around half-built constructions—steel rods protruding from their pylons—and around abandoned complexes already overcome by forest.

As the cavalcade neared the airport Grieve's driver slowed so that his vehicle was the last to come onto the tarmac.

The King Voar regiment fell into formation before the engine of a 747 and held their salutes. Their commander stepped out of his car and pulled down the elastic bottom of his tanker jacket, sand-coloured with two-starred epaulettes. Slowly he made his way over to them. First he shook hands and exchanged nods with the three chief benefactors of his work in Cambodia.

To General Monirith he said, 'Goodbye, friend.' To Ear Sohtireak: 'You look after that woman.' And to Meak Sakona: 'Go shit in your hat. And tell your wife she makes a mean coconut macaroon.'

'Thank you, General.'

'Pity about her face though '

Next was Elvis. They locked right forearms. 'I want you to have this.' Grieve unholstered his ivory-handled revolver and offered it in his palm.

'Hector, the Peacemaker?'

'It's been with me almost from the beginning. I want you to have it.'

'Hector, no. That's too much.'

'Good,' said Hector, and returned the weapon.

'You bastard,' Elvis smiled and shook his head. 'I'll see you mate.'

'In Valhalla, as on earth. Well, not yet. I'm going quite elsewhere.'

Grieve saluted as he stepped on and embraced forearms with KFC; with Pangolin; with Risotto; and with Groucho, his longest-serving private.

Then came Jerusalem.

'That hat,' said Grieve, inspecting its singular shape and shimmering embroidery. 'The first fruit of youthful war. Invaluable to the world. Cherish it.'

'I will, sir.'

'It should have been about you.'

'What's that?' said Jerusalem.

'All this,' Hector sighed, and shook his head.

'It was an honour, sir.'

Hector nodded and broke slowly into a smile. 'I know it was.'

He returned his straightened fingers and tucked thumb to his forehead. He cackled as he released the salute.

He put a riding boot onto the stair car and turned to give his men and the encroaching jungle one last look over. With the sun hot on his cheeks he looked skyward and then to the west. Momentarily he reflected that he could, if he chose, walk from here through Kafiristan to Scotland; could ride Selathoa around mountain passes to Oxiana; sail upriver to Peking; make pilgrimage to Annapurna; march to Damascus; overwinter in Liesena.

He with eyes downcast ascended to the flight attendants waiting inside the aeroplane's door.

'Welcome aboard, Mr Grieve.'

'General Grieve.'

NIBELHEIM

Chapter One

FROGSQVIRTERS

Hector Grieve lowered his head into a cramped galley of white plastic and purple light and instinctively he veered left. Abruptly and entirely his way was blocked by a young woman in a red dress, her neckerchief like a bouquet of parma violets. Grieve met the eyes behind her thick-rimmed glasses and took in the fullness of her cheeks—both flawless without makeup—the curvature of her top lip made carnal by crimson lipstick.

Instinctively the left corner of his mouth rose with its corresponding eyebrow. 'How do you do?'

Procedurally the girl's left arm rose with its corresponding fingers. 'Your seat's that way, sir,' she said, with a blankness born of deep resentment towards the constantly invading tribe upon which her livelihood depended.

'What?'

'Your seat's that way, sir. 33C. Thank you.'

'Do you know what that way is?'

'On the aisle, to your right, sir. 33C.' She spoke with haste, anxious to have the door closed behind him so that she could get the take-off, and soon thereafter the meal service, done with. 'Thank you so much.'

Hector turned his head halfway around and considered for a moment what manner of confusion was rearing its impertinent head. 'Back there?' he said, throwing his thumb over his shoulder. 'I don't think so.'

'*33C, sir,*' said the girl, nodding and reiterating with her hands that Grieve would absolutely find no seat beyond her. '*Thank* you.'

'What's your name?' said Grieve.

'Alice. And I'm looking after first and business class today. You'll be taken care of by Marc. Marc,' she called to a slight man in the aisle behind Grieve. 'Could you show this gentleman to his seat please? 33C.'

'Marc?' said Grieve, disappointed by the name. A haggard young person in black jacket and red tie said at his back, 'Welcome aboard, sir. This way please.'

Marc hurried back along the aisle and lowered a palm to 33C.

Hector furrowed the deep wrinkles of his forehead and turned to again devote his attention to Alice. A red curtain had been pulled across the entrance to where out of long custom he assumed he would be sitting. Not since flying to California to retrieve Sohtireak's sweetheart had he flown in any class but first.

'Sir!' Marc scowled.

Grieve drew the red curtain. Alice, only slightly shorter than he, stared up at him with grey eyes and something of a smirk.

'33C, sir. I promise it's behind you, *not* behind me.'

'Pinky promise?'

'Sir,' she smiled. Grieve peered around her—to the luxuriously upholstered capsules and vast leg-rooms, almost all of them unoccupied, the champagne glasses dancing with bubbles in erotic lighting.

'33C?' Grieve smirked back.

'Right beside 33B.'

'*Sir!*' Marc repeated, now almost shouting. 'Everybody's waiting for you.' Grieve smiled at Alice and said, 'I'll see you soon, kid.' He turned to shuffle towards Marc, immediately lamenting over the enclosure of heads vacuum-sealed in the galley before him. The door was closed at his surrender. He felt instantly cold.

'Fasten your seat belt for take-off,' said Marc. Grieve looked up at him with a disdainful grimace as he reached up and closed the baggage compartment. Hector lowered his snarling incisor as Marc moved along to the next seat, revealing thereby Carla, hunched on the other side of the sliver of an aisle.

'You're fucking kidding me.'

'I'm told we have a lot to discuss about you going home after so long.'

'Like fuck we do. If you say one word to me I'll hog-tie you at the emergency exit and pull the door to let the pressure suck you out.' Grieve swung his head back. The end of his nose was nearly at a television screen playing a cartoon of people instructing him on how to fasten a seat belt. The narration seemed to louden through the downlit confinement. Grieve looked to his left, and found a bare shoulder and the still face of a young man with a sleeping mask over his eyes. He grunted and sought consolation in the plastic undulations of the ceiling. Wishing that it would all just be over, he closed his eyes. He heard the rattle and rumble and roar of take-off. He thought upon Selathoa, and Christy's body, and riding through the dusk and the vivifying heat that had so instantly been turned to a cruel chill.

Shortly a dinging tone sounded. Seat belts were everywhere unbuckled. Immediately Hector was prodded in the arm.

"Scuse me mate,' said the young man beside him.

Grieve looked at him with little other than scorn. 'What?'

'He needs to go the toilet.' The young man pointed to the young man at the window, similarly bare-shouldered in an Angkor beer singlet and poised to stand up.

'We just took off,' said Hector.

'Yeah, the seat belt sign's gone now, so. Could you umm…'

'He didn't need to go fifteen minutes ago? You didn't need to go fifteen minutes ago? Hold it in.'

'Sorry, mate. Cheers.'

Grieve hesitated for a furious moment then looked at the tops of his knees. He shook his head with resentment. Until the appearance at his breakfast table of the woman now far too beside him, he had forgotten about the deep antagonism he felt towards his countrymen abroad. He contorted to squeeze himself out of his seat to let the supplicant and then his friend pass. He twisted to slink back in. Immediately the seat in front of him fell to his face.

A loud clear of his throat turned to a wet growl. After breathing for a time on the headrest, Hector banged it with his fist. Then he pushed it frantically with the balls of his hands.

'Are you right there?' snapped the woman who occupied it, rolling her head to the side.

'Put your seat back up.'

'The seat belt sign's turned off.'

'If the seat belt sign told you to rape a duck would you go out and look for one?'

'Excuse me!' said the woman, rising with nose scrunched and mouth agape.

'Look ahead of you. You have a smiling valley of freedom between your head and the next seat. But between your dandruff and my respiratory system is the crack of a starving builder's arsehole. Put your fucking seat up.'

'Put *your* seat down,' the woman said in a halting whine.

'*I* wouldn't do that to the person behind me. *I'm* not an inconsiderate frogsquirter. Put, your fucking seat back up.'

The woman withdrew the side of her face from the exchange and put in earphones. Grieve sensed the crotch of a pair of shorts at his right ear. He put his elbows on his arm rests and clasped his hands. He stared into the abyss that was the patternless red cloth at his nose and thought only of the fact that he was surrounded. Eventually he looked up at the incontinent young man, who in very large sunglasses nodded and pointed to his own seat. Grieve huffed and raised himself up and contorted his body out with especial difficulty. He squinted the cabin over once again.

When he sat he was graced with a conversation beginning with the phrase, 'Fucking Cambo.'

'Fuckin' Cambo ey,' said 33B beside him.

'Good birthday but?'

'Fucking *ge-rate* birthday, man. What a way to spend your thirtieth, ey? Fuckin' Cambo.'

To Grieve's side Marc pulled a trolley rattling with drinks. 'Something to drink?' he said to 33A.

'Beer please mate,' said 33B, holding up two fingers.

'Actually could we have two?' said 33A and Marc handed them each another.

'Something to drink, sir?'

'Whisky. Triple. Neat.'

'We do single whiskies, sir.'

'You do single whiskies?' Marc nodded impatiently. 'I'll have three of them.'

'One at a time, sir, if that's all right.'

'It's not all right. Whisky. Triple. Neat.'

'Sir, we only do single whiskies.'

'You gave them two beers.'

'Would you like two beers?'

'I'd like three whiskies.'

'Sir, we don't *do* triple whiskies.'

'You don't *do* them? Well can you *pour* them?'

'I can pour you a single whisky.'

'Three of them. Please.'

'I can pour you *one* single whisky, sir.'

'Three times.'

'Once.'

'You just gave them two beers, Marc, what's the fucking difference? Why can't you give *me* three whiskies?'

'We do spirits only in singles, sir.'

'Singles?'

'If we give you too much spirit we can't know what you'll do. Would you like one whisky, or can I serve everybody else?'

'One whisky, huh?'

'One whisky.'

'One whisky… Marc,' he said with a shake of his head and a smirk. He downed the dribble of liquid before Marc had pulled the drinks cart on. The brake was reapplied beside the row of the seat-dropping frogsquirter. In the lower shelf at the cart's rear were stowed unopened bottles of gin, vodka, whisky. Grieve watched Marc work until at last he leaned over to pass a tomato juice to the frogsquirter's window. He looked at Carla before pulling Johnnie Walker out and quickly putting him with the magazines in the netting between his knees.

'Waddya reckon Donut's doin'?' said 33A to 33B. They both gulped down the last of their first beers. 'Reckon she's still cryin'?'

'Hope not, the poor thing.'

'Steve don't make alone,' moaned 33A in a high voice. They both laughed. 'Can't believe she wrote y'a letter.'

'Steve don't make alone,' said 33B, reflecting upon a trip he could only in patches, and those of stupefication, recall.

'I never angry to you!' said 33A, shaking his head and affecting a wail.

'Three day you to near me like three years,' said 33B in impersonation of the heartbroken Cambodian girl who had taken a bus from Phnom Penh to Siem Reap just to see him one last time.

'Donut want baby with you! … How old you reckon they were?'

'I don't think I wanna know, man,' said 33A.

'Yeh true ey.'

'Fuck, I have to piss again.'

33B tapped Grieve at the shoulder. 'Sorry, mate.'

Hector squinted at the headrest. He had attempted to hear none of the screeching within the serpent's rib that was his row. In this he had, with most of the aeroplane, failed.

33B tapped him again and repeated his loaded apology. Grieve squinted fully and turned his head. 'What?' 33A was already standing at a crouch beneath the low plastic bulges.

'He's gotta use the dunny again.'

'What are you, 18 months old? You just went, hold it in.'

'Sorry, mate. I gotta go, ey.'

'Broke the seal,' said 33B.

With a very deep breath Grieve puffed up his chest. He slowly let it out as a gust of calming wind. He stood and 33A stepped over 33B and strutted off. 'Are *you* going to have to go to the bathroom?' he said as 33B tapped at the screen in the headrest in front of him.

'Nah, nah.'

'Are you fucking sure?'

'Yeah mate, I'm all right. He's like that, he pisses like a woman. Reckon he sits down to do it too.'

'If I sit down, and you have to get up to use the bathroom...' Grieve held his pointed index and middle finger at 33B's face. '...for the rest of this flight—'

'Are they guns?' said 33B, catching a glint from beyond the zipper of Grieve's tanker jacket.

'Ask me to stand up so you can use the bathroom. You'll find out.'

When his corner of return travel was seated again he leaned out to watch the goings on of the aisle. Flight attendants zipped about the galley, crouching and reaching and yanking drawers out and shoving them back in. He returned to upright and could hear between heavy taps at a plastic screen long and very loud breaths; could soon focus on nothing but the gale blowing out and the squall sucking in from 33B's mouth. Until all were surpassed in volume by the electronic sound of coins, clinking together somewhere behind them.

In 34D an ogreish man with a bald conehead was hunched over his phone. He held it in one hand and swiped furiously with the other. Each time his fingers met the screen the clinking sound repeated, in crescendo, until eventually there sounded a shower of treasure. At this the troll momentarily paused his rolling wrist and smiled at his achievement.

Grieve whipped his fingers at the man's tracksuited knee. 'Can I ask you a question?'

'What?' said the man, flicking Grieve his chin.

'Could you shut the fuck up?' Grieve broke their brief glance to scowl at his phone. With reaction of neither face nor posture the man returned to drool at his phone. Grieve snatched it out of his hand and sent it sliding down the aisle.

'Hey, arsehole!' said 34D as he shook three rows of seating in extracting his obesity from his armrests. The lull which followed the cessation of the coins was immediately broken by the apocalyptic wailing of an infant, screeching in a halter at its mother's chest in the seat in front of Carla.

'Shut that thing up,' Grieve pleaded, loudly so as to be

unmistaken in his target.

The woman turned from her loving gaze at a television screen. 'Are you talking to me?' she said, astonished that he might have been.

Grieve nodded once and said, 'Shut that fucking thing up.'

'That "fucking thing", thank you, is my daughter. And she's hungry.'

'Then flop an udder out and feed it.'

'For your information, arseface, I don't breastfeed my children.'

'Your choice or theirs? I wouldn't want my lips around a dragon's nipples either. Shut that thing up.' The mother looked down to her crying baby and soothed it with jiggles of her torso.

The taps at the television screen beside Grieve's now rerose to prominence. They became more rapid, more decisive. With them 33B's breathy tempest increased. Halfway through an exhalation Grieve clapped his hand over the offending hole.

'You breathe like that in the jungle you get your throat slit. Breathe fucking quietly. Like an adult.'

33B nodded. When Grieve's hand was uncapped from his face he said, 'We're not in the jungle, you psycho. Relax.'

'Oh are we not?' Grieve smirked.

33B was tapped on his left shoulder and 33A stood from his seat. 'Are you serious?' said 33B in a hushed panic.

'I gotta take a shit, man,' said 33A.

'Just siddown,' said 33B in a hush.

'I can't, man, I gotta take a shit. Oi, mate,' said 33A to Grieve. 'Mate?' He reached over and tapped Hector on the shoulder. 33B put his forehead in his hand. Hector slowly turned to squint at the window. 'I gotta use the toilet.'

'Irrumator,' Grieve smiled.

'Huh? I gotta use the toilet.'

'*Are* you fucking kidding me?'

'I went number 1's before. I gotta go number 2's.'

'Number 1's and number 2's? Are you fucking seven? You didn't have an inkling when you were pissing for the twelfth time in an hour that you might need to take a shit too? What the fuck, boy? Is this your first day off the potty? Or'd one of your ladyboys ruin things for you? I'm not getting up again. Shit in your hat. Shit in his hat. Or even better—Oi! Dragon with the baby. Can I get a nappy here for 33A?'

'Can you please be quiet,' said the frogsquirter.

'Oh, I'll be quiet,' said Hector. 'When selfishness and stupidity have been eradicated from this fucking aeroplane. Dragon tits! Throw me a goddam nappy!'

'You're really rude, man,' said 33B to Hector Grieve.

Hector grinned at him and shook his head. 'War is hell.'

Then he slipped into a mode that he had forgotten once constituted a large part of his character. It was, a very long time ago, his dearest mode, for it was once so that Hector Grieve was only ever charming when he was funny and only ever funny when he was angry. By it had he won the affections of his high school sweetheart and by it maintained among adolescent friend and foe an impeccable streak of entertaining argument. It was from it too that he had suspected that indignant words might play a part in his precocious literary pursuit. He had not in eight years of Cambodian exile been forced to relapse. Surrounded, here he was.

'And I'm not rude, you're a fucking imbecile. You can only be rude to your equals. Are you calling me an imbecile? Careful, kid. I've killed greater men for lesser insults. Tell unpottytrained Pete over there to sit the fuck back down and hold it in. And if you shit yourself, Pete, if I smell so much as a tinkerbell's fart from your direction I'll make a parachute out of mouth-breather's singlet and throw you both out the window without it. God damn it, can't either of you two behave like men? Only quadriplegics and retarded bulldogs breathe through their mouths and shit themselves. What's wrong with you fucking people? Pee-pants turns into Shits-himself, I've got a frogsquirter in a dentist's chair, this baby's crying from its mother's scaly tits and Golem the Treasure-Hunter's flicking his telephone's bean. I've been back among you purple-pissing savages for less than an hour and I'm already longing for the clash and sting of battle. The Pathet Lao once submerged me up to my chin for a week and fed me nothing but rat's tails. That was more pleasant than being in this whale's belly with you recidivists. Is this all you people do? Piss and shit and lie down in one another's laps and molest electronic devices? Back in my day you'd all be thrown under Panzer treads and if it were up to me you'd all be shanghaied into—'

'Chicken or falafel?' said an older flight attendant with high-pitched mechanical calm. She had arrived with a cart of shelved trays—her eyes like Arabian almonds, her hair dark-chocolate, her figure shapely and her smile sultry.

'What's your name?' said Grieve, simpering up at her.

'Cathy. Chicken or falafel?'

'You tell me, Cathy. I don't know what farfel is.'

'Chicken or falafel, sir?'

'Chicken.'

'Sorry, sir, we currently only have the falafel.'

'Why'd you offer me chicken?'

'Legally we have to offer two meal alternatives, sir. Chicken or falafel?'

'Chicken.'

'Sorry sir, we only have the falafel.'

'Cathy, you're offering me chicken.'

'Yes, legally we have to offer two meal alternatives, sir.'

'So no chicken?'

'Chicken or falafel?' she said as though for the first time.

Hector began to say chicken. He quickly thought better of it. 'Farfel?'

'Falafel!' Cathy chimed, then put a tray in front of him. 'Enjoy your meal, sir.'

The frogsquirter was told to put her seat up and Grieve unpeeled the foil from the plastic tub upon his tray table. He looked its contents over then lifted a bread roll from a plastic cup. He squeezed at it, found that it would not give, tapped it against his television screen.

'Cathy, what is this?' he called to her as she stepped along the aisle. 'Cathy!'

'Falafel, sir.'

'Is this food?' said Grieve, surprised. 'No, no, no, no, no. Look at this.' He banged the roll's hollow hardness against his arm rest. 'I've had food. This is not it. Look,' and he with a squeeze of his hands turned the roll into powder. 'Cathy! Where are you going? Look at this!' He took 33B's bread roll and threw it against the wall between the emergency exit rows. 'God *damn* it.'

Marc pulled up with the drinks cart.

'Something to drink, sir?'

33B spoke for 33A, whose mouth was stuffed with falafel. 'Could we have two beers please mate? Two each?'

Marc's hand and the first two beers passed over his tray table and Hector pinned Marc's tiny forearm against the seat in front of him.

'If you give either of these two bumhungries one more beer you'll shit bread for a week from the yeast infection you get after I shove a can up your—'

'Mr Grieve!' said Carla.

'What?'

Hector Grieve nestled into a black leather recliner and clinked his champagne glass against Alice's. She smiled, with one leg over the other, across the refreshing chasm of a first class aisle. His tanker jacket had been stowed and his sleeves were rolled up.

'I used to ride when I was a little girl,' she was saying, 'but Mum made me choose between going to a good school and the horse.'

'And here you are. A flight attendant,' Grieve smirked.

'Hey!' she said. 'I'm studying law, I told you that.'

'How far into it are you?'

'Far enough to know that these are illegal,' said Alice, running a finger over his ivory handle.

'They're definitely dangerous. I don't know about illegal though.'

'When was the last time you fired one off?' Alice reached in to put a full hand around its grip.

'Not recently enough,' said Hector.

'I imagine it's addictive.'

Hector stared into the grey eyes and returned her subtle smirk. 'Do you want to see it?'

'Might not be wise to pull it out with all these people around.'

'There aren't that many,' said Hector, looking around the first-class cabin and finding only a single pair of legs, four luxurious pods distant.

'But still, we should probably find somewhere private to do it.'

Grieve tilted his head back and smiled and nodded. 'I do think we should, yes.'

PEACEMAKERS

Hector's passport was handed back to him with the turn of an officer's head towards the large corridor which led from Immigration.

He walked slowly down a wide blue-carpeted ramp. As he passed between backlit billboards of koalas and people laughing at picnics and prancing on beaches and riding over vineyards in hot-air balloons and climbing mountains, two men in dark blue overalls and jackboots, brimming at the hip with instruments of violent subjugation, came out from the door among them and stalked at Grieve's shoulders.

He descended by a wide set of imitation alabaster stairs to the vast and sterile white of the Hall of Baggage Claim. An electronic panel told him that his luggage was to be collected from carousel eleven. As he strolled two more men emerged from a bare halogen-lit room to join rank behind him.

Grieve stood with his hands clasped behind his back at the centre of the length of carousel eleven. He watched with disdain as suitcases paraded beneath him—purple things with rainbow ribbons tied to every handle, Minnie Mouses smiling like devils on a Normande tympanum, enormous square clamshells of shining black plastic. A white-haired old lady wheeled a luggage trolley to his side and said, 'I wonder, young man, if you could grab that suitcase for me? The plaid one.' Hector smiled at her and said, 'Of course, ma'am.' He stepped forward and leaned down and pulled the thing from the belt and transferred it to her trolley. She thanked him and he smiled down to her and said, 'You're very welcome,' then he stepped back and reassumed his stance.

An armed man stepped into Grieve's line of sight. A black glove was poised at the holster on his waist. 'Mr Grieve?' Hector attempted to stare through him. 'Mr Grieve?' Then he announced, in a feeble attempt to sound authoritative: 'Please take off your jacket.'

Hector glanced sideways from the passing luggage and put his hands in his jacket pockets. 'Make me.'

'Mr Grieve, I won't tell you twice. Slowly take off your jacket and place it on the floor. Then put your hands behind your head and get down on your knees.'

Grieve looked over the man's crowded utility belt then stared for a time at his face, then at his thinning gel-spiked hair. He grinned and said, 'And who are you that's going to make me?'

'I'm an Australian Customs Officer, sir.'

'And I'm a Commander of The Royal Order of Sahametrei. So fucking what?'

'We have reason to believe that you're in possession of a concealed weapon. Slowly take off your jacket and place it on the floor. Then put your hands behind your head and get down on your knees.'

'On my knees?' Hector smiled. 'I don't fucking think so. And they're weapon-*s*. There are two. Not concealed, just under my jacket.'

'Please take the jacket off, sir.'

'Or what, masturbator?'

The officer leaned to his right and lifted his head. Several throats were cleared at Grieve's back. Hector looked to the ground behind his left foot and saw in his peripheral vision two more uniformed figures. He looked all the way around and inspected and scoffed at their armoury. He raised an eyebrow and looked over his right shoulder, there to smile at the fire power of the two officers he found there.

Slowly he unzipped his jacket and pulled it from his shoulders and let it fall to the floor. There, shining in his shoulder holsters, were the hammers and ivory and rosewood butts of his revolvers.

'Mr Grieve, you're going to have to come with us.'

Grieve ran his tongue along the front of his top teeth and lifted and slightly turned his chin. 'Irrumator, says fucking who?' He looked down to the officer's pistol. He wiggled his fingers at his sides. With slow rolls of his head he again looked over his shoulders.

'I'm just kidding, I'll come with you. I don't want to have a gun fight in an airport, it'll just make you look bad. Plus, your boyfriends might be watching.'

In a room in a distant and dark corner of the hall, Hector's holster was placed on the table before him as the balding officer flicked through his passport. He held each page out to catch the full white light of the halogen overhead.

'Mr Grieve, regardless of whether or not you have a permit for these weapons, you absolutely cannot carry them in an airport.'

'Says who?'

'Says the law.'

'Why, because some slobbering Tasmanian freak couldn't get his dick hard and decided to spray some tourists? They should be illegal in Tasmania, not here. No, Tasmania should be illegal. I wasn't going to shoot anybody with them. *You've* got guns.'

'We're Customs and Border Protection officers.'

'And I'm a Commander of the Royal Order of Sahametrei. A knight of the Guardians of Jayavarman the Seventh and a Most Honourable Captain of Indra Protector of The East. What's your point?'

'That just sounds like gibberish to me.'

'You look like gibberish to me.'

The door to the interview room was opened and a young man with a lanyard and laminated card at his neck stepped in and said as though he were impressed, 'Hector fucking Grieve. I don't believe it.'

'Brad,' said Grieve, elongating his name as a squawk.

'Hector Grieve.' Both men banged chests in a hug and slapped one another's backs.

'Brad, you got ugly.' His face had become a pale and meaty caricature of that which Hector remembered.

'Fuck you,' Brad laughed.

'How the fuck are you?'

'I'm really good, Hector. How 'bout you?'

'What the fuck are you doing here?'

'Thanks, Cam,' said Brad to the officer in the chair before taking his place.

'You're shitting me?' said Grieve as he watched Cam lean back against his hands at the wall. 'This guy's your boss?' said Hector to the officers around the room. 'I knew this guy when he had his head wrapped around a toilet six nights a week.' Grieve cackled and said, 'You remember that summer? Anchorman and Jägermeister. We almost got sponsored by them.'

'Summer and a half,' said Brad, nodding. 'Why are you in here?'

'Ah, these chubby-chasers didn't like I had my Peacemakers on me.'

With a single finger Brad raised Grieve's holster from the table. 'Do you have a permit for them?'

'I don't need a permit.'

'You've flown in from Siem Reap, right?' Grieve nodded. 'How did you get on a plane, not with them, Hector, but carrying them?'

'It's freezing in here,' said Hector. 'Can you feel that?'

'You realise you could be charged with smuggling firearms?'

'Who's smuggling? There's no smuggle. I walked onto the plane with them, clear as day. Had them on me the whole time. It's not like they were up my arse. Though that'd explain why these guys wanted to arrest me.' Hector looked around the room and wiggled his first two fingers at the ceiling.

'Carrying two revolvers, in an international airport. Hector. Do you think you're a cowboy? You can't carry these around, mate, and you definitely can't bring 'em into Australia. That's a federal offence.'

'I know all that, Brad,' Grieve moaned, tired already of the rigmarole.

'We have to confiscate 'em.'

'Brad! Come on! Do you know where I got these?'

Brad shook his head. Hector pulled out the seven-and-a-half-inch Colt Single Action Army and spun its considerable weight on the table so that its barrel faced his own stomach. 'This was a gift from Mel Gibson, Brad. He came to Siem Reap to scout locations for a film he was going to make. About me.'

'Mel Gibson was going to make a film about you?'

'About me. I took him riding, shooting, I took him on an... on an expedition. He had so much fun he sent me this as a thank you.'

'What happened to the movie?'

'Ah, the Cambodian government. They couldn't... Well, they wouldn't back a movie about what I was doing there. Do you know what the nicknames of these guns are, Brad? Peacemakers. The Gun That Won The West. Abe Lincoln may have freed all men, but Sam Colt made 'em equal. And look at this beauty.' He slid the five-and-a-half-inch across the table. 'A gift from the King of Cambodia himself, Brad. That's an ivory handle. From the king's own hunting grounds.'

'Ivory? Hector! You can't own ivory.'

'Says fucking who?'

'And you definitely can't bring it into Australia. This is quarantine as well now.'

'The holster's Javan rhino leather. Do you know how rare that is?'

'Javan rhino? Good God, Hector. Do you know how endangered those animals are?' Grieve pouted and shook his head. 'Hector, this table, right now, is international news.'

'I've been international news seven times.'

'We're taking them off you.'

'Brad, come on, it's me! I used to steal you bottles of Cointreau from over the bar. You remember? The Perseverance? You used to drink Cointreau, like a fairy. I'll tell you what, you keep the bullets, I'll keep the guns.'

'These are loaded!? Jesus fucking Christ, Hector! You're lucky you weren't shot.'

'They're lucky they weren't shot.' Hector unloaded the bullets from their chambers and slid them beneath his hand across the table.

'We have to go through your bag. Did you pack it yourself?'

'You're not going to like what you find in there.'

An officer lifted Grieve's army-green duffle onto the table and rummaged two surgical gloves through it. Very shortly he said, 'Woah,' and pulled out an M16.

'Hector!' Brad exclaimed in stern almost-disbelief. 'Are you fucking serious? Please tell me that's not real.'

'It's an antique. A gift for my dad. From a marine they captured during Vietnam. Did you know Cambodia's the most heavily bombed country in history?'

'And the AK-47?' said Brad with an open mouth as one was extracted and placed before him. 'Seriously?'

'For my brother. I took that, Brad, legally thank you, from a… Well, from someone who didn't need it anymore. That's an antique as well, see the serial number? Russian-made, 1950s. … And that one,' said Hector, pointing at the officer's latest extraction, 'is actually really valuable. Arisaka 38. Japanese, from the occupation. Look.' Grieve stood to show Brad the kanji symbols charred into its wooden body.

'Hector,' said Brad, very seriously.

'Brad.'

'Do you realise what you could be charged with?'

'Bringing souvenirs back for my family?'

'Conspiracy to commit an act of terrorism.'

'Terrorism? What the fuck does that even mean? They're not loaded, Brad. They're gifts.'

'They're guns.'

'*They've* got guns.'

'*They*'re federal customs officers. Hector, what are you *even* talking about? Guys, could you leave us for a second?' Those leaning against the wall and he searching Grieve's bag all sneered at Hector as they left the room.

'Working for customs, Brad?' said Hector with disappointed censure. 'What the hell?'

Bradley Nelson was never Hector Grieve's best friend, insofar as Hector Grieve could be said ever to have had one, but he was the friend with whom Hector had dreamt longest and largest. From sixteen until Hector's exile they had spent countless nights conjecturing at the stars, listening upon high cliffs to the crash of Bass Strait, philosophising at the sea, driving ocean roads to The Stones, encouraging and enlarging one another's aspirations— Hector's to write, Brad's to be a travel photographer.

'The youngest state director in the history of the department.'

'What happened to photography?'

'Photography? That was like ten years ago.'

'And our oaths? Remember that night we walked through the school at midnight swearing we'd never give in? Slaves to nobody, straight to the top, conquer or bravely die?'

'We were nineteen.'

'Ten years.' He exhaled the magnitude of the number. He had not ever thought about the duration of his life in decades. 'Wow we're old.'

'I get sore knees when the weather changes,' said Brad.

'I've got a bad back from riding.'

'What are you doing home?'

'Ah, Dad's sick. I have to… Well, I don't know yet.'

'Billy Boy? What's wrong with him?'

'Don't know yet.'

'What are you doing tonight?'

'Nothing. Drink? Jimmy's?'

'Jimmy's closed. Years ago.'

'Ah. … Dinner? Lion of India.'

'Closed.'

'Fuck.'

'How about I invite the boys around for a barbie and board games?'

'What's that?'

'It's a barbecue and board games.'

'Board games?'

'Yeah, it's fun! We'll have a few tinnies, grill up some snags. Maybe even crack out the Pictionary. Waddya say?'

'Will there be girls?'

'Oh there'll be girls,' said Brad. 'Now, Hector, what's in the box?' He lifted a flap on the cardboard container at the other end of the table to the assault rifles. 'Do I want to know?'

'It's whisky. Special whisky, very rare. It has a royal patent in Cambodia, and it's all I drink, and you can't get it anywhere else.'

'Well I'll tell you what… You've got twelve bottles in here. Your allowed limit for spirits is 2.25 litres. You have eight and a half. Four times the amount of spirit you're allowed. But you can keep the whisky if you bring a bottle of it tonight.'

'Deal.'

'But I can't let you take the rifles.'

'Brad!' moaned Hector. 'Come on!' He inserted into his protest a smile that infected it with danger. 'Remember in Munich when I stole that crate of Pol Roger and we got drunk six times in three days? Brad, it's me! Hector!'

'These two are fully automatic weapons, mate. They're just… You can't.'

'But I can keep the revolvers, right? You can have the ammo, I don't need it. But these guns, Brad. These guns are all I've got.'

'If you swear, *swear*, not to fire these weapons, or carry them in public, or show them to *anyone* while you're in Australia, you can keep them. For old time's sake. But you never tell a soul that they exist, and you never *ever* let them see the light of day.'

'I swear.'

'What's Mel Gibson like?'

'He's wild, man. He is hilarious.'

Brad escorted Grieve to the end of the 'Nothing To Declare' queue and they shook hands and said that they would see one another tonight.

High automatic doors of opaquely frosted glass opened before Grieve's baggage trolley. He entered the long and vast Hall of Arrivals and walked left. A crowd of Chinese people were assembled at a long barrier of plastic board and metallic railing— were peopling the cafes; everywhere tapping at their phones; collecting currency; ignoring the announcements made only in Chinese; holding up signs in Chinese; were everywhere pushing luggage trolleys loaded with Minnie Mouse suitcases; transporting taped and wrapped cardboard boxes across the shining white concrete.

Grieve muttered, 'What the fuck?' as he strode the length of the wide pathway. 'Where the fuck am I?' He found at its end Carla. 'Oh, fuck me. What the fuck are *you* still doing here?'

'I've also been told, Mr Grieve, you might have some trouble adjusting.'

'Adjusting to what?'

'Home.'

'Home you think?' Grieve gave a doubtful squint and a slight shake of his head. 'What makes you the authority on "home"?'

'I'm an accountant. How are you getting home?'

'I'll walk.'

'Don't be silly, I have a car waiting. Where are you going?'

'She-ferret, if the choice were between being carried over a mountain in the lips of an elephant with herpes, and spending ten minutes in a car with you, I'd let Dumbo the Prostitute suck me across Tibet.'

Carla shook her head at the reaction to her offer and Hector Grieve strode on, out into the crisp air and flaxen light of the afternoon.

WESTMEADOWS

WESTMEADOWS

1

With his duffle bag over his shoulder and box of whisky resting heavily between his hands and his stomach, Hector S. Grieve glared at the wide billboards and multi-storeyed car parks and on- and off-ramps and the cold breeze visible in the young gum trees that greeted him. He passed a caveless party of men settled into a lunch hunted from golden-arched paper bags and squinted up at a high billboard for Chinese wine before descending behind a seven-lane intersection and a McDonald's to climb an escarpment of crab grass.

Before him screamed a dual-carriage Acheron—wailing with unmuffled motorcycle and howling with construction-truck trailer. His gaze fixed ahead, looking neither right nor left, he crossed the first stretch of lane to come to a median strip of eucalypts. Beyond the second torrent of traffic he had a beer bottle thrown at his head. At last, a vista of chain-link fence, petrol tanker and ute.

In the distance hills of landfill rolled, grown over with drab green and yellow weed. Walking beside the freeway he entered immediately into a length of hip-high grass which trapped his ankles as he tried to step high, clouds of pollen puffing into the air as he brushed aside its heads. He followed the path of a shallow creek bed and soon stepped through the cobweb of the largest spider he had ever seen. He nearly dropped his box of whiskey as he swatted the creature from his thigh.

He veered away from the roadside as an off-ramp joined to form three lanes of speeding traffic. He followed the chain-link fence through pale ripgut which quickly became shoulder high and stabbed the backs of his hands. Between an overpass and a recycling depot the hillock dried out completely. White butterflies played in prickly lettuce. Then beneath his boots the terrain became a brown and grey crunch of ground thistle and dead grass. A brief respite from the trudging soon came in the form of a gravel path, fenced off at its visible end. He walked a length of barren and rocky dirt strewn with litter, saw pass underfoot the vertebrae and thin ribs of a lamb's skeleton, came to be above a bush of driest bramble at the barbed-wire corner of a sere meadow of highest ripgut daubed with the pale aqua of artichoke thistle.

Gellibrand Hill and its turning radar tower lay upon the horizon, falling gently across to low slate-grey roofs of houses in a creek valley. Hector dropped into a dry paddock. As slowly he traversed it the tone of his tanker jacket rendered him but a bending wind in the grass. Beside him, greeting cars on the freeway, a billboard advertising the Ring Cycle was stuck firmly into the soil beside a billboard for China Construction Bank. He stepped over another barbed-wire fence and walked a gravel road being thunderously prepared by large vehicles for the laying of asphalt.

A fly flew at his mouth, then at his ear, then three of them bounced at the contours of his head. He spat and convulsed and blinked and snorted as he struggled past a stretch of land that was now, where it had not been before, a car park fenced in at the furthest limits of the suburb. Birds chirped upon power lines as Hector swatted still at the tiny beasts. He stomped what should have been a stroll of freshly mown nature strips and gardens of cactus and wattle, of white rose and weed—houses of red brick and beige. Two sugar palms rose high behind the roof of the first house to invoke for Hector a memory—the traditional home of the gangly family of Alan Forney, the autistic kid whom through high school had been ridiculed for wanting to be when he grew up a spatula.

'No, a bachelor!' said Hector in Alan's easily imitated whine, smiling as he recalled the ancient teasing.

A woman in fluorescent jumper was almost as short and twice as fat as the pitbull she walked into the crescent that had long ago contained the house of the girl whose father repaired VCRs and whose golden high school reputation had in year 9 been irreparably sullied by the spreading of a false rumour that she was happily a sodomite. The park across the street had had its playground replaced with a collection of spongy protuberances. The small oval beside it was driest yellow and stalked by a squadron of magpies. The houses were unimproved; no front gardens more flourishing than Hector remembered. A brick fence had been replaced by a higher metallic one here, a lawn covered over with artificial pebbles there. Hector seemed to think that several large trees had been felled. He sensed an unsettling discrepancy between the craters of cracked dirt in each of the thirsting nature strips and memories of a verdant childhood.

There came the plastic white pickets of the house in which had grown up a football-playing contemporary of Hector's—now in alternating weeks a folk hero and a rapist—then, his own.

45 St George's Drive, Westmeadows. A short driveway opened to a double garage of red brick and green roller door; a front garden of rose, hollyhock, and fuchsia, all in the shade of the bottlebrush tree in whose drooping boughs Hector had so often played as a child. A path led between a lawn and a bird of paradise to the front gate. Hector left his box and kit bag beside the garage and used the brick of the western neighbour's house to spring himself onto and over the eternally locked gate which hemmed in the narrow passage beside the closed side of the house.

He fell onto his feet as softly as he could and stood in the shade of the green little alley. He pulled his ivory-handled revolver and crept forward to the first window. Slowly he leaned out to peer through curtains of heavy lace. He passed before them and crouched and crept to the floor-to-ceiling glass behind the kitchen table. He heard within the clinking of cutlery into an empty bowl and rushed past the width of the triple window to come to the back door.

He momentarily stepped out into the backyard; saw nobody in its length of bright lawn. With the barrel of his Peacemaker at his cheek he turned to the flyscreen back door. He lowered its handle as silently as he could and found it open; eased it towards himself and stepped up onto the concrete step. The brass doorknob too was unlocked. He eased in the heavy wooden door and was standing in his laundry.

He stalked past the dog food and vacuum cupboards and came to the staircase. He looked into the living room of familiar rug and sofas and turned to cross the macadamia tiles as quietly as possible. He came to the kitchen doorway and there was met by a man in a dressing gown. Hector snapped the barrel of his gun to the man's forehead and shouted, 'Freeze, y'old fucker!'

His face opened and convulsed with fright as he recoiled from the intruder. A bowl shot out of his hands and shattered on the floor.

Hector rose to uncontrollable cackling. He doubled over and put his hand to his belly then arched back to catch his breath, cackling still.

'I dropped my quinoa,' said the man, one hand on the kitchen table and one at his heart. He worked at catching the breath that had been frightened from him.

'Relax, Dad! It's empty. Look.' Hector cocked the gun and pulled the trigger to sound a steel clink. He twirled it backwards on his forefinger and opened his jacket to reholster it. 'Dad!' he said, imploring the man to embrace him. He stood him up by the shoulders and looked him over.

'What the fuck, Dad? You look like a scrotum.'

'Hector,' his father sighed, already enervated. 'What are you doing home?' He took a sponge from the sink and wiped up his lunch.

'Some spectacled dishcloth told me you were sick.'

'Dying.'

'We're all dying.'

'Not this quickly.'

'That's not how a Grieve talks, Dad.'

'Six months, Hector.' In his blue towelling dressing gown he ran the sponge under water.

'The dishcloth said something about not being able to afford treatment. What the fuck's she talking about?' His father stood at the bench and reassembled his lunch. His thin calves were blotched red and black between the hem of his dressing gown and his slippers. 'What the fuck are you eating?'

'My lunch.'

'That doesn't look like food. What the fuck is it?'

'Quinoa, goji berries, chia seeds, LSA.'

'None of that sounds like food. What are you, an astronaut? Let me make you a real breakfast.'

'They fight the cancer. They're superfoods.'

'And what's that bulldyke of a wettex on about? You can't afford your treatment?'

'I'm out of money,' groaned Hector's father. 'Broke.'

'Broke or broken? Where'd it all go?'

He shuffled around his son and the question. He had once been of equal stature to Hector. Neither had ever set foot in a gymnasium but both had always broadly chested and wide-shouldered. He was now so much reduced, hunched, and shrivelled, that Hector could see the top of his head—bald and mottled and sprouting with short needles of white hair.

'The Turk,' said Hector, and his father set off for the living room. 'I told you about her. Marry strange wives, Dad. Snares and traps and they *will* turn away your heart after their gods.' His father took to an armchair and raised its footrest and turned on the television. Hector went after him.

'What about Selathoa? I don't understand. ... Dad?' He snatched the remote and turned it off. 'Dad?! What about Selathoa?!' His father looked up at him in silence. Hector saw in his eyes a vulnerability he had not ever in another man encountered, not even one whose liver was bleeding. They were thinly lidded, resembled more a gecko's than a Grieve's. Without the thick head of black hair that Hector had known him to have his head was smaller than Hector imagined. His complexion was a sort of translucent grey, ethereal and cracked; his cheeks, as though he were malnourished, were sunken, and he had jowels, from which even his chin drooped.

'You really do, Dad. You look like a scrotum.'

Thus as testicles had William T. Grieve descended.

William T. Grieve had been since Hector's first memory a magnanimous man of action. Through Selathoa Property Limited, the company he founded shortly after marrying Hector's mother—that benevolent corporation on which he staked the continuance of his family's reputation and to which he devoted his life—William had campaigned across both the developed and the developing world, assisting the latter by wielding capital raised in the former. With vast reserves of kindly wealth—the type donated by Christian businessmen in America, invested by young businessmen in Australia, divested by dying businessmen in England—he had fought both openly and covertly most of the world's larger corporations and several of its more atrocious governments. He had taken Nigerian men out of the martial employ of Chinese oil and educated them to recruitment by BP; built Bosnian schools in Serbia and Serbian schools in Bosnia; rid northeastern Nicaragua of two strains of tuberculosis; facilitated the release and Indian shelter of thousands of Sri Lankan refugees; put roofs over the heads of doctors without borders in Iraqi Kurdistan; paved mountain roads in Burma so that whole Shan villages could vote; ensured the preservation of the jungle home of three hundred Sumatran orangutans.

William was on the national honour roll of seventeen democracies and four dictators had personally pinned medals to his chest. He was an inducted knight of eight chivalrous orders and revered variously as a lion, an eagle, and a rooster, in the tribal regions of three continents; possessed the keys to four cities he wished never again to visit; had been endowed with annuities by two now-overthrown provisional democratic councils. Fatwas had been declared upon him by three political parties of varying barbarity and eleven Russian corporations had prices on his head. His memory was invoked upon no less than six war memorials and a statue of an approximation of his likeness stood today in the churchyard of a village in northern Armenia.

Away from his young family for weeks at a time, Hector's bedtime stories had always been retellings of his father's travels— the height of rocket launchers compared to the Congolese children who carried them, the texture of Kenyan cow's milk when mixed with its blood, the sounds of the costumes of whirling Yemeni brides, the Jezebel eyes of parading Revolutionary Guards, the smell of the tents of Kazakh horsemen, the feel of the golden crests of Tibetan priesthood, the intoxicated laughter of old Khmer women who spat purple at his feet. Hector had not once detected fear or uncertainty in his father's demeanour nor had heard him speak tentatively of any project to which he had resolved to dedicate his energies.

Intensely proud of his family's history and wanting very much to pass on its ancient reputation, it was in this nimbic glow that William T. Grieve agreed to let his youngest son travel to Cambodia to see if the family business might assuage that increasingly embittered temperament.

So from William St. Clair, who died fighting the Moors in Spain on a quest to take the heart of Robert the Bruce to The Holy Land, to The Great Montrose whose motto was To Conquer Or Bravely Die, from the New South Wales Corps to the 2/9th Cavalry Command Regiment in North Africa—of Scotch and Swiss blood— from exemplar of vital goodness to internationally honoured man of action, from childhood hero to paragon of bosses—

Thus as testicles had William T. Grieve descended.

'What happened to Selathoa?'

'The Peshmerga.'

'What about them?'

'And the ATO took everything. And the Federal Police.'

'The Turk!'

'She stole my sperm and had a witch doctor put a spell on it.'

'You marry a Turk and this is what happens, Dad, I fucking told you. They bathe their children in bat's blood. You know that? Did you even read my letters?'

Correspondence with his son had long ago commenced a

decline into sad one-sidedness. William had not in five years read a single line. As Hector grew in experience, both in combat and command, he became more himself and took to chastising his father for remarrying, took to medieval insult at his father's selection of a Turkish woman as replacement to his mother, took to a condescending disavowal of his brother's decision to take up journalism. All were acts which Hector considered supremely disloyal to the upbringing of which he was so proud, both by the father who gave it and the brother who shared it. In his letters home he increasingly pontificated, berated, attacked. At last, the appearance of an envelope addressed by his son became to William occasions of repugnant distress. He simply slid them into the supermarket catalogues which he binned on his way back into the house.

'No more Selathoa?'

'Gone. The family has fallen. We faced charges of funding a terrorist organisation.'

'Shit.'

'Shit,' concurred William with quinoa dribbling from his mouth.

'Well we'll work something out. Where's Neville?'

'Neville? Hector.'

'What?'

'We put Neville down years ago.'

'You what?! What'd you do that for?'

'He got old and cranky, he kept snapping at people. He bit one of John's friends.' So ended a century-old succession of Grieve border collies.

William scraped the edge of his bowl with his spoon. When satisfied that no more could be gained from it he set it aside he picked up the television remote and pointed and clicked. A succession of low-definition video clips was playing, all of which involved an overweight male being struck in the groin. 'Turn that shit off,' said Hector and retook it and reswitched it off and threw it onto the tiles at the front door.

'That's *Ow, My Balls!* said William.

'Don't you want to know what I've been up to?'

'Why are you back?'

'To help you.'

'How are you going to help me?'

'We'll figure it out. I don't know.' A silence ensued. Hector looked around the living room. Not a decoration or item of furniture had changed. The ceiling was still of the same pine boards at which he had spent hours staring, seeing in their knots the eyes, ears, and snouts of deer, rabbit, dog. The walls still were adorned with William's photographs of faraway places. Shortly Hector said, 'I was kidnapped.'

'Mmmm.'

'Who got you again?'

'Mm hm.'

'Dad?'

'What?'

'Who got you?'

'Who got me?'

'When you were kidnapped.'

'Oh. … Umm… Boko Haram.' William was saddened by the memory rather than the fact.

'Ho!' said Grieve, impressed by the superior brutality of his father's captors. 'I didn't get it that bad. Pathet Lao. Sailors. Killed them all, the communist bastards. Hung the captain by the neck from his trawling mast. How'd you get out again?' William stared at the black screen of the wide television. 'Dad!'

'What?'

'How did you escape?'

'Escape from where?'

'When you were kidnapped.'

'Oh. … … Navy SEALs.'

'Nice. … Ever been fired on by a tank?' Still William stared. 'Dad, what the fuck?'

'Mnmnm,' William grumbled, shaking and lowering his head with anxiety. 'Enough.'

'Enough what?'

'Questions.'

'I haven't seen you in eight years, Dad! Don't you want to know what I've been up to?'

'Go and get the remote.'

'Don't you want to know where I got the revolver?'

'No.'

'What do you mean, No?'

'No more of the past, it stresses me out. Go and the get the remote, I want to watch the telly.' He slouched in his chair and stared.

'Dad, come on, this is temporary. The dishcloth said there's a drug that'll fix you, right?'

'Mmm.'

'You've turned into a miserable prick, haven't you?'

'Mnmnm.'

'You want a drink?' Hector went to the bar at the rear of the living room and poured himself two fingers from a fading bottle of Chivas Regal. 'Dad!?'

'What?!'

'Do you want a drink?'

'It's two o'clock in the afternoon.'

'Not for me. It's 10am. Time for a bracer.' Hector downed it and said, 'I'm going to get my stuff from out the front. Here. Have a play with this.' He handed his father the five-and-a-half-inch Peacemaker. 'Ivory handle, a gift from the King of Cambodia.'

William put the gun aside as Hector went outside, shortly to place the box of whiskey in the bar and to take his kit bag upstairs. Two of his own portraits and two of his brother still adorned the walls of the staircase, as did the last family photograph taken before his mother's death. The photographs of his father with the Dalai Lama, with Emir Kusturica, with an elated Maasai tribe—had been augmented by a handshake with Barack Obama. The sepia photograph of his great-grandfather's rural bank and its staff was still in place over the landing. The walls of his own bedroom were dark and bare. He stepped carefully through a floor of boxes and drew the blinds.

The Boyhood Of Raleigh, Lessing's *Last Crusader, Napoleon Crossing The Alps, Gordon's Last Stand, A Digger and His Roo in Egypt, The Sanananda Burial of Three NCOs*—all were stacked on their side in one corner. His single bed was on its side, jammed against the wall by boxes stuffed with possessions of varying exoticism—a Dogon mask, a scimitar, a fez, a ram's skull, gold plate—gifted all to his father out of personal, tribal, national, gratitude. He pushed with his boot a box in front of the door of his wardrobe. Bulging bags of thick plastic slid out. He shoved at the door with his shoulder to reclose it.

He opened the door to his brother's room and was immediately and comprehensively confused. The bed was draped in a pink mosquito net, its linen of printed Disney princesses, pillows and duvet covered alike in Ariels, Jasmines, Belles. Grieve's baffled look only intensified as he inspected the room. There was a three-storey wooden doll house between the foot of the bed and the wall, a corner of Polly Pockets, plush animals and wooden blocks, a Ninja Turtles van, a Tamagotchi and a GameBoy, an open bag of Legos with a half-ruined castle crumbling in its centre, two shelves of Beanie Baby, a rocking horse, a stack of colouring books and a tray of Derwents and an upright circle of connector pens.

Downstairs he found his father with his chin lowered to his sternum, staring up at the television.

'Did you have another kid?' William changed the channel, assessed its content, changed it again. Hector stepped into the bar and poured another triple. 'Dad?'

'Mm,' he grumbled.

'Did you have another kid?' Hector put his hand on his father's shoulder as he reached down to switch the television off.

'I was watching that.'

'Did you have another child?'

'No. Why?'

'What's with John's room?'

'John's room? Oh, the play room.'

'Play room for who? And where the fuck am I going to sleep? My room's full of crap. Where *is* Jack? What's he doing with himself? ... Dad?!' Hector pulled over an armchair and sat beside his father. 'What's Jack doing with himself?'

William handed Hector a tabloid copy of *The Age*. He eased himself out of his armchair and turned the television back on.

Hector found somewhere about the paper's middle a headshot of his younger brother with the headline beside it: 'Why I'm Fasting For Hashim al Katab.'

'Jesus,' said Grieve descending to concerned seriousness as he read. 'Does he actually believe this shit?'

'He'll be over for playtime later. You two can catch up.'

'Did you say playtime?'

'Mnm. ... You won't understand.'

'I have to eat something. Do you have anything in the house beside that crap you had for lunch? ... Dad!?'

'What!?'

'Turn... that fucking shit... off.' Hector stood between his father and the television. 'Do you have anything to eat in the house besides turtle food? Do we have bacon?'

'Everything's healthy since I got sick.'

'Do you have servants?'

William at last looked up at his younger son. With uneven

eyebrows he began shaking his head. 'No, Hector. We don't have servants. Go shopping. There's change on the microwave. Take the car if you want.'

2

Hector Grieve turned his father's unfamiliar car onto Western Avenue. What once were fields of grass now were on both sides warehouses and factories, enormous and concrete and bustling with forklift and gigantic truck, guarded and busied everywhere by fluorescent yellow shirt.

At the road's gentle bend a police car was parked in the middle of its two lanes. Red and blue lights twirled in the sunlight as a fluorescent officer waved drivers through on each side. At Grieve's approach the officer facing him stepped more fully into his path and waved an orange baton at her feet. Grieve slowed to a stop as she came to his window.

'You'd better be a stripper. What the fuck do you want?'

'D-d-d-Damo!' said Hector when the station's ranking officer came into the interview room and looked up from his clipboard.

'Hector Grieve? Jesus Christ. How the fuck are ya?' They shook hands as he sat.

'D-d-d-Damo.' (Not from Damien Boglight's own stutter had the nickname sprung, but from that of a much younger student, selected one day quite at random and picked up by the shoulders of his jumper and slammed into a locker.) 'What the fuck are you doing, you're a cop?'

'A station sergeant.'

'Remember when you put Nick in a wheelie bin? That was fucking hilarious. And you put that year 7 in his locker? Ha ha. It kind of makes sense that you're a cop actually, you did like putting people into things.'

'Driving drunk with no licence, mate?' As though he expected more from him, Damo winced as he asked.

'D-d-d-Damo. I haven't been in Australia for eight years. My licence must have lapsed. I'll get a new one, I can do it tomorrow. And the drinking … I'm definitely not drunk. What's .05? That's a number. And I blew *on* 0.05. Isn't there leeway? I've been in Cambodia for eight years. Do you know what I was doing there? I once drank a litre of whisky then got a call out to a raid by Thai special forces. Do you know what a Royal Thai Air Force Panther Squad is capable of, Damo? Seriously mean dudes. And after a litre of whisky I killed them all, with two revolvers, a torch, and a loudspeaker playing The Descent Into Nibelheim. I only had two drinks this morning. I've got jet lag. And I'm still on Cambodian time, D-d-d-Damo! Come on!'

'The way it works is, you have to pay the fines. When they arrive in the mail, they'll tell you when your hearing is. You can dispute the charges then if you want. But you won't win.'

'Whatever. Can I have my keys back?'

'You don't have a licence, mate.'

'What, I can't drive now? Is this Russia, I can't leave my house without being stopped by the fucking police? God damn it. I've been back for half a day and all that's happened is I've been told what I can't do. I killed two of those Panthers with my bare hands, Damo, dropped onto them from a tree. That was a litre of whisky. … Damo?'

His exploits falling on ears which considered them not only irrelevant but also as the ramblings of a particularly imaginative drunkard, Hector Grieve left the station and walked, under cloud like horizontal dark smudges on grey paper, up to that larger adjacent suburb in which he had spent so much time growing up, and into its very heart.

Chapter Two

GLADSTONE PARK

1

It was joked by the very few profound minds that passed through its vacuum that one dream died every minute in Gladstone Park. But this simply was not true. None of its inhabitants ever had dreams, insofar as a dream might be considered a conception of reality any different to that of its present unconscious depravity. All had what are termed 'goals', and all of those possessional—another car, a holiday house, the largest possible television upon which might be played the latest video game, the fastest conceivable computer upon which pornography of none but the highest definition could be enjoyed.

Cut off to the north and the east by valleys running with irretrievably polluted creeks, the geographical isolation which in other primitive communities led to bifurcations in language, to the specialised production of a tradeable handicraft, to a local divinity sacrificed to in common worship—had in Gladstone Park formed a particularly contemptible dialect of the national language, created a handful of aspiring mujahideen, sunken to the worship of objects obtainable from bank accounts made mystical by inexplicable fluctuations of balance.

The residents of this post-industrial village set their superbly modern lives not by the light of the sun but by the call of the work-bell and routine of the television guide—nine until five if one were lucky, more often seven till six, and their favourite shows at hourly and half-hourly intervals thereafter. The seasons were not of planting and harvest, nor even of cold and warmth, but of sitcom and drama, to which whole weeks were sometimes devoted. Their chief experience of travel, beyond repeated incursions into the hellish beaches of Altona and Bali, was traffic—the stagnation of the Tullamarine freeway their Silk Road, its Mickleham Road exit their Jade Gate.

And, its barely beating heart, fading in the southern sunshine, as quiet and outdated as a Christian graveyard—its shopping centre.

A single-storey sprawl of taupe tile and light blue wall, Gladstone Park Shopping Centre was bordered – past, present, and future – by a primary school, a TAB, a nursing home. Impervious either to gentrification or inflation, there was a supermarket and a few national banks but by and large its restaurants sold gruesome food at historical prices and from its retailers could be bought furniture and clothing that had changed little in cost or style since the fall of Saigon. Its stores were rotating cubes of hope, stock, silence, and loss. A handful persisted, mysteriously, through the decades—the growing debt or money-laundering operations of their owners the only logical explanations for survival.

There was an influx of obnoxiousness at midday, when a pimpley horde of senior students invaded to take their lunch, and one of tracksuit pant and pram at a quarter past three when the single mothers migrated thither after picking up their children from the primary school. At all other times the edifice was practically empty, its cracked tiles and mildewy walkways ghostly boulevards haunted by the elderly and the housewife, and—vastly more numerous—those taking sick days off work.

Hector S. Grieve came up a concrete rise of black chewing gum and cigarette butt. Beneath a portico of beige concrete and uncapitalled column he passed a huddle of cleft palette and foetal alcohol syndrome; of fluorescent-shirted and heavy-booted men in flat-brimmed caps and plaster-flecked wife-beater with Ned Kelly calves.

He entered through the automatic doors of its northern portal. He passed a barefooted woman in singlet and tracksuit, then a superclinic and a pharmacist and a man with a ponytail behind his head. At a dental clinic a woman with a throat bandage ran her wheel-carted oxygen tank into his leg. Then a podiatrist and a two-dollar superstore and a vending machine which dispensed Tarax Creamy Soda. Youths in his old school uniform loitered everywhere in packs. A family of native New Zealanders in oversized t-shirts and hooded jumpers were making bounce the timber of a wooden bench as they laughed at the mention of someone being kicked in the scrotum. In the centre of a low-ceilinged atrium was the podium of blue carpet on which he in kindergarten had sung Christmas carols. Then there crossed behind a dimly lit island, which still served thin milkshakes and old hot dogs, a figure Hector at first did not believe he had seen.

He slowed and waited till the apparition emerged once again from behind a wide blue column. The vision was confirmed.

The man wore a brimless white hat above a thick and low brow and sported a long moustacheless beard. His black vest was over a long white tunic and loose white trousers which fell upon leather sandals. Hector's face became entirely askew as his head turned to watch the man go into the supermarket.

From an aisle end of Vegemite Hector leaned slowly out to observe him browsing a rack of Tim Tams. He took a packet from a middle shelf and walked on. Grieve slid to the other side of the aisle-end to again await his reappearance.

'What are you doing?' said a voice at Hector's back. Grieve turned his head and found himself confronted primarily by the man's beard.

'Did you park your donkey out the front?' said Hector.

'Oh, you're very funny mate,' the man smiled with a thick subcontinental accent. 'Yes, I left him with my rocket launcher.'

'That was my next question. Or are you just here to slit a priest's throat?'

The man's smile widened and he began to nod. 'You're so funny, my friend. Actually I have a graduation party tonight, for my cousin. But I am not able to go home and change between giving my afternoon lectures and the party. Would you like to come? It has to be a small affair because she starts first thing tomorrow morning at the Children's Hospital. But you will have to change out of your battle clothings, she comes from a peaceful family. Where, might I ask you, did you park your tank?' Following the drop of the man's hand from the collar of Hector's jacket to his boots Grieve looked down at his own costume. 'You have a nice day, and peace be upon you.' He left Hector at the tower of Vegemite.

The layout of the supermarket was exactly as Hector remembered it, though the décor appeared darker. He strolled through the cold of the pre-packaged salads and the young coconuts and the mushrooms.

An old man in a beige Harrington jacket and flat cap rifled through onions. An employee came out to stack potatoes and immediately was assaulted.

'There's something wrong with your onions,' said the old man, crying out. Unheard, he repeated the accusation as he walked at the young man. 'I said there's something wrong with your onions.' He held one up.

'*What's* the matter?'

'I bought a bag of onions last week and I cut one in half for my dinner, and the next day I went to use the other half and it was all soft and shrivelled. There's something wrong with your onions.'

Grieve looked around to see if anyone was finding the geriatric's onionic gripe as amusing as he. He caught sight at the super-market's gated entrance of a couple holding hands, the female a short and heavily made-up blonde, the male a tall and slender East African in a check shirt. They discussed rolls before a bakery rack. 'Miscegenation?' said Grieve quietly to himself and lowered a concerned and investigative eyebrow. He watched as they laughed with one another before moving on to a refrigerator of European cheese.

'An onion should last at least week when it's been sliced,' said the old man, his discourse tolerated because it did not seriously disrupt the potato-stacking. 'When I was a boy an onion would last a fortnight. A fortnight! But these are only lasting a day. *Less* than a day,' he went on, in his booming and heavy Australian. 'Did you know the ancient Egyptians *worshipped* the onion? As a symbol of eternal life.'

Through the entrance strolled two men, in shorts and tight t-shirts, their hair cut closely to the sides of their heads and shining long with product on their scalps, their wrists crossed and hands holding.

'What the fuck?' said Grieve, as the pair went off towards the Vegemite.

'And if I'm paying four dollars a kilo for them I expect them to last at least two days. At *least* two days.'

The bakery section at Grieve's right appeared to sink momentarily into the ground. He looked over to it and found that it was in fact undisturbed.

'Where are they from anyhow? They're from bloody China, aren't they? That'd explain it? When I was your age we used to grow our *own* onions. Do you know how big they were? The size of your head, Sonny Jim.'

Now the pineapples and the mandarines began to falter. Whole patches of green and orange slid slowly as a blur from side to side. Hector blinked a few times and gave his head a violent shake and turned to watch a long deli case rock like a see-saw at both ends. He squinted hard and squeezed his eyes shut. He opened them on the packaged seafood fridge, whirling like a blue and salmon pin-wheel. The onions and the potatoes too—and the men castigating and stacking them—began to vibrate upon various unsettling axes. Hector pressed at his eyes with his finger and thumb and shook his head, then opened them as wide as he could.

'Hector bloody Grieve,' sounded long in an indelicate voice. He turned to it and found a young woman of uniquely familiar beauty and instant and unequalled nostalgia. 'I don't believe it.'

'Helen fucking Gricius?'

'Hector fucking Grieve. In Gladstone Park Shopping Centre. I never thought I'd see the day again.'

A basket hung at her folded arm. She was in yoga pants and fluorescent pink tank top, her hair in the ponytail that was to Hector, even after all those years, an object of visceral and especial arousal.

'Are you all right? You look like a crazy person.'

'I'm all right,' said Hector, looking at his surroundings with confused suspicion. 'What the fuck happened here?'

'What do you mean? Where?'

'There are immigrants everywhere. Gays, too.'

'Hector!' Helen laughed. 'You can't say that! What the hell are you talking about?'

'They're everywhere.' He shook his head. 'There were none before I left.'

'Of course there were, you idiot. Lauren's brother was gay. And Anton. Half the school were immigrants. I'm Lithuanian, you psychopath. Or have you forgotten about me?'

'I could never.' Hector subsided into vacant thought. Once again he looked around the open section of supermarket. Its tremors had ceased.

'So what are you doing home?!' she smiled. She was mildly excited to see him.

'Helen,' he said, smiling at her and shaking his head. He looked at the side of her head, gazed upon her so familiar ears, that delicate neck that had changed not a bit. 'Vicious Gricius.' He took in her deep-set eyes, Levant-thickened with mascara, her nymphic mouth, her softest top lip, high and fullest cheeks.

'Very funny.'

'You look good.'

'I feel good! *You*, look like you're about to invade Poland. What's with the boots?'

'Hm?' He looked at them and said, 'What's the matter with them?'

'No, nothing,' she teased. 'So what are you doing home then? How long you here for?'

'I'm not sure yet. It depends on Dad.'

'Billy Boy! How is he?'

'He has cancer.'

'Oh, Hector, I'm so sorry to hear. Are you all right?'

'He's the one with the cancer. What are you up to? How are you?'

'I'm *really* good, Hector, thanks. And I do hate to do this but I *really* have to run, I'm sorry, I have yoga.' She initiated her departure with a half turn away from him.

'What the fuck is yoga?'

'Still hilarious I see,' she said, dismissing the question as part of the feigned antiquarian ignorance she knew to be part of his humour. 'Will you call me? We *have* to catch up. How long's it been?'

'Eight years,' said Hector, in her presence again barely able to concentrate. 'I remember your home phone number.'

'Eight years! Wow.'

'Ummm…' he said, catching her as she again half-turned to leave. 'Brad, you remember Brad. He's having a barbecue tonight. You should come. All the boys are coming.'

'Ahhh,' she smiled awkwardly. 'I don't think so.'

'Why not?'

'I don't stay in touch with any of those guys. I haven't seen any of them since you left.'

'Neither have I. So what? It's the perfect time to catch up. I don't want to go alone. … Come on. … Vicious?' he said in playfully long and low syllables. 'Seven o'clock?'

'Let's catch up one on one. I'm free most weekends.' She turned fully towards him and stepped onto her toes to kiss him on the cheek. She hugged him and rubbed his back and said, 'So good to see you! You're at your dad's? I remember the phone number too.'

Hector watched her walk speedily to the front of the store. Her ponytail brushed lightly across her neck like gilt tassels over shimmering marble, the curtain hem of an abandoned temple of Venus on a hilltop in some remote outpost of a longed-for empire.

He emptied his pocket of change and totalled the gold and silver. At the refrigerated bays of plastic-wrapped meat he inspected prices. Legs of lamb were instantly excluded as beyond his budget. Chops were packaged in too great a number to allow him to buy the three he might have wanted, as were the dull pink sausages about which he had forgotten and whose nationally revered taste and texture he recalled as detestable. All cuts of beef had been valued as opulent. Even heaped zig-zags of mince meat he had to dismiss as luxuries. Pork belly, no—an extravagance; and the chicken breasts were so large as to weigh themselves out of his grasp.

At the case's far end, in a pool of diluted blood, he found a total that was more in line with the change his father had given him. He picked up the wet tray and read of its contents. 'Pet or soup bones.'

After walking most of the supermarket's aisles and marvelling at the strange diversity of its shelves, Hector arrived at the front of the store with a sliced loaf of home-brand white bread in one hand and smallest block of home-brand tasty cheese in the other. There was a single queue of overweight persons leaning bare arms at the handles of hulking and overflowing shopping trolleys. This wended from the open register's conveyor belt, past the Vegemite and beyond the adjacent ends of Doritos and bulk toilet paper. Grieve looked upon its still procession, at its offspring shouting at its whining elders, then turned to watch a curious expanse through which people with groceries were freely passing.

A kindly old woman in black woollen jumper approached him. 'Sir, if you'd like to use the self-serve checkout…' She held a hand towards the clearing.

'The what?'

'The self-serve checkout. This way.' She corralled him into the arena of space and movement. She directed him to a computer screen above a barcode scanner with a platform of shining metal on either side. As Hector read the screen a feminine voice sounded somewhere from it: 'Scan, or look up item.' He struggled to digest the unfamiliar configuration. He looked to his right and saw a woman scanning her own groceries before herself placing them in plastic bags. In imitation he ran the bread's barcode over the scanner. It bipped. He awaited further instruction. The screen told him to place the item in the bagging area. So he did. Instantly it told him to remove it from the bagging area. And he did. Then the screen, which had hitherto been green, turned red and a voice came from within: 'Please wait for assistance.'

He gave an impatient, 'Hm!?' and looked to the person beside him, running barcodes effortlessly over the scanner and dropping them into shopping bags without breaking her swing. The little old lady in the jumper came to his side and ran a scrap of paper over the scanner and tapped the screen. She said, 'There you are.'

A little display box showed Hector how to place the item in the bagging area while simultaneously imploring him to do so.

He again dropped the loaf onto the metal platform at his left and the red screen returned. It read, 'Item error,' and the machine's voice said kindly, 'Please wait for assistance.' He recoiled his hands from the whole system, fearing that somehow he was offending it. The little old lady stepped back to his side and scanned her piece of paper and tapped his screen. She inspected the bagging area and read through his digital tally of one item. Then she said, 'There you are.'

The bread now resting on chrome and satisfactorily accounted for, Hector S. Grieve with much caution passed the plastic sliver of cheese over the scanner. It bipped. He placed it very carefully on top of the loaf of bread and stood back from the arrangement and watched his screen. After a brief peace it turned red: 'Item error.' Then it intoned in its feminine voice, 'Please wait for assistance.'

'What the fuck?' said Grieve to it and patted a hand at his rib. They were there, though neither of them loaded. The man behind Hector was scanning and bagging like a veteran. The little old woman came again to Grieve's other side and looked back and forth between the bagging area and the flashing-red screen.

'Hang on,' she said, scanning her barcode and tapping at his digital list of items. 'Let's start again.' She handed Grieve his sliced loaf of home-brand white bread and his smallest block of home-brand tasty cheese and said, 'There we are.' As she embarked upon silencing somebody else's machine Hector thought of Jerusalem, and of seeing his men waiting as sentinels in the scorching sun. His screen returned to green and now read, as it had done so very long ago, 'Scan, or look up item.'

Hector tapped decisively at the 'Start' button, changing the screen to one which, without memory, implored him to scan his first item. He held the loaf of bread perpendicular to the surface of the scanner and with meticulous obedience drew it across. The machine bipped. Slowly he leaned down to place it with the utmost delicacy onto what he hoped was The Bagging Area.

He rose to upright again and saw that the screen had registered the new scanning. An animated box was instructing him on where to put it. Its display changed to, 'Please place item in the bagging area.' Grieve looked to that volatile region whereupon his item had indisputably been placed. He looked to the screen to see if there was not some delay in its processes. Then like Indiana Jones exchanging an idol for a bag of sand Hector raised the loaf from the booby-trapped platform. He looked up to his screen, saw that the order to place the item in the bagging area was unchanged, then relowered the sliced bread and snapped his hand back from it.

'Please wait for assistance,' sounded from the screen, rather more loudly than it had previously done. Grieve said to it, very loudly, 'Fuck you,' and hit it with his palm and picked up his sliced loaf of home-brand bread and smallest block of home-brand tasty cheese and walked out.

'Sir!' called the little old lady between chimes of, 'Please wait for assistance.' 'Sir!' she said again, scurrying after him as his striding boots echoed over the taupe. '*Sir!*' she said, catching up. 'Please wait for assistance.' Grieve turned and pointed the barrel of the smaller Peacemaker at her. The little old lady's palms rose to shake at her ears. 'Please wait for assistance.' Hector cocked its hammer.

'Sir, you have to pay for those.'

'Please wait for assistance.'

'Why isn't there someone scanning my things?'

'It's a self-serve checkout.'

'No. You shop, someone scans your shit, they put it in a bag. That's the system, it was flawless, what happened to it?'

'Self-serve checkouts, sir. You have to pay for those.'

'The self-serve checkouts don't fucking work…' He read her name tag.

'Please wait for assistance.'

'Silvia. They waste my fucking time. I was just working in a supermarket. Do you know how humiliating that is? Well, you do, you work in a supermarket. But I don't, and I was working in there. I don't want to work in a supermarket, d'you understand? *You* work in the supermarket, I shop at the supermarket. Employees work, not customers. You see? I'm sorry about the gun, Silvia, but I'm walking out with this loaf of bread, and with this tiny block of home-brand cheese, because I shouldn't have to work in a supermarket. Tell your bosses to get rid of those contraptions, and to get *people* scanning my shopping. So I don't have to waste half my fucking day trying not to upset a sensitive little princess of a dickhead machine. All right? We have other things to do. Real jobs. We don't want to have to work at the supermarket as well, OK?'

Silvia nodded and said, 'I'll tell them.'

'I really am sorry about the gun. I hope I didn't scare you. I would have shot the machine, but the gun's not loaded. See,' and with a pull of the trigger the hammer clicked onto nothing. Silvia's eyes convulsed to tightly shut and Hector reholstered the gun and turned to leave Gladstone Park Shopping Centre in something of a hurry.

2

Hector returned to a quiet house. He threw the bread (of which he had eaten half on his walk home folded around chunks of all the cheese—thinking, as he used so often to think, 'Why Westmeadows?') onto the kitchen bench and heard giggling upstairs.

He pushed open the closed door to his brother's bedroom and immediately his face contorted to one of extremest bemusement.

William T. Grieve lay on the floor. His older son was cross-legged in white t-shirt and denim dungarees. Between and surrounding them was an assortment of dolls and figurines and plush animals.

'Reach for the sky,' said John J. Grieve in a slow American accent. He shook Woody the Cowboy up at his younger brother.

'There *is* a child. Who had a kid? Am I an uncle? Jackie Boy!?'

'Ah Hector! It's playtime.' said his father. 'Join us if you'd like, or we'll be done soon.'

'Where's the kid? John, I'm an uncle? That's fantastic!'

John picked up a plush Ariel and smiled and sang in falsetto, '*Up where they walk, up where they run, up where they stay all day in the sun… Wandering free, wish I could be, part of that world.*'

'You have a lovely voice, Donut. Hector, doesn't Donut have a lovely voice.'

'Where's my niece? Who the fuck is Donut?'

William stood up from the rug and closed the door behind him. 'There's no child, Hector,' he whispered.

'So I'm not an uncle? What the fuck's going on? Why's John dressed like a four-year-old and playing with dolls?'

'I told you, it's playtime, part of John's treatment. It's called play therapy.'

'Therapy?' said Hector, loudly, and turned an ear to his father. 'I don't fucking think so. Therapy for what?'

'John's had a traumatic few years.'

'Traumatic? Has he had a horse shot out from under him at full charge? Has he had to throw a grenade back at the enemy not knowing how long the fuse was? I don't think so. Traumatic how?'

'Well,' said William, and compiled the incidents that had contributed to his eldest son's condition. 'Someone argued with him in another newspaper a few years ago. That set him on edge.

Then one of the muslims he was fasting for came out and said gays should be given the death sentence. That upset him quite a lot. He saw somebody get punched in the city…'

'Why are you calling him Donut?'

'John's taken a Western name.'

'What?' Hector growled.

'It's customary in Asian societies to take a Western name. You should know that.'

'First of all, donut's not a name, it's a fat person's biscuit. And Jack's not Asian, he's a Grieve. And John *is* a western name! What the fuck is going on, goddam it?!'

'At the start of the year your brother told me he's been having early premonitions of suicidal ideation. That's serious stuff, Hector. He needs this.'

'Dad…' said Hector, matching his father's prefatory solemnity. 'What the *fuck* are early premonitions of suicidal ideation?'

'It means he's thinking about thinking about killing himself.'

Hector paused to consider the sentence. Soon he erupted: 'What?!'

'The play therapy really helps, you couldn't *understand* how much it helps. He's able to wear jeans again, and he's eating hummus.'

'Men are above therapy, Dad, you know that. And I know that, and *he* fucking knows it as well.'

'Hector, that's just not the way it is anymore.'

'He is not a Grieve.'

'He's as much a Grieve as you are.'

'He is *not* a Grieve. You cannot change the definition of a Grieve anymore than you can that of a man. And he is fucking neither.'

'Oh, Hector,' lamented William as his youngest son returned to his oldest's bedroom.

'Stand the fuck up you weird little shit.'

'*I'm ready to know what the people know.*' John held the Ariel in both hands at his chest and rocked her from side to side. '*Ask 'em my questions and get some answers. What's a fire and why does it- What's the word? Buuuu-*' Hector slapped his hand onto John's mouth and grabbed a strap of his dungarees. 'Stop singing you fucking idiot. What the fuck are you doing? Act like a man. Stand the fuck up.' Hector attempted to lift him.

'It's all right, Donut,' said William above the commotion. 'Hector's a little bit angry, he's confused. He's been away for a long

111

time, remember? Hector's been riding horsey-worseys, haven't you, Hector? Don't be scared, John John. Hector, stop. Let go of your brother. You're not respecting his space. Hector! Donut needs his space. Leave your brother alone.'

'How the fuck can you even think about allowing this, Dad? Jesus Christ. Would you stand the fuck up?'

With terrified eyes John looked up from being shaken as there rose the sound of yapping at the front door.

'Hansikoko!' cried John in a high and elated voice after pulling Hector's hand from his mouth. He dropped the little mermaid and ran out of the room.

'What the fuck is *that* noise? What the fuck have you done?' said Hector to his father before they descended the stairs. 'This is *not* all right.'

At the entranceway a young man played with a navy blue baby halter at his chest. In it was breathing like a frantic rat a small animal which in some ways resembled, though it wore children's sunglasses, a dog. John wiggled a finger at the creature's furiously licking tongue.

'What the fuck is that?' said Hector.

'Hector this is Hansikoko. Hansikoko, my little brother, Hector.'

'I didn't know you had a brother,' said the young man as he slid himself out of the halter and passed it to John.

'What the fuck's your name?'

'Hansikoko,' he said, holding out his hand for Grieve to ignore. He was taller than Hector, the same height as John, with thick and straight black hair and olive skin.

'What the fuck kinda name is that? Is that your Western name too? God damn it.' Hector was resentful that he was using the term.

'My western name's Tomorrow. Hansikoko's my real name. Half German, half Japanese.'

'You're half German, half Japanese? … Fuck me, a little axis of evil. What the hell's going on, Dad? We just let the enemy into our home now?'

'And this little ball of cuteness is Foo Foo,' sang John as he placed the halter over his own shoulders. 'Say hi to Hector, Foo Foo.' He held one of the animal's paws and waved it at his brother. 'Hector, say hi to Foo Foo!'

'Neville would have killed that thing.'

'Which is why Neville was put down,' said John.

'*You're* the one who's been in Cambodia!' Hector glared at Hansikoko. 'I want to talk to you, about adoption. Foo Foo's all we've got till then, aren't you Foo Foo?' He put a hand at John's arm. 'But I just came by to drop the doggy-woggy off.'

The three Grieves went outside to see Hansikoko to his car. 'I'll see you tonight for iftar?'

'Three dates at sundown!' sang Hansikoko as he put on very small sunglasses and lowered his window.

'Fasting's so awesome! Isn't fasting awesome?'

'Why do you talk like that?' said Hector to his brother.

'Don't you think we should give Hector an Asian name?'

'Absolutely you fucking should not. Why the fuck are you talking like that? You didn't talk like that eight years ago, talk properly or don't talk at all.'

'Look at you three Grieves. All *so* handsome, but *he's* grumpy. Kisses!' Hansikoko backed out of the drive and William and John waved him goodbye.

Inside, John said, 'Hector will you look after Foo Foo for a couple of hours? I have to work, and Dad finds it stressful, don't you Dad?'

'Absolutely I will not.'

'Please, little brother? I have so much work to do.' John spoke as though he were talking to a baby: 'And Foo Foo does *not* like being ignored-y-wored, do you, Foo Foo?'

'John's writing a piece on the Ivory Bunker,' said their father. 'Aren't you, John?'

'Is that a nail salon?'

'The biggest economic crime in decades,' said his brother. 'Completely immoral. Do you not know about it? Of course not, you've been away. All the billionaires in Australia are pooling their money to build an underground bunker in New Zealand. Where they plan on escaping if ever there's civil unrest. This is how the rich spend their money.'

'I don't care.'

'John's Melbourne's most prolific journalist, aren't you, John?'

'Well bullshit does always abound. I'm fucking starving, can we eat something?'

'Not before sundown,' said John in a high and melodically annoying voice. 'I'm fasting. For Hashim al Katab. Do you remember him?'

'I do not. And I don't give a shit about your diet.'

'Well you should. He's being held on charges of conspiracy to commit an act of terrorism without a hearing. For two months.'

'Good.'

'That's a basic violation of our human rights, Hector.'

'His. Not ours. And humans don't have rights, they have obligations.'

After a pleading aside from his father, Hector sat in a metallic outdoor chair in the centre of the backyard, one ankle resting on the other, drinking the first of two beers he had found at the back of William's bar fridge. Around him, in wide panicked circles, sprinted Foo Foo, wheezing loudly as it deviated occasionally from its orbit in order to sniff something.

Grieve drank the last of the first beer and threw the bottle at the animal. Foo Foo dodged it, then grabbed the strap of its halter with its teeth and laboured to drag it to Hector's legs. It tried to lift its front paws onto Grieve's seat; waved them a few times in the air before falling back down. It put its head into the halter, withdrew, yapped, attempted again to climb onto the chair. It repeated the ritual (which normally induced the nearest human to don the halter) this time burrowing completely into its folds and wriggling around to poke its head out the top. It yapped again, and waited. Hector looked down at the critter and raised his eyebrows and said, 'As you wish.'

He stood from his chair and Foo Foo's breaths became through excitement even more rapid. Hector S. Grieve picked the halter up in one hand and walked over to the high wooden fence at the clothesline. Assuming that the neighbour's pool had not been filled in he tossed the halter and its contents over it.

And he sat back down and opened the second beer with his teeth and rather enjoyed it.

Chapter Three

BARBIE & BOARD GAMES

1

Hector heard familiar laughs before he saw the outdoor table of frosted glass at which his closest schoolmates were sitting.

'Here he is!' said Bradley Nelson and got out of his chair as Hector strode through the open gate between the brick garage and front corner of his house.

'Boys!' said Hector, as an electric guitar crunched from a speaker and a sinister male voice screeched: '*It ain't easy, living free…*' A series of 'Ho's and 'Jesus Christ's were exclaimed as there rose a flurry of excitement and wonder. Hector handed Brad the agreed bottle of whisky and turned to, 'Roger fucking Waybroke! Eighteen Twenty-Three. How the fuck are you?'

'You look exactly the fucking same,' said Roger, and the two men banged chests and patted one another's backs.

Hector said, 'Ozzy McOscar!' and embraced Oscar McAuliffe in a similar fashion.

'Absolutely amazing,' said Oscar. 'Hector fucking Grieve. Why you dressed like a soldier, man?'

'Why are *you* dressed like an eighteen-year-old?'

'Fuck you,' he laughed.

'Cambodia, Brad said?'

'Cambodia,' said Hector as Brad walked him over to the table. It was surrounded by young women, in the three chairs beside those left vacant upon his arrival. 'Now Hector,' he said, preparing to introduce them. 'We have Fiona. *My* fiancée.'

'Get the fuck out of here!'

'Engaged last Valentine's day.' In an indistinct gesture of greeting Fiona raised a hand covered by the jumper which also concealed her body mass. 'Fi, Hector. Went to school with everyone. Then we have Alicia, Ozzy's fiancée.'

'You're fucking shitting me?'

'And Jen, Waybsy's fiancée.'

'You *are* fucking kidding me. All three of you?'

'The boys are taking the plunge,' said Roger Waybroke with his hands at Jen's shoulders.

'Kids?' said Hector to Brad.

'Not yet,' said Fiona. 'Just us and Blackjack.'

'*We're* waiting till the house is ready,' said Jen.

Brad asked Hector if he wanted a drink as he brought a seventh chair down to the concrete triangle formed by the garage, the wooden patio, the front fence. 'Should we open this special Cambodian whisky?'

'No, no, don't open that. That's for later.'

'Beer then?'

'Beer's fine, Brad, thanks.' Hector in his shirt and tucked olive tie sat with his back to the street in a high-backed chair with a long green-and-cream striped cushion. Brad handed him a beer retrieved from the refrigerator in the garage. The rainbow of electric haze glowing from coloured bulbs nailed into the beams of the patio was augmented by the dim yellow of the lights in the house, emanating through glass doors and a window over the kitchen sink. The evening was already chilly, the backyard beyond the table almost invisible in dull-green darkness. That phlegmy voice screamed on: '*I'm on my way to the promised land…*' and Oscar McAuliffe said, 'So let's do this. Tell us everything. What's it been? Seven years?'

'Eight.'

'And what the fuck are you doing with yourself?'

'We haven't seen this kid in eight years,' said Roger to his fiancée. 'He just disappeared one day, didn't you?'

'The last thing I remember was a book?' said Oscar.

'Take us back, Hector,' said Brad. 'Come on.'

'Take you back to what?' said Hector.

'There was a book, right?' said Roger.

'There was. The Japs made me rich.'

'What's that?' said Oscar.

'The Japs. They made me rich. The book you're talking about.'

'Hector,' said Oscar. 'You can't really say that, man.'

'Can't say what?'

'That word,' said Oscar.

'Rich?'

He shook his head. 'The other one.'

'Japs?'

'Yeah, you can't say that, man,' Roger added.

'What do you mean I can't say it? One of you girls Japanese?'

'It's offensive,' said Fiona.

'How is it offensive? Offensive to who? There are no Japanese

116

people here.'

'You just ahh…' said Roger. 'You can't really say it.'

'I can say whatever I want. And I can call whoever I want whatever I want to call them. And those bastards killed my grandfather's two brothers, I can call *them* precisely whatever the fuck I want.'

'It's offensive to me,' said Jen, most indignant.

'You Japanese?'

'I don't have to be, I find it offensive.'

'Hashtag awkward,' said Roger Waybroke.

'All right,' said Hector, gently and slowly. 'Don't offend the fiancées. It shan't happen again. Jen?'

She put her hands together at her chest and bowed her head and said, 'Thank you.'

'Hector, you want the Wi-Fi code, mate?' said Brad, tapping his thumbs at his phone.

'The what?' said Hector, bemused still by Jen's usage of the sampeah.

'The code, for the Wi-Fi,' said Brad.

'What's Wi-Fi?'

'It's Bradley the tank 69. Bradley the tank's all in capitals, six nine.'

'I don't know what you're talking about. What's wifi?'

'Ha!' said Roger, looking down at his phone and squawking. 'What's Wi-Fi. Still the funny one.'

'Second funniest,' said Oscar. 'Thank you very much.'

'What about you guys?' said Hector. 'What are you up to? Brad's at Customs. Ozzy?'

'Teacher,' he said. 'Gladstone Park.' He pointed his thumb towards the back fence, a high and dark mass behind the silhouettes of four barbecues on the lawn.

'Bull shit,' Hector smiled.

'Nope. The Values Coordinator for all year levels.'

'What does that mean?'

'What does what mean?'

'What the fuck is a values coordinator?'

'I determine the school's values—in line with social trends and the needs of the market—and I design and implement programs to make sure those values are a part of the learning streams for the curriculum at all year levels.'

'That sounds like gibberish to me. What the fuck are values?'

'I've implemented a trinity. All related, all equally important.' Oscar counted them out on this thumb and fingers. 'Tolerance, Friendliness, Respect.' He smiled and reached across to put his hand on Alicia's.

'Tolerance. Friendliness. Respect,' said Hector, unable to withhold a smirk. Oscar so brimmed with pride that he added a nod to his smile. 'Whose fucking values are those? Ha ha!' Presuming universal likeness of thought Hector addressed the whole table. 'They're not value at all, they're weaknesses. Tolerance? Jesus Christ. Nobody should be tolerant. Stupidity is as universal as dickwarts on a Broadmeadows teenager. Should we tolerate stupidity? What about cowardice? Laziness? These should be tolerated? And friendliness? What the fuck does that even mean? You work at a hug factory or a school? You should be teaching virtues, Oscar, not values. Mercy. That's a virtue worth the striving. You know why? To be merciful you have to have power. Why don't you teach your kids how to become powerful?'

'We aah... That's not really how we look at things, Hector.'

'You believe this shit?' said Hector to Brad. 'Friendliness! Ha ha! What the fuck's that even mean?'

'I think friendliness is a very important value in the modern world,' said Fiona.

'Do you, think though?'

Fiona raised her right hand and flapped it in the air as she elaborated. 'Look at all the horrible things happening everywhere. If only everybody was friendlier to one another. Imagine.'

Hector stared at her with a dumb squint upon a deeply wrinkled face. Roger Waybroke brought four more beers from the garage and returned to his seat. 'What are *you* doing with yourself?' said Hector.

'Me?' said Roger. 'Sales manager at Fifty-One Mustang.'

'Sales manager. Fuck. What do you manage the sales of? What's Fifty-One Mustang?'

'Largest web hosting company in Australia.'

'I don't know what that is.'

'The internet.'

'You sell the internet?'

'I sell names that people have for their websites. Say you want... hectorgrieve.com. I sell you that name and store your website for you.'

'You sell the names that people can have for their websites? Can you hold that? In your hand?'

'I'm a sales *manager*. I manage one of the teams that sells the domain names. The Oceania team. You can hold the team.'

'You sell something that doesn't exist.'

'Define exist, Hector.'

'I can safely say, Roger, that you have *the* most boring-sounding job in the entire fucking world.'

'Excuse me?' said Jen.

Hector turned his smile to her. 'I said, your fiancé has *the* most boring job in the entire fucking world.'

'That's a bit mean.'

'Of course it's mean. It's us. How long have you two been together? Does she not know how we work?'

Though it was through the fate of classroom seating that the four boys met at fifteen, it was through a shared sharpness of wit that their friendship had commenced and by a like cruelty of humour sustained.

An uncanny similarity in the austerity of their upbringings meant that seamlessly they shared identical views on what was preposterous and what was not, what laudable and what laughable, new and old, cowardly and cavalier, what was wrong and what was right. In the schoolyard they formed a proud clique. Others came, and after orbiting about the fringes for a while, promptly and under impersonal ridicule went. Into young adulthood they persisted in their refusal to admit no outsider less excellent than they thought themselves to be. Each peculiar in both outlook and behaviour, all creative and all equally fond of drink, they had privately vowed to one another never to give in. At least twelve oaths had been sworn—many of them while sober—never to cease the pursuit of mastery in their chosen fields of acting, literature, photography, screenwriting. 'La garde meurt et ne se rend pas!' had been shouted from rooftop beer gardens. 'God favours the brave, victory is to the audacious,' had been offered to the sea from the flames of beach bonfire. 'To Conquer Or Bravely Die,' had several times been screamed from all four windows—much to the drivers' annoyance—of a taxi.

'And Brad works for customs,' said Hector in a sort of conclusion. 'What a regiment.'

'Youngest state director in the history of the department,' said Fiona, elaborating with a lifted and flapping hand upon her fiancé's success.

119

'How's that for a group of men, huh?' said Oscar. 'A state director, a sales manager, a values coordinator.'

'And Mike's a bank manager,' said Roger.

'Isenhammer?' said Hector. 'I haven't seen him in years.'

'Got us our loan for the house, didn't he honey?' said Roger. 'Works at the Commonwealth Bank in the city.'

Oscar repeated the amended list of occupations then added to it, '*And* a writer.'

'So what are you doing home?' said Roger.

'I came back to raise crops,' said Hector in a Scottish accent. 'And God willing, a family. If I can live in peace, I will.' His friends laughed at the return of a long-forgotten impersonation. Then Hector S. Grieve announced: 'I'm a soldier of fortune.'

Oscar cackled and said, 'Remember our fake jobs when we used to go out?'

'Oh, what were they?' Brad threw his head back as he strove to remember. 'Roger you were a samurai, I remember that. I was a rocket surgeon.'

'Dolphin trainer,' said Oscar. 'And Hector, you were always a shepherd.'

Grieve cackled and momentarily reminisced. 'How the girls loved that one.'

'All right boys,' said Fiona, sweeping her hand up and out to flap her fingers. 'Enough of the glory days. Let's take a picky.' She stood at the end of the table and held her phone up. All leaned in to be included.

'Send that to me?' said Jen.

'And to me would you, Fi?' said Brad. Shortly five phones dinged. Jen picked hers up and found that she had received the picture. She put her phone between her palms and lifted her elbows and bowed in Fiona's direction. Then Hector was left with his head high above the others as all exposed the backs of their necks to play with the image on their phones.

'Insta?' said Roger.

'Make sure you tag me,' said Jen.

'Oh I'm so sorry, I look *awful*,' said Alicia, and busied herself with deblemishing her face.

'Hashtag good times,' said Roger.

'Hashtag barbie and board games,' said Brad.

'Do you want it, Hector?' said Oscar.

'Do I want what?'

'The picture.'

An interlude of silence. Grieve moved his eyes around the table, his head jerking from person to person as he watched them tap their thumbs and slide their fingers. Eventually all six phones clicked and were returned to the perspex tabletop.

'Hashtag I am starving,' said Roger. 'Hashtag what's for dinner?'

'Is that four barbecues?' said Hector.

'Yeah Jen's a vegan,' said Brad, 'Fiona and Roger are vegetarians, and Alicia's a pescatarian and gluten intolerant, so all the food's on separate barbecues. Saves any hoo-ha, you know? I'll get the snags on?' He stepped up onto the patio and slid the glass door across and went inside.

'Vegetarian?' said Hector to Roger.

'I don't eat meat unless I know where it's come from. What farm, who killed it. Hashtag veg life. Hashtag animals are my friends. Hashtag I don't eat my friends.'

'Hector, Brad said you've been in Cambodia,' said Jen. 'I've always wanted to go to Cambodia. What's it like?'

'Hot and sweaty. Like my balls.'

'Oh, imagine…' she breathed. 'Angkor Wat! I have so much wanderlust. *So* much wanderlust. Don't I have so much wanderlust, honey?'

'She really does,' said Roger. 'I'm always telling her she has more wanderlust than anyone I've ever met. Hashtag wanderlust and a half!'

'The *most* wanderlust,' said Jen.

'You really do,' said Alicia. 'I've never met anyone who has as much wanderlust as you.'

'I just… There are so many places!'

'Show Hector your wanderlust tattoo, babe,' said Roger. 'Hashtag inked.'

'What the fuck is wanderlust?' said Hector, irate that they were profuse with a word of which he had never heard.

'It's just… Haawww,' breathed Jen. 'Just a burning desire to wander. You know? So many places in the world. So many journeys. All so different. So many cultures. I want to get out there and see them all.'

'And we're going back to Bali in July, aren't we babe?' said Roger. 'Hashtag so hung.'

'I can't wait! I need to *feed* my wanderlust.'

'What the fuck do you want to wander for?' said Hector. 'I had to wander once. Through the jungle for three days. I was taken hostage by the Pathet Lao. Communists.'

'You've been to Laos as well!?' said Jen.

'I had to wander through the jungle for three days just to find a village. There's nothing fun about wandering.'

'I can't believe you've been to Laos!' said Jen. 'My God, I'm *so* jelly! Oh.' She stopped to shiver. She put a hand to her cheek and shook her head. 'My wanderlust is kicking in. I can feel it.' She fanned herself with her fingers as Fiona refilled her wine glass from a box. 'So much wanderlust.' She put her palms together and bowed her head and said, 'Thank you.'

Brad emerged from the house juggling an armful of plastic containers and ceramic dishes. 'Fi, can you grab the falafels and the veggie kabobs?'

'Can I give you a hand there, Brad?' said Hector.

'Sure, mate, come on over.' Shortly Hector and Brad were joined on the lawn by all except Alicia and Jen, who set about quantifying the amount of wanderlust that Jen possessed.

'So Cambodia?' said Oscar.

'Cambodia,' said Hector, inspecting the four hot plates.

'How long for?'

'Eight years. I was there the whole time.'

'You have such a nice tan,' said Fiona, turning from a barbecue crammed with slices of onion and fillets of zucchini. 'Oh, I'm sorry.'

'What?' said Hector.

'What?' said Fiona.

'What are you sorry for?'

'What?'

'Why did you apologise?'

'Did I? I'm sorry.'

'Sorry for what? Why do you keep apologising?'

'For saying sorry.'

'But why did you say it in the first place?'

'I'm not sure. People tell me I say sorry a lot. Sometimes I think I'm actually living an apology.'

'You're living an apology?'

'No, *a* living apology. Sorry. Is that what they say to me, Brad?'

'You all right honey?'

'I'm sorry, I don't know what's going on. I think maybe I've had too much to drink?'

'What were you doing in Cambodia for so long?' said Oscar,

diverting the conversation.

'I live in Siem Reap. Thailand Conquered.'

'Writing, right? You never told us about the book.'

'No, I'm a soldier of fortune. Two-star general in the Royal Cambodian Army. A Dharmaraja of the Order of the Leper King and a Restorer of the Eternal Peace of Sangrama. Brad almost took my guns off me when I got to the airport this morning. Didn't you, Brad?'

Brad turned sausages and said, 'I literally saved Hector from becoming an arms smuggler.'

'What do you mean a general?' said Roger. 'Like an actual general?'

'A cavalry officer.'

'Tanks?' said Roger.

'Horses.'

And as the falafels dried out and the pink sausages charred and vegetable kabobs drooped, Hector failed to convince his old friends and their fiancées that he had not spent the last eight years in an office.

Brad transferred their dinner from barbecue to baking dish and called out, 'Fi, salads.' All sat down to by tong and fork hoard food.

Brad placed two burnt sausages onto slices of white bread and drowned them in tomato sauce. 'Hector, after dinner you *have* to come in and see the tiles we picked out for the bathrooms.'

'I do hope to,' said Hector, waiting for the others to finish serving themselves.

'They the ones we got you onto?' said Roger.

'*Like* your ones, but a bit lighter,' said Brad. 'Thermopylae blue.'

'You remember the ones you really liked, Jen?' said Fiona, 'But they didn't go with the fixtures?'

'Oh *those*!' said Jen. 'I really loved them.'

'Hector,' said Roger. 'You should come over one night this week and see the tiles we've put in the kitchen! Check out the house, maybe weigh in on the pizza oven debate?'

'Yes! Hector!' said Jen. 'You should definitely come! But not on a Tuesday. Tuesdays we watch New Girl don't we, honey?'

'Hashtag Winnie the Bish. Hashtag Who's That Girl?' Roger sang. 'What do you think, Hector? Come round, have a look at the new house?'

'No screenwriting, Roger?' said Hector, still struggling to digest precisely what had happened to his friends. He had come expecting girls and a riot. The last time they had all been together they stole a Porsche and went skinny dipping with a third of the Icelandic under-21s girls' volleyball team.

'Screenwriting?' said Roger as though he had forgotten the word. 'What about it?'

'You were going to be a filmmaker.'

'And Alan Forney wanted to be a spatula,' said Roger, almost laughing.

'What does that mean?'

'It means I grew up. Hashtag adulting, man! I'll always know it's something I could have done.'

'You've all given up,' said Hector.

'Given up?' said Jen, mocking the very suggestion. 'Roger's the sales manager for the whole of Oceania. Aren't you, babe?'

'For something that doesn't exist.'

'Brad's the youngest state director in the history of Australian Customs,' said Fiona.

'Hector, I'm twenty-nine and a Values Coordinator. Do you know how much of an accomplishment that is?'

Hector wheezed a laugh and looked around the table. His eyes glistened in the lamplight as his cheeks rose in a wide smile. 'You've all missed the point,' he laughed, and drank from his beer.

'I'm confused,' said Oscar. 'Did someone make a joke?'

'This is our lives, Hector,' said Roger.

'Who are you to tell us we've given up, mate?' said Brad.

'I'm someone who didn't given up,' Hector laughed.

'*Did* someone make a joke? said Oscar. 'What was it?'

'Our *lives*, Hector,' said Brad. 'You've got no right mate.'

'I'll tell you what,' Hector smiled. 'Before we eat why don't we have a toast?'

'Good idea,' said Brad, and raised his beer bottle.

'The whisky I brought,' said Hector. 'It's Cambodian tradition to toast with whisky before a meal.'

'They must have *so* much culture there,' said Jen.

Hector returned from the garage with six shots of his whisky and one of Johnnie Walker, poured for himself from an assortment of half-empty bottles on the concrete bench beside the refrigerator.

Jen accepted hers with a bow, Alicia with an apology. Hector raised his own and said, 'Audacity, bravery, honour.'

'That's so beautiful,' said Jen. 'Hashtag good times,' said her fiancée. 'Hashtag cheers.'

'To old friends, and to… fucking fiancées.' Hector chuckled and said, 'Choul Mouy,' and drank his scotch.

'Is that Cheers in Cambodian?' said Jen. Hector nodded and repeated the salutation. All attempted to imitate it before drinking. Hector with a grin turned his shot glass upside down. 'Now let's dig in,' said Brad, and all did.

'What a banquet,' said Oscar.

'And you're going with the same tiles in the en suite are you?' said Roger to Brad.

'Is this all they ever talk about?' said Hector to Alicia at the corner beside him.

'Pretty much,' she said, forking salmon from its charred skin.

'How the fuck do you stand it?'

'Ha,' she laughed and nodded. 'I just think about being a mermaid.'

'What's that?' said Hector, as though he hadn't heard her.

'I imagine I'm a mermaid. Just swimming all day, the ocean in my hair. Or a unicorn. Imagine what it would be like to be a unicorn! Adulting's so hard, don't you think? *Too* hard most of the time.'

'We were thinking about going for the Thermopylae blue in the downstairs bathroom but then we realised that all our towels are almost that *exact same shade*.' said Roger. 'It just wouldn't make sense, would it babe?'

'It really wouldn't,' Jen laughed.

'And what about the feature wall,' said Brad to Roger. 'What are you gonna do with that you reckon?'

Persisting with Alicia, Grieve asked her what she did for work.

'Me?' she said, almost surprised. 'Oh I'm between jobs. I can't figure out what I want to do with last year. I am enjoying it though. Getting into art again, spending a lot of time drawing pictures of myself. There's just *no* better feeling than going to bed at night and not having to set an alarm in the morning though, you know?'

'No better feeling?' Alicia forked at slices of tomato and smiled and shook her head as she squeezed them into her mouth. 'Ever taken part in a dawn raid?'

'Is that like a fun run? I've done the Colour Run. I was meant to do Tough Mudder too this year but I think Oscar wants to go to Bali with Roger and Jen so… I've never been to Bali, have you? They have a mermaid swimming academy there. You can go swimming, *as* a mermaid!'

'You like mermaids, don't you?'

'I *love* mermaids. I think I was one in my past life.'

'How do mermaids have sex? You ever think about that?'

'Excuse me?'

'Everything's flat. There's no penis. There might be a vagina, but where?'

'That's a bit inappropriate I think.'

'Do you think, though?'

Offended, Alicia turned to join the bathroom tile conversation. Grieve sat back in his chair and chewed at a tasteless mouthful of blackened plastic casing and still-pink meat on white bread. He watched his old schoolmates and their fiancées for signs betraying the onset of the whisky—inspected Oscar's top lip for involuntary overbiting, Jen's eyes for wandering. All smiled and laughed as they discoursed at incredible length upon the dilemmas of Thermopylae versus Zama blue. The light from the kitchen seemed to brighten across the table. Hector squinted at the new intensity of glare then turned his head from the pulsating which seemed to begin from the coloured bulbs nailed to the patio. The outdoor table sunk at one side then almost overturned on its other. Grieve closed his eyes and rolled them back in his head and tried to breathe calmly. He drooped his shoulders and rattled his head back and forth.

An electric guitar twice sounded two notes from the stereo and was followed by the rising crash of a cymbal. The succession was repeated a few times until a dopey voice sang, '*If the sun… refused to shine.*'

'Hang on, hang on, hang on,' said Fiona, lifting her hand to wave and dangle her fingers as she tile-quibbled with her fiancée. But her quarrelsome hand seemed to keep on rising. Her eyes followed it with amazement through the air as it appeared to become a black and metallic blue butterfly. Her head meandered around the party as the shining insect fluttered across the table.

'Y'all right?' said Brad.

'Yeah, why?' She turned back to her fiancée. From his eyes sprouted and descended thick green tree roots. 'What's wrong with your face?'

'What do you mean?' said Brad. 'Have I got tomato sauce on my cheek?' Brad wiped his fingers at it then held them out to inspect for ketchup. They were bleeding, crimson seams of haemoglobin rising from his skin and running down into his palm. He wiped his hands with a napkin. The blood reappeared. He sucked at his middle finger; still the hemorrhage would not stop.

Seeing Roger's gaze frozen with fright at the roof of the pergola—he was monitoring a crouching samurai—Hector brought out the bottle of Cambodian whisky and poured them each another shot.

'I'm still so hungry,' said Oscar, rocking back and forth and gripping with both hands his ribcage, which he was very concerned to discover turned to dust in his fingers.

Jen's appalled mouth shot open—and was held agape—as Generalfeldmarschall Erwin Rommel appeared to hand her a drink.

For as the Greeks discovered their God-filled heaven on libations of amanita muscaria so the Khmers long ago conceived of their glacial hell—ice-cavernous and populated with snow devils—by a tea brewed of psilocybe cubensis. Hector raised his own shot of Johnnie Walker—standing at once a merman bearing a trident, a Nazi giving a heil, a shepherd with his crook—and all cheered and drank. Hector smiled and nodded and sat back down to wait for the more extreme effect of the second dose of the rare distillation that he had for years received in grateful tribute from the mushroom-gathering monks of Beng Mealea.

'Is that Mary Poppins?' said Bradley Nelson, the first to perceive Helen's entrance at the gate. '*Juuust aaaaa… spoonful of sugar helps the medicine…*'

'For every job that must be done,' said Fiona, watching the backyard of her home turn corner by corner into an enchanted wood.

'Helen,' said Hector, turning his neck. 'You came.'

'Let me get you a chair, Sherry Bobbins,' said Brad and stepped onto the patio. He descended to the grass and spun a chair at a waltz singing, '*Supercalifragilisticexpialidocious…*'

'What the hell's going on?' said Helen, smiling.

Hector stood up and slid Brad's chair over to his. Fiona was trying to catch single specimens from the swarm of fairies that had descended on the party; Roger's chin was glued from fright to his shoulder as he stared up at the pitter patter of samurai boots upon the pergola; his fiancée scowled at Hector, whose eyes were glowing red and upon whose top lip a toothbrush moustache was spinning like a spool of black string; Oscar pulverised his ribs between his fingers and his thumbs and was telling everyone how hungry he was; his fiancée was quite certain that she was underwater and now swam with glee.

'Quite the party. What is this, charades?'

'Do you want a drink? There's beer and wine. They're all drinking whisky. You don't want the whisky.'

'Why not?'

'It's got magic mushrooms in it.'

'They don't know it has magic mushrooms in it do they?'

'They do not.'

'You drugged them?'

'They are literally the most boring people I have ever fucking come across.'

'They're your friends.'

'Not anymore. I don't know who these people are. They're all engaged.'

'Only engaged?' said Helen, drinking from Grieve's beer bottle.

'Ridiculous right? And you're going to drink my beer are you? Thanks for coming. You hungry? I don't think there's any food left.'

'I'm actually starving. But it's all right. I'm good with wine, I can't stay long.'

Hector poured her a glass of white from the box in the centre of the table.

'Do you know where I get the whisky from?'

'Where? Cheers.' They clinked glasses. 'Welcome home.'

'There's a temple 75 miles northeast of Siem Reap. Have you been to Cambodia?'

'Nope.'

'Called Beng Mealea. Thai soldiers laid siege to it in '014, they wanted to take the tympanums out and sell them to the French. Beautiful carvings, eight hundred years old. But soldiers won't touch monks, so they waited at the cardinal entrances hoping they'd surrender, which they didn't. So I rode my regiment, you know I'm a two-star general, right?'

'Have a look at her,' said Helen, and pointed to Alicia. She was prostrate with her arms at her sides, flapping her legs as though they were a fin-ended tail.

'She really wants to be a mermaid,' said Hector. 'She told me so.'

'Board games!' screamed Brad. He had set his four-legged dancing partner on the lawn and was sitting upon her, staring at the embers of the barbecues.

'Board games!' screamed Fiona, and ducked beneath a plague of dragonflies and went inside to get some.

'I am actually starving,' said Helen.

'I rode my regiment out to this temple and entrance by entrance my men and I galloped through the jungle, we'd painted ourselves completely white, and we galloped through the jungle in the night appearing here, disappearing, reappearing there. They all fled, terrified. Their commanding officer called it off. We didn't kill a single man. And the monks were so grateful we didn't spill any blood on holy ground that they send me five boxes every year of the whisky they make with the mushrooms picked from the trees that overgrow the place.'

'You did what in Cambodia?'

'I'm a two-star general.'

Fiona came out through the sliding kitchen door with a stack of board games and a phone book. She was quite taken by the black and green and red of the Scrabble box and came to stare so closely at it that she could lick it. Then she did.

'The King of Cambodia gave me an ivory-handled Colt Single Action Army. Do you know what that is? A revolver, a very famous gun. As a gesture of free reign in Siem Reap Province.'

'And you're in Gladstone Park.'

'West fucking meadows and Gladstone fucking Park.'

Fiona stood at the other end of the table, snapping the halves of a Monopoly box like the jaws of a crocodile. 'I gotta take a wizz,' said Hector, disappointed that his bragging had had so blank an effect. 'I'll be back in a second.'

'I'm *sooooo* hungry,' said Oscar, watching his petrified skeleton turn again and again to puffs of ash as he punched his fists at his torso.

'I'm hungry too,' said Roger in a low whimper, afraid the samurai might hear, and upon hearing, decapitate him. 'I just want to eat meat again before they get me! One last time,' he quietly whined.

Hector patted Brad on the shoulder as he walked into the darkness of the rear of the house. He poised himself at an olive sapling in the corner of pine fencing. As he micturated he heard organic snorting from beyond the back door.

A searchlight shone at a small lattice enclosure, at whose top railing glistened a snout. A piglet, black and pink, rocked its head from side to side and appeared to smile as it looked curiously up at Hector.

Oscar was shouting still, 'I'm so hungry!' Roger was in a rising whisper repeating his plea that he wanted to eat meat just one last time before the samurai got him. And Helen *had* said that she was starving.

Hector opened the back door and stepped up into the kitchen and found a knife block beside the microwave. He pulled its most prominent handle, found that it was a bread knife, returned it. On the refrigerator were photographs of Brad and Fiona at the tile store, of the couple in Bintang singlets drinking cocktails in a swimming pool—held fast all by fridge magnets moulded of and emblazoned with 'Bali.' Hector unsheathed the knife from the widest slit and held it upside down to inspect the fineness of its blade.

Helen gripped at Jen's wrists in a struggle to hold them back from her cheeks, which Jen thought were those of a soft white rabbit. Alicia was beside her, clapping her fingers together as though they were pincers, now quite certain she was a Jamaican seacrab. Roger 'Eighteen Twenty-Three' Waybroke had watched the gathering army of samurai make the ten-foot jump from the pergola onto the concrete and had failed desperately to keep track of them as they dispersed into the backyard. His eyes were tightly closed, expecting at any moment a ninja star to enter his neck. Oscar 'Ozzy McOscar' McAuliffe held the Yellow Pages like a hamburger to his mouth and was attempting to fit his teeth over it in order that he might satisfy his burning hunger. Fiona tried to pry it from him, for it was, according to her screams, 'a stingray made of gold that was going to bite him like Steve Irwin.'

Hector S. Grieve leaned his head out and hissed in an attempt to gain everybody's attention. Neither his second nor his third, 'Psst,' had an affect on anyone, not even Bradley 'Brad' Nelson, saying with deep suspicion, 'Dragons,' to the barbecues.

From the cream-brick corner of the house Hector held out the carcass by its hind legs. He shook the thing so that the movement might attract their attention where his voice could not. When Brad finally looked over and saw the dripping gorge in the animal's throat the volume of his scream turned the whole party to the direction in which his horrified finger pointed.

'Blackjack?' cried Fiona. 'Blackjack!'

Jen began immediately to wail. Helen was unable to prevent her from grabbing her with both hands by the head. After a fourth scream she shrieked, 'I'm a vegan! I can't see that! I'm a vegan!'

Hector crossed the lawn with the carcass swaying at his outstretched hand. 'Roger, you can eat this, you know where it came from. Oscar? You said you're still hungry, right? Suckling pig!'

'Blackjack!' screamed Fiona. 'My baby. Blackjack!'

'Pigs are as smart as dogs!' yelled Jen. 'I'm a vegan! Pigs are as smart as dogs!'

Hector caught sight of the blood dripping onto the concrete of the patio. He stepped back onto the lawn and stood, variously in the harsh porch-light of the frigid evening, as Mr Donald Trump, Narcissus, a ronin in his suit of plated armour, a shepherd, the sea-witch Ursula, the devil—curly-tailed and pitchfork and all.

'I think we should go,' said Helen.

'Yep.'

'Pigs are as smart as dooooogs!'

The steel cries of a harmonica bent through the air as they left and a guitar was plucked behind a husky voice. *'I come from down the valley, where mister when you're young…'*

Hector closed the gate behind him. 'Did you drive here?'

'I walked.'

'I'll walk you home.'

'Leave the pig.'

'Really?'

'Yes really, you psychopath. You're not walking me home with a dead pig.'

Hector concealed it in Brad's front hedge and beneath a starless night blanketed with yellowish cloud they rounded the footpath of a long and silent bend of parked cars, past the grey silhouettes of the paper trees on the nature strips. Darkness emanated from houses with windows shuttered as though upon fortresses. Open lawns and wide desolation—desert shrubs and chain-link fences and bricks of cream and roofs of mission brown; drizzle set in and the road began to glisten.

2

'You still live around here?'

'In my parents' old house.'

'With Jules and Vlad? No!'

'No, they sold it to me. I'm 30 years old, you think I still live with my parents? They moved to Bali and gave it to me for next to nothing.'

'What are you doing with yourself?'

'I'm a teacher.'

'You too. Marvellous.'

'At Gladstone Views.' She smiled at him, knowing he would be amused by the fact.

'Jesus. Our primary school? How the hell'd that happen?'

'I can't afford a car and it's close.'

'Do you like it?'

'Mn,' she sounded as a high grunt. 'You said you haven't been back in eight years?'

'Eight years. And I have *no idea* what the fuck has happened in those eight years.'

'You said that, what do you mean?'

'My Dad's company's gone under. He's broke, and he's dying. He looks like a fucking scrotum. Some Turkish whore ran off with his semen. I probably have an autistic Turk half brother doing burnouts in carparks and slaughtering goats in Roxburgh Park. *I'm* fucking broke. My brother's in play therapy, whatever the fuck that is. He thinks he's a fucking eight-year-old girl. And all my old friends are as boring as a field of disabled eggplants whose girlfriends want to wander off and be Balinese fucking mermaids. Who invites people around to play board games? Seriously. Roger Waybroke's engaged! That kid had a foursome in a caravan park when he was fifteen! I can't carry my guns. I can't have a drink and then drive. There are Taliban and homosexuals at the supermarket. Nobody has a sense of fucking humour anymore, not even my goddam dad. You remember how funny he was. I pulled a gun on him this morning and he didn't even laugh. Not a chuckle, not a tee-hee. Eight years and the whole place has been turned upside down. The whole world's gone fucking boring. Sales managers and values coordinators. What the fuck is a values coordinator? Fuck tolerance. Toleration of differences is a denial of their importance. Every man knows that. A man needs war, not tolerance. These boys should be fighting, not talking about bathroom tiles with their fucking mermaid fiancées. Maybe I can start one. I almost started two wars with Thailand, and one with Russia. They sent a sniper after me, you believe that? Sneaky little fuckers. He shot me in the shoulder.'

'Aaaaand, back in the real world. You're doing what while you're here?'

'Wait, are we…?' Hector sensed a forebodingly familiar assemblage of scenery. He and Helen stood now before high gates of green iron. The oval was to their left, the gym to their right;

sheets of rain moved like shoals of fish in its spotlight. Beyond the basketball courts, the office and G block—where Hector had sat for home economics, metalwork, textiles, art. At their feet, in golden letters, the three-word slogan whose teaching Hector Grieve had not in six years of schooling found evidence: 'Knowledge Is Power, huh? … How much better our lives would have been had we gone to *any other school.*'

'Still a drama queen I see.'

'I am not.'

'You are a drama queen, you always were.' They walked on in the drizzle. Hector growled, and pulled some gum leaves from an overhanging bough. 'You gonna get a job while you're here?'

'A job? What for?'

'You said you're broke.'

'Yeah, but…' He scoffed: 'No.'

'Are you staying though, or back to Cambodia?'

'I can't go back to Cambodia, it's too expensive.'

'I thought Cambodia was cheap.'

'Not for a soldier of fortune.'

'Hector.'

'What?' He smiled at her.

'What were you doing in Cambodia?'

'Have you not listened to me?'

'You were not a soldier of fortune.'

'I *am* a soldier of fortune. I'm a two-star general. I'm a Commander of the Royal Order of Sahametrei.' He counted his titles out on his fingers. 'A Knight of the Guardians of Jayavarman the Seventh, a Most Honourable Captain of Indra Protector of The East, a Dharmaraja of the Order of the Leper King, a Restorer of the Eternal Peace of Sangrama, a Teahean of the Dynasty of the Seven Southern Lords *and* a Mahasena of the Most Exalted Order of the Lotus Pond.'

'All those?' she teased.

'Do you want to know how many people I've killed?'

'I don't.' Hector had unknowingly walked with Helen to the beginning of the gauntlet of feral widow and illiterate youth that was Khartoum Crescent, that fear-doused boulevard of welfare and child cruelty.

'I normally have my guns on me. Two Colt Peacemakers. One was a gift from the king of Cambodia, the other one's from Mel Gibson. Seven-and-a-half-inch model. He's a nice guy. A bit crazy, but I like crazy people. Much better than the boring fuckers I just had dinner with. After every battle we slaughter a pig. Whoever fights the bravest gets to slit its throat. Last it was Jerusalem, four days ago. You should have seen how this kid rides. Brave like a crusader.'

'I think you need a girlfriend, buddy.'

'What?' he smiled. 'Why?'

'You realise what's happened?'

They came to the end of the garden path which ascended to Helen's front door. Hector grabbed her by the arm and pulled her to his chest and pressed his mouth against hers. Immediately he had it pushed away by her hands at his stomach.

'Hector, I'm married.'

'Bull-shit,' he said in high voice.

'And you have blood on your hands. Literally.'

'Married to who?'

'His name's Nick.'

'Seriously?'

'What?'

'Have you *ever* met a Nick that wasn't a cunt?'

'You don't even know him!' said Helen, laughing.

'Imagine if I did, I'd hate him even more. Where the fuck is he?' Hector pointed to her house. 'In there?'

'We're separated.'

'Good.'

'It's not good! He's my husband.'

'It is good! Come on! You know what I know.'

'What do you know?'

'We're meant to be together.' He grabbed her arm again and stepped towards her.

'No, Hector,' she whispered, looking up into his eyes.

'Yes.'

'No.'

'No?'

'No.'

'Why not?'

'Because you literally sound like you've turned into a psychopath. I haven't seen you in eight years, after you ran out on me without a single word. Not even a goodbye.'

'And why do you think I'm back?'

'Not for me, you idiot. Don't even begin to pretend that's why you came back.'

'I love you, Helen. I always have.'

'You are an actual psychopath.' Helen jangled her keys from her purse and walked to the golden searchlight above her white door. Two houses down, domestic yelling started up like uneducated chainsaws. 'Goodnight, Hector.'

'We're going to run away together you and I,' he called after her.

'I assure you we are not,' she returned as she went inside.

Hector looked left, and saw a car whose wheels had been replaced by bricks, and right, at a mutilated shopping trolley and a rat. He poked out his bottom lip and raised his eyebrows before retracing the path by which he had entered so notorious a crescent.

He pulled from Brad's hedge the freshly slaughtered micro-pig. He slung it over his shoulders, his left hand pulling at the front legs, his right at the back, and walked through suburban silence and uncomfortable darkness, home.

LINGCHI

Chapter One

GREENVALE

1

Returning slowly from her dawn stroll in the rose garden, a woman in a thinly belted sun dress, printed all with fading lilies of brown and orange and leaves of lime, clasped her knuckley fingers at the sharply scaled naga head of a wild rosewood walking stick. Its end crunched into the drive's sandy gravel with each slow step.

The grey and mauve flecks of her silvery perm resisted by hairspray an icy wind. She held with her other hand two corners of her silken krama, checked in white and turquoise. She passed the translucent sheet of water which cascaded from the fountain of rearing hippocamps and looked to the staircase and concrete portico at the centre of the two rounded wings of her leaden-painted home. A man sprung from its automatic front doors and kicked the heels of his slippers from each step as he hastened to have his feet crunch in gravel. 'I put it to any man whom my words may reach,' he orated in a panic and with a finger in the air. 'However they may reach him, that he owes it to the future of the country, not to be stinting in what he will do now for Australia.'

The woman glowered back at him as she put a foot onto the staircase. An orderly in dark blue scrubs descended to give chase and caught him at the fountain. She threaded an arm under his and began the sequence of questions which the staff ran through in order to calm him whenever he got like this.

The stern and stately figurine, who if it were not for the spirit burning in her eyes would have appeared frail, put one foot beside the other as she ascended. On the landing of polished tile she was greeted by a nurse, one arm across her stomach, the other not letting a cigarette further than three inches from her mouth as she pivoted it by the elbow. 'How was your morning walk, Margaret?'

Margaret stood up as straight as her arthritis would allow. She turned her head to the young woman and squinted angrily at her. Then she returned it to the glass doors before her. 'Lovely, thank you.'

She tossed up and caught her walking stick (a souvenir from a visit to the war graves of Kanchanaburi) by its middle as the doors opened and she was presented, in a lobby of thin blue carpet over thick concrete, with the residents of Greenvale in disappointing formation between the thick square pylons which at mealtimes dictated the table arrangements.

She inspected their front rank—one end of Asian orderlies, the elderly gentlemen with balding heads and fraying collars, the portly assortment of white-haired ladies.

Then Margaret tucked her walking stick under her arm and turned to the centre of the assembly.

'This… is a day of unique importance. The Anglicare fête is the campaign that ensures we have enough money to see us through the summer. This week, as always, we do God's work. I implore you to do it today as though it were your own, for by that work we *will* continue to live, by standards that make us the envy of the world.' Margaret paced with her head turned to her audience. 'We've doubled our booze rations in a year. We eat like emperors. Let us never remit from the labour which ensures this unique prosperity; the ethic that alone ensures that we are… The Lucky Country. We all remember the stringiness of the roast beef which once was fed to us at tea time. We all remember the drubbings the lawn bowls team used to get at the hands of the grub-sucking snail-lickers at Old Broady Retirement Village. We all, I'm very sure, remember the dryness of the lamingtons,' she said with heightened emotion, banging the handle of her stick into a pylon, 'that the café used to have for morning tea. These have we fought against. These have we conquered.

'I ask of you this morning that you bake with all the effort required of any great and terrible undertaking. Measure accurately, taste often, feel consistencies through your whole body. I would ask that you knit with haste, with determination, precision—may fury of wrist and sturdiness of finger be your weapons. And I ask you all to make your jams and relishes as though they were for your very own grandparents themselves.'

Margaret came to the end of the formation and there addressed at their too-casual attention the comparatively young Sri Lankan, Cambodian, Filipino, women. 'Orderlies, where are you all from?'

'Thailand, Margaret,' they said, in unharmonious accents.

'And how do we say hello where you're from?'

'Sawadee Kaaa,' they returned in high pitched chorus.

'Very good. The mango sticky rices that you sell bring in the highest profit. Make each one exceptional. Sweeten that coconut milk. Smile as though you live in a tropical fucking paradise. Bow as though you are meeting the very Dalai fucking Lama, or whichever animal-headed demon it is that you people worship. For only by this tribute do our peoples coexist in peace.

'You *will* enjoy the fête. Your grandchildren *will* come. But only after you have earned that enjoyment. Prosperity is of all things the costliest, bought only at the price of eternal vigilance. Discipline has gotten us this far. Discipline will keep us here. Greenvale… Dismissed.'

All shuffled about in their slippers and in a hundred confused directions doddered to their morning tasks.

Later, Margaret left the sunlit splendour of the paperwork in her office to make her inspections.

In the common room seven women sat in leather armchairs, clinking their knitting needles together. On the coffee tables at their rug-covered knees were the products of their labour—baby booties, phone covers, football scarves, beanies, tea cosies. By the rubbered end of her walking stick Margaret raised one of these last.

'Who made this?' she said with suspicious calm.

'I did,' said Wilma, a lovely though ever-vanishing woman.

'Wilma, Wilma, Wilma.' Margaret dangled the tea cosy in her face. 'I expected this from Rhonda. Not from you. Why are there such big gaps in your reverse stocking stitches? Is this a tea cosy, Wilma? Or a condom pinpricked by a foreign whore so she gets pregnant by her white boyfriend? Hm? No gaps, Wilma. As tight as your ninny after your husband pulls his pindick out. Save the holes for the handle and the fucking spout. This is a tea cosy, not a sieve, Wilma. Do you understand?'

'Yes, Margaret. Sorry, Margaret.'

'Don't be sorry, Wilma.' Margaret shook her head. 'Just don't do it again.'

In the café's small kitchen three ladies were at various stages in the manufacturing and jarring of a relish, a chutney, a marmalade.

'You wrinkly old slut,' said Margaret, dropping onto the bench the teaspoon by which she had tasted Fanny's pickle and onion relish. 'Do you want us all to go sober this summer? Fanny? Look at me. Who's going to buy this after tasting it, hm? It tastes like it looks, Fanny. Like a Moroccan crapped his dinner onto a leaf. If you don't fix this fucking quick-smart you'll be on Sustagen and baby food for a month. My God, woman, do you understand me? I've tasted your piccalilli, Fanny. I know what you're capable of.

And it's not this. Fucking fix it.'

Margaret thanked Tess, the maker of a divine apricot chutney and then stared from some distance at objects of instant repulsion.

'Gertie,' she said, very gravely.

'Yes, M—'

'Shut the fuck up. What is this?'

'What?' said Gertie, surprised that Margaret had without tasting it found fault in her marmalade.

'Don't you What me.' Margaret lifted a jar and turned the label to its author. 'Do you know *why* people buy marmalade from old ladies, Gertie? Hm? Do you think it's because marmalade tastes nice? Fucking *no*, Gertie, that's not why. Marmalade tastes like compost. It tastes like rotten fruit, because it *is* rotten fruit. They buy marmalade from old ladies because of the calligraphy on the fucking labels. I've told you this a hundred times, now what is this shit?'

'I'm sorry, Margaret.' Gertie looked down at her interwoven fingers. 'It's my Parkinson's.'

'Oh, it's your Parkinson's is it? How *dare* you use a tragic disease as an excuse for *this*. It looks like an unusually dumb monkey wrote it with his toes. Did Muhammad Ali ever use Parkinson's as an excuse? He was freeing hostages in Iraq with Parkinson's and you can't even loop your fucking l's. Look at your slant lines, Gertie. You have Parkinson's, not cerebral palsy. Are you using a fineliner?' Margaret picked up the felt-tipped evidence and growled: 'You little Arab. You need a pen with a flat nib, Gertie. For fuck me's fucking sake. Jar-labelling rule number one.' Margaret threw the pen into a corner and pointed the serpent head of her walking stick at Gertie's face. 'Take your medication, find a new pen, and start again. And I had better be fucking breathtaken by your penmanship.'

In the main kitchen three old ladies and an old man were in aprons at a stainless-steel counter.

Margaret stopped at the first woman and looked over her tray of untopped vanilla slices. She dipped a fingertip into the custard and transferred it to her tongue. 'Exceptional, Coral.'

'Thank you, Margaret.'

'Eeeexceptional.' From her pinky she sampled a mixing bowl of shining chocolate batter. 'Too many walnuts, Glenda. Nobody likes hedgehog with that many walnuts.'

'Yes, Margaret,' and Glenda set about adjusting her ratios.

The third lady was unceasing in the dipping and rolling of her squares of sponge cake into cocoa butter and desiccated coconut. Without breaking rhythm she handed Margaret a finger of the final product. 'I knew I could count on you, Ethel.' Ethel nodded humbly and continued constructing her lamingtons.

The chubby man at the end of the line, in his red-and-white-checked apron, slowly handed Margaret half a scone already slathered with cream and strawberry jam. He had been nervous since her entrance. Margaret bit into the thing and paused. It was some time before she spat it from her mouth. She looked blankly at him; he looked sheepishly down at his baking tray. When shortly he glanced up beneath flamboyant eyebrows Margaret flung the remainder of the scone past his ear. His shoulders clenched with fright and his eyes slammed shut and he quivered at the neck.

'Dick, are you fucking serious? Do you even remember what your wife's scones tasted like? Like a walk through an English garden on a wet spring morning. Do you know what *your* scone felt like, in my mouth, Dick? Like a mummy farted dust into it. Like four-thousand-year-old pyramid dirt was puffed into my throat by the sphincter of a mummified boy king. Was the recipe burned with Agatha's body, Dick? Did you have the recipe cremated too? Did all moistness die with your wife? Well obviously not, you're crying. I put you in charge of scones out of respect to Agatha. They're our biggest bakery item, Dick. Start again. And the next batch had better be so fucking moist that I drown in them like a vampire in a hemophiliac's crotch. Jesus Fucking Christ, Dick. You should be ashamed of your self, baking like that. What would Agatha say? Hm?'

She took a swig from a milk bottle in order to remoisten her mouth before storming out of the kitchen to take her morning gin and cigarette.

At the end of G-wing's corridor a disarmed emergency exit opened onto a path of ochre gravel, shaded by arches dripping with purple wisteria. Beside this a perfectly groomed lawn, hemmed in by two high fences draped in Italian jasmine, ran to a brick-paved terrace that overlooked the entire width of a valley. Margaret stood upon this promontory with her long gin and tonic and her slender menthol cigarette. She put the sides of her first and middle finger at her mouth and inhaled deeply. She finished the last of her lightly iced drink and rattled its remaining contents to call for another.

'Antoinette here to see you, Miss Margaret,' said Lucie, the orderly who served as her attendant.

Margaret nodded and said, 'Send her out.' She took up her

walking stick from its lean at the archway and met on the path the administrating nurse of Greenvale. 'What can I do for you, Antoinette?'

A sturdy woman, with a short bob and a confusion of lanyards at her wide chest, she said, 'We need to talk, Margaret.'

'I always make time for you, you know that. Walk with me.' They ambled across the lawn, around the border of very rare flowers planted by an eccentric young gardener called Athelstan whose grandmother Margaret had known through Lion's Club. Lucie brought Margaret's drink; Antoinette declined to join.

'It's about our split.'

'Oh is it now?'

'This fête's looking like it'll bring in more than ever. We've already had to buy more raffle ticket books. The nurses want their split upped to 35.'

'Antoinette,' said Margaret, smiling calmly. 'Do you remember what this place was like before I arrived? Do you remember what the residents were like? Shitting themselves four times a day, urinating at the dining table. Do the girls want to go back to being slobbered on every time they take someone's blood pressure? Need I remind you of the sexual crimes that used to be the entertainment in the dementia ward? I fixed that, Antoinette, just like I turned this place into a haven for resident and staff alike. *I* fixed it. Me. Alone. These people had *no* self-respect before I arrived. I've given them that. I've brought this community hope, and I can take it all away like that,' she said, and stamped her walking stick into the grass.

'Life expectancy has dropped 7% in the last three years, Margaret. I'm copping that heat. It's the work.'

'Work is the law of life, Antoinette. They may be dying a little sooner but their last years are happier, fuller, and *cleaner*. And do *not* pretend that new blood isn't your chief source of income. We both know that every resident who dies makes room for a nice new superannuation to go in your coffers. Any raise in the nurse's cut comes directly out of your end. I *don't* like talking politics in the morning, but you come here and you interrupt my workday to ask for things to which you are not entitled, Antoinette.'

'Who do you think you are, Margaret?'

'Who do I think *I* am? If it weren't for me these bed-shitting old—'

'Miss Margaret,' whispered Lucie, always afraid of the furore that might come of interrupting her.

'What?'

'There's somebody here to see you.'

'Well who is it?'

'He wouldn't say, Miss Margaret.'

'Well is he a resident?'

'I don't think so, Miss Margaret.'

'No more visitors this morning. Tell him to come back after supper. … Who do I think *I* am, Antoinette? If you—'

Across the lawn, with open arms and an excited smile, there strode then jovially yelled, Hector Grieve.

'Grandmaaaa!'

2

Margaret sat beside her grandson in one of two low deck chairs of green cloth. The two Grieves surveyed the wall of suburban homes rising gently across the valley in terraces of sticky dark grey and bleached mission brown.

'How's your gin and tonic, dear?'

'Just fine, Grandma,' said Hector, taking it up again from the table between them. 'Thank you.'

'Lucie,' said Margaret, calling over her shoulder.

'Miss Margaret?'

'Lucie my darling, what is this?'

'Your gin and tonic, Miss Margaret.'

'Is it?' Margaret sipped slowly from it, then smashed the glass on the patio. '*That* was tonic water with a dick-splash of gin. Is that how I take my morning drink?'

'Sorry, Miss Margaret. It's just…'

'Just what?'

'It's your nurses.'

Margaret turned instantly dour. 'What about them?'

'They asked me to help you.'

'Help me? Lucie, I take my gin and tonics how I take my gin and tonics. If they are not how I take them then they are not gin and tonics. They are an oriental cocktail mixed of selfishness and stupidity. I've taken them like this for sixty years. My drinking habits are older than your country. *I* tell the nurses what goes on and what doesn't. If you pour me one of these again I'll have you wiping shitty arses and mopping up drool before you can say, "My country very poor." *Do* you understand me?'

'Yes, Miss Margaret. I'm sorry.'

'You will be.' Margaret eyed her attendant off as she returned to the drinks table at the front corner of the terrace. 'More and more of them every day,' she said. 'But they work for nothing and they're grateful. Gratitude is rare. *And* they bring me their newspapers in English. How *is* Cambodia, dear?'

'There is no more Cambodia, Grandma.'

'What about those lovely horses I was always seeing in the papers?'

'Ahh they've probably already been sacrificed and their blood smeared across their savage faces.'

'And that book? It's been such a long time since I've seen you. I tell everyone I have a grandson who's a novelist.'

'That was nine years ago, Grandma,' Hector lamented. 'The book stopped selling. That's kind of why I'm home, I'm out of money.'

'Oh, money can always be gotten from somewhere, dear. There's certainly enough of it in the world.'

'I have to see a bank manager today,' he bemoaned, and drank.

'It's the bloody Irish,' stated a wobbly voice from somewhere behind them. 'Papists the lot of them. They're taking this country and giving it to the Pope!'

'Never mind him, dear. That's Arthur. The dementia ward's just behind us. He'll be gotten to in a second.'

'You hear me?' said Arthur, his danglings slapping against his thighs as he made high-kneed leaps for the patio. 'The bloody Irish. We shouldn't let 'em in. God knows who'll be next!'

But Arthur was not gotten to. The orderlies who arrived to retrieve him did so in time only to witness his stumble from the bricks at the edge of the terrace.

'Good work, old cock!' said Margaret as her grandson stood to watch Arthur's naked body tumble down a valley walled with nettles. 'He almost never makes it that far. Good on him.'

'What the fuck has happened to this place?'

'How do you mean, dear?'

'We used to be such a proud people, a fine people. Manly. Now it's like we live in a… Well, it's like we live in a n…'

'In a what, dear?'

'In a nursing home.'

'Well,' breathed Margaret after taking a large sip of her more perfect drink. 'There are worse places to be spending your twilight years.'

'I'm twenty-nine, Grandma!'

'And a ray of sunshine in the morning, too. How long are you home for, dear?'

'Depends on Dad.'

'What about him?'

'He's sick.'

'Still?'

'Do you not know?'

'He hasn't visited me in a year. And I won't see your brother, not now he's given up. Still sick? Oh dear. With what, the poor thing? Heavens. But I'm glad to have you home. Family's so important. You may not have much money, but at least you have a family who loves you and a roof over your head. They're the main things. And you wrote a novel. You have your achievements as well, don't despair.'

'You don't know he can't afford his treatment?'

'Can he not?'

'You heard about Selathoa?'

'I read about the Turk in the papers.'

'I tried to tell him. For years.'

'You should have met her. Eyebrows like Mehmed the Conqueror and a moustache to match.'

'Grandma, you can't umm…'

'Can't what, dear?'

Hector smiled cheekily at his grandmother. 'You can't umm…'

She smiled back at him. 'I haven't a penny, Hector. All our money went to putting me in here. I've had to work for years just to get drink and decent food. This place was *awful* when your dad put me in here. Really it was. Like an Egyptian prison. But I live a life of privilege rather than of wealth. I can get you anything you want *in here*. Do you want a lamington?'

'No thanks, Grandma,' he smiled.

'Won't John be getting something from his new book soon?'

'What new book?'

'Your grandfather's war memoirs.'

'What?' snapped Hector, suspicious instantly of the combining of a brother in play therapy with a manuscript for which he had an unmatched fondness.

Margaret was distressed by their mention. 'John's publishing the

147

lot of them. He went through them earlier in the year to edit them down. Brought me the manuscript to see if I approved. I did *not* approve.'

'Why not?' Hector said with mounting gloom.

'Let's go inside.'

On the day that news reached Mildura that France had fallen and photographs appeared all over the world of Hitler and his boobies strutting before the Eiffel Tower, the three Grieve brothers volunteered for the Second Australian Imperial Force. Their father knew the enlistment officer and asked that they be split up. They were assigned to divisions in the order opposite to that of their birth.

The oldest, Andrew, was drafted into the 7th and trained in Palestine. Four months later Rommel was laying siege to him as a Rat of Tobruk and for a time he garrisoned a fort in Damascus. He survived the deprivations of the Kokoda Campaign to get it two months later in the ambushing of a New Guinean knoll of no strategic value. His muddy funeral on a hilltop at Sanananda was sketched through tropical rain by Ivor Hele and immortalised in oil on canvas. The painting's recumbent dead hung still in the galleries of the War Memorial in Canberra.

Malcolm, the middle brother, was with the 8th Division in Singapore when it was surrendered, prisoner without having fired a shot. After three months of eighteen-hour days cutting through hard stone with soft tools he was executed by samurai sword for attempting to disappear into the jungles of western Thailand.

And Robert E. Grieve, youngest, selected for the 9th Division Cavalry and sent to chase Fascists from Egypt to Tunisia as a gunner in a Crusader tank. When his division was called home he hoped to join Andrew in New Guinea, unaware that his brother's funeral had already been painted. He was sent to Far North Queensland where his regiment was demechanised and retrained as jungle commandos. A year later he was a guerrilla behind enemy lines in East Timor and had stormed undefended beaches in New Guinea and Borneo when the atom bombs called abruptly an end to his service.

When he felt the end of his long life approaching, Robert Grieve set about turning his memories into a memoir—to retell for his grandchildren and all who might be interested in such archaisms the most exciting years of his life—those spent 'squinting into the golden glare of death,' listening to flak blow through steel, watching the desert stars disappear behind tracer rounds, hearing 'the wet thud of .30 caliber shred the torsos of his closest friends.' By the diary retrieved from Andrew's body he included his brother's voyage through war. After expensive investigation and the interviewing of as many of Malcolm's fellow inmates as had survived into old age he pieced together and narrated his middle brother's slavery until death.

He called the book *Grieves At War* and this remained the name of the manuscript which Hector now held in his hands. John had left little besides its title unaltered.

'That fucking little shit,' said Hector as he read what was labelled as an introduction penned by his grandfather.

'Take it with you,' said Margaret. 'I don't want it here. I'd throw it away but it's the only copy I have. I can tell most of the parts that Bob wrote and sometimes I read them and hear his voice.'

'This is *not* happening, Grandma. I'll talk to John about it. I'll fix it, I promise.'

'Do, Hector. It's not what your grandfather would have wanted.'

'Yeah well, none of this crap's what Grandpa would have wanted. God damn it, this country's going to shit.' Hector tucked the manuscript under his arm. 'All right, Grandma. I gotta go. I have to go and see my agent. This place is nice, no?'

Margaret's sitting room had a high ceiling and white walls. Upon them were hung a sepia photograph from her wedding day, an oil painting of her husband and his brothers in uniform the week before their departure for service, a bust photograph of her in her late twenties at whose sighting all said, 'You looked exactly like Grace Kelly.' Two Edwardian fauteuils of mint-green embroidery, which Hector remembered from their old house, were at a card table by the window. The family's grandfather clock stood beside the doorway; a bouquet of red roses rested in a familiar vase on the closed bureau between the small television in the corner and the door to her office.

'It's *really* nice in here, Grandma,' said Hector. '*I* could live here. You happy?'

'Always.' Margaret was kissed on the cheek. 'Now, don't you let your brother publish that.'

'I won't Grandma, don't worry. I love you.'

'I love you too, dear.'

Chapter Two

A GRECIAN ROME

1

Hector strolled down Marlborough Street—the rolling main road of this older side of Westmeadows at whose rising end was Greenvale. Practically not a house was without a flash of juvenile or adolescent nostalgia. Half the children he went to primary school with had lived there. Its courts were many of those up and down which he had spent whole weekends gallivanting on bicycles.

There was the family friend's house where Grieve had morning tea with his parents the day the creek broke its banks; the house that had been host to most of his sleepovers in his first year of high school; the primary school to which Brad Nelson and a large proportion of his schoolmates had gone; the house where his first fencing coach lived, the house where that kid lived whose British bulldog always had eczema and died of cancer.

At the height of a gentle hill there stood the bluestone church, now more than a century and a half old, which had long ago been the local house of Grieve worship. Its front car park boomed with some kind of rapid music and crawled with young people. Hector stopped to admire the simple building, to remember the warming glow of midnight service, the excitement of Reverend Stuart's narrative sermons. Its front garden was much drier than Hector remembered, barren even, and into its cracked soil was stuck a metallic billboard quartered with photographs of laughing youth and centred with the words, 'Lifehouse Church.'

'Watcha reading there?' said a slender young man in t-shirt and shorts, appeared among the shrivelling agapanthus to point at the manuscript in Hector's hand.

'It's an instruction manual,' said Hector. 'On how to fuck off and leave me alone.'

'Woah!' said the young man, raising his palms in beaming submission. 'Only asking a question, mate. I got a thought though. See all these recreational activities? Would you like to join us? We're recreating. For God.'

'Absolutely I would not.'

'You sure?' He pointed at Grieve's stomach. 'We've got a

sausage sizzle going,' he said, as though this enticement above any other would persuade him. 'See that jumping castle? Pretty fu-un. Some of the girls are knitting for the raffle we're gonna have in a coupl'a 'ours! A few of us were thinking of a friendly game of two-on-two. You shoot hoops?'

'I shoot people like you.'

'Best way to spread the Word of God is through recreational activities. Waddya say?'

'I say go fuck yourself you happy freak.'

'Woah, you *are* an angry young man. That's not kindness. Let me ask you a question. Do you know where anger comes from?'

'Talking to you.'

'From denying God's love. Join us, just for a half an hour. Why not? Could be fu-un. My name's Rupert.' Hector looked down at Rupert's outstretched hand and then up at his smiling face, red from exercise. 'Can I get you a lemonade? Ice-cold. Why not?'

'Why not?'

'Yeah!' breathed Rupert.

'Irrumator, when the Israelites first entered Palestine they were ordered to slaughter the Amalekites to the man, to utterly destroy all that they had, to slay both man and woman, infant and suckling, camel…' Hector pointed his first two fingers at the young man before slowly finishing: '…and ass. God did not order them to play basketball and have sausage sizzles. My God is a god of action, of righteousness. And under His wings do I walk at liberty, for I have *kept* His precepts.'

'We believe that God is a God of love.'

'Oh, He's a God of love all right. He loves poets, priests, and warriors. He doesn't give a camel-jockey's malodorous fuck about ignored gag reflexes like you. Play your basketball, squirt, and sizzle those sausages—God *shall* forget thee.' Hector tilted his head back and almost lapsed into that apoplectic mode about whose enjoyment he had until three days ago entirely forgotten. He cut short a nascent nod to shake his head.

There was the house from which Hector had left a pool party early when the sixteen-year-old revellers fell into vomiting on one another before it was even nine o'clock; the tiny house which used to belong to the weird old lady in whose derelict backyard Hector's mother had for a time kept her horses; the court at whose end he had spent the larger part of two summers playing cricket with a power pole for wickets; the house that that kid lived in who used to chase garbage trucks down the street screaming the words to *Jingle Bells.*

Hector knocked on the front door of a house that held no memories and asked the old woman who answered if he could use her phone to call the police. 'I think I just saw a house being broken into.' She led Hector past the living room's blaring television to a kitchen that reeked of cat shit. 'Do you have the number for the police station? Quicker if I speak to them directly.'

The old woman, who smelled likewise, pulled a business card from beneath a fridge magnet. Eight times Hector wound the clicking dial of the wall-mounted phone. 'Hi, I think I've just seen two men jumping the fence behind a house in Hopetoun Court. They were wearing balaclavas. Number 17.'

And the house whose driveway he and his friends used to cordon off with witch's hats for no other reason than that Tim Ferrett lived there, and the house where he swore he had seen a family of dwarves living. Hector passed under the gum trees before the park where he had once been unable to control his laughter as John was pinned down and terrorised by a magpie and strolled past the memorial honouring the men who served The Empire in the Great War—remembered that it was the monument from which he had taken all the character names for his precocious novel—Kingshott and the four Gage brothers, Shankland, and Fuzzard.

A police car sped by with its lights flashing and no siren and at the very bottom of the street, beside the stone bridge and the pub that were the suburb's second and fourth-oldest constructions was its third—Westmeadows Police Station—tiny, of bluestone, and adjacent to Hector's kindergarten. William's car was the only one in the lot of unmown grass. Hector pressed a button on its spare key and unlocked its doors. He threw John's manuscript onto the passenger seat and backed slowly out of the gravel drive and made for the freeway.

2

Not five minutes into the journey Hector S. Grieve braked the car to a stop. Before him stretched a long and rising bend of unmoving cars, the open space of Essendon airport flat and fenced off beside him.

The lights turned green in the tiny distance ahead; a few cars eased their way forward. Row by row their places were taken—the four-lane stagnation allowed a brief but glorious interlude of onward rolling. After much delay Hector too was granted two yards of movement. Almost instantly he pulled up again; sat and waited.

He pressed the volume dial of the car's stereo. The centre of the dashboard lit up and the radio started. He cycled through an ostentation of vacuous presenters and a succession of idiot songs before smacking it back off. He checked his rear view mirror. He was now not anywhere near the end of the procession of drivers, unseparated of nationality by alike frustration. Through the windscreen of the car behind him he saw a woman waving him forward. Soon she pushed at her horn. A car length had opened up before him. The brake lights of the queue momentarily disappeared and all edged on to stop a little further towards the vacant road. Hector watched his mirror—the woman's hand still waving, her head shaking, mouth raging on. She tapped a few times at her car horn. Hector smiled and allowed the gap before his car to triple before waving and smiling back at her.

'Laugh it up you inserter of stoats.' Grieve laughed gently to himself as the woman attempted to change lanes in still traffic.

Eventually the light returned red. No cars drove across the road that all hoped to soon enter, yet there before it everybody was, amassed. 'Just go you fucking idiots,' Hector growled to himself.

Half an hour later he was first in line between the traffic lights. At its final green change he drove up the rise onto the exalted other road. He straightened the car from its right turn and was called immediately to a halt by a pair of traffic lights turned red.

'Are you fucking serious?' he said to the windscreen.

Not a car could be seen before him. The four wide lanes of his side of Mount Alexander Road were empty. He looked to the car beside him—a woman waiting contentedly with both hands on the steering wheel—then again to the red light. He surveyed the only two intersections which he could surmise fed onto the road ahead. Not a car was using them. He looked to the red light again, to the empty carriageway descending to Moonee Ponds, the city rising in the distance to dark blue-grey storm clouds. He checked his rear view mirror for police cars and found none. He eased his father's car forward until he was half a length over the thick white line. Then the light turned a liberating green. He accelerated, and was free. Until twenty metres on a pair of red lights called him to a halt.

'You have got, to be fucking, kidding me.'

Still the first car in line, the road ahead was clear and could not have been rendered otherwise—he had passed the only two junctions which might feed vehicles onto his own. He again checked his mirror for police cars. None had been added to the queue. The woman in the car beside him was singing and shaking her head as manically as her lungs and neck would allow. Hector squinted and said, 'What the fuck is wrong with these people?' It had seemed far too long a time to be sitting at a red light which held him back from a vacant road. He eased the car forward and was shortly half a length over the thick white line. He was about to accelerate from the illogicality of the coloured dictators of his progress—began to lower his toes toward the foot well—when the car behind him flicked on and off its siren and startled him to a halt. In his mirror a man shook his head and pointed to the police lights on the far side of his dashboard. Hector waved in abdication and reversed.

Thusly did Hector S. Grieve that morning advance, in drips and fits and over-excited delusions of manumission, until in the early afternoon he came to the St Kilda Road offices of Debbie Bodeswell, his literary agent.

3

'You don't remember me at all?' said Hector Grieve, taking a seat in an office of cluttered desk and floor-to-ceiling and wall-to-wall shelves of paperback.

'You do *kind* of look familiar. Were you on Masterchef? What's your name again?'

'Grieve,' he said impatiently. 'Hector Grieve. You took my novel to Hachette nine years ago.'

'Grieve, Grieve, Grieve,' said Debbie, rising to browse her bookshelves. 'Ahh, here we are.' She pulled a thick paperback from its row. 'The Big and Many Battle of the Seabird.'

'What? My book was called Cormorant War.' She showed him the front cover. Plainly Hector could see an approximation of his own name.

'I remember this book!' she declared in high and slow recollection. She handed it to him; he had seen neither its cover nor its title, but there his name almost was.

He opened the unfamiliar soft cover of his own pubescent novel—the very pages which he had dropped out of a master's degree to attempt; this initial literary flowering of his insolence; his precocious attempt at writing a long novel after having read only a handful of short ones. It cost him twelve months of desk-chained tedium to finish the first and second drafts. Hitherto infectiously exuberant, by the end of a year of unbroken solitary work he was somebody else entirely—irascible, rancorous, sulky—and took to every other day rereading Hamlet before his unhappy self had something of an epiphany.

Evening after youthful evening of reading memoir and biography—of Villehardouin and Dandolo, Polo and Kublai Khan, Byron and Chateaubriand, de Marbot and Bonaparte, Chinese Gordon and Peachey Carnehan, Freddie Chapman and Orde Wingate—in immediate contrast to days of sedentary labour, Hector came to formulate, then to accept, the unwelcome conclusion that the man tapping away at his keyboard was in no way the equal of him wandering the wilds of God's earth with a war to fight.

In four weeks he rewrote the whole book, retroactively introducing the theme that was to briefly lift him into the dim spotlight of cultured Melbourne—that of the necessary and lamentable difference between a writer and a man of action.

The writer, a young Hector Grieve argued as he rewrote, wishes to be great but knows that only men of action can ever truly be so. The author may spend his life admiring them, even creating them. He cannot ever become what he most wishes to be. 'Men do; his inferiors think,' became an early Grieve maxim. In light of his several months of mental labour he set about convincing himself that the completion of an audacious novel could fit into his nascent desire for a life of sensation and he finished the thing. Through the innumerable connections of his father he found it an agent and soon thereby a publisher.

So well-received had the story been, so deeply did its appended theme strike at a vein of restlessness among his own and older generations, that the book, for two months, looked as though it might take off. The independent press ran stories on him. He was photographed, interviewed, briefly televised. But still that original unnerving dichotomy festered in the recesses of his mind. The unpleasant (and he thought undeserved) success coincided with the death of his mother. As a pretentious new author he told people who inquired of his diffidence that he could cope easily with the latter but not abide the former. He became increasingly cantankerous—professionally insulting, personally arrogant—at last deciding he would not have domestication form the central tragedy of his adult life. So Hector Grieve renounced the pen and asked his father if there might be a place for him investing capital in hopeless economies and left for Cambodia a voluntary and enthusiastic exile.

Looking over his work, which the young Japanese editor of an art magazine had long ago thought would very profitably resonate with the Japanese market, he found that it was to him entirely unrecognisable. He opened *Cormorant War* to its middle and read.

'Paw took off the table arose highly and return on that very same position of his seatings. Looked he with lick doom upon the wall attempt find many time units illuminated he's plumbing. With very great ahead work of with the one primary digit—weightful heart with a bad—he pressed the keys of the primary story for informational length in the job of the same type longways that for him then had been intergalactic... What the fuck is this?'

'I *think*...' Debbie began, but was cut off by Hector's enraged reading.

'Everybody not who watched the snail-like and not very interested to do it! Musical construction can be estimate highly of its worth and a history glimpse.' Hector looked up from page one and shook his head. *'Of myths to be lowly given in the best tradition of the sale said over and over again in shops of a said out of recall books to the fondness. Eternally the best sushi in the he-suey ever remember one for hundreds of cutter paste; the time second of an instant, when the big leather shoe started on good makings. ...* Seriously, what the fuck is this?'

'So yes, if I remember correctly...' said Debbie, piecing together a history of Grieve's novel from the manila folder she had kept while working with him. 'You asked us to destroy the manuscript and the proofs when you pulled out of your Australian contract. ... So we did. ... But the Japanese translation had already taken off. Then... here. Australian bookstores ordered a second printing but we didn't have the proofs of the original, so we had to get it translated from the Japanese edition, back into English.'

'This is in Chinglish?' Debbie raised both of her eyebrows and smiled. 'Are you telling me I've written the first novel in Chinglish? . . . I don't fucking think so, are you kidding me?'

'I actually like this idea.'

'And the Japanese aren't buying their translation?'

'The views contained in the story, Henry, are at—'

'Hector.'

'Hector?' said Debbie, most surprised.

'Yes,' he said, holding the cover up.

'Oh yes. Hector Glieve, sorry.'

'Grieve,' said Hector, his voice rumbling.

'The views contained in the book, Henry, in light of Japan's recent attempts at reconciliation *with* China, though yes, traditionally revered there, have kind of fallen out of fashion.'

'*Push gather,*' Hector continued, his outrage swelling with each adulterate page, '*large animal London. Not a deal been made to happen much only to the president that have in jail been made to house. Larger temple than revolution gunji decapitate, by black superman named Beni the Jew of Russia who railing at the staircase. To talk without going up not for goodness they say, he is drunk when his offspring try to see him, but democlacy head of city rady say most un normal. Lovely spring weather bubonic plague raging.* What the fuck!?' He threw the book at the wall behind his agent. 'This is the fucking book I wrote?'

'Unless you have a copy of the original, we can… But yes, that's the book you wrote. It's actually a really great idea, Henry. It's never been done before. We've had picture books, with Chinglish signs and menus. But never a whole novel. The first novel in Chinglish. It's an awesome idea. Especially with rising numbers of Asian readers. We can release it for Christmas, stocking fillers sell *tens* of thousands of copies at Christmas.'

4

Hector pocketed his hands in his jacket as he stepped out into a wind that spiced his face and a cold that ached his kidneys. The oak- and palm-lined footpath along the clamorous quadruple carriageway of St Kilda Road took him past the bubbling fountains and grimly bare façade of the National Gallery. A long banner advertising an exhibition on prostitution faced the sculptural confusion upon the lawn of the Arts Centre. Around its windows were bill posters advertising a woman conducting Wagner, a cabaret cast with men in women's underpants, The Nutcracker.

Around the gravelly wall of Hamer Hall Hector came into sight of glass skyscrapers and the unembellished green and yellow dome of Flinders Street station. On Princes Bridge he ignored the pleas of the homeless for even more change and looked up at the height and number of the buildings by which he was encircled. At the bridge's end, a gothic revival church whose façade implored the welcoming of more heathens into the country. He watched between sliding and dinging trams the scurrying of people into and out of and up and down the camouflaged contortions of Federation Square. As he walked on, the heavy square end of a thin metallic pole swung around and sideswiped his head.

'Woah, sorry mate,' said the assailant, raising a supplicatory palm.

Hector stopped and turned his head to squint at the young man who had swung at it—he in knitted green shirt, its sleeves and v-neck unhemmed, his hair in a knot atop a wispy face.

'Sorry, mate. Just takin' some photos.'

'Of what?'

'Of myself, mate, sorry. Hashtag selfie wanker, right? We just want the church in the background.'

'Photos of yourself? What the fuck for? You look like a hipposcrotum.'

'What's a hipposcrotum?'

'The scrotum of a hippo, you imbecile.'

'I'm sorry mate, all right?' The person's girlfriend pulled in tight to wrap an arm around him and pout her face beside his. He extended his hand and they looked up to the rectangle at the end of his stick. 'How old do you think it is?' he said.

'Organised religion's *so* evil.'

Like chimpanzees trying to seduce a zookeeper into giving them food they showed to their stick's end the various aspects of their lips. The couple spun upon their hind legs to change the background of their courtship and as Hector stepped on he was again tapped on the crown. He reached an arm around and threw a wrist over the stick as he turned into this new enemy to yank his weapon from him.

'Sorry, mate! Sorry! I didn't mean to, yeah?'

'You didn't mean to take a photo of yourself? You know you could just go to a zoo and take photographs of a hipposcrotum there. How about a three-day-old rat carcass? That about matches the hair on your fucking face. Have this coked out degenerate purse her shaft lickers next to that. You actually own a stick whose purpose is to enable you to take photographs of yourself? My fucking God. The French staged a revolution because their king was vain and ended up dethroning half the world. What should the kings do now, that the people are so in love with them-fucking-selves that they devote whole days to photographing their own faces. Vanitas vanitatum, irrumator. Bring back the guillotine and send *you* to the fucking scaffold. But first just the top of your mongoloid head, to cut that ridiculous ball of hair from it. Then we'll stuff it in your mouth and push you up a bit and off with your little bauble of pride that you call a head. Execute the fucking vain. And we the kings shall come to the brightness of that rising.' Hector broke off the heavy end of the stick and tossed it into the street.

'That's my phone, mate,' said the male, backing towards it as Hector loomed.

Grieve whacked the side of his knee with his own stick, sending him to genuflection. Then he hit him in the neck. The dim young thing went sideways to ground and Hector put the broken end of his stick to his throat.

'This, is a magic wand.' Hector lowered his voice to a growl and put a boot on either side of the prostrate's ribcage. 'If the spell you're trying to cast is to be a vain little fuckwit who takes photographs of himself. What happened to humility? What part of the world needs reproductions of your peasant's face? Aren't there enough gay chipmunks on the internet already? And you,' he said, pointing the new sabre at the girlfriend. 'Why don't you just shave your head and start nosing beaver? This isn't a man. This is a dickwizard. A dickwizard who owns a wand that turns himself into an idiot.'

'It's a selfie stick,' she said, yelling at him.

'It's an idiot wand.'

Passing by shops which sold camel's meat and shops which sold strap-on dildos and mouth gags and stores of Ethiopian groceries, Hector snarled at dozens of Chinese people in surgical masks and a caravan of covered women and their countless veiled daughters. He passed by McDonald'ses and innumerable KFCs and shops selling figurines from Japanese cartoons and a homeless saxophonist playing *Run Through The Jungle* being danced at by a hefty drunk woman in a muumuu. Then shops selling American candy and a restaurant playing gangster rap and selling Turkish food, and he came to the revivalist mess of arches that was the façade of the Old Stock Exchange building and the Commonwealth Bank which occupied its ground floor.

He ascended into a hall of malachite columns, rising high to wide pointed arches. White and multifoiled with gilt teeth, they dropped from a blue-bordered heraldic ceiling. Maroon carpet was everywhere underfoot. At his left, the length of the hall daylit by quartets of lancet windows and cinquefoils—to his right, open partitions of walnut with desks and computer screens and upholstered chairs between them—a row of cubicles before a pair of automatic glass doors set into a glass wall. Yellow lamps glowed beneath a ceiling of frosted white glass over the long stalls at which tellers sat and customers stood.

A queue of people waited in the space between the partitions and the tellers, its course determined by golden bollards and red rope. Hector strode the walnut partitions, searching. He found at the third desk along the vaguely familiar face of Mike Isenhammer. He slapped on the shoulder the chubby man sitting opposite him and said, 'You. Out.'

'Excuse me?'

'Let's go. … What have you got your husband's juice in your ear? Get the fuck out.'

'Excuse me, I will not "get the fuck out",' said the man, flustered. 'You can stand and wait in line like the rest of us.'

'Jocksniffer, listen to me. I know the cup size of the first girl who sucked this man's winky. Get the fuck out of here, we won't be long. Jesus Christ, you selfish prick. Why don't you listen to people when they talk to you? Do as you're fucking told. Go take a photograph of yourself.'

As the jocksniffer rose he hit away the hand that was handling his suit's shoulders. Grieve took his seat.

'Mike fucking Isenhammer. A motherfucking bank manager.'

'Loan manager,' said Mike. 'Hector fucking Grieve.'

'I could not think of a more fitting profession for a boring son-of-a-bitch like you.'

Mike smiled and shook Hector's hand. 'Born to manage loans, wasn't I? You proo-bably shouldn't have told that guy to fuck off though. He's quite wealthy.'

'He had it coming, he sniffs jocks. Old time's sake, uh?'

'How long *has* it been?'

'Eight years, Mike.'

'And let me guess… You're in… marketing?'

'What the fuck is marketing?'

'You were creative. Not marketing then? PR?'

'I'm a soldier of fortune, Mike' Hector leaned back to put an arm over the back of his chair. He smiled as he pushed it onto its back legs.

Mike laughed and said, 'Soldier of fortune, I like that. Remember the fake jobs you guys used to have when we went out?

You were always a shepherd. How the fuck are you, Hector?'

'I'm good, Mike. Listen I need a favour.'

'Shoot.'

'I was having dinner with Eighteen Twenty-Three last night…'

'Who?'

'Eighteen Twenty-Three. Roger Waybroke. Waybsy. Told me you got him his home loan.'

'Waybsy! Yeah I did! 30-year fixed rate.'

'Thirty years? Jesus, that's older than I am. You know my great-great grandfather managed this bank? Long time ago.'

'Is that a fact?'

'"Tis a fact. Anyway, Mike, I need a loan.'

'For a home?'

'No.'

'For what?'

'Do you remember my dad?'

'Bill! Of course! Love that guy.'

'He's sick. Very sick.'

'Sorry to hear.'

'Cancer of the blood.'

'I'm very sorry to hear, Hector.'

'And I've come home to find out that he can't afford the medication that's going to save his life, some rare drug. And that, Mike, is where you come in.'

'Oh, Hector,' said Mike, preparing him for what was to come. 'We go back a long way.'

And so they did. Mike Isenhammer was Hector Grieve's oldest friend. They had played together as six-year-olds, slept over at one another's houses to watch cartoons and play Forty-Forty Home then Goldeneye. Their first semester of high school came; the immediate commencement of Hector's rebellion against stupidity coincided with an intensification of Mike's obsession with animation. Inseparable as children, as adolescents they found little in common. Their friendship groups increasingly diverged. Through the years they were in some of the same classes, played football against one another at lunchtime, attended some of the same parties, ran into one another's parents in the shopping centre. When at eighteen their social lives began to revolve around the pubs and bars of Maribyrnong they even managed to share the occasional pint. But Hector long considered Mike to be astonishingly boring. A drunken and obviously sarcastic inquiry into his accounting degree had been the last conversation between them.

'But that *would* be considered a personal loan,' said Mike. 'I don't really do that kind of stuff.'

'You manage loans.'

'I do.'

'Good.'

'Ummm…' Hector was not the first schoolmate to appear begging at his place of work, though he was the first to deny the simple logic by which he saw off familiar supplicators. 'How much are you thinking?'

'I'm not sure. How much does cancer treatment cost? I don't know. He has to have a course of Humilitotyn, do you know what that is?'

'I don't.'

'Well how much can you give me?'

'Errrmm… Well, how much do you have for a deposit?'

'A deposit?'

'A deposit.'

'Why do I need a deposit?'

Mike laughed. 'I can't give you a loan without a deposit. That's universal.'

'But I need the loan because I don't *have* any money.'

'Errr…'

'I need money, Mike.'

'Hector, it's just…'

'It's just what? In order to get a loan I need to have money?'

'In order to get a loan you need a deposit.'

'A deposit is money. So in order to get money I need to have money. How the fuck does that make sense? If I had money I wouldn't be asking for money.'

'Do you have a job?'

'Of course I have a job.'

'What is it?'

'I told you, I'm a soldier of fortune.'

'I thought you were kidding. What even is a soldier of fortune?'

'I'm a two-star general in the Royal Cambodian Army.'

'I can't tell if you're being serious.'

'Of course I'm being fucking serious! I'm a two-star general, Mike. A Commander of the Royal Order of Sahametrei. I'm a Knight of the Guardians of Jayavarman The Seventh *and* a Most

Honourable Captain of Indra Protector of The East. Do you know what that *means*?' Hector counted them out on his fingers. 'A Dharmaraja of the Order of the Leper King, a Restorer of the Eternal Peace of Sangrama. I'm a Teahean of the Dynasty of the Seven Southern Lords, and a Mahasena of the Most Exalted Order of the Lotus Pond. Genuinely, Mike—I'm a two-star general in the Royal Cambodian Army, commanding officer of The Royal King Voar Regiment. And I've never once lost a battle.'

'That all just sounded like gibberish. Do you have an employment contract that I can sight?'

'An employment contract?'

'For this job of yours.'

'There's no contract. I have an agreement with the Cambodian generals, and a financial arrangement with the politicians. It's all unsaid.'

'It's not really a job though, Hector. Especially not here. It *would* explain the clothing though. What's the salary?'

'A fortune!'

'Do you have payslips?'

'What the fuck is a payslip?'

'Hector, I'm going to give it to you straight, mate. You don't have a deposit, you don't have a job. In,' he said loudly, hoping to be allowed to explain himself before causing offense, 'Australia. I can't give you a loan.'

'Fuck you.'

'Hey, calm down.' Mike smiled. 'There are loan criteria, OK? And I have to put those criteria into a computer. It's the computer that decides, not me. If you get a job, here, a regular job, recognised by the computer into which I enter your loan criteria, *then* I can waive the deposit, for a higher interest rate.'

'A job?'

'At the very least. A real job, with an employment contract. For me to even consider giving you a loan.'

'How do I get a job?'

'You interview for one.'

'That's a job interview isn't it? I've heard of those. How do I get one?'

'Are you serious?'

'I've been in Cambodia for eight years, Mike. I was a soldier the whole time. Job interviews aren't... I became a soldier by walking into a general's office and telling him how incompetent his army was.'

'How 'bout I get you a job interview?'

'You'd do that?'

'Do you remember the night after Jimmy's when we broke into EKC and went swimming at two o'clock in the morning?'

'Of course! Helen gave me an underwater blowjob. They don't feel as good you'd think, by the way.'

'That was the best night of my life, Hector.'

'*That* was the best night of your life?'

'All because of you. You made me drink absinthe from the promo girl's tits, remember? Roger passed out in the toilet so you had space in the car for me. I can still remember climbing the fence and trying to run the pool cover. Best night of my life.'

5

Hector stepped down onto the coal-grey pavement of the street and contorted his face into a look of sharply disgruntled ire. 'A job.' His neck burrowed further into the ribbed collar of his jacket and he set off for his father's car.

He passed a shop selling Chinese bubble tea and three selling souvenirs; a shop selling objects which facilitated the smoking of marijuana and a bar at which people paid to play board games. There was a shop which sold crystals carved as dick-and-balls— purported to heal one's heart chakra—and a vegan leather store and a café at which one paid for the privilege of smashing one's own avocado. Hector crossed Elizabeth Street without looking left or right. At the opposite kerb he was intercepted by two police officers in fluorescent bibs.

'Sir, are you aware it's illegal to cross a road within twenty metres of an intersection that has pedestrian lights?'

'Heh?'

The first officer repeated his question as the second scribbled at a notepad. 'Is there any particular reason why you didn't cross the street at the pedestrian crossing, just there?'

Hector looked to where the officer pointed and back again. 'No.'

'Jaywalking,' declared the officer. 'Officer Stacey and I just witnessed you crossing a road within twenty metres of an intersection that has pedestrian lights.'

'Good for you and officer Stacey. I hope he buys you a candlelit dinner to celebrate.'

'Sir, are you carrying any concealed weapons?'

'What the fuck are you talking about?'

'If we have reason to believe you're carrying a concealed weapon we have the right to search you.'

'Marvellous news, gentlemen. Good day.'

'I'm informing you that we are issuing you today with an on-the-spot fine for jaywalking. When crossing a road within twenty metres of an intersection that has pedestrian lights you must use the pedestrian crossing. It's for your own safety.'

Officer Stacey tore a completed sheet from his notepad and offered it to Hector Grieve.

'What the fuck is this?'

'If you refuse to accept the notice of infringement, you will be liable for a fine.'

'If I don't recognise your right to tell me that I can't cross the street where I want to, I get a fine.'

'That's correct.'

'What the fuck is wrong with you? What the fuck's wrong with this fucking country? Why don't you fine them?' Hector pointed to a trio of people sprinting to cross the street beside him.

'They're Chinese.'

'So?'

'They probably don't speak English.'

'So because I speak the language of this country, I'm the one that has to follow your pointless fucking rules?'

'Please don't swear, sir.'

'I'll swear, and I'll swear well. Now because I speak the language I'm the one that has to follow your pointless fucking rules while foreigners do whatever the fuck they want because they can't speak English?'

'Pretty much, yep.'

'Plus,' said officer Stacey. 'If we fine them, they won't pay it.'

'What if I won't pay it?'

'Then you'll be liable for a fine. And then we'll seize your property.'

'*Plus*,' added the first officer. 'If we fine them, their dads might stop investing in our country.'

'And they *are* the future,' said Officer Stacey.

'What am I then?'

The first officer raised his eyebrow and clicked his teeth with uncaring uncertainty and said, 'Have a good day, sir.'

As the officers walked on Hector held the pink piece of paper between his hands and lowered his forehead to crumple it in his fingers as he calmed himself with slow breaths.

He crossed through the winds of Princes Bridge and passed the palm trees of Queen Victoria gardens. He raised an eyebrow to the equestrian statue of Edward VII and sighed and raised both of them in tiredness at the landscaped clock before it. Opposite a fountain dancing with water a person in an akubra and with long green sleeves under a fleece vest stood at the front tyre of his father's car. The man tapped a stylus at an instrument in his palm and stepped around to inspect and record the vehicle's number plate. Then he tapped some more.

'What the fuck are you doing?' said Hector.

'This is a two-hour ticketed parking zone.'

'Good for you.'

The man offered Hector a folded piece of paper in a sealed plastic slip.

'What's this?'

'A parking fine.'

'What the fuck for?'

The man pointed down the street with his mock pen. 'Two-hour ticketed parking zone. You don't have a parking ticket.'

'Where does it say that?'

The man repeated the vague indication of his instrument as he photographed the front of the car with his phone. 'On the sign.'

'Down there!? That's in fucking Frankston! How could that sign possibly apply to me?' To this the man made no reply. Hector unwrapped and unfolded his pink fine. '*Two hundred dollars?* I don't fucking think so. I'll buy a parking ticket. I've only been here for what? Ninety minutes?'

'Sorry, mate. That's not the way it works.'

Hector stepped into the man and growled: 'Make it the way it works.' He scrunched up the fine and threw it in the man's face. 'Do something on your little machine there.'

'Infringement notice has already been logged. You can apply to the court to have it disputed, but you won't win.' He turned to check the next car's licence plate against his machine, which Hector promptly slapped out of his hand. 'Abusing a City of Melbourne parking officer carries maximum penalty of a two-thousand-dollar fine or imprisonment,' he said, picking up his machine from the gutter. 'We have the right to a safe and secure working environment too.'

'A safe and secure working environment? I was once hunted by a Russian sniper for six hours. I slashed his liver with mine own hand but his knife. A safe and secure working environment? What's the fine for being a fuckhead? Tell me that and I'll write *you* a ticket. What do you think? You can come to this country and fine its inhabitants for parking in their own streets? Who employs you fucking people? They don't have jobs for parking inspectors in Bombay?'

'I am from Sri Lanka, sir.'

'Good for fucking Sri Lanka. I sat in traffic for two hours to get here. Do you know the average speed that is? That's six kilometres an hour. I shit faster than that. And I drove here at shitting speed for you to tell me I can't park in the streets of my own city?'

'You *can* park here, but you have to buy ticket.'

'How am I supposed to know that?' Hector droned impatiently.

'The sign over there says it *very* clearly.'

'That sign is nowhere fucking near me! Where do I even buy a ticket?'

'At machine,' said the officer, raising his stylus to the sky.

'Machine is further away than sign! Undo the fucking fine.'

'I'm sorry, sir. I cannot. If you want to dispute the infringement the instructions on how to do so are on the reverse of the fine that you scrunched up and threw at my face.'

'I'll throw more than a piece of paper at your face in a minute. Fix it. Aren't you a public servant? I'm the public. Serve me. Get rid of the fucking fine. I'll buy a ticket. All ninety fucking minutes' worth.'

'The palm pilot does not let me undo infringement that I have already logged.' The man was pleading, hoping Hector would understand the obvious simplicity of his situation. 'Please, sir. You can tell your story in a letter to the city council.'

'My story? You don't know half my story my sub-continental friend.'

'Sri Lanka is an island.'

'One that perhaps you should have stayed on. Two hours I drove here to find out that I've written the first novel in your God-damned language, then I went into a bank that my great-great-grandfather used to manage to be told by a boring granny's-fart that I'm too poor to get a bank loan. This, my country. Then I was told where I can and cannot cross the street. What has fucking *happened* to this place?'

As Hector entered that beloved mode about which until his flight he had forgotten, the parking inspector tapped away at his palm pilot with his instrument.

'Traffic lights tell us when we can and can't go, even though there's no fucking traffic. I can't cross the street without a cop telling me it's illegal to do so, and the Chinese skip all over the place eating noodles and I can't park my fucking car anywhere. Why do we even have roads? What's the point of even living in this fucking place? I imagine it feels free for you, Gunga Din, but for someone who grew up with clean drinking water among rolling hills of pasture it feels a little bit like we're regulating ourselves out of existence. Only to be replaced by snivelling brownwarts like you, grateful for breathable oxygen.'

At Grieve's inferences the parking inspector looked up from his device and presented to Hector widely provoked eyes. 'You're really rude, mate.'

Hector squinted and grinned and shook his head. 'War is hell. ... Do you even have any self-respect? Look at the job you're doing. Why would you even come here? *We* don't want to live here. We *don't* live here. Not in the true sense of the word. It's a fucking prison. Its open spaces are regulated down to the millimetre. *Do* any Australians even live here anymore? And then we have to import cheap labour to enforce the regulations we've placed on ourselves that make us not want to live here in the first place. This, is a cycle of history. Civilization has so overgrown us that we employ rickshaw drivers to come and tell us what we can and can't do. This, a Grecian Rome. Not by your strength. Not by your strength shall we be conquered, but our weakness. I don't come to your country anymore and tell you what you can and can't do. What the fuck are you doing here and pretending you're Australian in your little hat there?'

'I have been an Australian citizen for eight years.'

'Eight years? Wow. My great grandfather built half this city with his benevolence and his money. What do you do with the money this sinecure gives you? Send it home to your forty thieving children so they can get IT degrees? What did your great grandfather get up to? Sacrificed children to Kali. You've been here eight years and now you're telling *me* what I can and can't do? I don't fucking think so. What are we doing to ourselves here, people?! Really I mean no offense to you, ultimately. I'm sure you're just trying to make a living for your orientally large family. I'm just… I mean *what* are we doing to ourselves?' Hector turned to the crowd that he sensed was encircling him. He yelled, 'Am I right?'

None of it responded, though those who were not already filming on their phones now poised their devices and began doing so.

'Why don't we put in regulations that say we *can* do whatever we want, wherever we want to? And then let the wisdom of the individual decide what's worth doing and where? Would that be so fucking revolutionary? Start legislating *for* freedom rather than against it? Do you not all agree with me? Or are you just all on your phones all the fucking time? You are. You don't care. You're going to stay on your phones aren't you? Yep, there it is. Fuck me. I mean what's the point in having a country if that country is composed completely of foreigners who are here to do nothing but enforce the fucking ridiculous laws that make its inhabitants leave the country in the first place? You know what Alexander the Great said? You, with the idiotic fucking bun of hair on your head. Do you know what Alexander the Great said? He said the people of Asia were enslaved because they'd never learned to pronounce the word "No". I've been here for a day and all I'm wondering is what shameful subjugations we're going to keep on saying Yes to. I can't leave my house without being stopped by the police. I can't drive anywhere because traffic lights hold me prisoner. I can't cross the street where I fucking want to, and I can't park the car once I've actually managed to get it anywhere. I can't have a drink before driving. I can't carry my Peacemakers. Where the fuck are we going, people? Ask yourselves. Not by their strength, but by our weakness. Clearly nobody here's having kids anymore. Have you walked around the city lately? It's all Asian people. We've built a country that *we* don't even want to live in, so why would we have children? And the kids we do have either leave or turn into boring idiots who do nothing but take photos of themselves and save all their money to take holidays in the countries that all these people are moving here from. What the fuck is going on!? Who, can abide a Grecian Rome!? Are *none* of you listening to me!?'

And off Hector Grieve went, on a rather predictable three-minute tirade against parking officers, bureaucracy, and the growth of his own civilization.

Chapter Three

KHARTOVM

1

In the furthest corner of his backyard Hector Grieve sat in a camping chair with his back turned to the house and the world. Despondent in shirtsleeves, his guns at his ribs, he passed between one hand and the chair's mesh cup-holder a red can of tasteless beer—the only he could afford with the change he had found in the seat crevices of his father's car.

He gripped with his teeth at his second-last Cohiba, letting waft its spiced and now-precious smoke. Occasionally he broke from his stare and leaned forward to turn the spit that was roasting Blackjack the micro pig over coals at his knees.

Presently a frigid change seemed to set in. He moved onto the balls of his feet and turned his cheek to the warmth of the raised pit he had constructed. He closed his eyes and found that no thought but of Cambodia would come to him—of Elvis' sacrificed boar after the defence of Beng Mealea; of the bacchanalia which followed the burning out of Bayon, of Jerusalem's cavalry charge seen from the high and otherworldly heat of Phnom Bakheng.

He felt a fleck on his cheek and wiped it away, thinking it would instantly burn his skin. Then another, slightly larger on his forehead, wet and cold. He could hear between the hissing and cracking of fat onto embers the fast and heavy thud of charging hooves in Cambodian dust. Then a hiss shot from the coals, loud and accompanied by a curled ribbon of smoke. Then another, until his shoulders were being spat on. Like a stick against a dusty rug, rain beat at his smouldering fire. A wall of white ash was lifted by steam to the piglet's skin and very quickly the coals began to dull from raging orange to dead white. The rain stung and the new wind pierced his shirt. He pulled his riding gloves from his back pocket and unwound the butterfly nuts from the ends of the spit and lifted the crisped animal from the contraption and hurried it inside. He stepped from the lawn onto the bricks of the path at the side of the house and the downpour stopped, instantly and completely. Hector S. Grieve raised slowly his dripping chin to the treeline, then to the sky proper, and said softly, 'You motherfucker.'

The high clink of an iron latch; the gate at the front of the house swung in. John J. Grieve's bare knees were almost at his chin, his sandalled feet oversized in the plastic stirrups of a stroller.

William T. Grieve pushed him to the porch and stepped backwards up onto its first step. Roasted piglet in hand, Hector looked on. His seated brother rolled his smiling head from side to side and sang *Do You Want To Build A Snowman?* William pulled the stroller towards himself until its back wheels were touching tile. He strained to raise the thing up the first step, then the second.

He held open the wire door with one hand and pulled Hector's brother back to the wooden ledge of the front door; he levered the rear wheels of the stroller against it with all his strength and pulled him inside.

John unbuckled himself and said in a high voice, 'Yippee!' and ran upstairs. William staggered to the kitchen table and put a hand at his sternum and struggled for breath. Hector put the pork and its steel skewer on the chopping board beside the sink and caught his father by the arm as his legs gave way. He helped him into the living room and into his armchair.

'Dad?' William closed his eyes and reached for the television remote. 'Dad?'

'What?' he exhaled quietly. Immediately he was lost in a television show. Hector tried to make sense of its concept. He soon concluded, correctly, that it was a show consisting of people watching people watching people watching a television show.

Hector snatched the remote and threw it with a bang into the corner of the living room. 'Dad, how much does this course of Humilitotyn cost?'

'Hm?'

'The medication for the cancer. How much does it cost?'

'Fifteen thousand dollars a month,' said William, slowly overcoming the anxiety of having his television show turned off.

'Jesus. Is it not covered by Medicare?'

William shook his head and said, 'Hardly anything is anymore. Too expensive.'

'Too expensive for a whole country to pay for? Yeah right. That's a fucking crime. And I bet you—I mean, how rich are rich people now? How many billionaires do we have in this country? … Dad?'

John descended to the foot of the stairs and there unrolled a carpet and placed an iPhone and tripod at the front door.

'Dad!?' William took up a book and scribbled at its paper with a connector pen. 'What the fuck are you doing? Are you colouring in?' Hector pushed the book towards his father and read its cover. *Jungle Wonderland: a colouring book adventure.* He looked at his father's vacant eyes and shook his head. 'Dad, how many billionaires do we have in this country?'

'I don't know,' he said, frustrated.

'And what do you think they're worth? I mean… And what's Medicare's budget? Do you know what their combined worth is? Dad?!'

'Hm?' said William, rotating the page one way and his wrist the other as he stroked a felt tip at a peacock's breast.

'What do you think these billionaires are worth?'

'Hmm?' William tilted his head and poked out his tongue as he rotated the book.

'The billionaires, you fucking vegetable. Pay attention when I fucking talk to you. What are they worth?'

'John'll know.'

Hector called to his brother. 'John, how many billionaires does Australia have?'

'Twenty-seven,' he returned, standing from his knees to adjust the height of the phone.

'And what's their combined worth?'

John fiddled at the tripod and said, 'Seventy billion.'

'And do you know what Medicare's budget is each year?'

John pressed at its screen and took off his sandals. 'Hundred and forty billion.'

'Half! Fucking hell. That's half! Twenty-seven people could cover half of Medicare each year, and we can't even afford the food that probably gave you the cancer in the first place. That's a fucking crime against humanity. John…' said Hector turning once again to inquire of his brother.

A barefoot John J. Grieve loomed over one end of his carpet. His eyes were closed and his head was rocking back and forth. 'John?' He dropped to his knees and fell forward to hold his forehead to the other end of the carpet. 'What the fuck are you doing?'

He came back onto his shins and with closed eyes mumbled something to himself. He again fell forwards and rubbed his forehead into the carpet. Then he was kicked in the side by his younger brother. He whined and rolled onto his back.

'What the fuck are you doing?' said Hector.

'I'm praying, you a-horn, what does it look like?'

'You're a fucking disgrace.'

'Daddy! Hector won't let me pray.' Hector shook his head and looked down into his brother's cowering eyes. 'I'm praying for Hashim al Katab. I have a Solidarity blog. I'm sticking up for what's right.'

'Do you know *why* Dad's medication isn't covered by Medicare? My own fucking family, dressing up like babies and letting civilization crumble around us. Look at your fucking self. Going everywhere over to the fucking enemy. We've lost our identity. You take away a nation's collective identity and you can do whatever you want to its lost and homeless individuals. A Grecian Rome, divided and conquered. Except you tell them they've become individuals! And that only their individual wants matter. Let 'em go shopping twenty-four hours a fucking day,' Hector smiled as he shook his head, 'and they'll never even see that their country's been given to the enemy. Why do you think America doesn't have healthcare?'

He spoke at his brother and father; neither of them listened.

'Because they're not a people, they're just an enormous group of individuals. Who were the first countries to implement national healthcare? Australia, New Zealand, Canada, Britain, Scandinavia. And which nations are now dismantling it? The no-longer Anglo-Saxon countries of Australia, New Zealand, Canada, Britain. Why, Jack my boy? Because we're no longer a nation of people. Look at you. We haven't got a single thing in common. Two brothers, one a warrior and one a coward. And no white man's going to be OK with paying for a Chinaman's throat surgery after he's smoked Chinese cigarettes his whole damn life, and no Chinaman's going to be OK with paying for a white man's triple bypass after he's eaten burgers and pizza his whole fat life. You lose collective identity, you lose national healthcare. National spiritual decline *will* be followed by physical. And their replacement by the Xerxian hordes, grateful for clean water and a home loan in the suburbs.'

'You're so racist,' said John.

'You shut the fuck up, little baby. You will *not* accuse me of being anything, for you *are* nothing. I listen to no opinion from lesser men than I. What the *fuck* are you doing down there, praying like a Turk? *And* by the way…' Hector stormed into the kitchen and shortly threw their grandfather's manuscript onto his brother's stomach. 'What the *fuck* is this?'

'You know what it is.'

'Do you know about this, Dad? … Dad!? God damn it!' William was scribbling still at his colouring book adventure. Hector slapped it out of his hands and tore it in half and threw his connector pen at his oldest son. William jolted with fright and looked up with toothless fear.

'What are you doing?'

'What the fuck are *you* doing?! Why are you colouring in!?'

'It helps with the cancer, it's the art of mindfulness.'

'It helps with cancer? Bull fucking shit. A colouring book never cured anything. Money's going to cure you, Dad. *That's* going to turn you back into a fucking child. Just like your little girl of an older son. Do you know what he's done to Grandpa's war memoirs?'

William closed his eyes and through his nose exhaled an unnerved breath.

'He has raped them, Dad, with feelgoodery and filthy fucking cowardice. Listen to this shit…' Hector strode back to his brother and lifted the top page from his stomach and read:

'*I'm not proud of the battles I fought, nor of the men I killed. When I was in the army all I ever thought was, 'Why can't we all just get along?' It seems to me that war is the stupidest thing that mankind has ever undertaken, that war is the easy way out, that conflict should be resolved by dialogue and democracy. I look forward to the day when war at last is revealed to humanity for the childish stupidity that it truly is.*'

'Your grandfather was a great man.'

'He *was* a great man. He was a soldier, a proud soldier. Grandpa was a warrior. You were a warrior. I'm a warrior. And John's a fucking—'

'If John can do some good with his writing, then—'

'Do some good? Dad! This is fucking cowardice. It's weak and unheroic, and I *know* you don't equate those things with good.' Hector threw a few pages from the stack and read again. '*As I near the end of my life I can truly say that I fought Fascism so that love, the law by which the garden of mankind is tended, would triumph, and hate be defeated. I fought Fascism so that all men could marry one another. …* Dad, do you know he's done this shit?'

'It's what Grandpa *would* have said,' said John, standing at the doorway to the living room with his rolled carpet under his arm.

'*Would* have said? Under what conditions? If he was tortured by an army of camp donkeys into saying what *you* wanted to hear? If he was made to lie by a cowardly government ruling a selfish people who want nothing but rising wages and newer televisions?

Hm? Boring little wankers who think that war is detrimental to their investment portfolios? This is *not* Grandpa's voice. It's the voice of a coward, and it sounds remarkably like your voice, John, you puddle of spoiled oyster. And I'll tell you what…'

Hector threw what was left in his hand of the manuscript onto the living room's jade rug and unzipped the fly of his khaki trousers.

'You're wizzing on Grandpa's memory,' said John.

'Oh am I now?'

'You're wizzing on Grandpa's war service.'

William shook his head and closed his eyes and lowered his brow to the inside of his hand.

'I'm pissing,' said Hector Grieve, 'on your conception of Grandpa's war service. I'm pissing on your abuse of his memory. If you publish this book, John, I'll kill you.'

'Hector!' said their father, very sharply. 'You *don't* say things like that.'

'I've killed men before, brave men, soldiers. Cowards die easy.'

Yapping arose from beyond the front door and the gate latch clinked up and down. 'Hansikoko!' John sang in a high voice and waited behind the fly-screen door. They kissed as Hansikoko stepped across the threshold.

'What the fuck?' said Hector, his stunned eyes darting from side to side.

'Does it smell like urine in here?' said Hansikoko.

'Did he just kiss you?' One side of the living room seemed instantly to sink into the ground. It sprung back up, unsettling the armchair closest to the doorway, which seemed now to stretch towards him. 'Why'd that unitchable rash kiss you on the lips?'

'Why do you think?' said John.

'Wait, are you serious?' said Hansikoko. 'Is he serious?'

'Tomorrow, I think he's serious,' said John.

'Why do you think I wanted to talk to you about adoption?'

'To adopt a baby with some Chinese-Russian wife. This can't be for real. Dad, are you fucking serious? You let this shit happen under your own roof? … Dad!?'

William had retrieved the halves of his book and was oscillating his wrist and a green texta, rotating the pages as he coloured the peacock's tail. Hector's mouth was turned down in disbelief. He said, 'I thought people like you shot yourselves.'

'You have to come to terms with my lifestyle, Hector. I'm your brother.'

'Like fucking fuck you're my brother. Dad, can you weigh in here? This is some fucked up shit I'm having to deal with.'

'That's ignorance,' said John. 'You're ignorant.'

'And you know what you are? You are not a Grieve.'

'*You* can read my driver's licence. John Donut Grieve. You need to stop being so mean. I'm in a pram now because of you. Does that make you feel good?'

'You're in a pram because you don't want to grow up and face the real fucking world. The world of men. The world of good, and of evil.' He moved his pointed first two fingers from his brother to Hansikoko and back. 'You don't believe in evil, do you, Donut? You believe in what you want. That's it for you, the purpose of the universe. And you're in a pram because you want, to go around making things nice and colourful, so you can play with your dolls and suck on your dicks.'

'You're a fascist arsehole with no friends.'

'If people are like you, then who the fuck wants friends? This is fffffffffucked! Dad, how can you let this shit happen under your own God-damned roof?'

'You're making Dad sicker,' said John.

'*I'm* making Dad sick? I'm pretty sure the disappointment in his oldest son is killing him. He probably doesn't even have cancer. He's dying of a broken heart. At having brought *you* up. This, the final product. A fat man's biscuit. This, the weak excuse for a man who has no conception of anything higher than himself. Who wants to make his own cowardice legislation and his country a refuge from greatness. A journalist. Such failure would break any man's soul.'

'Do you really think Dad has a soul? Ha ha. I mean, how out of touch are you? We're born, we die, and in between we should do whatever we want. That's the only recipe for happiness. The soul!' John smiled and he and then Hansikoko gave grinning scoffs of laughter. 'Dad's proud of me. He tells me all the time, don't you Daddy? But imagine how he feels having brought up someone like you. A Nazi with no friends.'

'Someone like me? You mean someone who's *not* in play therapy and being pushed around in a pram? Someone who's *not* more concerned with praying for a beheader of teenage girls than with his own father's health? Someone who's *not* OK with having someone else's tiny half-Asian balls on his chin.'

'You actually are an arsehole,' said Hansikoko. 'And a homophobe. That's ignorance.'

'You shut the fuck up,' said Hector, unholstering his ivory-handled revolver as he crossed the landing to hold it almost to Hansikoko's forehead. 'Get the fuck out of my house.'

'Hector!' said John after squealing. 'Dad!'

'We don't use violence to resolve our problems,' said Hansikoko.

'Do we fucking not?' said Hector. 'Yes we fucking do.'

'Hector, *you* have to leave,' said John. 'Not Hansikoko. He's welcome because he welcomes others.'

'Like fucking fuck I do. This is my house. And I welcome any man who strives to live up to the name.'

'Daddy,' said John, deferring to their father in a quivering voice. 'Daddy, look what's happening!'

Hector switched his aim to his brother and widened his eyes. 'What's happening?'

'Hector, you should leave. Daddy doesn't need your temper in his life, or your hatred. You're a homophobe. That's cowardice. Intolerance is cowardice. *You* are a coward. You should have the courage to be tolerant.'

'What the fuck?' said Hector, above all saddened. 'Your tongue speaks evil.'

'There's no such thing as evil, Hector. There's only miseducation. Daddy?' John called out.

'Stop calling him that,' said Hector.

'Daddy, Hector's bringing bad juju into the house.'

'What the fuck is juju? Is it this?' Hector pulled his seven-and-a-half-inch Peacemaker and pointed it at Tomorrow.

'Where do you think you are, Hector? *When* do you think you are? Daddy!'

'Hector,' called William, gruffly as he labored to lift himself out of his chair. 'Hector,' he said again, faster and with more severity as his youngest son edged his hostages towards the front door. Finally he boomed: 'Hector!'

'What?'

Then his father at last said something with the conviction for which Hector had always known and revered him. 'Please leave.'

'This doesn't concern you, Dad. Sit down and keep colouring.'

'You're upsetting John. He's in a pram now because of you. And you're not doing my health any good either. Everything was just fine before you came back.'

'Everything was fine? Nothing here is fine, Dad. This country's going to hell in a Chinese-made handbasket filled with polka dots and rainbows. *I'm* upsetting things? An angel of discord in a discordant world is an angel of peace.'

'Hector,' said William, approaching him calmly. 'Things are changed. For everyone. You either accept the changes, or you leave, it's that simple. Everybody was getting along just fine without you. You've become detached from modernity.'

'I'm not detached from it, I'm staring it straight in the fucking face, and I do *not* care for it.'

'Please, Hector. Leave.'

Hector S. Grieve turned his head from the barrels of his revolvers and looked upon his father. William T. Grieve pushed both hands at the walls of the living room doorway. He could barely hold himself up. 'Hector, leave.' Then he nodded, once. 'Please.'

'Dad,' said Hector, imploring his father to regain his senses. 'Dad?' he breathed insistently.

'Hector, just… please.' William raised his lowered head. Hector lowered his guns; his shoulders followed.

'Dad?'

'I'm sorry. You should leave.'

Hector stood almost limp.

'Anyway,' said Tomorrow as he and Donut went into the kitchen. 'You should have *seen* the shawls we were looking at today. Weren't they *awful* Foo Foo?' He gripped one of the animal's paws. 'They really were so ridic, Donut, you would have *hated* them! And the colours! Ergh! So I told him. I don't care if they're handwoven by little Indian girls, they look like something an Untouchable would wear. And if an Untouchable would wear them, then I won't touch them. Isn't that clever?'

'You're so clever, Tomorrow.'

'I'm sorry, Hector,' said William, shaking his head. 'We were doing just fine without you.'

'And what is *that*? Oo, is that a roasted pig? A piggy wig! Yummy! Look at all the yummy crackling.' Foo Foo strained from its halter to flick its rattish tongue at Blackjack's perfectly roasted skin.

2

Westmeadows at dusk was a downhill stroll of high fence and weed-bed. Where non-synthetic lawns could be glimpsed they were yellow. A single house attempted an archway; the rest had no design principle but economy. A lifeless silence was broken only by the wheezing of an air-conditioning unit or, more frequently, the tearing of a car exhaust in the high distance of Mickleham road.

Across the street from Hector's house had once been a plot of land used for the stabling of horses. It was now a division of three driveways, each lined with dozens of stacked units of the same imitation slate, not a one of them owned by its occupants. This, the first in a series of invocations that Hector found he could in Melbourne nowhere escape—neither house nor glance was without some memory.

He passed the house where the dad with one arm used to stand watering his lawn with his sleeve buttoned at the armpit; the house where Iain Muir lived, who still worked at McDonald's and whose mother worked at a dog food factory; the path which led down to the bend in the creek where Trent Ptarmigan had discovered a dead body on his walk back from football training.

Over the horizon of grey- and terracotta-tiled roofs there towered a rolled-up newspaper sculpted of plastic—the printing house and distribution centre for the tabloid in whose pages John was so prolific a journalist—the proud blue-lit symbol of the organ by which the traditions of one's upbringing were transformed into the opinions of one's income bracket. A court at the bottom of the hill led to the path around the artificial lake that in Hector's absence had been surrounded by factory and warehouse. Seven flies came to Hector's arms, his cheeks, his orifices. He slapped at them, flicked them, whipped them with his fingers; spat and shook his head and made raspberries with his tongue in order to shoo them from his lips. Still they would not unfollow him. He stopped in the middle of the court and screamed, 'What the fuck!?'

Across Mickleham Road, stationary with cars where it was not terrifying with trucks, Hector soon passed the shopping centre. To take a step was now to venture deeper into the warrens of Gladstone Park, to leave behind stagnation and delve into several circles of decay. To cross Beersheba Drive was altogether to wander into a hostile wilderness.

Law and order prevailed in this fringe of darkness only insofar as the police made twice-daily visits to remove under arrest those men, women, and children whose chief impulse to life was the spreading of violent tribalism as far as their abilities allowed. Theoretically this should not have been far. The criminality which deprived them of employment should also have deprived them of the time and resources necessary for the rearing of offspring. They were not deterred. Free from any prejudice against having a national government pay for the sheltering and nourishment of their young, they used the brief intervals spent out of police custody as precious fornicatory windows, their mating season determined not by menstruation nor seasonal overabundance, but by parole, lack of evidence, false testimony.

Slowly but sadly, year after year—another addicted teenager's successful application for commission housing, another mortgage secured by the equity of a forklift licence—the spoliation by laziness and desertification by savagery crept. It was no longer uncommon for a car driving along what was once a sort of demilitarised zone to have a bottle hurled at it from a sofa upon a porch; for a cycling child to be shot; for an elderly pedestrian to be abused as an Australian.

And at the palpitating heart of this lost world, Khartoum Crescent, that feared and fabled bend—at feeding time aflutter with the mumblings of Maori jabbering and the piratical hocking of Arabic abuse. Hector turned into its northeastern entrance and was instantly on edge.

Khartoum Crescent. The traditional source of all the poorest children with whom Hector had gone to school—they who filled whole classrooms with the smell of pissed-in blanket and soiled uniform, whose hair was always shorn rather than cut, those miscreant boys and girls who looked and reeked as though their skin was every morning powdered with a dust ground of the contents of their inebriate parents' ashtrays.

The sun had abandoned Hector and with it the shadows. The whole desolate row languished in toneless grey. With sharp turns of his head Hector checked his flanks. He pulled down his jacket's zipper until only its stops were joined and he stalked with scanning eyes the footpath. He passed an engineless and bootless car with a swivel chair on its roof, a stack of cut and dying tree branches, a blood-stained suitcase, several mounds of dirt being played in by human children. Between a telephone pole and letterbox tied with matching ends of police tape he startled at the coming on of a burglar alarm. He eyed off the rear of a caravan in the front yard of the house that had always been rumoured as the home of a girl who in primary school took in the space of twenty-four hours the virginities of five eleven-year-olds. Then he passed with a hand at his ribcage the graffiti which encased the park that had long ago seen one resident start a nationwide gang war by shooting another resident in the stomach. After nature strips of two charred and melted rubbish bins, a boat on bricks, a barbecue and washing machine, a rocking horse with mange, a workout tower and a very soiled mattress—Hector at last came to the sloping and cultivated front lawn of Helen Gricius' childhood home.

'Hector?' said Helen, finding it he who had knocked on the door.

'Can I come in?'

The thick glass of a Molotov cocktail shattered against the front bricks of her next-door neighbour's house.

'We're just having dinner.'

Hector's face glowed red in the flickering light of the projectile. 'I really need to come in.'

The house smelled of vinegar, vegetable oil and onions. Muslin curtains and shag carpet abounded. The walls were turning from painted white to stained yellow. Helen led Hector into the kitchen, where at a table clothed with lace then covered in clear plastic an old woman and a young boy awaited the completion of a banquet.

'Babushka, this is Hector, an old friend.'

'Who are you?' demanded the woman from the head of the table. Her brown hair was in a sort of curly crew cut. Her look upon inquiring of Hector's identity was one of violent hatred. Electric blue eyes were slightly curtailed by epicanthic folds. Her Eastern accent rumbled from a mouth that barely had a chin.

'And this is David,' said Helen, making kind her voice. 'David, this is Hector.'

'How you doing, little man?' Without a word David put his miniature hand into Hector's and had it shaken.

Helen stood at the stove and finished preparing the dishes that had not yet been tabled.

'Who *are* you?' the old woman repeated across the kitchen as though she had not been heard.

'Hector and I went out, Babushka. Just after high school.' Hector inspected the beige surroundings of Helen's wooden spoon.

'I don't remember you. You are not important. This is before you could get your dick hard?'

'Babushka!' said Helen, turning from a pot.

'I could get it hard then,' Hector grinned.

'Sit down.' The old woman pointed with bulbous knuckles. 'Eat

181

zis. I make it.'

'What is it?'

'What do you care vod it is? So many qvestions. If I tell you, you won't eat it? It is kartoshka. My special dish. Three hours you must cook.'

'It looks like potatoes.'

'Ah, you are genius and botanist. Of course it is potatoes. Taste.'

Hector sat and tasted a droopy cube of yellow and said, 'Oily.'

'Your vocabulary. Why did you break up with Yelena? Let me guess. Because you knew she would never amount to anysing. And vot have *you* amounted to?'

'Grandma,' said Helen. 'Enough, please.'

'The big little boy is at my dinner table. I want to know who he is. Why did you break up with Yelena? Tell me.'

'What makes you think I broke up with her?'

'Please, I know my granddaughter. Who would vont her? In high school she was fat face, no hip. Like box for telephone.'

Hector swung his head around in disbelief and smiled up at Helen. 'I went away.'

'You are laughing. Vhy did you go away? To get away from here?'

'I moved, to Cambodia.'

'Cambodzha,' she said, as though she were about to spit on the floor. 'You Australians with your Asia. Do you know what Asia is to Russian? Prison. We send criminal to Asia. But everybody here *vont* to go to prison. This whole country should be *put* in prison! Complaining so much, everybody, make you criminal. Babies you are, crying, crying. "Give me vot I vont, give me vot I vont."'

Hector pouted his bottom lip and nodded. 'Did she say Russian?'

'She did.' Helen put a bowl of creamy white salad onto the table as she sat.

'Of all the horrible words, why that one?'

'Hector, you knew this.'

'Knew what? You're Lithuanian.'

'Russian, from Lithuania.'

'Russian?' said Hector. He looked around the room with a frown and a wrinkled nose. 'I don't know how I feel about that.'

'I don't know how I feel about you!' said the old woman. 'English vaginar.'

'Babushka! David.'

'Did your grandmother just call me an English vagina? Who is this woman?'

'What you are asking here for? You can't understand me? She can't even keep husband, don't ask here. Thirty years old she has and not even own a house. When I move to Australia I voz twenty-two and I own a house vizin less than two years.'

'That was 1958,' said Helen. 'A house cost forty-seven dollars.'

'What's your excuse, English vaginar?'

'Babushka! Please. David.'

'There's no 'r' in vagina,' said Hector. 'Just so you know.'

'But there is a 'u' in Don't correct my English".'

'No there isn't.'

'Ohh, but there is one in Shut up.'

'There are two.'

'So shut up, English vaginar.'

'Babushka!'

'Let the boy hear, Yelena. David, you are Russian. Never forget this. Here, is English vaginar. You come from the last Europeans. We alone can fight the Turk. They have men. We have better men, because we have warrior soul. It dies with every Russian killed, and is reborn in the soul of every Russian boy and gyirl. American, English, Australia—they say they want to fight, but they will not die. They will not die for what they vont, so they vill not get it.'

'What's your name? Babushka?'

'It's Russian for Grandma,' said Helen.

'I am called Anastasia.'

'*You* don't say much, do you, little man? Tough to get a word in with this one scaring the bejesus out of you?'

David put down his fork and rested his hands in his lap. 'If you listen carefully people tell you exactly who they are.' Then he returned smugly to his potatoes.

'Where'd you learn that?' said Hector.

'Ever read a book?' said David.

Hector smiled and laughed silently and said, 'All these angry little Russian people.'

'Who knocks on dinner time at door?'

'Sorry about that.'

'Sorry,' said Anastasia in doofus imitation. 'Always apologising. I don't want your sorry, I want you to talk to me!'

'I am talking to you.'

'You call it talking, I call it vining. Say something worth hearing! You have no mind of your own. You are a voman.'

'What are you?'

'I am Russian. Eat this.' Anastasia passed Hector the bowl of white salad. 'I watched Yelena make it, it should not be horrible. Potato salad. Do you know the problem with your country, little boy? Your politicians, they want only one thing. To sell your country to China. They sell your tomorrow for the sake of their pocket today. Russian politicians are corrupt, but they are patriots. Your politicians are corrupt, but they only love themselves. This is democracy. Your democracy has only today. Russia also has tomorrow. We will survive. You have only today, but Russia also has yesterday. You are not allowed to remember. I have seen. Your streets are full of Japaneses, your enemies of yesterday. And your streets are filled with Chineses, enemy of your tomorrow.'

'Thank you for the scary politics lesson, Babushka.' Helen forked three small pancakes onto Hector's plate after serving David. 'These, Hector, are the *best*. Draniki. Potato pancakes.'

'Potatoes,' smiled Hector.

'And here,' said Anastasia, passing him a small bowl of purple soup. 'My borscht.'

'Let me guess. Made from…'

'Beetroot,' said Anastasia.

'The potato's purple cousin.'

'Do you have problem with potato?'

'I love potatoes.' Hector was smiling still at Helen.

'You *do* have problem with potato! If you were a vegetable, potato would have a problem with you.'

'What exactly does that mean, Potato—I mean, Anastasia?'

'It means I think you hate potatoes.'

'No, I love potatoes! Truly.'

'I'm sorry, Hec-tor,' she said, deliberately overpronouncing his name and rolling his r. 'My table has too many potatoes for your English vaginar. Maybe potatoes are all that we can afford. Or maybe potatoes are most glorious vegetable in the whole entire verld! Do you know how old I am? I am one hundred and forty-six.'

'Grandma, you're eighty-seven.'

'One hundred forty-six. And why am I still alive? Potatoes. Our table *used* to be filled with caviar and champagne. But German government stop paying my Holocaust pension. They tell me I have to give them one more document for to keep pension. Do you know where that document is, Hec-tor?'

'I do not.'

184

'In the dirt of Buchenwald with the ashes of my father and mother! So I am sorry if we have too many potatoes for your English vaginar. You are a nudzh.'

'What?'

'You are a nudzh to me.'

'Nudzh? Is that the word you're saying, scary Cossack? Helen, can you translate here? What's Russian for "scary old lady"?'

'Anastasia,' said Anastasia, pointing to her cardigan and cackling. 'Nudzh is my word for you. You are a pest.'

'It's Yiddish,' said Helen. 'It means pest.'

'Yid—. … It's a what word?'

'Yiddish.'

'Yiddish?' Hector looked to Anastasia and squinted. She squinted violently back at him.

'You are blind *and* dumb?'

He looked at Helen's face, and at David's. Behind the boy's head a small silver Menorah rested on lace at a side table beside the kitchen bench.

'Does that…? Wait, really?'

'Really what?' said Helen.

'I had absolutely no idea.'

'Hector, you knew this, come on! We went out for two years, I know you knew this.'

'Here. Vodka,' said Anastasia, slamming a tumbler onto Hector's cork placemat. 'Drink.'

'That's vodka!? Jesus, I thought that was water, lady. Look at the size of your glass. You've had three full ones already.'

Anastasia clicked her tongue and said, 'You want to tell me I've had too much to drink? You are drinking vite vine like a voman.'

'I'll drink vodka with you, she-bear. Don't you worry.'

Anastasia sniggered. 'I like you, English vaginar. You are funny. Yelena, don't fuck it up again. You know what I think? I think you have a Jew face.'

'I have a what now?'

'You have a Jew face.'

'I don't have a Jew face, you have a Jew face.'

'Hector!' said Helen, surprised by the reciprocation.

'I am a Jew,' said Anastasia. 'But I think you are a Jew too.'

'I'm definitely not a Jew.'

'But you have a Jew face, Jew face.'

'Helen, what the fuck is wrong with your grandma?'

Anastasia smirked at Hector and closed one eye and mouthed the appellation once more. Shortly she added a nod to her smile and began to murmur, then to snigger, then to cackle.

After dinner they sat in the living room and watched without subtitles a biopic about a female Russian sniper. Anastasia laughed and cursed every time a German was killed and Hector laughed and cursed every time anybody was killed. When very quickly the bloodshed became too much Helen put David to bed.

'You be good to my granddaughter,' said Anastasia from the armchair imprinted with her outline. 'I give Yelena much shit, but she is a good voman. The boy is good too. Better actually. Hyer husband is a fucking Australian rat. Are you Australian rat?'

'I am not.'

'Well be more than just Australian. Be a man. Look after hyer. Get hyer the fuck out of this place. We are surrounded now. African, Arab, the black ones from New Zealands, Australian scums. No Jews, no Russians. No tsivilitsation. Get hyer out of here, Hec-tor. You can do this?'

'I shall try. But I'm not sure umm… Well, I'm not sure Helen wants me to.'

'Umm, umm, umm. Who you are, Huge Grant? You *are* English vaginar. Be a man, Hec-tor. Tell hyer what you want. Tell hyer what *she* vants. I know Yelena, if you tell her you want to take hyer, she will let you. If—'

Steps sounded a return along the corridor. Anastasia closed her eyes and opened her mouth and threw her head back. 'How long's she been asleep?' said Helen.

Hector looked at Anastasia and said, 'Can we go outside?'

3

'What's up?' Helen sat on the bench in her tiny backyard of concrete, clothesline, and potted cactus.

'You have a kid,' said Hector in half statement, half question.

'I have a son.'

'You didn't think to tell me that?'

'You were too busy trying to tell me how many people you've killed. And trying to kiss me.'

'What happened with the ex?'

'Left me for my best friend. Apparently they're now very happy.

We had a house. I came home early from work one day. She was in my bed, with him. Actually, inside of him, which I never knew Nick was into.'

'And you live with your grandma, in Khartoum Crescent.'

'The Holocaust pension story's true. She couldn't afford her old place anymore so my parents said that if I let her live with me, I could have their place.'

'She's terrifying. But she's also the only person I've heard talk any sense since I've been back. How is that possible?'

'You're a hundred-and-forty-six-year-old Russian Jewish woman?'

'I may as fucking well be. Mike Isenhammer told me today I can't get a loan because I don't have a real job.'

'Of course you can't, you psychopath.'

'But I have a real job.'

'And what's that?'

'I'm a soldier of fortune.'

'Hector, for God's sake be serious.'

'I am being serious!' he smiled and almost yelled. 'Have you been to a job interview?'

'Hector, everyone has been to a job interview. You poor thing.'

'Poor?'

'Listen to you.'

'What?'

'You've become just like everyone else.'

'Like fucking fuck I have. Why are you smiling?'

'No home, no family, no money. My little writer, the boy who used to clean my Dad's rifles and wash my car in the sun with no shirt on. We who fell in love while rolling around on the floor of your parents' kitchen. Who was always above everything, who loathes happiness, and who without so much as a goodbye up and left me to go riding horses in Cambodia… Hector Grieve, just like everyone else.'

'Like fucking fuck I am. I'm the same person I always was. Except everything I had's been taken from me.'

'Taken from you, or given up? You left. If you'd have stayed it might all still be yours.'

'If I'd have stayed I would have had Gladstone Park and fucking board games and vegetable kabobs. Instead I came home to find out that I have no fucking income, my book's been translated into fucking Chinglish. A year's worth of work, turned to gibberish. I find out that my brother's turned my grandfather's war memoirs into a show pony for cowardice. And he's a homosexual. *And* a journalist. I can't get a loan to get my dad his medication because I don't have any money to actually borrow money. I need a real job for that, whatever the fuck that means. And I'm literally no longer welcome in my own fucking home. Proof at last. Greatness and happiness are incompatible. Here, anyway. In one day I get a parking fine *and* a fine for jaywalking, I get hit in the head by a sad excuse for a buttcousin with a stick that enables him to take photographs of himself. This is the pettiest, most babyish fucking… place I've ever goddam come across. God, fucking, damn, it.'

Hector sat forward with jaw clenched and nose scrunched. He stared at the plain concrete of Helen's backyard. By Helen unanswered and ignored, he heard himself. Eventually he listened.

'Fffuck this. Have a fucking listen to me, I sound like a goddam coward. Complaining like a conscientious objector. This country's no obstacle to me. A piss in the pool. A job? I could do any one of the made-up preschooler tasks that these pissants call jobs. Eight years of soldiering, commanding real men, and not once have I lost a battle. I can become a fucking sales manager of shit that doesn't exist. I'll coordinate values until there are no more fucking values to goddam coordinate. A job?! I'm a Commander of the Royal Order of Sahametrei. Do you know what that means? And I *will* get that fucking money and save my god-damned father and rescue my grandfather's memory from the pen of a cowardly humhungry. They want to kick me out of my own fucking house? What do they think, I've never slept under the stars? I once stayed awake for thirty-two hours in the jungle, waiting for that Russian fuckface to show himself. I am a *knight* of the Guardians of Jayavarman The Seventh, a Most Honourable Captain of Indra Protector of The East. I'll fucking find somewhere to live if they fucking want me to. How hard can that goddam be? I once had a palace laid at my feet, I'm a Restorer of the Eternal Peace of Sangrama and a Teahean of the Dynasty of the Seven Southern Lords. I'm a fucking Mahasena of the Most Exalted Order of the Lotus Pond. I'm Hector fucking Grieve, and I *will* get you back.'

'What?'

He turned to look into Helen's eyes. Coldly she met his gaze. Then he moved across to kiss her. She recoiled and shook her head and insisted: 'No.'

'What do you mean, No?'

'No!'

188

'We're meant to be together, Helen. We have the same initials!'

'Listen, you psychopath. We went out for two years and you didn't know I was Jewish *or* Russian.'

'So?'

'We went to at least two Russian Jewish funerals while we were together.'

'I have no recollection of such exotic ceremonies.'

'I don't know what or how you've remembered, Hector. But David's my life now. You,' she said, pointing, 'need to think about starting your own. You need a job, and you need a girlfriend. I'll set you up on a date with someone. A friend.'

'I don't want to go on a date with one of your friends. I'm a fucking Dharmaraja of the Order of the Leper King. I don't go out with the idiot friends of the girl I love, I want you.'

'You don't want me, Hector. And stop saying you love me, it's manipulative. You don't know who I am. Two years, you didn't know I was Russian or Jewish? You want me ten years ago, Hector. And you don't even know who I was back then. You want your idea of me ten years ago. Or maybe you just want ten years ago. I'll set you up with someone. I know just the girl, you'll love her.'

'Helen.'

'What?'

'Shut up.' Grieve attempted again to kiss her.

'Hector!' She weaved her face from his and shook her head. 'Do you not listen to what other people say to you?'

'You're scared.'

'Yes. You left without saying goodbye. Do you have any idea how that felt? You just disappeared. My boyfriend of two years, gone, into the jungle, and never coming back. You were like the kid out of Jumanji. I can't trust someone who's even capable of doing that.'

'And now I'm back, I've come back for you.' Again he reached across to pull her head in for a kiss.

'Hector, you fucking psychopath! You need to leave. Now.'

'I don't have anywhere to go.'

'I'm sorry, you're out. You're not listening to anything I'm saying. You hear only what you want to hear, and what you want to hear is how the world is very much exactly as you remember it. I'm not who you remember, Hector. I'm not who you want. I don't want to confuse David and I don't want my grandma asking questions. Or calling me a slut, which she very often does. I'm sorry. You've gotta go.'

'You and I are going to run away together,' said Hector, smiling as he rose to leave.

'You're a crazy person. Goodnight.'

4

Marlborough Street ascended, Hector Grieve's boots crunched onto the gravel, white in the evening blue around the moonlit rose gardens. Lights were switched off and the water shimmering aquamarine onto the rearing hippocamps, went dark as he passed them.

Margaret answered Hector's knock in curlers and quilted night gown, tied by a silken bow at the neck. A Noël Coward record played upon the card table.

'Dad kicked me out.'

'Why am I not surprised, dear?' She pulled open the door and stood back to let him in. In the amber light of the table lamps a piano waltzed beneath a warped orchestra: '*It's time for little girls and boys to hurry home to bed. For there's a new day...*'

'I was just about ready to get into bed.'

'Sorry, Grandma.'

'Would you like some tea, dear?'

'I fucking hate tea. Thank you though.'

Margaret took a folded blanket from the back of one of the arm chairs and handed it to her grandson. 'I've only got the chairs, unfortunately. But there's a blanket for you.'

'That's all right, Grandma, I like sleeping on the floor. It's good for my back.'

Margaret switched the first of the lamps off and said, 'We'll talk in the morning?'

'Goodnight, Grandma.' Hector took off his boots and prostrated himself in the corner with his feet almost touching the legs of the card table.

'*Night is over, dawn is breaking; everywhere the town is waking.*'

He tucked the woolen blanket under his heels and pulled it up to his chin. He instantly recognised its feel and its smell. He could see it even in the low lamplight, knitted into squares of bold colour divided by black lines, and a flood of nostalgia washed over his closed eyes. Hector pictured the blanket on his grandmother's lap in her leather armchair, shelling peas and peeling potatoes amid the sweet smell of boiling corned beef; could see it on the back of the chintz chaise longue in the sunroom in his grandparents' homestead.

'*The thrill has gone, to linger on would spoil it anyhow.*'

He could feel the scorching sunshine of rural summer and smell the chlorine of their swimming pool; taste the ice-cold lemon cordial made for him and John and the cool of the butter in her cucumber sandwiches.

'*Let's creep away from the day, for the party's over now.*'

FORTITVDE
SOVTH

Chapter One

GRIEVE INTERVIEWED

1

His wrinkles from idleness wide and deep and his hair from sleep a high and furry entanglement, Hector Grieve's head and bare shoulders were crowned by beige bathroom tiles as he continued through puffy eyes to stare at himself in the mirror.

For some time now no words had come to him. Lately he had thought much, done little. Not at all feeling his Cambodian self, he was barely even feeling his youthfully cantankerous pre-exile self. He turned his cheek to inspect the several chins which appeared to overnight have folded themselves upon his aspect.

'Well here you fucking are,' he eventually said. He pulled back his forehead to inspect a red triangle that a pillow had made in it. He ran the underside of his knuckles down over his stubble and groaned. Soon he said, 'A hall of mirrors. Twenty-nine-years fucking old. … And all purpose taken from you. By who? By men and women who don't respect the rules of war. Men and women who probably don't even know those rules exist. … An army is only as strong as its commander is perceived to be. This you know. The enemy, in their lowness, do not even perceive you *as* a commander. … Your army's gone. An instrument of surrender was signed less than halfway through your war. Wealth, memory, family—Versailles. Seek a new command? There is no other way. You, my friend, were born to lead and a born commander always finds a ready army. The enemy fights, though he does not know who, and he does not know why. But he fights. Shamefully. Kicking his foe in the balls. But he fights. And in any place where they fight, a man who knows how to drill men can be king. So drill your fucking self, and conquer this goddamn shit.'

Hector closed his eyes and saw in their darkness Preah Khan, Holy City Of Victory—the first Khmer temple with which he had fallen in love, that triumphant citadel built to honour his father by Jayavarman The Seventh over the battleground on which he defeated the Cham invaders. He breathed slowly and deeply.

'You were atop the highest mountain. Now, fucking here. Where the mountains are nothing but piles of mermaid dung topped with snow made of fuckwit's dreams. But there, General. There. You see it? Across the valley. Another mountain gleams, higher. A father healed, a fortune restored. A job, a house, a girlfriend. Honour. Victory. War. The sting and clash of battle. Christy's arse. All the busty rhinemaidens you and Elvis can get your hands on. Oh, German women! And yes, to get to that mountain you must go down into the valley where there is no peace. And yes the valley contains a village to which all the other villages have sent their village idiots. Guarded by journalists, overseen by accountants, where everyone speaks fucking Chinglish. So wretched they'll let anyone walk within their walls. Infidels. Russians. People who denounce war. But denouncing war, they *are* defeated. Hector fucking Grieve. Get off that fucking mountain made of fuckwit's dreams. You cross that valley and you climb that fucking mountain. A job, a house, a girlfriend.

'The end is glorious, the striving cannot but be worth it. When talent is paired with resolve triumph is inevitable.

'Do not take counsel of your fears. God favours the brave. Victory…' Hector's eyes shot open. 'Is to the audacious.'

He nodded once to himself and took two steps backwards and lowered himself onto the grey shower seat. He turned the dial at his shoulder. A woosh of icy water fell onto his naked body and Hector Grieve washed with his head held high, his eyes level with the handrails of yellow plastic and the toilet booster seat and the big red button for the emergency alert system.

In jacket and tucked tie he strode the corridor of his grandmother's nursing home. He breathed through an open mouth so as to receive none of its acidulous smell. He passed a tall man dragging one leg along as he hobbled. He passed a doorway wherein an ignored woman was clapping as she chanted, 'Hello. … Hello. … Hello.'

Early sunlight over the valley streamed through floor-to-ceiling windows into the dining room. Without breaking stride Hector passed through a sea of white hair and wrinkle and took his seat with Bill, Keith, and Pat—all of whom since Hector's arrival had taken to wearing their medals at mealtimes.

'Boys!'

Keith in his RAAF blue looked up from his cornflakes and said, 'Morning, Hector, me boy.' His mottled forehead and white moustache twitched with life.

'Have a look at that,' said Pat in khaki shirt. All three followed his gaze as it followed Jenny across the room.

'You tried it on yet?' said Bill, alone in civilian jacket and tie.

'I was thinking about it yesterday,' said Hector. 'But then I saw her wiping apple sauce from Gay's stubble. Got a bit turned off.'

'Bull *shit*,' Pat scowled. 'Look at that sit-upon.' The boys did as it rose and fell in her tight blue scrubs. 'Do you know what we'd *give* to be able to get it in there?'

'*Both* testicles,' said Keith, and leaned into his compote. "Cos all they'd do is get in the bloody way.' The table chuckled. 'Here, here,' said Bill.

'Now you bloody well get up there,' said Keith. 'And we want details.'

'All right,' said Hector. 'I'll see how I get on tomorrow. So tell me boys, what am I in for?' Jenny put his breakfast in front of him. 'Thank you, Jenny,' he said, looking up at her with boyish simplicity.

'Say, Jenny?'

'Yes, Keith?' She pulled at her lanyard and smiled.

'Hector hasn't got any sugar for his cornflakes. Why don't you give Hector some sugar?'

Jenny looked down at Hector, whose head was hung and gently shaking. 'Hector can't have sugar on his breakfast, Keith. He's already sweet enough. But he could have sugar *for* breakfast. If only he knew how to ask for it.'

The three older veterans made muffled exclamations of excitement as Hector's head rose slowly from the table to look into Jenny's long- and thickly-lashed eyes.

'I'll work on my asking skills.'

'Do. … Sugar.' Silence ensued as they watched her return across the room to the trolley of shelved breakfasts.

Bill pointed his spoon at Hector and said, 'I bloody told you. She's bloody up for it.'

'Tell me boys, what am I in for?'

'How do you mean?' said Keith.

'Old age. What am I in for?'

'Ahh!' groaned Pat. 'No different really. But you know all that peace and quiet you've wanted your whole life? You get it. To the point where people ignore you entirely. … It's fucking brilliant. You can steal things. I haven't paid for a condom in twenty years.'

'And he hasn't had occasion to use one for twice that long!' Bill boomed.

Keith and Hector laughed and Pat said, 'That's not true, Billy boy. Your wife *always* made me use protection.'

'Oooooh,' said Keith and Hector.

'You can get away with bloody murder,' said Pat. 'Literally. I've killed three people in the last five years and nobody's suspected a thing. Killed more men in retirement than I did in wartime.'

'And you know what,' said Bill. 'You'll like this, Hector, I know you're fond of quotations. When it comes down to it, there *is* only wartime and retirement. If you're not at war with something, with anything, you're retired. My advice is, fight while you still can, boy. Fight and fuck while you still bloody can.'

Hector spent his morning in the library reading Sallust and Fitzroy Maclean. On his grandmother's lawn in the noon sunshine he and his friends smoked Belgian cigars and drank limoncello in their undershirts and played bocce with the Sicilians.

He took afternoon tea with Margaret in deck chairs. Hector picked up a cucumber sandwich from the silver tray between them and they stared out over the valley; listened to the mellifluous chatter of birds and the swaying rustle of eucalypts baking in sunlight. Lucie brought their second gins and tonic and took away their empty firsts. Hector stirred the wide slice of cucumber around his glass and found its first long mouthful perfectly refreshing.

'It's a good life, Grandma.' He lowered himself further into his chair and looked to the sky, clear and babiest blue.

Margaret turned her head slowly to look at her grandson. She pursed her lips and gently shook her head. 'Hector...'

'What is it, Grandma?' He closed his eyes and smiled.

She repeated his name in a high prefatory tone, but broke off.

'What's up?'

But instead of applying to his current habitation the scowling disapproval of common sense she said, 'There's bingo tonight in the games room. *My* bingo. High stakes. And it's not bingo, it's roulette. You interested?'

'I can't tonight, Grandma,' said Hector Grieve. He opened his eyes and rose in his chair. 'I have a date.'

2

'Sorry I'm late.'

'Mmmm,' Hector growled, having watched this young woman say, 'Sorry I'm late,' to the restaurant's three other unattended males.

'Are *you* Hector?'

'Mmmm,' he by an identical growl conceded.

'Sorry I'm late.'

'You said that.'

'I'm June,' she beamed, both through ignorance of and obliviousness to Hector's visceral distaste for tardiness.

He shook her hand as she sat and said, 'Helen told me your name was May.'

'Sometimes I change it. Have you *eaten*?' she said, leaning in with intensely wide eyes.

'Why would I have eaten?'

'Oh, you're right. I don't know why I asked that.'

'So your name *was* May but now it's June?'

'Mm hm!'

'Is your next name going to be July?'

'No, I think it'll be Olympia. But I'm not sure yet. They'll tell me.'

'Who?'

'My girls.'

'What girls?'

'My past lives. I know I haven't been an Olympia yet.' She looked at the ceiling. 'But I haven't been a Sequoia either. I *really* want to be a Sequoia.'

Hector took in fully the girl's appearance. She was thick of eyebrow—so thick that he could not recall having ever seen strips of hair quite so solid upon the top half of another face. Plucked to a point, they made her look vaguely sinister. Her nose was small and curved to a cute button, a diamond affixed to one nostril. Her eyes, caked with mascara, seemed to bulge and contract with her pulse, making her look on every other beat like a slow loris. Her hair was parted in the middle and fell in unnatural shades of blonde over her temples, making her look daft. She wore a piece of black lace around her neck as though a leash might be attached to it and bony shoulders were bare above pleats of flowing white cotton.

Hector squinted dumbly. He said with little kindness: 'How do you know Helen?'

'We went to yoga teacher training together. Have you been here before?' She turned over her plastic-covered menu.

'I have not.'

'It's the *best*.'

Hector looked his menu over. 'Do they *only* serve toast?'

'What else would they serve?'

'Any other foodstuff.'

'But the restaurant's *called* Toaste!'

'My favourite restaurant's called Ganesh. They don't serve only elephant. They don't serve any elephant. I don't understand, is this a breakfast restaurant?'

(A decade a sheesha bar, the establishment had suffered the damning sequence of a fortnight of drive-by shootings then several newsworthy anti-terrorism raids. Sensing that perhaps their time had come, its owners sold up and went back to Libya. After a year of dereliction its new owners set about making the space feel as much as possible like an Ardennais farmhouse. Heralded across the city as genius pioneers of the restaurant industry, they were to base their latest venture's entire menu—had successfully staked its prosperity—on warmed slices of bread and correspondingly rustic décor.)

'No!' said June, excited again. 'But I'm vegan and lactose and GMO free. But luckily *not* gluten.'

'You're not gluten? What do you mean?'

'I'm *not* gluten! Thank God. And the bread here is other-*worldly*. The best. Bread's my favourite thing in the world. What's yours?'

'Bread is your favourite thing in the world?'

'Mm hm. Bread and baby pandas.'

'Wait, is this…' Hector at last fully concentrated on his menu. 'That's twenty-four dollars for two pieces of toast?'

'Organic, fair-trade, GMO free.'

'I don't know what you just said. Twenty-four dollars? How?'

'And everything's locally sourced.'

'Except the waiters,' said Hector as one arrived to take their order.

'Any question?'

'Yes,' said Hector to the waitress. 'Does the Dalai Llama take a shit on the toast before it comes out?'

'What you saying?'

'I'm wondering where twenty-four dollars comes from, as a price, for two pieces of toast, with butter. *Did* the Dalai Llama take a shit on it? Was it in Barack Obama's armpits for a time? Have the slices touched Angie Dickinson's nipples?'

'Who nipples?' the waitress said.

'He's being hilarious,' said June, taking command of the exchange. 'We're on a first date and I think he might be hilarious. *I'll* have the Otway Sourdough, four slices, I'm *starving*, with the Yarra Valley olive oil, smashed avocado and activated almonds.

Hecty? How about you?'

'What did you just call me?'

'New nickname.'

'No. Do you actually just serve toast?'

'No, of course not.'

'What else do you have?'

'We have bread.'

Hector put his elbows on the table and rubbed the fingertips of both hands at the centre of his forehead. 'Do you have bacon and eggs?' The waitress pointed with her pen to the bottom of the menu as June gave a long and high screech of, 'Nnnnnnn…'

'What?'

'Bacon's meat.'

'Bacon *is* meat.'

'I'm a vegan.'

'Forty-five dollars!?' said Hector, following the waitress' pen. 'Were the eggs laid by a golden fucking goose?'

'They chicken eggs.'

'A golden fucking chicken. Just give me toast, two slices.' Hector grinned at her as he rattled his head from side to side. 'With butter.'

'Alrighty! And to drinking?'

'Beer,' said Hector.

'I'll have…' June began. 'Ooo, should I have a nutrition bomb? What do you think?'

His frustration was mounting. He breathed: 'What's a nutrition bomb?'

'Alkalising greens, Hecty. Flavonoids. They explode goodness into your system.'

'I think maybe they explode bullshit into your mouth.'

June laughed and said, 'No, I'll just have a sauerkraut juice. Thanks.'

Hector watched in squinting disbelief as the waitress took their menus. 'Sauerkraut juice?'

She bulged her eyes and said, 'Mm hm.'

'Actual sauerkraut juice?'

'One of the best things you can *possibly* drink! Do you have *any* idea the amount of enzymes it contains? And the flavonoids!?'

'Flavonoids?' Her eyes again bulged like that elated slow loris trying to see in extremest darkness. 'And what the fuck is an activated almond? Is there a deactivated almond? What about just almonds?'

'All part of my plan, Hecty.'

'Please stop calling me that. What plan?'

'To be the first person to live to a hundred and fifty.'

'Who the *fuck* wants to live that long?'

'Everyone.'

'No, they don't. Can you imagine the world in 2130?'

'I wanna go to Mars.'

'Mars?'

'Mm hm,' she smiled and bulged.

'Well you are a space cadet.'

'I wish!'

'A hundred and fifty?'

'No?'

'Life, February, October—June. Life is one protracted operation of jungle warfare. In which you are shot repeatedly and you never fully heal, and each one of your fellow soldiers either dies before you or turns out to be a coward. The longer it goes on, the worse gets your trench foot, and the more likely you are to get malaria and shellshock and to turn coward yourself. One hundred and fifty years, I'm afraid, is too long on this earth.'

'You're *such* an old soul!' she said, astonished by the new discovery. 'Just like me! I'm an old soul too. *Such* an old soul. What do you do?'

Hector sighed and huffed out his bottom lip and sneered around the restaurant. All were buttering toast with smiling enthusiasm. Instinctively he put his right hand to his left ribs. He was unarmed. He contemplated standing up and walking out. It would have saved him at least thirty-five dollars. But he had little else to do with his evening. He had already missed his grandmother's poker game and would only make it back in time to watch a Jerry Lewis film with the demented insomniacs. Plus he was very fond of breasts, and May, or June, or Baobab—whatever it was that the voices in her head were telling her she was called—in abundance possessed them.

'I used to be a writer,' declared Hector Grieve, angrily subduing his reluctance to talk about himself.

'*That* explains it! A writer. It makes so much sense! You old soul! I *love* to write, but I don't get to do it very often. My *dream* is to just disappear in the woods for a few months and write. Is that crazy?'

Hector grinned and said, 'I'm sure it's not only your dream for you to disappear into the woods.'

'I know right!? Ha ha. You *are* really funny. And smart, too. I can see you as a writer! *Such* an old soul, just like me. We should write together. We should run away together! Into the woods!'

'You like the woods.'

'Oo, no, you know what you should do, mister smart and funny old soul?' She was pointing at his eyes. 'You should become a journalist!'

'Should I now?'

'Do you know who my *favourite* journalist is?'

'I do not.'

'John J. Grieve, have you read his work?'

'I have not.'

'I *love* his writing. He's so insightful and so deep. Smart and funny like you. An old soul. Like you too! He's like the best writer in the whole wide world right now. You haven't read what he's writing at the moment?'

'I have not.'

'The Ivory Bunker,' she announced.

'And what is that?'

'You haven't heard of it? How have you *not* heard of it?! You won't believe this. Australia's richest people are all putting their money together to build an underground bunker in New Zealand.'

'I'd rather snorkel in a pond full of turds than spend a second in New Zealand.'

'I *love* New Zealand!'

'You would.'

'And kiwi *fruit*! What's *your* favourite fruit? Mine's avocado. Hashtag avocado's life. They're building a luxury bunker. Like a super-yacht, but underground. They're going to escape there when the revolution comes. I've always wanted to start my own revolution. A creative revolution. *We* should start one, mister old soul writer man. And a secret society. But isn't that atrocious?'

Hector closed his eyes and raised their brows as high as they would go. He soon sprung them open and said, 'What do you do for work? You're a yoga instructor, right?'

'For most of the year, yep. But my big business is writing retreats.'

'Retreats?'

'All over the world! People come and we spend a week together and explore our spirituality and creativity and we do lots and lots of healing and writing.'

'Retreats?'

'Mm hm.'

'Only cowards retreat.'

A woman in a t-shirt which read, 'The Future Is Feminine,' had sidled meekly to their table. She apologised to Hector before saying to June, 'You're Truth-Rainbow, aren't you?'

'Oh. Hello,' said June, smiling timidly up at her. 'I am, yes. Hi.'

So exhilarated that she was barely able to breathe, the woman put her hand to her heart. 'Can I just say, that I follow you, and you are my absolute hero, you changed my life, your words, they have such… such healing powers. I feel like they warm my soul. I just had to say thank you for being such a hero, to me and to so many people.'

The two women smiled into one another's eyes for a time. Soon June started nodding and the enthusiastic woman began to cry. Eventually she became too overwhelmed and shook her head and walked away.

'What did that nutjob call you? I thought your name today was June.'

'She called me her hero,' said June, protective of the asserted role. 'Can you believe that? I love hearing that stuff. I'm someone's hero, Hecty. I love changing lives. There's nothing more… Mmm!'

'Truth-Rainbow?'

'That's my name on Instagram. And the name of my yoga school.'

'Cowardice has a hundred names, while honour's simply honour called.'

'Who said that? Is that poetry? My favourite poets are Cummings and Plath. Do you like them? You're such an old soul, quoting poetry on a date. I,' she declared, then paused. 'Have to go to the bathroom.'

'What's taking these people so goddam long?' Hector looked over his shoulder to the kitchen. 'All they have to do is put toast in the toaster.'

'Silly! You don't put toast in a toaster, you put bread in a toaster.'

'Go to the bathroom.'

She set off for the rear of the restaurant, only to return almost immediately and say before taking one, 'I just need a sip of life juice.'

Hector squinted at her hurried gulps. 'You mean water?'

'Mm hm,' she beamed as she gulped. 'Life juice. You should drink more life juice. I haven't seen you drink any. Do you know how *good* water is for you? Do you hydrate? You should. Sorry if I stink by the way.' Her nose met her bicep halfway. 'I'm armpit detoxing. Do I stink?' She sidestepped to Hector Grieve and lifted high her elbow.

'Go…' he said, turning his head from her, 'to the bathroom.'

'Grum-py.' And she did.

Her glass of sauerkraut juice was brought to the table. Hector sniffed it and gagged and drank long from his beer. Immediately after the placing onto their table of six pieces of toast she returned.

'Now what were we talking about? Work. Retreats. Yoga. Yes! I have to give a workshop this weekend for Pride Week. Are you going? We should go together!'

'Am I going where?'

'To Pride Week.'

'What's Pride Week?'

'Pride Week.'

'Pride *week*? We have a week dedicated to a sin? I don't understand.'

'Did you just call homosexuality a sin?'

'I called pride a sin. Which it is. Where do homosexuals come into this? I'm confused.'

'What the hummus are you talking about?'

'What are *you* talking about? A week dedicated to pride, you said, right?'

'I know for a *fact* that in one of my past lives I was a Venetian courtesan and I was bisexual and some of my closest friends were a secret society of gay costume makers who gave all their money to the poor. Pride week's a chance for people of all walks of life to be proud. L. G. B. T. I…'

'M. M. L. J. Zed. You're just saying letters. Why are you saying letters to me?'

'*And…* to have a dancing parade! Who doesn't love a dancing parade?'

'Who indeed. But I don't understand, what are they proud of?'

'Of being gay.'

Hector stared at her. Then he tilted his head back and squinted. 'That's not an achievement. Do *you* feel proud when you put a knob in your mouth?'

'How much turmeric do you eat? Maybe you're not an old soul. But you're dressed like one, so you probably are.' She smiled and said, 'I don't understand you. I think maybe you eat too much turmeric.'

'I don't eat any turmeric. What the fuck are you talking about? Who eats turmeric? And I don't know what an old soul is, September, but to be honest, if being one means dancing through the streets to show people I celebrate not just any sin, but the beginning of all sin, then I am most certainly not one.'

'I have to go the bathroom again.'

'You just went,' Hector snapped. 'Why don't you hold it in?'

'Because my poos are ready to go,' said June, shaking her head. 'I can't *not* obey them, my body'll get angry at me.' Hector's eyes fell closed and his head began to drop upon his shoulders. 'Are you all right?' June said. 'Are your poos ready to come out too? In one of my past lives I was a medieval proctologist, and the things I learned then have *really* helped me with my gut nutrition. *And* my decision making. You know the saying, "Follow your gut?" "Your gut instinct?" See, if your gut is healthier, then you make better decisions! Makes sense, right? You should listen to your gut, because you're actually listening to your poos. And they know everything. *My* poos are telling me that they're ready to come out right now.'

Hector tongued with some force the inside of his cheek and then opened his mouth as a growl commenced its rise to a moan of furious distaste. He looked up at the chesty blonde standing opposite him. She bulged her eyes and sipped at her sauerkraut juice and said, 'Yummy! I can *feel* the enzymes having sex with the flavonoids. Their babies are my poos.'

He stretched his jaw as far it would go. Soon he said, 'Fuck this.'

'What?'

'Fuck. This.'

'You wanna fuck? Here?' she said, leaning in and looking around the room with an excited look in her bulging eyes.

'Fuck. This.' Hector Grieve stood from his chair and lifted his plate of toast onto his hand and flung it across the room into the brick wall.

'You *are* an old soul. Like a Viking. Do you watch that show? You should give a workshop at my next retreat, on how to awaken your old soul. It'll be *so* awesome! Yes! I'm seeing it now!'

3

'No, no, no, no, no, no, no,' said Hector to an answered security door.

'Oh it's you, cowboy boy,' said Anastasia from behind it. 'What do you vont?'

'Mongol hag, where's Helen?'

'She doesn't answer door at night time. She is scared, like the deer that is afraid of getting stung by bee, so turn to run away and is mauled in face by bear.'

'You are a weird sociopath, lady. Where's Helen?'

'Yelena! GI John Vain is here.'

When eventually Helen took the place of her grandmother Hector said, 'No, no, no, no, no, no, no! God damn it, Helen. What the fuck?'

'What?' Helen stepped out of the house in a slip of orange satin.

'That's who you think I should be going out with?'

'May?' Helen led Hector from the house, under the arbor to the garden bench.

'It's June now. Did you not know? She changes her name every thirty-five fucking minutes depending on what the voices in her head tell her.'

'She's quite famous, Hector.'

'So's Rain Man. That girl has an undiscovered syndrome. Dickheadylococcus. I can't even *begin* to describe... The... the modernity of that thing.'

'Calm down.'

'I can't calm down, my temper's too tied to my reason. I mean, she was a fffff... My God!'

'I thought you liked blondes.'

'I like intelligent human beings who just happen to be blonde. She was a babbling storm of retardation in a teacup of fucking daffodils. I like civilized people, Helen. She was one step removed from Mowgli's mongoloid sister. She had a bone through her nose. Eyebrows like Saladin. I like blondes, Helen, when they're not dumber than a kindergarten full of Lebanese cucumbers. I like *you*, Helen.'

'Hector,' she said, warning him not to start. 'Did you come around at midnight just to abuse my yoga teacher?'

'I came by at midnight to talk to you. And to thank you, very much, for introducing me to that anti-person. Can we please just go away now?'

'And where shall we go away?' she smiled.

'*Any*-where.'

'And how do we afford to do that, hm? You have no money. You have no job. I have less and I'm in debt. And I have a son.'

'Plus all the potatoes you have to buy.'

'Exactly.'

'But what if I get the money?'

'Good for you.'

'Good for us.'

'Hector,' she pleaded with a breath. 'There is, no us. There hasn't been for a very, *very* long time.'

'What if I get a lot of money? I need some for my dad, you can have the rest. What then?'

'I'm too tired for this conversation. Do you need a place to stay?'

'I do not.'

'Where are you staying?'

'At my grandma's.'

'In Essendon?'

'Greenvale.'

'The nursing home?'

'A retirement community.'

'Hector, are you living in a nursing home?'

'You wouldn't let me stay here would you?'

'You can't live in a nursing home.'

'But you can live in Gladstone Park?'

'It's not a nursing home.'

'Greenvale *is* a nursing home, yes. For people. And Gladstone Park *is* a prison, for dreams. You're better than Gladstone Park, Helen.'

'Do you *know* how that makes me feel?'

'Does it make you feel like you should leave and come away with me?'

'It makes me feel horrible about myself. I'm building a home here, Hector, and you telling me that I'm better than my home, is rude. I'm *not* who you think I am.'

'You're Vicious Gricius.'

'My surname is Pudding now. I took Nick's name.'

'Pudding?' Hector smirked instantly.

'Shut up.'

'Pudding?! Your surname's Gricius.'

'It's Pudding.'

'Don't be ridiculous. Vicious, Gricius.'

'You live in a retirement home. *That's* ridiculous, so who cares what you say? One of the other teachers at school is looking for a housemate. Do you want me to put you in touch with her?'

'What's that?'

'What's what?'

'A house *mate*?'

'You don't know what a housemate is?'

'I've lived in a palace for seven years.'

'In a palace?'

'A colonial villa, I had seventeen bedrooms. And maids. Is that what you mean? A house-*maid*? I don't want to be someone's maid. Why would I want to do that?'

'House-*mate*, Hector. You live with people, in a house, with your own room. In a place that is not a nursing home.'

'With strangers?' said Hector, recoiling from the very word.

'Yes, with strangers. Do you know all the decrepit and drooling people in the nursing home?'

'Hey, I have friends in there! Keith flew in the Battle Of Britain, thank you very much. Pat was on the Kokoda Trail and Bill was in North Africa with one of my grandfather's brothers. And unlike my old friends, who live for bathroom tiles and taking photographs of themselves, they're real men.'

'And they're what, ninety years old?'

'Age is more enviable than youth. Age is wise, calm. It doesn't drink sauerkraut juice or call itself Truth Rainbow or talk about its poo. Age is a condition to which we should all aspire.'

'You need to not be living in a nursing home, Hector. She's a lovely girl, lives with two other people and one of them's moving out next week. I'll put in a good word for you.'

'I don't want to live with anyone else. And I don't want to go out with anyone else. I want to go out with you.'

'Tough. You're looking at the house tomorrow.'

'I can't tomorrow. I have a job interview.'

4

Hector strode into the high-ceilinged, open-planned, grey-carpeted lobby of a Queen Street office building. In dark green jacket and khaki shirt and tie he said to the shapely young brunette woman behind the ground floor desk, 'I'm here for a job interview?'

'Hector Grieve?'

'Hector Grieve. Can I ask you a question?'

She smiled up at him from behind her long barricade. 'What?'

'Have you done a job interview before?'

'Of course,' she said, playfully suspicious of where the strange line of questioning might go.

'What are they like?'

'You mean here?'

'In general.'

'What are job interviews like? What do you mean? Have you never done one?' Hector shook his head. 'Oh, they're the worst.'

'The worst what?'

'Just the worst anything. *The* worst. Let me see your CV?'

'My what?'

'Your CV. Your resumé.'

'What's that? Should I have that?'

'Are you serious?' The girl tilted her head and waited for his lack of seriousness to break. 'You're joking?' she smiled. 'You're joking.'

'Has anybody ever told you that you're a very pretty girl? What's your name?'

'Marlene.' She leaned back in her chair.

'Lili Marlene?'

'What's Lili Marlene?'

Grieve lilted in his flat singing voice: '*So wollen wir uns da wiedersehen… Wie einst, Lili Marleen.*' The girl leaned forward onto her elbows and smiled. '*Wie einst, Lili Marleen.*'

'What's *that*?'

'Just like then, Marlene. Just like then. I'm going to see you again. But first, a job interview.'

'I'll see if Dave's ready for you.'

He was eventually led up what seemed like floating white stairs, along a wide grey-carpeted corridor, and into an office.

He decided on their feeble handshake that he was going to give the characterless 'Dave' nothing that he did not have to labour to extract. Dave sat behind his desk and flattened his tie and looked Grieve and his crookedly contemptuous posture over. 'So you know Mike?'

'I know Mike.'

'How do you know him?'

'We go back a long way, Mike and I. How do you know him?'

'We go to Comicon together. Both big Game of Thrones fans. You watch it?' Hector stared at him with a clenched jaw. 'No? All right then… Why don't you…' Dave tapped his fingers at the edge of his desk. 'Why don't you tell me what makes you think you'd be excellent at management consulting?'

'Why don't you… tell me a little bit about what management consulting is?'

Entirely opposed to Hector's application, Dave stared at him. He soon said, 'Do you mean what we do at Floss & Well specifically? Or what actually is management consulting?'

'What you do here specifically.'

'And then you can tell me your strengths and weaknesses.'

'I have no weaknesses.'

'Good to know. Floss & Well, Mr Grieve, specialise and excel in a range of management consulting services. We do workload capacity analysis, administration review, long- and short-term feasibility studies. We do advanced spending levers, procurement reports, governance frameworks, best practice contract management. You brought your CV with you?' Dave was uncertain as to where Mr Grieve might be hiding the traditionally unfolded document.

'What *is* that? Your receptionist asked me for that.'

'Your resumé.'

Hector shook his head and said, 'Nup.'

'All right. Ummm, why don't you *tell* me about your work experience.'

'For the last seven years I've been a soldier of fortune.'

'Here?'

'In Cambodia. A two-star general.'

'A soldier?'

'An officer. A two-star general and I've never lost a battle.'

'And back in the real world, why don't you tell me about your actual work experience?'

'That is my actual work experience. All I've ever done. Well I wrote a novel but…' Hector counted his qualifications off on his fingers: 'I'm a Commander of the Royal Order of Sahametrei, a Knight of the Guardians of Jayavarman The Seventh, a Most Honourable Captain of Indra Protector of The East, a Dharmaraja of the Order of the Leper King, a Restorer of the Eternal Peace of Sangrama, a Teahean of the Dynasty of the Seven Southern Lords, and a Mahasena of the Most Exalted Order of the Lotus Pond. Commanding officer of The Royal King Voar Regiment. Cavalry. Horses. Seven years of soldiering and I never once lost a battle.'

'That sounded like gibberish to me. What does any of it have to do with management consulting?'

'Management's the same as commanding. Not quite as manly, but how hard can managing employees be compared to leading an army on the field of battle?'

'I like to think it can be very hard.'

'You like to think, or you need to think? To justify spending ten hours a day in this room to do a job that probably doesn't actually exist. I've come across people like you before, "Dave." My ex-girlfriend was a management consultant. Let me tell you a little about how I work. The success of my generalship is defined by one maxim—Don't tell people *how* to do things. Tell them *what* to do, and let them surprise you with their genius.'

'That's a very good corporate management strategy.'

'Yeah, no shit.'

'Where'd you get it from?'

'History, Dave. All the lessons a commander of men can need are found in history. Read it often and read it widely.'

'All right. *But...* You don't have a millisecond of experience in management consulting.'

'Do I need it? I just told you about the soldiering.'

'Ummm,' said Dave, momentarily looking to the floor. 'Do you have a business degree?'

'I have a flawless combat record. Not a single soldier lost to the enemy in seven years of command. How's that for a degree?'

'Do you, have any idea, how the real world works?'

'I tell you, I'm very quickly getting one.'

'And do you have any idea what it takes to get a job, in the real world?'

'To be honest, you all just seem like a bunch of idiots. Like you have your heads stuck up your arses and that's your vantage point for the world. I figured a smart person could get a job anywhere. When talent's paired with resolve triumph is inevitable, and I *am* talented. None of you actually do anything that requires a brain, do you? I mean, what's contract management? Seriously. Workload capacity, feasamalleability procurement advanced masturbation spending. It's meaningless. You can tell me it's meaningless, Dave, it's all right. They're just words you came up with to give yourself something to do, aren't they? "Jolly planing phlebotomy tingle-frunch." What's that? Don't know. But I'm going to do it today and I'm going to call it my job and I'm going to make people pay me for it. You're not a soldier, Dave. It's the only job there truly is, and I'm an exceptional one. You tell me the what and I'll figure out the how. I need this job. And back in my day all a man had to have was talent. Talent always rises and it's talent that conquers, and in talent do I abound.'

'Back in your day? How old are you?'

'I'm twenty-nine.'

'We're the same age.'

'And what have you done with your life? Gotten a job and grown a goatee.'

'What have I done with *my* life?' Dave turned a defensive ear to Hector. 'I have a job, which is more than we can say for you? I have a house. A French bulldog. See this watch? Four thousand dollars, mate. And I've met both my heroes.'

'And who might they be?' said Hector, already almost laughing.

'Dave Hughes and Angeline Jolie,' said Dave, very proudly.

'You've met Angelina Jolie?'

Dave thrust forward a framed picture of the woman, smiling awkwardly as he, dressed as a tomb raider, squeezed his arm at her shoulder.

'I slept with her,' Hector grinned.

'Don't be ridiculous.'

'Best piece of arse I've ever had. Best piece of arse she's ever had,' he added, pointing to himself. 'I had an affair with her in Cambodia.'

'I've travelled too. Sooo…'

'Let me guess.' Grieve sat back in his chair and grinned. 'Bali and Thailand.'

'No, thank you very much. Bali and Phuket.'

'You're an unnoticed skidmark, Dave.'

'You're not getting this job.'

'I'm sorry, what did you say?' Hector put a hand behind the top of one ear. 'I don't speak dickhead, what did you say?'

'Get the fuck out of my office.'

'Suck a fat one, Dave. I don't want your fucking job. Not if I'd have to work for an Irish-looking paedophile like you. Fuck you and everybody that looks like you. I don't need this shit, you dicksniffing turtle-licker, you're not a man. Look at you. Like the shadow of a real man farted and not of the earth but from that stinking silhouette vapour were you born. Love foreswore you in your boring mother's womb, didn't it, Dave?'

213

'How'd it go?' said Marlene when Hector emerged striding.

'Exceptionally.' He pulled a cigar from his jacket. 'Your boss is a tired old granny far, you know that right? But I do have a few questions.'

'Shoot.'

'Have you ever changed your name?'

'Me? No, why?'

'Do you listen to the voices in your head?'

'What voices?'

'Do you drink sauerkraut juice?'

'That's disgusting.'

'And do you remember that song?'

'Which song?'

'*Wie einst, Lili Marleen.* Wie einst. Just like then. I told you I'd see you again. And I want to see you again. What are you doing tonight?'

'You're taking me out for drinks.'

'Do you eat meat?'

'Every meat you could possibly think of.'

'You pick the restaurant?'

'Deal.'

'Marlene '

'Hector.'

Grieve put his last Cohiba in his mouth and lit its end as he stepped through the automatic glass doors onto the dark pavement. 'Shit.'

5

Two hours later he was in a musty and shag-ridden den—the dimly-lit and progressively decorated living room of a Pascoe Vale sharehouse. He was seated before Athena, Helen's co-worker (a gawking mouth arranged with teeth like well-polished headstones) and her housemate (a fuzzy-moustached and man-bunned toothpick of a person wearing fluorescent Ray-Bans though he was indoors and tiny shorts and a white shirt that said, 'Close the camps').

Hector glared again at the unframed canvas portraits of a fluorescent Joseph Stalin, Mao Zedong, a red-white-and-blue Barack Obama. He redoubled a mild effort to prevent disdain from radiating at his frown and crumpled nose.

'We *are* looking for someone on a similar schedule to us,' said Athena after Hector told them that he was currently looking for work. 'Fabian works two jobs and's doing his PhD, so he's barely home. And I work at the school with Helen obviously and I have yoga two nights a week and netty two nights a week, so no one's really home most of the time. What do you do outside of work, when you have a job?'

'I go riding I suppose.'

'Cycling's life,' said Fabian. 'Isn't it mate?'

'Horses,' said Hector. 'Walers. My own. The Waler took part in the last successful cavalry charge in history. Beersheeba, Palestine.'

'Free Palestine! Am I right? I'm allergic to horses,' said Fabian as though the information might be to Hector wondrous.

'I didn't doubt it for a second.'

'And what about your rental history?' said Athena. 'Do you have references we can call? Helen said you're delightful but we *would* like to speak to people you've lived with before, you know, just to get an idea of what you're like as a housemate, rather than as a friend.'

'References?' Hector thought momentarily upon the congregation of dropped crocodiles by which he had ejected the succession of girls of whom he had grown irreparably tired or whose loyalty he had begun to suspect. 'I don't have them *with* me. Is that a problem?'

'Umm… Where did you live before?'

'I lived in a house. In a villa. A colonial villa. In Cambodia, Siem Reap.'

'And how many housemates did you have there?'

'I had a staff of around thirty. Maids, pool cleaners, drivers, zookeepers, mahouts, a monkey that shined my shoes, a valet.'

'How much was that a month?'

'It was leased to me by the army.'

'The Cambodian army?' said Fabian. 'Does that mean you're OK with genocide?' Hector yawned at the boy, who was several years older than he. 'I did genocide studies at uni, mate, and we *studied* the Cambodian genocide, I'm not OK with that.'

'The Russians raped a million women on their advance to Berlin.' Hector waggled his thumb at the prints on the wall. 'But you and the world seem to be OK with Communists. I moved to Cambodia thirty years after the genocide, "Fabian".'

'Yeah…' said Fabian, preparing his rebuttal. 'Bu-ut! The army was—. Wait! Stay there!' Fabian rushed from the couch and lifted his phone from his lap. He poised the object at Hector's head.

'What the fuck are you doing?'

'Stay still, you have a Pokémon on your head.'

'What?' Hector flinched from Fabian's outstretched hands. 'What the fuck are you doing? Sit the fuck down.'

'Stay still!' Fabian shrieked. 'You have a Charizard on your head! Do you even *know* how rare they are?'

'Ffffuck this!' said Hector. He stood and slapped the phone out of Fabian's hand and punched the sunglasses (though not the man-bun) from his head. He picked up the chair upon which he had been interviewed and threw it against the portraits on the wall with enough force to turn it into kindling.

6

'Much more civilised,' said Hector, nestling warily into an armchair in a raised and not-horribly-lit corner of a Fitzroy restaurant. 'Odd name for a restaurant though, no?'

'It's *such* a nice place, don't you think? I thought it'd be perfect. Doesn't it feel like you've gone back in time?' The warming contours of Marlene's beauty, her plump cheeks and her smile lines, were raised tenfold by the glow of red-shaded lamps.

Billie Holiday's voice wafted with Count Basie's piano through the crimson darkness of the terraced booths. '*I've been around the world in a plane, settled revolutions in Spain.*' 'Shall we drink champagne?'

'Oh yes please,' said Marlene. 'And we'll take the banquet,' she said to the waiter before even a menu had been handed to her.

'I like that,' said Hector.

'A woman who knows what she wants? I know exactly what I want.'

'And what's that?'

'Apart from champagne? You'll have to wait and see. Isn't this *so* much better than Tinder?'

'Better than what?'

'Tinder.'

'What's that?'

'Are you serious?' she smiled, again inspecting Hector's face for the emergence of a smile. 'You've never heard of Tinder?'

'I have not.'

'You're such an old soul.'

'Don't call me that.' He shook his head. 'Please.'

'Well it's just so nice to meet someone the old-fashioned way, you know? In person. And for that someone to be a man and to have the balls to ask me out to my face. All I get nowadays is dick pics.'

'You get what?'

'They just don't make any sense. Like, yes, thank you, I'll take *that*, how fast can you get here?'

Not at all having a clue what Marlene was talking about, Hector smiled and nodded with a hint of embarrassment as the champagne arrived in a plastic bucket. He popped the cork and poured. 'To the good old days,' said Marlene, grinning with glowing eyes as they clinked glasses.

'I'll drink to that,' and both they did.

'It's seriously impossible to meet a real man nowadays. They're either arrogant pricks who feel you up at nightclubs, or whiney little mummy's boys. Where have all the *men* gone? You know what I mean?'

'All my old friends do is play board games and eat vegetable kabobs and take photographs of themselves.'

'Like what happened to chivalry? Not the chivalry of just opening a door for a girl. Men think chivalry now's letting a woman pick what they want to have for dinner. I mean, tell me what to have! Tell me what to do! Boss me around! I'll boss you back, but I just love a man's man, a man I can expect things from and who can expect things from me. I'd fulfil a man's *every* physical desire if only he'd behave like a gentleman. Do you remember that word?'

'Well.'

'Really, I had the worst day at work today, besides meeting you. It's so nice to be here with you. Cheers. To men. To real men.'

'Chahik si chahik,' said Hector, meeting her glass with his. 'Men of men.'

'The *worst* day today, honestly. It's Thursday but I still feel like I'm Tuesdaying. D'you ever get that feeling?'

'What feeling?'

'Like you're Tuesdaying, but on a Thursday. Last week I was Mondaying all the way up to Friday. *That's* the worst. Then I couldn't even Friday on the weekend 'cause I was still Wednesdaying up till Sunday! Then it was back to Mondaying again, and that lasted three fucking days.'

'Huh?'

Marlene sat back in her chair and crossed her legs and looked out over the restaurant. 'Sometimes,' she said, becoming wistful, 'adulting's just too hard.'

Hector turned his head and frowned with curiosity at this newest new verb. 'Adulting?'

'I'd *love*… to just be a fairy mermaid zebra.'

'Oh, fuck me. Not you too.'

'Or a unicorn! Well I *am* a unicorn, just so you know. You've got yourself quite a catch here. Oo, you know what I'd *love* to be?'

Hector looked blankly at the girl and drew and dropped a heavy breath. He said with an admixture of fatigue and disinterest, 'Apart from a fairy mermaid zebra?'

'A zebra *unicorn*! Can you imagine? A zebra unicorn!? Or,' she said, very excited by this new fantasy, 'to have sex in a mermaid lagoon. Where can we find one, ey? Do you think mermaids get their anuses bleached?'

An arrived waiter interrupted Marlene's speculation by transferring several plates from his arms to their table.

'Yummy!' said Marlene, as though she were alighting a waterslide. 'What's this?'

'These,' said Marlene, moving in with chopsticks, 'are with chilli and lemongrass.'

Hector surveyed the banquet. He recognised most of the dishes. 'They're silkworms.'

'And *these*, are the *best*,' said Marlene, swirling her implements over the table. 'Termites with soy and ginger. Oo, *so* good!'

'Where the fuck are we? Why are we eating insects?'

'Plague, silly billy! It's like the coolest restaurant in Melbourne right now. I told you I eat every meat there is. Did you know that each year the world's population grows by seventy *million* people? Bugs are the only protein we can eat now with a clear conscious. Please tell me you love the environment.' Marlene dropped an eyebrow to a shoulder and awaited Hector's response. She put a chargrilled locust halfway into her mouth and crunched and swallowed the thing. Then in a very high voice she called out something which resembled, 'Lop lop, lop lop, lop lop.'

'What the fuck is wrong with you?'

'Lop lop, lop lop.'

'What's that noise!?'

'That's the noise a zebra makes. A happy zebra. After she's eaten a chilli locust. Have you ever *seen* a zebra? I *love* zebras. But not as much as babies and puppies. And cuddles. Zebras are number four. Or maybe baby pandas. You try.' Marlene repeated her high-pitched lopping and with a stab of her chopsticks beckoned Hector to replicate the sound.

He put an elbow on the table and into his palm slammed his forehead. 'We're out of champagne,' he said with closed eyes. 'I'll go to the bar.' He sighed and laboured to raise himself out of the armchair.

'Something to drink?' said the bartender.

'Give me a second,' said Hector, staring into the mirrored wall behind the shelf of whisky bottles. It seemed to begin to tilt. Sinatra's voice danced between a flute and the ascension of a dance band: '*And even when I'm old and grey, I'm gonna feel the way I do...*' He squeezed his eyes shut and tried to shake it off. He reopened them. The bartender appeared to be walking downhill.

'Hector Grieve,' declared a voice at his side.

He turned his dazed eyes towards it and said, 'What?' Immediately his face transformed—his bottom lip fell, his eyes widened with boyish attraction.

'I don't believe it,' said the woman. 'Knight of the Guardians of Jayavarman the Seventh, Captain of Indra Protector of The East.'

'Dharmaraja of the Order of the Leper King.' Hector smiled and said, 'It's about fucking time.'

'What are you doing home?'

'Home? No. I'm homeless. Friendless, penniless,' he grinned as he shook his head. 'Sexless, jobless. Who might you be?'

'Australians call me Polly. But my name's Apollonia. Apollonia Lupazzoli.'

'Apollonia? Piacere.'

'And with perfect pronunciation. I knew it.'

'Lupazzoli. The lone wolf. Where you from, Apollonia?' She pointed at the ceiling and its crescendo of instruments. '*Pickin' up lots of forget-me-nots! You make me feel so young...*'

'Sicilian.'

'You don't say.' Her eyes were as wide and dark as her cheeks were gibbous and high; they glowed in jade green. Her hair was pulled loosely forward over one bare shoulder, curling like ribbons of darkest shining chocolate; lips magenta and full and curved as two baroque scrolls. 'What brings you to the bar?'

'Who the fuck brings a date to a bug restaurant?'

'Who the fuck brings anyone to a bug restaurant? Who *eats* at a bug restaurant? They eat these in Cambodia because they're dirt poor. And now what? It's cool to suck maggots? What's wrong with you people?'

'You people?' said the woman, taking a very detectable step forward. The black silk of her dress rubbed at Hector's elbow.

'Everybody I come across here. You seem normal, some of you even seem smart. Like orbs of Carrara marble. But then I scratch the surface with a little pin and the paint comes off, and you're not an orb of Carrara marble, you're a painted pink balloon. Then the surface gets scratched a little more, and the balloon pops and everything implodes and becomes a floppy deflated idiotic mess that wants to be a fucking mermaid. The one I'm here with doesn't even speak English. Literally, for five minutes, I couldn't understand a word she said.'

'I don't believe it,' said Apollonia, staring eye to eye with Hector and smirking.

'What?'

'Hector fucking Grieve. Real as day, and next to me at the bar. Did you say you were homeless?'

'I did.'

'And sexless?'

'Mm hm.'

'I find that *very* hard to believe. The boy I'm here with hasn't shut up for ten minutes about how easy it is to get girls to come round to his apartment late at night. From what I've read, and I've read as much as I could get my hands on, you, Hector Grieve, *are* a man.'

'The last.'

'I think I can take care of your situation.'

'Which situation would that be?'

Apollonia raised her Aperol spritz to her mouth and extracted its skewer. She ran her lips over its olive. 'Homeless,' she said, and slid the fruit along with her teeth. 'Friendless,' she said, holding it among the magenta lusciousness of her lips. 'Sexless,' she said, and drew it into her mouth.

'I just have one question,' said Hector.

'What's that?'

'Do you bruise easily?'

Apollonia Lupazzoli pulled Hector Grieve by his tie as she reached back and slid open the shoji doors which led to her bedroom. She slammed her body into his and held his bottom lip between her teeth.

'Careful,' warned Hector in a mumble. 'It's my natural instinct to meet violence with violence.'

She slid his tie from his collar and unbuttoned his shirt. 'It's my natural instinct to meet violence with submission.'

'So shut up,' he said as he pushed her onto her back. 'And submit.'

'I'll shut up if you make me shut up. And what is that?' She reached into the trousers she was unzipping. 'Oh yes, let me take care of *that*.' She pushed Hector towards the ceiling and rolled him over and straddled him. 'You said you were jobless?'

'I did.'

She took his right hand and put it around her neck. 'Take care of me and I'll take care of that too.'

7

Hector Grieve ran the ends of his fingernails back along the side of his wet and combed hair. He pulled the windsor knot of his cornflower blue tie up to his white spread collar and turned his face to inspect in the mirror the closeness of his shave.

Apollonia Lupazzoli, wearing nothing at all, came into the bathroom and opened his grey pinstripe jacket and slid it up onto his shoulders. She reached under his arm and moved a hand across his waistcoat—squeezed him at the ribs, bare both of holster and revolver. Hector put his hand over hers and lowered his cheek to offer it for the kissing.

'You ready?' she said.

'Born ready.'

'Give me an hour?'

'What's the name of that book?'

'Propaganda.'

Hector sat with his ankles on her balcony and read Bernays while she fixed the mess he had that morning made of her.

A short time later they struggled through long shoals of suited people darting instinctively to their places of work. Hector and Apollonia veered from the insentient procession and stopped outside the ground floor of a Southbank office building.

'Can I go in alone?' said Grieve, looking into the building's empty lobby and seeing a receptionist behind a desk. 'I've always wanted to say this.'

'Say what?' said Apollonia.

'I'll tell you afterwards.'

Automatic glass doors parted before him and Hector S. Grieve strode the polished concrete floor. He stared at the lowered head of the young woman distant behind the curved white reception desk. He slowed as he neared her. He came almost to the bay of elevators behind her and found that still she had not looked up.

Apollonia watched from the street. Hector turned about and came halfway towards her before turning again. He re-approached the brunette crown and stepped his black brogues harder and louder onto the floor. Still the receptionist would not be moved from whatever work she was with pen and paper doing. He turned about again and came almost to the entrance. He shrugged his shoulders at Apollonia and she shook her head and shrugged hers. He stamped a foot as he turned around to make his final striding pass. He made each step as loud as possible. He cleared his throat. At last the young woman raised her head and peered over her white pillbox to see what all the noise was about. Hector Grieve walked directly at her and locked on to her eyes as he neared.

'Can I help you, sir?'

'No you cannot.' Hector broke off his stare and veered towards the elevators 'I'm an employee.'

And with the push of a riding-gloved thumb he called a lift.

Chapter Two

GRIEVE EMPLOYED

1

In an open-plan office with exposed ceiling, its chrome ventilation and yellow sprinkler system hanging from bolted strips of steel, morning light shining white and viscous onto its sealed concrete floor—there was working no one.

At three long drawerless tables of unlacquered pine, notorious for splinters, and in sixteen wheeled chairs of metallic black mesh between two partitioned glass walls—there sat no one.

And at eight back-to-back pairs of computer screen and sixteen white keyboards and four rows of mice—there was, typing and clicking, nobody.

For the entire staff of Messina Media & Communications were in the conference room being given by Bradley Dinkle, their Human Resources Manager, a seminar entitled, 'Kindness in the Workplace.'

'Kindness is the foundation of strong and long-lasting business relationships,' Bradley had begun. 'Kindness is the only thing a person needs in order to achieve corporate greatness. Kindness makes *you* a true hero in the world of business. It is the all-encompassing happy-making rainbow of glitter that makes our days truly sparkle with profit. As part of the new worldwide "Rebuild the World with Kindness" initiative, we—'

'What a load of goat semen,' a voice sniped, slowly and very loudly from the back of the conference room.

'Excuse me?' said Bradly, unsure of where precisely the shot had come from.

'I said, What… a load… of goat semen. Sit the fuck down, "Bradley". Let me talk to them.'

Hector S. Grieve rose from his seat and buttoned his jacket as he took the room unopposed.

'Kindness is the biggest swindle pulled over mankind since universal suffrage. And just because Lenny told Sarah that he thought a kimono was a dumb thing to wear to work, we have to sit through this preposterous discourse on dickheadery?'

'Kindness makes the world a better place, Hector,' Bradley insisted as he took the empty chair beside Apollonia at the side of the room. 'The United Nations just released a report on it.'

'Can you even hear yourself, boy? What a ridiculous fucking sentence. *Kindness makes the world a better place.* While mankind inhabits this earth it will never be a better place than when they didn't. You want to make the world a better place, you take power from your enemies and you hold it and you wield it and you make damn sure that it's your country that the world's insuperable bullshit is serving and no one else's.

'The world is *not* a kind place and never will be. Mankind is wicked. Russians are even wickeder. Leave it to your mother and your fucking boyfriend to be nice to you, "Brad." Expect everyone else to be purple-pissing sons of bitches. Keep them in their place, get what you want from them, and you'll never be caught off guard. Kindness? 1943, Sicily. The Germans were surrendering under white flags. The Americans were kind to them, Bradley. Kind. And when the GIs got close enough to accept the surrender the Germans shot them. That's kindness. That's where kindness gets you. Those Hun bastards should have been shot where they stood, white flag and all.

'*Rebuild the world with kindness.* ... A load of fucking goat semen. All great things are built on bloodshed, and they always will be. The blood of the Roman legions was the bed soil of its empire. The blood of the martyrs was the seed of the church. Greater deaths win greater portions. The greatness of the British Empire depends on the volume of blood that its sons are willing to spill in order to civilize this savage world. It cost the lives of nine hundred thousand American, British, Canadian, Australian young men to save our civilization from the Jap and the Hun. Sorry, Sarah, I know you're half Japanese. But it's true.

'We did *not* go to North Africa or to New Guinea to kill our enemies with fucking kindness. We went there to spill their living guts before they spilt our own. Some of us were put on this earth to succeed, Bradley, and some of us were put on this earth to be kind to one another. The two are incompatible.

'Now I know that bloodshed does appear to have a bad reputation among you people. But there are many things worse than bloodshed. Slavery is one of them. New Zealanders are another. Russians, are a hundred times worse than bloodshed. ... Where was I? ... Kindness.

'I know I've only been here for a week, but I see a lot around me that doesn't make any fucking sense. Daily performance reports, first of all. I couldn't think of a bigger waste of anyone's time. One of your ideas, no doubt.' He pointed at Bradley with his first two fingers. 'You, should be put in front of a firing squad. Kindness is the falsification of your true feelings towards another human being. People *are* idiots. Being kind to them allows their idiocy to not only persist but to thrive. Telling a person that you like their kimono, when clearly that kimono makes them look like a Senegalese in an Amsterdam window, is not kindness. It's lying. Being kind, and telling someone you value their opinion, is a lie—and one that only serves to confirm that idiot in their idiot opinion.

'Furthermore, being unkind to people, is hilarious. From what I can gather, you all love humour. You actually don't seem to take anything seriously except your own opinions. But you will find the strength of character and the perceptive candidness required in order to be unkind are both vastly more amusing than are their opposites. That is—weakness, and the sugared words of poisoned tongues.

'Kindness is a load of goat semen. Nobody needs it. Nobody wants to receive it, and you definitely don't want it near your face.

'I'm proud to be leading you wonderful people into business. Do your duty. Be unkind. Only good can come from it. Victory, is to the audacious, not the kind. God favours the brave. He does not favour the kind.

'Now get back into that office and let's do some goddamn work. We conquer today as a team.'

All except Bradley Dinkle and Apollonia erupted into smiling applause. One by one they rose to give a standing ovation.

As the clapping died down and the staff filed slowly out of the conference room Apollonia Lupazzoli stayed behind and shook her head as she slunk towards Hector. She had warned her employees that their new COO was going to introduce a different style of management, that he was unorthodox though brilliant, stern but well-meaning—that bringing him across to their industry from his was exactly the kind of revolutionary thinking that MMC should be applying to all of its work.

His motivational tirade had exceeded all expectations that she had held for a young man whose generalship she for years had followed on obscure Southeast Asian news websites and history-buff and war-nerd blogs.

'Exceptional,' she said, her head shaking still.

'You think they liked it?'

'They loved it.'

'It was a fine speech. One they sorely needed.'

2

In the afternoon there came a knock at the window adjacent to the door of Hector's office. 'James,' he said, looking up from the manila folder tucked under his keyboard. The edges of Hector's computer screen brimmed with post-it notes reminding of his day's, his week's, his quarter's objectives. A framed reprint of Napoleon Crossing the Alps hung at his shoulders. His Peacemakers were mounted in a glass case on the wall. 'If you've come to tell me again how much you hate Mondays, I'm telling you, James, I don't want to fucking hear it.'

'Oh,' said James Truman. 'But…'

'Ah!' he said, cutting James off with two fingers. 'Now you may think that I'm negative, Truman, that I dislike too much. But do you see me sitting around having actual conversations with people about how much I dislike certain days? No. Each day, James, brings new opportunities to conquer one's enemies. No day's worse than any other and none are better. Complaining, James—about anything—is cowardice. I dislike a lot, it's true. But there never has been a time in which there was so much to dislike. Complaining is at the forefront. Laziness, disorder, Russians. Bradley. I hate them all. And yes, I do hate much, but I complain little. You must *act* on what you dislike, James. Conquer it.

'I don't care about your feelings, be sure of that. *Especially* when it comes to Mondays. I only care that you do your duty. That is all that God, and I, can ask of you as my team leader. I don't want to hear how much you hate Mondays, or that you have a case of them, or that on Tuesday that it still feels like one. Days do not have feels, James; anymore than Russians have feelings. Now do you have anything you want to talk about relating to the RCA account?'

'No. Just…'

'That'll be all.' The March of the Grognards sounded loudly from Hector's iPhone. He said, 'Dismissed,' to James and answered it. 'Speak to me, Monty.' He rubbed his neck and held the device to his ear and leaned back in his swivel chair.

At five-minutes-to-five the entire staff was roused to excitement when a man bearing seven flat white boxes walked the hallway which passed the glass walls of the office from the elevators.

'Are they…?' said James.

The polo-shirted man came to MMC's open door.

'Oh my God, they are,' said Sarah opposite him, welcoming with closed eyes their cherished aroma.

Hector came out of his office carrying a box of his own. He gestured his chin towards the long pine table at the back wall. 'Just set them down over there.' He thanked the delivery driver and set down his own and extracted bottles of etna rosso from it. He spread the cartons along the length of the table before turning to address the office.

'I have been informed … that your distaste for Mondays … is equalled only by your love for pizza. I couldn't think of two more trivial things over which a person could obsess, but nevertheless, you did good work today. And good work will not by me go unrewarded. When all of you believe that your day's work is complete and that you have done your duty according to the standards that MMC and God expect of you, you may feast.

'Bradley, I ordered a pizza made out of kindness especially for you. It's right here…' Hector lowered his arm to an empty space at the end of the banquet. 'Between the salad made out of bullcrap and the cake made out of little girls' wishes. Thank you. And enjoy.'

The employees gradually overcame their uncertainty as to whether or not they were allowed to knock off. Self-satisfied, Sarah rose meekly. Then Pook. These two crossed slowly to the pizza boxes and inspected the toppings. Soon they were followed by three more. Then all had risen from their workstations, to each present a glass to Hector and receive from him a lashing of wine.

3

Friday morning, Hector received into the conference room Matt Wallop and Linda Lapaine. 'How are we both?'

'Yeah, really well,' said Linda, a fish-lipped young blonde woman with freckled skin who smelled of woodchips and sweaty hair.

'And you both know Apollonia.'

'Of course,' said Matt, a brown-wearing stretch of pale-covered bone and hairless gristle.

Hector took the room. After a week of investigating the philosophy and methodology of his new career, of being astounded by the depravity he found there, and of chafing against what precisely Apollonia Lupazzoli wanted his maiden project to achieve—at last of following her orders (she being his only superior at MMC), the moment had now arrived. It was time for Hector S. Grieve to give his first ever client presentation.

He was not afraid. The aggressive ambiguities and malicious deceptions of the young century were but naive simplicities compared to the eternal extremes of battle, so familiar to him. The carrying out of corporate orders, the winning of a public relations war—slivers of a toddler's birthday cake to a young man who once saw off with a hunting knife the Russian sniper who had six hours previously shot him through the shoulder.

Standing at the front of the conference room and staring long in silence, switching his clenched jaw from Matt, to Linda, to Apollonia, to the empty chair beside her—Hector Grieve could even convince himself that he had once again found his war. He maintained that No, his vocation had not been abandoned, nor had it been altered. It had merely changed theatres and had gone behind closed doors. Where once he gave warlike speeches before the city of the King of the Angels, that which once counted a hundred and twenty kings under tribute and put into the field an army of five million men—once prepared men for battle before the Gate of the Age of Kali, in which the Brahmins are prophesied to be ignorant and the times of darkness, the people enslaved not by other men but by passions that are their own—he now orated before Matt Wallop and Linda Lapaine in a halogen rectangle of blank plaster and imitation-wood and plastic chair. Where once Hector Grieve commanded a cavalry regiment in the Cambodia wilderness he now manoeuvred over blue-grey carpet, won clients instead of skirmishes, slew growth targets instead of enemy soldiers. Here, at last, had he recovered the madness of action— this enlarged cubicle, adorned not by Kala, devourer of all things, nor Apsaras, delighting nymphs of the clouds and the waters, but festooned by framed photographs of graffiti and meek slogans of encouragement—merely his other, newer, Preah Khan, the Holy City Of Victory, that triumphant citadel built to honour his father by Jayavarman The Seventh over the battleground on which he defeated the Cham invaders, where now nature and art were engaged everywhere in ferocious battle and in stone was Shiva, destroyer and creator, being destroyed by his creations.

He had not laid down his arms: the nature of his weapons had changed. He once with revolvers and on horseback defended the past. He now charged with disinformation into the future. Hector Grieve, Commander of the Royal Order of Sahametrei, knight of the Guardians of Jayavarman the Seventh, Most Honourable Captain of Indra Protector of The East—had exchanged soldiering for management and was now a chief operations officer in the largest standing army in the world. How provincial the horse-riding and the gunfights seemed when compared to commanding the ideological battles of tomorrow. How easy a foe the Thais in contrast to the complex minds of whole economies of consumers.

Hector understood little of the cowardice that had over the last eight years abandoned, betrayed, and overturned his traditions of family, nation, manhood. Now, Coriolan-like, he had abandoned his own traitorous people for these corporate Volsci and without even so much as a whiff of vendetta was fighting their battles as they—with thought to no consequence but money.

Casually dressed, shamefully pallid, neither an honourable nor a martial bone in their bodies—Linda and Matt he did not even see as the bottom-feeding dreamcatchers as he might once have dismissed them. They sat before him now as officers in the air force with whom his shiny new army was taking part in combined operations.

So from William St. Clair who died fighting the Moors in Spain on a quest to take the heart of Robert the Bruce to The Holy Land, to The Great Montrose whose motto was To Conquer Or Bravely Die, from the New South Wales Corps to the 2/9th Cavalry Command Regiment in North Africa, from his father—exemplar of vital goodness and internationally honoured man of action—of Scotch, Swiss, and English blood—to two-star general in the Royal Cambodian Army—from broke soldier with a dying hero to Chief Operations Officer of a mid-level strategic communication processes company. Thus had Hector S. Grieve ascended.

Undoubtedly he was still at war.

And so he was not afraid.

Among the decorative plastic and deified vandalism his voice sounded large and full.

'The Refugee Council of Australia wants the contribution of refugees to be celebrated and the voices of refugees to be heard. This we know. But before this can happen, we need to silence the voices that are louder than theirs.'

Hector pulled back his window-pane check jacket and put his thumbs at the arms of his waistcoat. 'Matt, Linda, I present to you,

Operation Guilt-n-Shame. A two-pronged attack. We're going to hold them by the balls and kick them in the arse. Australia, not the refugees. Now, holding them by the balls…'

He paced slowly at the front of the room as he switched his war face from Linda to Matt and back again. 'I've spoken with the Deputy Commissioner of VicPol. He agrees with us, as I knew he would, that racial profiling is nothing but harmful to minority communities and prevents them from successfully integrating. He's a good guy, I've met with him. And he's agreed to hold back from the media all qualitative statistics pertaining to petty crime, armed crime, gang-related violence, membership of terrorist organisations, and rape—gang or otherwise. This includes a total gag on crime-related information that might in any way lead to cultural or racial bias. There's not a damn hope in hell that any Australian's going to know just how prevalent is the raping of their women by young men from immigrant communities—no matter how much they want to believe in it. We impose our imagined future onto their true present, and by this imposition wipe out all resistance to change. That's holding them by the balls. Now to kick 'em in the arse.

'We've reached out to several journalists at The Herald Sun and The Age, and we've gotten onto that TV show with that immigrant kid and the girl with a dry pole up her arse, and they've all agreed to run shaming stories on *anybody* that we tell them is speaking out against refugees. New or old—the fresh-off-the-boats and the established minorities. We've got James watching the media twenty-four hours a day—I don't know where James is this morning, he's meant to be sitting there, but I don't know where he's gotten to—but James has got his team watching parliament question time, reading all the newspapers, watching television from five till ten, and he's going to bring to me the names of anyone, famous or otherwise, who in any way expresses an opinion on refugees that does *not* celebrate them as the brave and virtuous individuals that we know them to be. I give those names to our journalists, the journalists shame them as racists. Not only will Australia not know the truth about who these refugees are or what they're getting up to—we've got them by the balls—but they won't be able to speak out against them for fear of being called a racist—kicking 'em in the arse.

'It's a sound strategy, and what it does, Matt, Linda, is all the negative work. The negative information's withheld, and in its place, we put positive. It leaves us, I hope together, to then do all the work to really get this media machine going and to make Australia see that these people, fleeing unemployment, prosecution, inflation, not only deserve employment, immunity, and low prices—but that by those things they *will* truly make Australia the great country that it thinks itself to be.

'And that, ladies and gentlemen, is Operation Guilt-n-Shame, as well as what Messina Media & Communications hopes to do for you in the future.'

Matt and Linda and Apollonia applauded as Hector scowled at the empty chair in which his team leader was supposed to have been sitting.

'Where the fuck is James?' said Hector to Pook, who sat beside him.

Pook leaned back from her computer and looked up beneath a mousy fringe and over thick-rimmed glasses. 'I think his girlfriend broke up with him.'

'So?'

'He came to work and went straight into the tearoom.' She whispered: 'I think he was crying.'

Hector stood up straight and puffed his chest out and turned his head to the direction of the tearoom. He squinted one eye and heaved loud breaths through his nose.

'James!' growled Hector as the tearoom door banged against the wall. 'What the fuck are you doing?' James was slouched in a chair at the end of the long table, staring into the distance. 'James, what the fuck are you doing?'

'I can't take it,' he whimpered.

'Where were you for the RCA presentation? You were supposed to present our long-term perception management strategy.' James shook his head. 'We're part of a team, James. And each of us plays a vital role in that team. You're my team leader. That makes you a captain.' Hector loomed over him. He took his riding gloves from his jacket pocket and twisted them in his fists. 'How does it look when one of my captains doesn't show up to a client meeting?' James' head fell from its fragile gaze into his hands. Soon it was jolting up and down. 'Soldier?' Then Hector heard it. 'James, are you crying?'

'I don't know why she broke up with me,' he wailed into his palms. He looked up at Hector with red and waterlogged eyes and

231

shook his head. 'Everything was going so well. I just can't take it.'

'What did you just say?'

'I can't take it.' James rehung his head and his shoulders began to convulse.

Hector looked with furious alarm around the empty room. 'Why you're nothing but a goddamn coward.' James looked up at him with a wide frown and dripping cheeks. Hector's eyes bulged with rage. 'Stop your crying.' Hector raised his voice and growled: 'Stop your crying goddamn it!' With the backs of his fingers he tapped James on the side of the head. James put his hands over his ears. 'You yellow bastard,' Hector said almost under his breath. 'Look at you. Sitting here crying while everybody's out there working. Act like a man! Act like a goddam soldier!'

Such was the volume of Hector's initial growl that the staff had assembled at the tearoom door to see what was going on. Those late to the incident were on their tip-toes trying to catch a glimpse between the heads of those earliest.

Hector grinned and said very calmly: 'I won't have cowards in my office.' Then he roared: 'I said you stop your crying!' before hitting his team leader twice in the side of the head with sweeping slaps of his riding gloves.

A short time later Bradley Dinkle knocked on Hector's door.

Hector squinted up from his work and frowned

'Hector—'

'Shh sh sh sh sh.' Hector rolled his chair over to his encased revolvers. Bradley took one of the vacant seats on the far side of his desk. 'Do you know what these are, "Bradley"? Colt Single Action Army. Peacemakers. The glass case here?' Hector put a finger at its bottom and lifted the front flap. 'It's unlocked. The Gun That Won The West. This one was a gift from the King of Cambodia. Ivory handled. From the king's own hunting grounds. And this... a present from Mel Gibson. We're good friends, he and I. And they're both loaded, "Bradley." Irrumator, what *do* you want?'

'You have to apologise to James.'

'What the hummus-eating fuck for?'

'You slapped an employee, Hector. In front of the whole office.'

'I disciplined a coward.'

'You slapped James and now he says he can't face his coworkers.'

'That yellow-bellied little...' Hector growled. 'Have you

apologised?'

'To who?'

'To everybody you've ever met, for being alive.'

Bradley conceded with a dull nod that there was no comeback for that. 'Hector, you have to apologise to James. In front of the office. He's been in the bathroom for the last hour and—'

'He's still not working?'

'I've spoken to him, and he said he'll come back to work if you apologise in front of the whole office.'

'Oh, I'll apologise,' Hector grinned. 'You bring that yellowbelly to me.'

Hector Grieve came to the doorway of his office and announced, 'Could I have everyone's attention please?' Those facing it looked up from their computers; those with their backs to it spun their chairs around. Hector eyed Bradley Dinkle off as he escorted a diminished James Truman to his workstation. Then he stared over the assembly. Their attention was his. Apollonia emerged at the doorway beside him and leaned against its jamb with folded arms. Hector broke with his gruff voice a strategically protracted silence.

'This morning, most of you saw me attempting to restore in someone a sense of his own manhood. I had no intention of being harsh or cruel in my treatment of the… employee… in question. I wished only to remind him of his obligations as a man, and as a coworker. James was upset because his girlfriend broke up with him. What do we all think James' ex-girlfriend would say if she saw, today, that he was a blubbering mess in the tearoom? What would James' girlfriend say, what would anyone's girlfriend say— ladies what would *you* say—if you saw the pathetic spectacle of your boyfriend weeping into his hands over a little rough patch? You would say, and James' ex would say, Thank God I broke up with that bedwetting piss-ant who doesn't have the gonads to accept rejection with his chin up and his chest out.'

'You are a bully,' said James, rising meekly from his seat.

'You sit down. You *sit* down! I'm not finished. A bully is someone who picks on the necessarily weak. You *choose* to be weak. I'm not a bully, you're a coward. Now, I freely admit that my method in attempting to restore James' self-respect was wrong, but I hope you can understand my motive. No woman worth her salt would ever go out with a man who talked baby talk in the office, and no woman worth her salt would ever go out with a man who could break down in tears, and in doing so, neglect his duties as an employee. I trust that you will here, especially the female staff, concur with my estimate of what it means to be a man. Ladies, the sooner you stop letting your men behave like show poodles on a sparkly carousel made of unicorn farts, and start demanding of them, on pain of abstinence, that they start behaving like men, the sooner such incidents as today's will cease to interrupt our work. Back to it. Thank you all.'

The female employees recommenced their typing with grins on their faces. The male employees returned to their browsers with fearful frowns and quite a lot of thinking to do.

'Where the hell have you come from?' said Apollonia, backing Hector into his office.

He stared into the distance and momentarily became wistful. 'World War Two was the defining moment of my life.'

'And drinks with everyone tonight, right?'

'You bet your ass. I've got a surprise for them.'

'Another one?'

At five Hector placed two labelless Black Douglas bottles on the refreshments table and again addressed the office.

'Friyay,' he said. 'To me a new concept. One which, if I understand it correctly, appears to be in direct contrast to everything that you so dislike about Mondays. The weekend is here. I trust that you will all spend it doing what is most of service to God and to your country. But before it begins, a very special ceremony.

'I've spent a lot of time in Cambodia over the years, done some agreeable work there. If any of you have been to Siem Reap you will no doubt have seen the glorious ruins of the ancient city of Angkor. 25 miles northeast of Siem Reap, there's a temple called Beng Mealea. The Temple of the Lotus Pond. An immensely delightful place. The monks there make their own whisky, and for the last few years they've given me bottles of that whisky in exchange for some work I once did for them. Today, on this, my first official Friyay as your COO, I invite you all to join me in a drink, of this rarest of blends from the Temple of the Lotus Pond.

'When drinking this very special whisky it's Cambodian tradition to play a little game we call Burmese Standoff. A simple game. You take a shot of whisky. You let it burn. And instead of chasing it with a beer, you chase it with another shot of whisky. Bang Bang. A Burmese standoff. Who's my first shooter?'

Apollonia put her hand in the air and crossed the room from her office. Hector mumbled, 'Managers last,' as she came to his side. 'Trust me.'

'Those are pretty big shots, Hector,' said Lenny with bounces of his volunteering head.

'Says who?'

'I think it's more than a standard drink,' he smiled and twanged. 'Don't you?'

'Any man who tells another man how big his drink should be is a Fascist.'

'Well I think it's the government that tells us what a standard drink is, isn't it?'

Staring into Lenny's beady eyes, taking in the length and thickness of his black hair and the untidiness of his face, Hector began drafting in his head the speech that would introduce his new regulations on workplace grooming standards. 'Well there you are.'

When forty shots of Cambodian whisky had been downed Hector poured himself and Apollonia two half measures. Most of the office, on beer and wine, began to chant, 'Friyay, let's go out! Friyay, let's go out!'

Hector and Apollonia led them down to Southbank and followed them along the river into a waterfront bar.

'My lips are cold,' said Apollonia, her shoulders hunched almost to her ears by the chortling crowd in which they both stood.

She touched a finger at her top lip and an amorous gaze overtook Hector. He again beheld her Arabian eyes and goddess' hair, curling like the black cashmere of a temple curtain, her cheeks as largest cherries concealed beneath scarves of white silk. Two men pushed past at her back and spilled beer on her arm. Hector looked around the room and said, 'This is a bar, right?'

'Yes, it's a bar,' she smiled, at the feigned antiquarian ignorance that she was discovering was a part of his sense of humour.

'Why the hell would anybody come here? It's loud, dark, you can't move. You may as well have a drink in a coffin. There'd be less people.'

'People come here to be social.'

'In order to be social you need society. This is not a society.' Hector waggled his finger at her. 'This is just a collection of people with nothing in common but the desire to make money.'

'Come on. Outside's quieter.'

They struggled through a sea of polyester and chardonnay and came to a thick wooden bar overlooking the two-way human traffic before the quay.

'I'm telling you my lips are cold,' said Apollonia. She smacked them twice together. 'And not from the wine. It's like they're frozen.' She wriggled her mouth around and ran her tongue back and forth across her top gum.

'That's the whisky.'

'What's the whisky?'

'There's a reason I only let you have one shot.'

'Why?' she said, instantly wary of what he might be about to tell her. 'Hector?'

'There are magic mushrooms in it.'

'What?' she snapped in a low voice. 'Hector, did you drug the whole office?' A naughty smile drew back across her face.

'It's not really drugging them. They'll... things'll just seem a little more interesting for a while. To them *and* us.'

Apollonia looked to the inside of the bar. She said, as though she were disappointed in both men, 'Hector, Lenny's staring at the ceiling.'

'He'd be doing that anyway, that kid's lost.'

'He's staring at it like he's in love with it. Aaaand Dan's shooting people with a machine gun. Great. Oh, God, and look at Susan,' she sighed. Hector watched Susan whip an invisible horse as she cantered it through the crowd.

'Let's get out of here.'

'Back to your place?' said Apollonia.

'I don't think so,' said Hector, shaking his head and smiling.

'Why not?' she moaned, collapsing a little.

'I have too many housemates, I told you.'

'How many's too many? More than five?'

Hector thought momentarily upon the drooling choir at sing-along time and the musty crowd that very slowly flocked to classic movie night; the flabby aquacising classes he had a few times now taken because Jenny led them in a bikini. 'More than five. And your place is so much nicer. It's like I'm back in the Orient. Plus the view, the bar. Do you not like me at your place?'

'I love you at my place.'

'Careful with that word.'

Hector's imperial ringtone played from his jacket pocket. He pulled the contraption out and looked at its screen. 'I have to take this.' He stepped down from the wooden decking of the bar and crossed through a gushing wind to the riverside. 'Dad?'

'It's Donut.'

'Fuck off. What do you want?'

'Dad collapsed.'

'Into a pram?'

'Hector, this is serious.'

'What do you want me to do about it?'

'He wants to see you. Can you come to the hospital?'

'No.'

'Any episode like this could be his last, Hector.'

'He kicks me out of his house and he wants to absolve his guilt before he dies? I don't fucking think so. Even if he was dying do you think I want to spend his last moments standing with you and that half-caste?'

'You shouldn't say things like that. They're not good for my—'

'You're a fucking disgrace. You're a coward and you are not a man, and *not* a Grieve. You're what's killing him. Forget about the fucking cancer, everybody gets cancer now. But not everybody loses a son. Put him on the phone, you prolonged case of botulism.'

'I can't take the phone into his room. It's a radiation free zone. And please stop saying things like that. They make me upset.'

'John, listen to me. You tell Dad to hold on. You tell him I've got a job and I'm getting a loan. First thing Monday morning. And we can start that treatment straight away. He's going to be fine. Are you listening to me? We can afford his medication and the cancer will be gone and Dad'll be fine. And you tell him that I'm working at Messina Media & Communications, in the city, and I'm in the office ten hours a day. He can get his pansy arse out of bed anytime he wants and come and visit. John, I've got the loan on Monday. I have a job and an employment contract and an appointment. He is *not* going to die. You tell him exactly that. John?'

'What?'

'You tell him that.'

'I will, jeez.'

'Don't you "jeez" me you lisping drop of leopard's lactate. You tell him what I said. You tell him that the body can do anything it wants if the mind is willing. You remind him that God favours the brave, and that victory's to the audacious. And you tell him that I have the money he needs for his goddamn medication and he'll be fine. And John?'

'What?'

'Don't suck any dicks in front of him.'

'Fuck you.'

'Fuck you too. Go fist a mongoose.'

4

Before dawn on Monday, Hector Grieve woke in the red and black silk of her bed beside Apollonia. He looked out to the bay, calm and ashen, waves like bars of white silence advancing from the horizon. He put his hand into the thick softness of her hair and felt the delicateness of her neck. Wanting her instantly he slid onto her back and with a firm squeeze at her hip and with his bottom lip on her shoulder he woke her.

The sea was washed over in russet morning as Apollonia squeezed her sheet with both hands, soon to release them in bliss at full writhing stretch.

Hector turned on the hot water. When it ran he mixed it with cold and Apollonia with her hair tied above her head stepped in and wet her chest and said, 'Again.' Hector pinned her against the wall—by both hands above her head, by his mouth pushed firmly against hers; at last by her waist with his own. He pushed the shower head away so that it would all be of use. Of the few occasions for which Hector Grieve took delight in rising before dawn his second favourite by far was shower sex.

Afterwards she lathered his chest. He said, 'You don't own any crocodiles do you?'

'Crocodiles?' she smiled. 'Why?'

'Just asking.'

'Should I own crocodiles?'

'It's probably safer if you don't.'

Before the shoals had begun their morning's currential migration, and before even the building's receptionist was at her desk, Apollonia and Hector crossed the Southbank lobby with take-away coffee cups in hand, in silence and a foot apart, to the elevators. They stood beside one another as they waited. She tapped at his dangling left hand with her finger.

'No,' he said, warning her playfully.

'Come on,' she said. 'They already know.'

'Do you think?'

'Surely.'

A ding, and open doors. Closed doors, and Hector held his coffee cup away from his body and pressed Apollonia against the elevator's wall and kissed her.

He sat on the other side of her desk with an ankle on his knee as she turned and tucked the pages of Hector's employment contract, signing as she went.

She looked up from the last page's signature. 'Nobody will be here for another half an hour.'

'Mm?'

'Again.'

'No,' he said with a grin. 'I have to go and save my father's life.'

In triumph did Hector ascend the steps of the Collins Street branch of the Commonwealth Bank. He strode into the vast edifice of white wall and malachite column and took in the sunlit detail of the room—crimson carpet and gilt arches, golden capitals and coats of arms, gryphons at the cornices and gilt fleurs-de-lis, its blue- and silver-baubled Christmas tree. He joined a queue behind a young Chinese woman and a man in a white kaftan and immediately noticed four men in short-sleeved grey shirts with holstered pistols at their belts. They crossed the bank's carpet from the entrance to the rear. Each held out one arm to counter the weight of lugging a filled duffle bag. They went through glass doors and their heads disappeared as they descended into a room with a white vaulted ceiling.

Shortly they reappeared clutching each in their hands an emptied duffle bag and strode out of the bank. A few minutes later they returned, each again bearing a full bag. They conveyed them across the room and took them again beyond the automatic glass doors. As he watched their labour Hector came to the front of the line. He said to the young bank employee in black skirt and white shirt, 'Yes I do have an appointment. Mike Isenhammer.'

In triumph did James Truman walk the sealed concrete hallway, newspaper in hand, which led from the elevators to the offices of Messina Media & Communications. Into the glorified cubicle of his CEO he pranced—there to place before Apollonia Lupazzoli the front page of the day's *Herald Sun.*

'What's this?' She leaned in and up from her chair and read the tall white headline. 'Racist Poet Warlord Abuses Refugee Parking Inspector.'

'He's dressed like a World War Two soldier. I didn't recognise him at first.'

Bordered in black and surrounded by his own quotations, a very blurry image of Hector Grieve appeared to be giving a Roman salute.

The young woman returned from Mike Isenhammer's desk to the front of the queue as *The March of the Grognards* erupted from Hector's pocket.

'Hello? ... ... What? What do you mean? ... You're fucking kidding me. ... No! ... That had nothing to do with refugees, that was about parking inspectors. ... Insulting a group? ... How is that a crime? ... Inciting discrimination? I did no such thing. ... What do you mean, filmed? ... James, that little coward. ... That was a tirade against my own people! I said very clearly, "Not through their strength will we be conquered but by our weakness." Ap—.'

But she had hung up.

Hector looked to the long wooden barricades which stood between the tellers and their queues. As though their patch of earth suddenly turned floppy, all seemed to sink momentarily into the ground. The jade columns at the far side of the room became wavy lines of green crayon. The glass which lined the rear of the hall appeared to melt and overhead the shields of Victorian commerce rushed at his face then bounced back as though attached to bungee cords. Hector blinked quickly then held closed and opened his eyes and shook his head. Still the ceiling loomed, then sped away from him, loomed again.

He looked at his shoes, which seemed very far away, and then thought that he could faintly hear being very slowly and very deeply mumbled: 'Mike's ready to blee bloo blow.' He stared at the girl's face; it seemed to zap in and out of transmission. He followed her, his eyes darting from left to right with wide-eyed suspicion of the soundness of the building's construction.

His mouth was dumbly open when he came to the walnut partition in which Mike Isenhammer was entrenched.

'Hector!' said Mike, standing to offer his hand. 'You all right?'

'Mike,' said Hector. He exhaled loudly while staring at Mike's crotch. 'Mike,' he breathed again, and cleared his throat. Shortly his focus partially returned. The two old friends shook hands and Hector sat. 'Mike.'

'Y'all right, mate?'

'I'm very well.' He put an ankle at his knee and looked once again around the hall. The four uniformed guards had returned, laden. He watched with a gentle squint their procession across the bank's floor.

'Now, Hector, this…' he said, recalling Hector more fully to attention. 'Is a loan form for two hundred thousand dollars. You brought your employment contract?'

'I did.' Hector handed it to him and he flipped through its pages.

'Now, if you want to look over the loan form, make sure all the repayment information is correct, I just have to call…' He read from the very newly defunct contract. 'Messina Media & Communications, to confirm the validity of the sighted contract.'

'What, you don't trust me?'

'Of course I trust you. It's just procedure, for the computer. I have to click a box here that says I spoke to your employer and confirmed the validity of the sighted contract. You were a soldier, you understand procedure.'

'All right then,' Hector sighed. He put the ends of three fingers and a thumb at his temple. Mike lifted the telephone to his ear and pushed at its buttons. Hector turned from him. Those guards were bringing in another train of loaded duffle bags. The phone conversation at Hector's right quickly faded into silence as Mike's tone dropped from an inquisitive one to a concerned. Then there resounded through the hall a high clink.

The bottom of one of the duffle bags had torn. From it tumbled a pile of golden bricks. Three of the guards stood watch around the stack as he whose bag had ripped hurried out to retrieve an intact one. He transferred the contents of the ruptured to the fresh and they soon reformed their column and its march.

'Hector?'

'I fucking know,' he said, very loudly. 'I only found out two fucking minutes ago.'

'Hector, you understand that…'

'Oh, come on, Mike! For fuck's sake. They literally fired me two minutes ago. For something I didn't even do.'

'Insulting a group, Hector?'

'What does that even fucking mean? A group? If there are four people in a corner and I call them stink badgers, does that mean I've insulted a group? Come on! I have experience now. I got a job in a week of trying to get one, I'll get another one this week. Can't you just pretend you made the phone call after I'd signed the loan form? You know why I need this money. Dad collapsed on Friday night. If he doesn't get the drug that this money's for he *is* going to die. Bill! Billy Boy! He used to drive us to Jimmy's together, you remember? He's dying, Mike. *My* father.'

'I'm sorry, Hector. I just can't. It's the computer.'

'Ah, fuck you, Mike. Fuck you with fucking bells on.' He banged the ball of his hand against the table as he cursed. 'Fuck you with ribbons of dicks and balls made of polka dots and fucking retarded moonbeams. Just fuck it all.' Hector leaned back in his chair and gave a frustrated growl. He shook his head and ran the edge of his index finger back and forth at his top lip. He looked around Mike's cubicle and shortly said with a rearward head toss, 'What's with the gold?'

'What gold?'

'Those security guards are bringing in gold.'

'Oh that,' said Mike. 'You've heard of the Ivory Bunker?'

'Nnn,' he groaned from the back of his throat. 'What is it?'

'Australia has twenty-seven billionaires, right? And 'cause of all the unrest lately, they've all agreed to pool their money to build this luxury bunker in New Zealand. A retreat kind of a thing, so they can fly there if there's a revolution. But none of them trust one another, so they're putting a gold reserve with us so and we're financing it for them. Combined collateral of the country's twenty-seven richest people. Exciting stuff, no?!'

'Gold bullion,' said Hector, squinting as he watched the guards again walk light-handed from the rear of the bank to its front doors. 'Thanks for your help, Mike.' Hector turned and offered his hand. 'I understand. Really I do.'

'I'm sorry, Hector. I really am. It's just…'

'I know, I know. The computer tells you what you can and can't do, because you're not a man. But nobody seems to be anymore. If you want something in this life, Mike, you've got to take it. Because it's plain as Australian day that nobody's going to fucking give it to you—not unless you're a Muslim woman or a gay refugee.'

Hector descended into the room at the rear of the bank. The Corinthian capitals of six granite columns held up a high ceiling, partially vaulted. Its walls were lined with triplets of false lancet windows; all was in marmoreal white. A small doorway halfway along the room was guarded by two men in cheap black suits and cordoned off by red rope between golden bollards. Beyond them Hector glimpsed a descending stairwell. He circled the room for a time, inspecting the carving work and the stained glass, waiting. 'Always this quiet?' he asked one of the men.

'Few tourists every now and then.'

'Nice room,' said Hector to the ceiling, and the guard nodded.

He stepped out into the grey day of Collins Street and its green elm leaves. The sunshine hit warm and full on his cheeks. He closed his eyes and lifted his face to the sky and could feel the thundering of cavalry into Cambodian earth. He heard the engine and creaking tracks of an enemy tank, saw its turret turn towards him—pulled hard at Selathoa's reins to race to outflank it and his eyes burst open. Across the street a skyscraper's ground floor was signed with the Chinese logo of the largest bank in the world.

He saw his race to the Thai border and their ambushing of the Swiss' aeroplane; the bright yellow and joyous green of young rice fields, open plains of sugar-palm, the dense blue of summer sky. Dripping with sweat, he remembered smiling for no other reason than that he was happy, recalled the heat which makes the Khmer feel more alive at his chessboard than did ever a European except on the field of battle, as he watched from above Jerusalem charge alone and at full speed a Walker Bulldog. He looked down to the intersection of car traffic. A tram ascended for King Street, stickered all over with advertising for a Japanese department store.

He looked to his left and found that a high building adjacent to the Commonwealth Bank left no gap. He walked up Queen Street. He found a gate of red iron closed across a short alley which led down to the tiled floor and stained glass he had seen at the centre of the bank's rear. Three slowly scanning security cameras watched from brackets fixed high on the brickwork—one looking north, one south, the lowest covering a front-lift bin of ribbed blue steel halfway along the alley. The very word 'adventure' returned to him in flashes of heat and danger.

He could smell frangipani and rumduol and spit-roasting pig and the gun smoke from his Peacemakers. He felt on his face the ice-cold of his swimming pool at dusk; by its waters was washed of red dirt and blood. He held Christy's tiny waist by her wet skin and looked into the eyes which he often told her were the most beautiful he had ever seen and he called her Sook. Another tram descended for Elizabeth Street, covered entirely in a beaming marketing campaign for a German financial services company.

'A Grecian Rome,' said Hector, and saw the sun rising in twists of coral and honey, veined with cyan, curling to the heavens over the northern baray—heard the booming shots of his Single Action Armies and the thin taps of the hammers when their chambers had emptied—felt the coarse hair of Selathoa's neck and breathed her ancient scent of chocolate dust—welcomed the searing heat rising from the stones of The City Of The King Of The Angels, that which once counted one hundred and twenty kings under tribute and put into the field an army of five million men, whose wealth was built on the sapphire feathers of the halcyon kingfisher, a temple indebted for its splendour to the greatness of the Leper King, its once-gilded towers the work of zealous giants, said even to have—

Two police officers in fluorescent vests stopped at a red pedestrian light. One was short and fat, and one was fat and short and had a black scarf covering, save for a circle around her face, her entire head. 'A Grecian fucking Rome.'

—built themselves; their stone lotus-buds rising triumphantly from the earth, those five peaks of Mount Meru almond-coloured in the dawn and the jangling of tack coming to rest before the gate of The Age Of Kali, in which the Brahmins are prophesied to be ignorant and the times of darkness, the people enslaved not by other men but by passions that are their own. He saw the flaming arches and spiny laterite halls asphyxiated by gigantic trees—his mounted farewell to the King Voar regiment at Preah Khan, Holy City Of Victory—the first Khmer temple with which he had fallen in love, that triumphant citadel built to honour his father by Jayavarman the Seventh over the battleground on which he defeated the Cham invaders; where now nature and art were engaged everywhere in ferocious battle and in stone was Shiva, destroyer and creator, being destroyed by his creations; where were more guardians of holy places than at any other Khmer temple; that Holy Sword onto whose roof at dawn Hector Grieve often climbed and there among birdsong contemplated the desuetude of a whole crumbling city covered in turquoise.

'Who could abide a Grecian Rome,' said Hector Grieve. 'Fffuck this.' He pulled his phone from his jacket pocket. It rang long. Eventually someone answered. 'Elvis?'

'Sir!'

'Are the men battle ready?'

'Always, sir. I'll have to round them up, but they're ready.'

'Get them to Melbourne. Operation Overlord. You remember it?'

'Two at a time. Succeeding days, from Phnom Penh.'

'I'll see you tomorrow.'

'Yes, sir.'

'And Elvis?'

'Sir?'

'The gold bar.'

'What about it?'

'Do we still have it?'

'Of course.'

'Bring it. And bring cash. As much as you can get your hands on. And Elvis?'

'Sir?'

'Whisky. Bring whisky. A lot of it.'

RHEINGOLD

Chapter One

OVERLORD

1

Between two long baggage carousels a young Cambodian man in civilian uniform of pleated grey trousers and bright pink Angkor Wat t-shirt, in thickly-rimmed golden aviators walked a luggage trolley through the hall of baggage claim towards fortifications of chrome bollard and black retractable strap. His trolley was stacked with a duffle bag atop two cardboard boxes—drawn all over with Chinese characters and taped up as though they needed to be waterproof. In the hall's urine-yellow halogen he eventually managed to locate the end of a gigantic queue. He was some ninety minutes wending within it.

At its front a uniformed officer read his customs declaration. He took one look at his luggage and said, 'That way,' and at the end of another improbably long queue the young man was greeted coldly by another officer who took with surgical gloves his passport.

'Sros Rath?'

The man smiled and nodded.

'Mr Rath, is this your luggage?'

'I mister Rath.'

'Yes, Mr Rath, is this your luggage?' Mr Rath smiled and nodded and was asked to lift the first box onto a chrome table. 'I'm going to look inside this box, OK?'

'Is medicine.'

'There's medicine inside?'

'Is medicine.'

The officer took a safety knife and sliced through three thicknesses of tape in order to open its top. He lifted a brick of bubble wrap from the box and saw within only several other bubble-wrapped bricks. He cut open the extracted one and beheld eight small jagged bottles of amber fluid, labelled in Khmer script.

'Mr Rath, what are these?'

'Is medicine.'

'What kind of medicine?'

'Is medicine!'

'Yes, what *kind* of medicine?'

'Is medicine!' Mr Rath gave the officer a pained look and laboured to rub hypothetical ointment into his bicep.

The office spoke as though to a child: 'Cambodians bring a lot of medicine into Australia when they come here.' He rifled through the box and found it to be filled with nothing but bubble-wrapped bundles of the same purported ointment.

'Is medicine.'

'And what's in this box?'

'Same same. Medicine.'

'There's medicine in there too?'

'Medicine my friend.'

'Is medicine. Mr Rath how long are you planning on visiting Australia for?'

He showed a single finger to the officer. 'I here for one mun.'

'And what's the purpose of your visit?'

'Holl-i-day,' he said in three identically low-toned syllables.

'Do you have family here?'

'Fam-illy no.'

'And who do you know here in Australia?'

'My friend.'

The officer turned his back on Mr Rath and handed his passport to an officer seated among partitions of frosted plastic. They mumbled to one another about Mr Rath's boxes of medicine, about the photographs that they had without permission taken of their girlfriends the other night while they were 'dogging' them.

'Is medicine Cambodi-aaa,' said Mr Rath, squinting behind his sunglasses in one long and loud syllable.

When the officers were finished showing one another the images, they handed Mr Rath back his passport and shooed him away.

Waiting for him at the far end of the domestic terminal, in riding breeches, boots and formal jacket, Hector Grieve said, 'Where the fuck have you been? I've been here for two hours.'

'These customs idiots are worse than backpackers,' said Elvis. 'Wouldn't know their ends from their arseholes.'

They loaded the boxes into the boot of a taxi.

'How's home?'

'It's not good. Monirith has the men on traffic duties.'

'That donkey's butthole.' Hector shook his head. 'Victoria House?' Elvis looked across the back seat and shook his own. 'What?'

'A hotel.'

'Already?!'

'The day after you left. Three hundred dollars a night.'

'Those sons of bitches. The horses?'

'I let them go, at Phnom Kulen. Happy Ranch rounded them back up.'

'You're fucking kidding me. Trail rides to tourists? What a fucking waste. Selathoa, a tourist attraction. Overlord?'

'Groucho and KFC tomorrow, Risotto and Pangolin the day after, then Jerusalem.'

Late that morning they were on the southern side of Collins Street beside the Melbourne headquarters of the Industrial and Commercial Bank of China, sitting at bad coffee in the ground floor window of the Hotel Bastogne.

'Ready?' said Hector, bidding Elvis to look outside.

'What?'

'Wait for it.'

Shortly two dark bay Thuringian Warmbloods came up the street in reflective-banded boots and with visors over their eyes. They were mounted by police officers in full helmets and fluorescent jackets. 'See that?'

'The horses?' said Elvis.

'The riders. See how they sit? They're too comfortable. Man without war is lazy. They're barely in the stirrups. If the horses bolt they'll come out of their saddles.'

'And?'

'They pass the bank, right there, every day at eleven o'clock.'

'A problem?'

'The solution.'

Hector and Elvis watched as the Warmbloods each bowed their heads and tapped a front hoof as they waited at a red traffic light.

'You don't think robbing a bank in broad daylight and using horses for a getaway is a bit… Well, a bit old-fashioned, sir?'

'Robbing a bank is something thieves do to finance their own greed. But a raid, Elvis—a raid on an enemy's supply lines is an operation befitting the finest regiment. The horses aren't a getaway, they're a diversion. One of two. We'll have these people looking all over their Grecian Rome for their money. But we're going to leave it right where it is. When near, appear far; when far, appear near. We lure with bait and strike with chaos. You know who said that?'

'Who?'

'A Chinaman. So it must be true.'

2

A week later, Hector Grieve in full battle uniform strode through the early evening sunshine a wide path beside a strip of eucalypt parkland, surrounded all by towering chrome sculptures and gigantic new buildings of blue glass and grey steel. With his helmet under one arm and his gloves in his hand he squinted up at the logos which graced their top floor corners—of domestic financial services companies and three of the country's four largest banks, its oldest and largest retailers. He returned his confidently excited gaze from the heavens to the footpath and was instantly run into by a sweating person, hitherto jogging in fluorescent peacock leggings and a pink lycra shirt.

'Where you going?!' said the young woman, agitated by the interruption of her exercise. 'This line for running,' she pleaded, and swung an arm along a lane of footpath demarcated with white paint and marked by an arrow. Hector stood with his shoulders high and his chest out.

'We speak English in this country.'

'I speaking English, yes! You walk in line for walking,' she insisted in a flustered breath. 'This lane for running.' Grieve stared at her with his jaw clenched. 'You must move!' She shooed him with a wave of her hand. He grinned and waited. The girl repeated her sweeping gesture and added to it a nod. 'This line for running!' She pushed an open palm towards the road. 'You must move!'

Seeing that her obstacle would neither move nor engage she shook her head and clicked her tongue and jogged on. 'This line for running! You must move!'

And Hector Grieve recommenced his strut.

The retractable windows of Bopha Devi were drawn all the way back. Into the restaurant Hector stepped. A modern space of long thick tables of darkly stained wood with green footstools for seats and red lanterns for lighting, only the enormous photographs on the walls of carved and dancing Apsaras and Preah Khan and Angkor Wat betrayed the nationality of its kitchen.

Hector went behind the bar that concealed the till and kissed on the cheek Chantrea—Elvis' third cousin and somehow Pangolin's aunt—and asked her how she was.

Strategically late, he found the reassembled King Voars feasting in the restaurant's back room. All stood to attention. Hector saluted and said, 'At ease,' and took a spring roll from the table as his men retook their footstools. Elvis went out and pulled across the restaurant's front windows and locked its door. Then he switched off the function room's lights.

'Good to see you, men. Welcome to Australia. I hope you're all taking full advantage of how reasonably priced everything is here.'

He took the front of the room and stood before a projector screen. Shortly a square of white light came up beside him, then his first slide.

'The standard gold bar. Ten inches by three inches by one-and-a-half. Twelve-point-four ounces of pure gold. At today's price, fifteen thousand dollars a piece. And I've found a goldmine full of them. And that goldmine belongs to the enemy. We're going to steal a hundred and fourteen of them. 1.7 million dollars. Men, a hundred and fifty thousand dollars for each of you—your families, your villages, the rest of your lives—taken care of by one final King Voar operation. Operation Willy Wonka.'

Elvis hit a button on the projector.

'This, is the Collins Street branch of the Commonwealth Bank. We all know the Khmer proverb: the thief who steals from the thief gets a hundred years of pardon. Inside this bank is currently being held, in gold bars, the combined collateral of this very rich country's twenty-seven richest people. They are all of them billionaires. No man has ever needed a billion dollars. If God did not want them shorn he would not have made them sheep—our genius for war is to be our shears. This…' Hector turned to the projection of the bank. '…is our shearing shed. We raid it at ten-forty-five on Monday.'

He outlined in meticulous detail the order of battle for Operation Willy Wonka. He told his men that he had too much respect for their intelligence to tell them *how* to purchase, obtain, or construct the necessary materiel, that he would merely tell them *what* they needed to purchase, obtain, construct—and let their individual genius figure out the how. He told them that as the nature of warfare changed so would the battlegrounds on which it was to be fought. He told them that as the enemy came evermore to appear as a benevolent friend, the methods by which he was to be destroyed would have to become increasingly sophisticated. He told them that war is the only place where a man truly lives, and that while every day the enemy grew in number and influence there would be more than enough life to be had for all.

'The people bend before us,' he said, reciting something, though he could not remember what. 'We turn the battle in the field of the brave. We look on the nations, and they vanish: our nostrils pour the blast of death.'

He told them that God expected that they would not merely do their duty but excel at it; that the end was glorious so the striving could not but be worth it; that when talent was paired with resolve triumph was inevitable. He reminded them they were not just men, but Chahik si chahiks—men of men. And he told them that he would be proud to lead them in battle anytime, anywhere.

'That'll be all.'

Then followed a week of preparation, during which each young man of the King Voar regiment not only performed his duty according to his individual genius, but by that genius excelled at it.

3

The night before the operation Hector went to Helen's for dinner.

'Potatoes again!'

'Laugh it up, funny boy.'

'Not laughing, Anastasia! Delighted, thoroughly.'

'Why don't you like potato?' she grumbled.

He banged a hand on the table and leaned forward and smiled at her. 'On the contrary, my crumply Siberian beast, I *love* potatoes! I've told you that repeatedly. They're absolutely my favourite thing about coming here for dinner. After you, of course. I am left wondering though, what it is that you people will do *next* with potatoes. Oh look! You've put it on toast. What's *this* hefty white delicacy called?'

'Here,' said Anastasia, thumping a tumbler of vodka beside his hand. 'Drink this and shut up, please. Stop smiling.'

'The drink is white too, Anastasia! I *love* it here, so much. Not a colourful foodstuff in sight.'

Helen was seeing in him smiling flashes of the infectiously exuberant self for whom she had so long ago fallen. 'Y'all right, Hector?'

'Vicious Gricius! More than all right! I was afraid there might be something green tonight! But nope. And nothing red neither, no nor orange. Just the occasional hint—always welcome—of a soft brown. David, you know you've said one of the smartest things I've ever heard anyone say? And I've only met you once. Don't let this old bag of Soviet grandma scare you into silence, will you? Her heart's filled with love, I'm sure. Well, maybe not filled with love, probably filled with potatoes. But there's got to be some love in there, surely. And Helen. Helen, Helen, Helen.'

'Yelena, is cowboy boy drunk?'

'Hector *are* you drunk?'

'Just happy, baby.'

'Happy,' Anastasia instantly lamented. 'Australians. Always with the happy. You have no right to happiness, what have you done for it? You are the richest purple in the world, and you never have even worked. Not like my Josif. He was a real man, a great man. Every veek he give me his pay cheque, never ask a kvestion. He would come home from factory, hand it to me. As long as his family ate and vent to school and were safe, he voz happy. He did not kyair about money. But you people, only are happy if you have money. Do you know who we say is the only happy person in village? The idiot. You smiling, must be idiot. Desire for happiness is great disease of mind.'

Hector wooshed his head to Anastasia and smiled wide at her. He broke into a joyous cackle and laughed: 'You're pure evil!'

4

In the latening dusk—crickets, and a firmament halved by orange cloud and electric blue—an ambulance drove without lights or siren up the long hill of St George's Drive and backed into the driveway of William T. Grieve's house.

A paramedic opened the back doors. She was shortly illuminated by the headlights of Hansikoko's bumblebee-yellow hatchback as it pulled in behind her. She and her partner slid William out of the vehicle. They helped him to sit up on the gurney then slowly slid him forward until his slippered feet touched the ground.

Hansikoko took a stroller from the boot of his car and unfolded it at the passenger door. He reached in and took John by the armpits.

The paramedics took William by the bent elbows and turned and lowered him into a wheelchair. One opened the front gate and the other wheeled William through. They both worked at pulling him up onto the front porch and getting him inside. They were soon followed by Donut, ringing a sleigh bell and singing in his sandals and denim dungarees, *Do You Want to Build a Snowman?* Hansikoko pushed his stroller through the gate and laboured to lift and pull him into the house.

'Daddy, you're home!' John assured him as his father was helped into the living room and his armchair.

William switched on the television and stared and nodded as the paramedics left. The stroller was put beside his chair and John put a blanket over his own knees and a hand on one of his father's.

'You're going to be OK, Daddy! Tomorrow we'll go and get new colouring books, and then we'll feed the duckies at the park. There's meant to be sunshine and showers, Daddy! Maybe we'll see a rainbow!'

5

On a dark corner made yellow, made red, made amber and green by a succession of electronic lights, a garbage truck screeched to a stop beneath the pair of Venetian windows carved out of the western façade of the Collins Street branch of the Commonwealth Bank.

Wearing dark blue and fluorescent orange, Jerusalem and Pangolin hopped off its running board. They worked on the lock which secured the chain at the iron gate guarding the alley behind the building. When Pangolin had it picked they swung in both gates. With the push of a button KFC lowered to the street the stinking blue dumpster that rested on the truck's rear forks. Jerusalem and Pangolin pulled the alley's dumpster up to the kerb; guided its replacement from the forks then eased it down into place, halfway between the gate and the glass doors. Pangolin rethreaded the chain and relocked its lock. He and Jerusalem pushed the unmodified dumpster onto the truck's fork and when it was raised from the ground they hopped into the truck's cab and away KFC drove.

6

After a dessert made of potatoes Hector asked David if he wanted to see something cool. David nodded that he did. 'Helen, is it all right if I show David something in the backyard?'

As Helen washed up she realised that as far as she knew Hector Grieve did not actually own very much that might be considered cool. She downed her putrid sponge and went to the back door, arriving in time to be temporarily deafened by a gunshot and to see her son sent stumbling backwards by its recoil. David fell elatedly onto the seat of his pants.

'Hector!'

'Cool!' said David as he picked himself up.

'Yes my love?' Hector took the smaller Peacemaker from him and reholstered it under his arm.

'How is that showing David something cool?!' she fulminated.

'Was that cool, buddy?' David nodded and beamed as Hector rubbed the back of his head. 'See.'

'You give my son a loaded gun?'

'I put one bullet in it. Told him the back fence was a Sudanese kid trying to steal his iPhone. What's the harm?'

'What's the harm!? He could have shot himself!'

'How? He's not a retard.'

'And when the police turn up at the front door?'

'Rerax! There's a shooting on this street every thirty-five minutes. Gunshots are like wind chimes here. The kid should know how to defend himself.'

'David, you *go* inside and brush your teeth.'

'Am I in trouble?'

'Of course not, little man. I'll calm her down. She's going to yell at me though. Should I be scared?' David bulged his eyes and nodded. 'More scared than I am of your grandma?' He shook his head and smiled. 'Go brush your teeth, and next time I'll bring two bullets and you can shoot two guns at once? Like this.' Delighted by the idea of imitating Hector's clicking thumbs David ran inside to get ready for bed.

'Not cool, Hector.' She hurried him into the house.

'I think Hector very cool. It's the first time I've seen him smile.' Helen walked Hector through to the front door and the garden bench on the lawn. 'So what would you do if I had that money tomorrow?'

'What money?'

'The money I told you I was getting. What if I have it tomorrow? And half of it's for my dad and the other half's for you. You'll come away with me, right?'

'Hector.'

'What?'

'Do you not listen to me at all when I talk to you?'

'Of course I do. Why?'

'I live with my grandmother.'

'So do I.'

'Yes, but I have to take care of mine. And I live with my son.'

'Who will have a much better life, *anywhere else in the world*, than if he grows up here. I'm coming into some money, and I want to use it to help the people I love. Your grandma can move in with mine. Greenvale's lovely. They'll get along fine. They'll quarrel, but old people like that. What else do we have to live for but quarrelling?'

'And Apollonia?'

'Who?'

'You're really going to lie to me like that?'

'How do you know about her?'

'Am I right in assuming you don't know what social media is?'

Hector shook his head. 'I've heard of it.'

'You're now a hashtag.'

'What does that mean?'

'And your little Apollonia posted a picture of you sleeping, with her head on your chest.'

'She mailed you a photograph? What kind of a person is that?'

'Don't tell me you love me, Hector, just to get me to do what you want. That's not fair. Especially when you're seeing someone else.'

'You told me to see other people. You set me up with that stink badger, the yoga instructor.'

'And just because one girl doesn't work out doesn't mean you can come and spend your in-between time with me.'

'*They're* my in-between time. You're the one I fucking want to be with, I've told you that. Why don't you listen to *me* when I talk to *you*? I'm getting money, Helen,' he intoned. 'A lot of it. My dad'll get this medication and you can have the rest and it'll get you all out of Gladstone Park.'

'I don't *want* to get out of Gladstone Park, Hector,' Helen droned back at him. 'My whole life is here.'

'You use the word life very loosely,' droned Hector.

'Fuck you!'

'Fuck you!' he chimed, and smiled. He impersonated: 'You know, you look mighty pretty when you get mad.'

'It's insulting when you tell me my life isn't good enough. Can you understand this?'

'But it's *not* good enough, Helen. And I'm an insulting person, it's who I am. I see a horrid truth, harming someone I love, and I'm going to point it out to her. Gladstone Park is a circle of hell and you need to get the fuck out of here, if for nobody's sake than David's. We'll have a small fortune. We can go anywhere. Don't you want to get the fuck out of here?'

'No I don't,' said Helen, in the playfully angry tone that had dominated their conversation. Then she added something about impracticality and impossibility; and something about the pointlessness of entertaining childish dreams when one had to raise and feed an actual child. She mentioned how she very much liked living in Melbourne, even though she was a little too far from the city and the beach. And spoke at length about how devastated Hector's flight to Cambodia had left her 21-year-old self, and how she didn't think she could ever really trust him—about how after what happened with her husband she might not be able to really trust any man again.

And on they talked for forty-five minutes, though Hector barely listened.

He had already heard exactly what he wanted to hear.

Chapter Two

OPERATION WILLY WONKA

1

Hector Grieve strode into the chrome and unvarnished-pine lobby of the Hotel Bastogne. In tucked tie and shirtsleeves he carried his green duffle through a one-sided avenue of tropical flowers to a reception desk of imitation marble.

A tall and slender young woman with big eyes and mousy hair pulled back tightly into a bun said, 'Good morning, sir, how can I help you?'

'I have a reservation. Hector Grieve. I asked for an early—' He looked down into the girl's amethyst eyes and simpered. He recommended slowly, 'I asked for an early check-in.'

Her eyes darted about her computer screen.

'Hector Grieve.'

She found his name and said, 'Yes! Welcome, Mr Grieve.'

He watched her azure nail polish as she took from a draw his keycard and almost said, 'General.' He furrowed his brow and by a manoeuvre of his throat deepened the timbre of his voice and said, 'What's your name?'

She lifted a dawning smile. 'Diana.'

He looked very intently into her eyes and soon said, 'That's a very pretty name. You're not Russian are you?'

'Argentinian.'

'Thank goodness for that.'

She smiled up into his eyes and asked why.

Upstairs he threw his bag onto the bed and took from it his shoulder holsters. He armed himself then went to the window. It commanded a comprehensive view of both streets. He retrieved his binoculars and inspected the ground floor of the bank. Then he watched the foot traffic passing the Queen Street alley. Opposite, a small white van was parked with its rear to the bank.

Then up Collins street, in ashen suit, white shirt and red tie, a bespectacled Elvis conveyed a navy blue duffle bag. He ascended the steps of the bank's portico.

Inside, he crossed the maroon carpet and told the woman in charge of the queue among the golden bollards that he was Mr

Tobtabeetle Suksawang to see Mr Garlick. 'I have an appointmeeent,' he assured her in his mock Thai accent. Mr Garlick was retrieved from somewhere within. He shook Elvis' hand and asked him how he was and led him through the rear glass doors and into the Gothic-revival hall. There Mr Garlick explained a little of the bank's history.

'Go,' said Grieve into his radio microphone. Groucho and Risotto, in felt-bottomed sandals and white kaftan and songkok—with wispy goatees glued onto their chins—came side by side up Collins street. They ascended and joined the rear of the cubicles' queue.

'This is the cathedral room,' said Garlick standing in its centre and rounding the cornices with his gaze. 'The columns are made of granite from Bendigo. And as you can see, all quite beautiful. It was once the trading room of the Australian Stock Exchange, Mr Suksawong.'

'Suksaw-aaang,' Elvis screeched, and pushed at the bridge of his transparent aviators.

'Suksawang?'

'Suksaw-aaang, yes. I know, I sorry. Thais have so stupid name. This room is very beautif-uuul. We do not have anything look like in my cun-tree.' Elvis craned his neck until at last Garlick finished doing so. 'Please we can?' he said, and looked down to the bag in his hand.

'Of course,' said Garlick. 'This way.' One of the armed guards at the room's inner doorway moved aside a golden bollard and Elvis followed Mr Garlick down a spiral staircase.

In the bank's foyer a young boy pulled at Groucho's kaftan.

'What do you want? Ah, you little shit you got the kaftan dirty!' The child's hands were covered in dried chocolate ice cream. Lines of it dripped from the corners of his mouth and joined at his chin. 'Keep your hands off.'

'Are you here to rob the bank?'

'What?' said Groucho, momentarily alarmed. 'What the hell are you talking about?'

'My name's Billy and I'm here to rob the bank.'

'Good for you, kid.' The child gave two big nods of his head. 'What are you going to rob a bank with?'

'My gun.'

'And where's your gun?'

'Right here.' Billy pointed two fingers and a raised thumb at

Risotto before jabbing them into Groucho's kaftan.

'Oi!' Groucho raised his arms and jolted his thigh from the boy. 'Stop dirtying the kaftan!'

'I don't need to rob a bank,' said Billy. 'I play guitar.'

'Where the hell's your mother?'

'Drinking champagne.'

'It's eleven o'clock in the morning, your mum's drinking champagne?'

'She said it's five o'clock somewhere.'

Groucho bent down to meet Billy eye to eye. 'Kid, you're annoying the shit out of me. Bugger off.'

'You said a bad word.'

'How about we make a deal? If I show you *my* gun, you shut the hell up and go away.'

'Groucho, who the fuck are you talking to?' said his commanding officer, the whole exchange broadcast over their radios.

'This kid's dirtying up my kaftan.'

'Who are you talking to?' said Billy, unused to people speaking to him in the third person.

'I don't care if he's rubbing shit on your shoes, soldier,' said Hector in his hotel room. 'Focus.'

'You have something in your ear,' said Billy.

'So do you. What is that, chewing gum?'

'Blu-Tack.'

'That's disgusting.'

'Groucho!' said Hector as Billy nodded. 'What the *fuck* are you doing?'

'I need this kid to leave me alone, I can't focus.'

'Tell him to shove off.'

'How do I tell him that? He's like—. How old are you, kid?'

'Eight.'

'He's eight. What do you tell an eight-year-old?'

'Tell him… not to take counsel of his fears.'

'Don't take counsel of your fears, kid.'

'God favours the brave, victory is to the audacious.'

'God favours the brave.' Groucho turned his pocket to the child and pulled it open and showed him the handle of the Beretta resting therein. Billy's eyes and mouth flung wide open with amazement. 'Victory is to the audacious. Now wipe your face, you look disgusting, and get the hell out of here.'

Billy grabbed Groucho's kaftan and put it to his mouth and

shook his face on it and ran off.

'You believe that kid?' said Groucho to Risotto.

At the end of a long corridor of painted-green concrete Elvis stood with his back to Garlick as the vault's code was keyed into a wall unit. Garlick spun its spoked handle and heaved open its shining steel door. There it was: stacked on steel shelves and lining all sides of the vault.

'How long will you be holding your deposit with us, Mr Suksawong?'

'Suksaw-aaang. Two week, if that's be OK. I have business to make with Chinese associ-aaate. I need here for secur-ity.'

'Of course, we understand perfectly.'

'So much gold you have. All of it unlabelled, and stacked in… twenty-seven pile.'

'Four from each pile,' said Hector over the radio. 'Plus six remainder.'

'These,' said Garlick, pulling a gold brick from one of the low stacks, 'are one of the most exciting projects we've ever been a part of. Have you heard of the Ivory Bunker?'

'Ivory?' said Elvis, becoming animated. 'I get you ivory!' He moved to the innermost wall of the vault. Following, Garlick turned his back to corridor. 'Ivory you want?!'

'Never mind. Mr Suksawang, do you mind if I take one last security measure?'

'OK, khap.'

'May I handle your gold?'

'OK, khap!' Elvis put his duffle bag on the safe's concrete floor and unzipped it. With an open palm he implored Garlick to help himself.

'Go,' said Hector, watching the front of the building through binoculars.

Groucho and Risotto excused themselves and smiled and bowed their heads in apology as they shifted through the people who had amassed behind them in the queue. They rounded the last bollard and turned about and went through the automatic glass doors at the hall's rear. They glanced at the cathedral room's security guards then craned their necks as they sidled across the mosaic floor. When they hit their rehearsed marks they turned inwards and kicked downwards to put the security guards on their knees. They each struck an elbow to a neck and put a gun to a scalp and said, 'Make a fucking noise and your children are orphans.' They disarmed the men and dragged them into the stairwell, putting in place the rope and bollards behind them. Halfway down they bound and gagged and left them.

Garlick bent down and pulled the centremost gold bar from Elvis' bag. With a drop of his forearm he weighed it. Then with bends of his elbows he compared its weight to that of a bar taken from the shelf. He nodded. Then he clinked the two bars together, twice—putting his ear to the precious collision and listening for suspicious tones. He handed Elvis back his gold and reshelved the other. 'You never know, do you? They could be made of chocolate.'

'Chocol-aaate! Ha ha ha!'

Groucho and Risotto stalked the concrete corridor in their sandals bottomed with felt. Elvis laughed with Garlick and nodded and said that yes, they *could* be made of chocolate! He remarked upon the meagre worth of his own deposit compared to that by which they were surrounded as Groucho put his Beretta to the back of Garlick's neck and cocked its hammer. 'Hands on your head.' Risotto grabbed Elvis by the collar of his jacket and with a fist to his chin pushed him into the corner. 'Say one word and your boyfriend's single again.' Elvis acquiesced in silence and allowed Risotto to turn him around and bind his wrists with cable ties to the upright poles at the corner of the shelving.

'Do you have any idea what you're stealing?' said Garlick as he was similarly bound. Groucho punched him in the mouth and said to Risotto, 'Bags.'

Risotto reached into the pockets of his kaftan and undid the Velcro straps within. He birthed three duffle bags, which he and Groucho spread open on the safe floor and stacked with gold. They started at the piles closest to the doors, took four from each of the twenty-seven stacks, returned to make up the remainder.

'Do you have any idea who you're stealing from?' Garlick cried out, and Groucho punched him in the mouth.

'We go, we go,' said Risotto when the three bags were full.

Groucho spoke in bouncing gibberish as he zipped his bags closed and picked them up and carried their considerable weight out of the safe and along the green corridor.

'Do you have any idea what kind of a crime you've committed?!' Garlick said, and was punched in the mouth. Risotto zipped Elvis' bag shut, then his own, then followed Groucho up the staircase. As he stepped over the bound and gagged security guards Groucho informed Grieve that they were exiting the cathedral room. Hector gave the order for KFC to reverse the van to the alley.

The edge of a gun barrel rested on its lowered rear window. Laser-guided balls of opaque paint shot at and hit each of the security cameras. Jerusalem said, 'Go,' and KFC hit the accelerator harder. The van's outswung rear doors perfectly obstructed from the street all view of the laneway. Jerusalem and Pangolin—in white kaftan, songkok, and goatee—hopped out and descended at a sprint to their dumpster.

They took the steel caps off the tops of its ridges as Groucho and Risotto came up through the automatic glass doors and lay at their feet a hundred and fifteen gold bars. All hurried to slide the plunder down the chutes which fed into the dumpster's base. Clink after clink sounded as the bricks dropped to sit end on end in the floor and the walls of the steel bin. Groucho and Risotto took up the empty bags and hopped into the back of the van. Jerusalem and Pangolin replaced the steel caps then were tossed three stuffed green duffle bags and one navy blue. Groucho and Risotto pulled closed the van's doors and were driven away.

Risotto sat back in the van's rear and wiped his brow with his songkok then leaned down and took a bar from Elvis' duffle. He peeled back its flawless gold wrapper; smiled and bit off a chunk of its corner.

'Fat bastard,' said Groucho.

'Mm hm,' Risotto smiled, and took another bite.

Jerusalem and Pangolin each wore one bag as a backpack while carrying the other up the alley and down Queen street. Hector watched on as at the corner they came eye to blinkered eye with the Thuringian Warmbloods. The mounted officers took just as much interest in the bags dangling at their side as in their unusually mischievous faces. Jerusalem pulled from his kaftan's pocket a flare gun. He fired one across the horses' muzzles. The first horse's eyes bulged and the animal sprung briefly onto its back legs. The second horse staggered in its place as its rider struggled to keep her steady. Jerusalem shot a flare past its eyes. The closer horse, then the further, reared fully and punched with their front legs. Both riders came out of their saddles and thudded onto the road. The King Voars grabbed each a rein and pulled themselves up onto horseback; pulled hard at the tack and turned the horses about and with a pair of 'Hya's galloped down Collins street. With one duffle between their legs and one at their backs they reached Parliament

House. Police sirens started up in the distance behind them as they passed St Patrick's and hurried on through Fitzroy Gardens.

Soon they came to the wooded grassland of the Yarra River at Collingwood. They dismounted and slapped the horses' thighs to move them on. They pulled off their kaftans to reveal jogging outfits—fluorescent t-shirt and tiny shorts; took running shoes from their bags and poured the rice that had filled them out into the river and set off to jog to Northcote.

Hector Grieve grinned out over the amassing blue-and-red-light chaos of police car, fire engine, ambulance. He picked up the phone on the table beside the bed.

'Is Diana there? ... Hello, Diana, this is room one hundred and twenty. Yes, Hector Grieve. ... I was wondering, does your restaurant or your bar have Pol Roger? ... Excellent. ... No, no, don't send it up. I was wondering if you'd like to bring it up. ... Yes, exactly like that. ... See you in a minute.'

When his full morning's work was done (twice) Hector S. Grieve took afternoon tea at Greenvale.

2

'Ah, Grandma!' he said, wriggling back into his deck chair and sighing happily.

'What is it, dear?'

'Why *do* all the wrong people have money?'

'Because the right people know what it costs.'

'Grandpa did good with it though, didn't he? And Dad. There *is* good to be done with money, there must be. There must be more good to do with it than there's ever been. Just look at this fucking place. From the top down, from the accountant politicians to the inert matter of the historical process. The only people who have money don't know what good is—or they openly repudiate it and work against it. Poverty, Grandma. A divine gift. Poverty is our closeness to God. Money, our obscene affair with the devil.'

'You don't *really* sound like you know what you're talking about, dear. Why so philosophical?'

'What would you do if you had money again?'

'What *could* I do? I'm a dying member of a dying breed. I have my final comforts, everything I need is here. Though not for want of hard work, mind you. What else could I want? Why, you about to be rich?'

'Not rich. I've gotten a loan for Dad's medication. It goes through this week and I might have a bit left over.'

'Good, you can move out of my drawing room.'

By this was Hector genuinely surprised. 'Do you not like having me here?!'

'It's a nursing home, dear. It's fucking weird that you live here. And I know you've been fucking Jenny.'

'How do you know that!?'

'Old people know a lot more than you think we do, young man. I've seen the spring in her step. That's a spring that can only come from a really good fuck.'

'Grandma, goddam it! That's disgusting!'

'What is dear?'

'Don't talk about sex! That's gross!'

'Just don't *waste* the money, dear.'

<h1 style="text-align:center">3</h1>

Mr Tobtabeetle Suksawang had already been an hour in the interview room.

A baby-blue-uniformed detective stared across a table at him while a besuited one hovered at his sides. 'Why you think me!?' said Elvis, feigning alarmed offence. 'I have money stolen alsooo. They took from me every golds I hab. Twenty-four bar gold!' he pleaded, squinting. 'Three hundred sixty thousand dollaaaar!'

'How much?' said the circling detective.

'Three hundred sixty thousand dollaaaar.'

'Twenty-four gold bars?'

'Chai! Yes!'

'Were they made of chocolate?'

'Chocolaaate? Why you say?'

'How much is a gold bar worth, Mr Suksawong?'

'Suksaw-aaang. Gold bar, fit-teen thousand doll-aaar.'

'Is gold especially cheap in Thailand?'

'I Thai but live Cambodiaaa. What you talking about?' said Elvis, leading the detective down his own line of questioning. 'Why you say cheap?'

'You have a bag full of gold that you use for international transactions and you have no idea what it's worth?'

'I know! In my country,' Elvis pointed to himself, 'three hundred sixty thousand dollaaar. One bar fit-teen. How much for here? Is bet-ter?'

'A standard gold bar is half a million dollars, Mr Suksawong.'

'Suksaw-aa,' said Elvis, his insistence evaporating as he calculated.

'US. Has been for a decade.'

'Half a million?' His fake accent disappeared as his brow discernibly lowered. 'That's…' He looked to the floor and calculated. 'Twenty-four gold bar… twelve million doll-ar. Twelve million doll-aar?!'

'Twelve million dollar.'

'Oh no, I lose so much more!' He squinted and squirmed in his chair. 'Twelve million dollaaar!' He put his hands on his head. 'No hab insuraaance! They take from me twelve mill-iahn?! No! Maybe bank hab, I no hab! Twell million?! Four hundred twenty million bahts! Oh nooo!'

4

The Queen Street alley behind the bank was cordoned off with blue and white police tape. Since half-past eleven a pack of detectives had been re-enacting the morning's events. A team of forensic specialists had been working to find and lift as many fingerprints as possible from the building's interior and exterior. The tapes of the tens of thousands of CCTV cameras within three blocks of the bank had been collected and were being watched in a police van. Two gaggles of blue-overalled police officers scoured with wooden poles the corridors of long grass on the banks of the Yarra River, one walking north from where the Warmbloods had been found, one walking south. Two pods of police divers dredged the river in fishing waders with nets that looked like lacrosse sticks—all in search of even the tiniest fleck of evidence that might assist in piecing together where the thieves had gone after ditching the horses.

As the day latened and a cold dusk set in a young man in dark blue three-piece pin-stripe suit, with red Windsor knot at his semi-spread collar, in shining black shoes and with golden watch chain at his stomach—made his way through the mess of parked police cars and news vans and lifted the police cordon to descend the laneway.

'Whose crime scene is this?' he called out in his Whitlamite accent. His wavy hair shone black and was combed across his tall forehead. He had barely any lips between oversized ears and an almost perfectly square jaw.

The minotaur who had interviewed Elvis looked up from a clipboard and said that it was his.

'Not anymore,' the young man announced. 'United Nations Special Detective Roger Sherwood.' He held up a leather wallet and the shiny badge therein.

'United Nations? What the hummus do you have to do with this?'

'There's a war going on, detective, a world war. Your men been through this bin?'

The older detective stared impatiently at the younger. 'What do you think? We're standing here and we haven't looked in the bin? You sure you're in the right place?'

'There's no point in talking to you. How many Instagram followers do you even have? I'll take it to the people that count.' Sherwood walked back up the laneway and out into the street and stepped into the spotlights of two dozen news cameras.

'Good evening. I am United Nations Special Detective Roger Sherwood. As I'm sure you all know, there *was* a robbery committed here this morning at approximately eleven am. But this was not just a robbery of anybody's money. This was a very specifically targeted violent crime—a deliberate attack on everything that makes this country great. A very small number of people were attacked, for no other reason than that they all have the same thing in common. This makes it a hate crime. And not only a hate crime, it's something much worse. It's an economic crime. There's a war going on, a global war. It's happening, in our streets, in our newspapers, in our occupied houses of government. The war, against the rich, by the poor. Today's crime was, as part of that war, a deliberate and violent attack on the wealthy—those men and women whose hard work and generosity ensures that this is indeed The Lucky Country—those gentlemen and ladies whose brilliance radiates from their business interests like light from the very sun. Those men and women whose goodness is *proof* that if God actually existed we could only conclude that their near-divinity was the reason they have so much money. As such, according to Article 19, section 24 of the United Nations Declaration of the Rights of the Wealthy, this morning's atrocity is being investigated as a war crime.

'The men who carried out this injustice *will* be pursued and caught as war criminals.'

5

In Westmeadows John J. Grieve sang *Colors Of The Wind* as he came home from work, skipping from the driveway to the front door. The sun had almost finished setting over a blue-grey sky of gale and cloud cover. It would soon be time for iftar. He was most excited. Hansikoko was bringing over a feast of Turkish food.

'*You think, I'm an ignorant savage...* Daddy!' he called. 'I'm ready for playtime!'

John found his father asleep in his armchair with a colouring book open at his stomach. The laughing track of a new sitcom roared rhythmically from the television. A chainsaw buzzed somewhere in the near distance; the hollow jangling of wind chimes rang out loudly in the wind.

'Daddy, wake u-up!' he sang as he sat in William's lap. 'Daddy!' he chimed, and tapped him on the cheek. 'Daddy?' He picked up his father's dangling hand from the side of the chair. 'Daddy!' It fell back down again. He hit his father a little harder on the face before raising his cheek and inspecting it. William T. Grieve looked cold. John put two fingers at his neck and eventually found a pulse. It was weak and slow. 'Daddy!' he cried. Then he called Hansikoko, who told him to call an ambulance.

6

At the top of the northern wall of the valley which protected Hector's side of Westmeadows from rural Victoria and the infestations of Craigieburn, a break in the barbed wire led from Mickleham Road onto acres of potholed scree, overgrown with weed and high grass. Successful navigation of a path of unlabelled drum and burnt-out mattress brought one to a wall of boulder and earth over which a single width of soil had been raised to allow vehicles to surmount the barrier. After driving what in the day was a pleasant stroll through forestland of magpie and kangaroo one drove underneath a flight path and followed a gravel road beneath the western slope of Gellibrand Hill until coming to a seeming wasteland of breast-high artichoke thistle and ubiquitous ground weed, aflutter all with the white tail-puffs of feral rabbits.

After a long rise beside a chain-link fence one descended into what was once a bluestone quarry. Veering again from the vague path, one came to a promontory above that quarry, which in the day glistened with turquoise water.

In the night it was a forbidding undulation of oil-black beneath restless glimmers of moon and wind.

The lights of the airport sat high in the distance as headlight beams passed along the freeway beyond this young lake. At intervals two jet engines roared then gave deep screams as aeroplanes rose to take-off speed. Yellow and red tail lights flashed as they ascended and banked.

Standing in a frigid breeze upon the promontory, Hector S. Grieve waited with a sledgehammer over one shoulder between Jerusalem and Pangolin, all in battle dress and smoking cigars and grinning.

'Where the fuck is Elvis?' said Hector, turning his pocket watch to the moonlight.

'No idea, sir,' said Jerusalem, looking down to the tree branches protruding almost invisibly from the water.

'I haven't heard from him all day,' said Pangolin.

High and wide headlights lit up the horizon behind them. A truck came over the hill. Its horn blared twice through the biting air. It lit the chain-link fence red and white as it braked to ease its way down the veins of red earth and sandstone towards the torch in Jerusalem's hand. Hector raised a hand and with waves of his fingers beckoned the truck to him. Gravel crunched under tyre until at his commanding officer's palm KFC brought the truck to a stop.

Groucho and Risotto hopped out of the cab, in costume still as Melbourne City Council garbage men. Hector kicked a wooden chock under each of the front tyres. KFC used his mirror to lower the blue dumpster behind him to a metre from the ground. Groucho called out, 'That's good!' Shortly all came to stand around it.

With the swing of his sledgehammer Hector knocked out one of the bolts which held in place the custom-made dumpster's floor. He walked around to its other side and readied the sledgehammer behind his head. 'We ready for this?'

A car engine sounded over the gravel behind them. Then headlights shone across the horizon. The soldiers unholstered their sidearms and watched the bumps of its approach.

'About fucking time,' said Hector when Jerusalem's torch hit Elvis' face.

With a second swing Hector knocked out the other bolt. Instantly a clamour of steel onto gravel, then a jackpot of gold upon gold—the sweet sound of a hundred and fourteen standard gold bars cascading at their feet.

'Listen to that, boys!' said Hector. 'That's how you stand up against the rising of the tide.' Elvis stepped out of the car. 'Pick 'em up, bring 'em here. Where the fuck have you been?'

'They interviewed me for hours.'

Hector took a blanket from the boot of the car and placed it folded in half on the ground. He kneeled and stacked the loot as his men handed it to him.

'Do you know *why*?' said Elvis, crouching beside him. 'Because I didn't know how much a gold bar was worth. Even though I was in possession of twenty-four of them.'

'How do you mean?'

Elvis took a knee and lowered his voice. 'Do you know what these are worth, Hector?'

'Yeah.'

'How much is a gold bar worth?'

'Twelve hundred dollars an ounce, and they weigh twelve-point-four ounces. Twelve-point-four times twelve hundred. Fifteen thousand U.S., depending on the market.'

'Hector, they weigh twelve-point-four kilograms.'

'Mm?'

'Which is what in ounces?'

'I have no idea.'

'Four hundred and forty.'

'So?'

'They're twelve hundred dollars an ounce, at four hundred and forty ounces.'

'So they're... four hundred and forty times twelve hundred? Wait, that's...' Hector looked across at his aide-de-camp—the King Voar with whom he had gallivanted longest and largest, the young man at whose side he had once broken from the tree line with six-shooters firing in order to steal ten gold bars. 'That's five hundred and thirty thousand dollars,' he whispered angrily. 'They're half a million each?'

'Half a million dollars each.'

'Did I just accidentally steal fifty-seven million dollars?'

'You did, sir.'

'Fuck!'

'A hundred and fourteen, sir,' said Groucho as he handed Hector the last.

He placed it neatly on the interlaced stacks and rose to stand over their haul. In a single instant his cut had gone from five hundred thousand to seventeen million. 'Seventeen million dollars,' he thought. Elvis would take ten. His men had six million each. 'Seventeen million dollars?' he thought again. He said, 'Shit.' Then he addressed his soldiers.

'Men! Congratulations. A perfectly executed manoeuvre. A fully successful raid on an enemy's supply lines. War, the only place where a man really lives, has returned to us. How gloriously have we welcomed its revival, how victorious have we today been. Now what I'm about to tell you is going to be rather life-changing…'

7

In the back of an ambulance somewhere between Westmeadows and Melbourne, William T. Grieve was prostrate on a gurney. Oxygen pumped through a mask strapped to his face and various solutions ran through tubes in his forearms. He turned his head from side to side as he struggled to retain consciousness between agonised draws of precious breath. His eldest son held his hand and watched over him in a panic.

'We're almost there, Dad, OK? Just hold on. Please hold on.'

'John,' William exhaled.

It was the first word John had heard from his father since discovering him in his armchair. He leaned in and said, 'Dad? What is it? I'm here.'

'Hector. … Tell Hector… to come… and see me.'

'I will, Dad. I'll call him as soon as we're at the hospital.'

'I want… my son.'

'I'm here, Dad. I'm here for you. Just hold on, everything'll be OK.' Then he sang. '*Do you want to build a snowman?*'

'Shut… the fuck…,' William almost silently wheezed.

'*Come on let's go and play.*'

'Up. … Please. … Just shut… the fuck up. I want… my son.'

'I'm here, Dad. I'm here. Can you feel my hand?'

273

'I want… my manly… son.'

'Dad?'

'Not… you. … I want… to see Hector,' he almost didn't say. 'You… are a disgrace.'

8

With his men readied at the garbage truck's rear, Hector stepped up into the cab and released its handbrake. He jumped down onto the gravel and knocked out the chock from the driver's-side tyre. He rounded the front of the truck and called, 'Ready?'

'Ready,' said Elvis. Hector hit the second chock with the sledgehammer and ordered, 'Go!' The King Voar regiment pushed; the truck began to roll, then to gain speed. Hector joined them in running with outstretched arms against the raised dumpster.

In the darkness of cold night Hector shouted the order to stop as the truck's front wheels passed the edge of the cliff. A slide of dirt and rock began as tyre and axle scraped against the side of the quarry. A whooshing splash shot up as the truck's front hurtled into the water. The dumpster at its rear teetered and quickly toppled. A louder crash sounded as the length of the truck's top slapped the black surface.

The wreck seemed to hesitate in sinking.

'Go, go, go, go, go,' Hector urged. Jerusalem gave it his spotlight and all watched as the truck slowly sank. Shortly not a tyre could be seen.

Water covered the swirling of the tumult and the last bubbles blurped to the surface. The quarry's water returned to its undulations of oil-black and its glimmers of wind and moon.

Hector lit a Cohiba and slung the sledgehammer over his shoulder and smiled. He pulled his phone from his trouser pocket and said, 'I fucking hate these fucking things.' He threw it into the lake. 'Now let's feast.'

Chapter Three

THE RHINEGOLD

1

Through the tepid pinpricks of an evening rain shower a young couple walked the wooden boardwalk beside and above the still and littered waters of Docklands.

'What about *here*?' said the boyfriend, pleading in the direction of a round fortress of glass which looked as though it might be an Italian restaurant.

'I don't care!' said the girlfriend.

'Well you *do* care, because the last three places you said No to.'

Windy, overcast, and lukewarm, it was an unimpressive dusk beset by drizzle and made all the more infuriating by crowds of couples who were not arguing, but kicking their feet out as they ran their tongues at scoops of ice cream.

The girlfriend clenched her teeth and said, 'I didn't say No at all. I just didn't want to eat at the restaurant where I found you with that fucking slut from Bali, all right?'

'And what about the first and the third restaurants? I never took her there, did I?'

'You're such an arsehole.'

'Yeah, and you're a seawitch. I don't care how often you dress up as a mermaid. You're not Ariel, you're Ursula the fucking seawitch.'

'Would you just shut the fuck up? Can we eat, I'm fucking hangry!?'

'Don't! Fucking! Yell at me!' he droned. 'God damn it, people are watching.'

'And they'd be yelling at you too, if they knew how much of a little bitch you are.'

'Oooh,' said the boyfriend, then broke into offended laughter. '*I'm* the bitch?' He lowered his lips to a frown and scrunched up his nose and put on a high screech: 'I don't care where we eat, we can eat anywhere. Oh, but not here. No, and not there either. No, not there, that's where you took that *nice* girl. *That* place doesn't have good décor. *That* place charges you for bread. *That* place my ex-boyfriend used to take me to.'

'You're gonna fucking cop it.'

'Yeah, what are you gonna do? Not not have sex with me? I'm really fucking scared.'

'Well if I hadn't have caught you messaging your little slut again, maybe I'd put a bit of effort into entertaining you at night, wouldn't I?'

'You can't let it go, can you?' He put his intertwined hands on his head and smirked. '*What* about here? Cambodian food. It's meant to be very good.'

The girlfriend folded her arms at the end of the laneway. 'Fine.'

'Fine,' said the boyfriend, rescrunching his nose and bringing back his screech. They stomped towards their finally chosen restaurant. 'That's all you can come up with? Fine? Not, "Yes, this would suit me very well for our dinner this evening." "I haven't had Asian food in a long time. Thank you for suggesting that, I'm really looking forward to having a nice dinner with you."'

She smirked and said, 'I'm going to fucking—'

'What? What are you gonna do? Hm?'

They were greeted by a piece of white paper taped to the inside of Bopha Devi's front door. '*Closed for private function. Sorry for inconvenience.*'

'Are you fucking kidding me?' said the girlfriend.

'Oh, this is bullshit!'

'Can we just go home?' said the girlfriend, looking dejectedly at the pavement.

'Are you serious?'

'I'm cold.'

'I told you to wear a coat.'

'All right! I didn't know it was going to rain did I?'

'I told you it was going to rain. Me telling you wasn't enough information for you?'

'Well you're not God are you? You didn't *know* it was going to rain.'

'And yet, I knew you were going to be a bitch all night. Maybe I am God.'

'If God's dick is as useless as yours, it's no wonder there are no Christians left.'

Beyond the retractable floor-to-ceiling glass doors, in the room normally set aside for parties of twenty or more, with enormous photographs on its walls of Angkor Wat, The City Of The King Of The Angels—that which once counted a hundred and twenty kings under tribute and put into the field an army of five million men, whose wealth was built on the sapphire feathers of the halcyon kingfisher—coals beneath the wasted ribcage of a roasted pig had long cooled to light brown. The enlisted men of the King Voar regiment stood raucously over the low dining table, each with an Emirates flight attendant at both arms. The table was littered with empty bottles—of Pol Roger and Angkor beer and two of Black Douglas. Its centrepiece had for an hour now been a Kla Klok mat.

Wads of hundreds were slapped with violent throws—onto the fish, the gourd—Groucho always the cock, Elvis the crab—or onto what most of them, because of the Beng Mealea whisky, were seeing as a king voar. Jerusalem put the dice cup against his palm and to a crescendo of excited humming and table-banging he shook it. He slammed it upside down into the centre of the mat. All eyes dilated to see what luck was contained within.

Two king voars and a prawn.

Pangolin and the girls at his arms threw their hands in the air and smiled and yelled. They kissed one another as he leaned in to take from the table his considerable winnings.

In the main dining room, empty and lit only by the lamps from the kitchen, the function room, the laneway—Hector S. Grieve sat with his ankles crossed on a chair. His back against the wall, his head was centred beneath a six-foot-wide photograph on canvas of a turquoise and lilac Preah Khan dawn—The Holy City Of Victory, the first Khmer temple with which he had fallen in love, that triumphant citadel built to honour his father by Jayavarman The Seventh over the battleground on which he defeated the Cham invaders...

Hector listened to the revelry from the Kla Klok game and inhaled large from a newly lit Cohiba. He took the cigar from his mouth and lifted and swigged from a bottle of Pol Roger. As he rolled its perfumed effervescence over his tongue he saw a hairy and hook-nosed dwarf scurry out from the kitchen. 'What the fuck?' he said softly to himself as it crossed the dining room and scampered out the front door. Grieve squinted and rolled his eyes and rose from the couch.

Outside, the glistening concrete smelled of wet earth. A dark cover of cloud concealed both the colour of the sun's setting and the height of the buildings which encircled him. The landscape was one of neon bank and insurance logo and of the girders of a football stadium adorned with the name of an airline operated for the profit of a Sheikhdom—along the quay, the varied signage of corporate hospitality. Hector set off after the bristly-legged dwarf and came to the water's edge.

The black sea was made argent by the lamplights of a downramp which turned to become a jetty. A pulsating swarm of jellyfish glowed white between the path and the boardwalk. Into this wafting field of underwater lantern there appeared to swim in flowing robes of white three elegant young females. They glided by, a foot from the surface, and the last turned onto her back and winked and clapped the fingers of one hand to wave up at Hector Grieve. From the height of the quay he shook his head, asserting to himself their unreality. Then he waved bashfully back. 'Mermaids?' he whispered. He tried to relocate them in the calm below. 'Not mermaids.' But they were gone. He could not quite remember if they had fins. 'Water-nymphs?' He darted his eyes suspiciously around the harbour. Briefly he searched the crowds at his back for the scurrying dwarf who he seemed to remember had been carrying a blacksmith's hammer.

A foghorn sounded loud and low and crisp from the mist to the south. Hector turned to its unsettling volume. There drifted across his field of vision an enormous white prow, sharp and steep and several stories high. It sailed slowly in, revealing in colourless night a first deck and the yacht's cursive name—*The Rhinegold*; then a higher second deck, then the highest third, each set back from the other. At last, its antennae and bulbous navigational equipment and again it blasted its horn as it came to rest and finally was the landscape. Hector scrunched up his nose and looked all around and could find neither wicked dwarf nor attractive water-maiden. The jellyfish too were gone. He sighed and his shoulders drooped before the towering vista of white steel or carbon fibre or titanium or whatever it is that super-yachts are made of.

2

Aboard *The Rhinegold*, on the long curve of cream-coloured couches in its fourth-largest dining room, three billionaires breathed atrociously loudly.

The first, wheezing, was Carbuncle Tempest—Australia's richest man, just past middle age, with black peas for eyes and an Armenian's nose. A pelican's gullet ran in two lines of drooping tissue from under his rounded goblin ears to meet at his necktie. The volume of his respiration, rather softer than that of his company, was due to nothing more than an obnoxious and lifelong habit of mouth-breathing.

Two people over from him there sat croaking Hiram Semenov, with a bulbous nose and wide forehead of albino skin rising high to a thin helmet of burning orange fluff. Australia's second-richest man, were Mr Semenov any shorter he would only have been accused more often than he already was of being a native of Loompaland. In truth he was physically incapable of breathing quietly. The warts which plagued his throat like toadstools on a tree trunk had turned his oesophagus into a kind of infested flute—the consequence of a benign virus given to him by a prostitute, though he could not pin down precisely, of the thirty-five hundred of whom he had availed himself, which.

And in the centre of their bend of Javan rhino leather—for it was her yacht—there gasped and screeched Adipose Rhinegold, Australia's richest person and by a factor of ten its richest woman. Were it not for her lipstick, her string of pearls, the length of her thinning hair, she would very often have been mistaken for a malicious and mannish slug. The deposits of fat which enveloped her neck made her throat screech and hiss like the stretched mouth of a squeezed balloon. Their thickness crushed at her larynx, their looseness made her self-conscious of shaking her head—their folded arrangement meant that she had once discovered between their chins her Benz keys.

As *The Rhinegold* dropped anchor Hiram Semenov said, 'I hunger.'

'I want to dine,' said Carbuncle Tempest.

So Miss Adipose Rhinegold, in concurrence and summons, twice banged a fist on the table.

At its sounding there came into the dining room Michel, Miss Rhinegold's personal chef.

'Oui, Madame?' said Michel, his head dramatically bowed, for after a decade of service he was still unable to look at Miss Rhinegold for longer than a fraction of a moment. Though he had worked on the yachts of two ducs d'Enghien, and of the reichsgraf von Himmelstaun of Hohenlohe-Ingelfingen-Lich-Babenburg, and on that of the Visconte di Scack, and on Filbert James Heathcote-Drummond-Spit, 4th Earl of Ancaster's lecherous catamaran—Michel feared beyond all else the crude materialism of his current employer.

'Menu,' Adipose strained to grunt.

'Bien sûr, Madame,'and Michel bowed and withdrew.

Shortly he and his two sous-chefs wheeled in three perspex enclosures, each containing wildlife.

'Zis evening we av for you, Madame, ze Sunda pangolin. Ranging from Burma to Java, zey are critically endangered, partly due to ze illegal trade wiss China, though really because of people's stupidity. Zey sink ze foetus is a cure to prevont miscarriage, so zey boil hundreds of babies into soup and give it to ze pregnant muzzer. It also is mixed wiss ze bone of tiger and wine and zey drink as tonic to prevont cancer. Very, *very* endangered, and I prepare in ze style of Thailande, wiz sweet basil, lemongrass and red coory pest.'

'Did he say penguin?' said Carbuncle Tempest.

'I think he said Panga-uin,' said Hiram Semenov. 'He's pronouncing it wrong. You're pronouncing it wrong.'

'That doesn't look like a penguin,' said Tempest.

'Who wants to eat a penguin anyway?' said Semenov. 'Gristly old birds, and they taste like fish.'

'Yeah,' growled Miss Rhinegold. 'Not the penguin. What's next to it?'

'Not ze pangolin? Very well.' With a wave of his hand Michel turned to introduce the first alternative. 'Here we have ze orangutan. Deliciooce. I use only ze breast and ze 'and, grilled or roasted. Orang-utan are found only in Sumatra and Borneo, and zeir numbers have eerrr… declined, by eighty percent in the ze last seventy-faff years, due to the clearing of 'abitat for ze makking of Doritos, and z'innate tendency of mankinds to destroy all zat it come across.' The animal moved its lips over a half-peeled orange. It switched the leg by which it was preventing itself from sliding down the wall of its enclosure and with a finger and thumb went on peeling what might very well have been its last snack. 'Zis is an adolescent, it have two years of arge, and I serve ze breast flambéed in eerrr, in eerrr… rosemary and truffle, and in ze very oil by which it is maked endangered. Ingeniooce, and, truly delicious.'

'I've had orang-utan,' moaned Semenov. 'Tough to get right.'

'I don't wanna eat no monkey,' said Carbuncle, saving instantly by his vote the animal's life.

'They're an ape,' said Miss Rhinegold.

'What?'

'They're an ape, not a monkey.'

'Aren't they the same thing?' said Carbuncle.

'Not the monkey!' said Semenov to Michel, and the Frenchman stepped to the last and largest of the plastic cages.

'Ze saola. Only discovered in 1992, zis mystical creature has already been declared as critically ondangered. It is one of ze rarest large mammals on earce, living only in ze forests of central Vietnam, and it's referred to as ze Asian eerrrr… 'orse wiss one 'orn. How do you say eet? Ze errr, ze unicorn! Ze Asian unicorn.'

'Unicorn!' said Mr Semenov, enthusiastically growling his vote.

'Yes!' said Tempest, 'Let us eat the unicorn!'

'I like the sound of that, Michel. Cook the unicorn!'

'Very well, Madame.' Michel bowed and the enclosures were wheeled from the dining room.

A knock came at the door which led in from the upper deck. Through it walked United Nations Special Detective Roger Sherwood.

'Boy!' said Miss Rhinegold. 'Where's my money?'

'Where's *my* money?' coughed Mr Tempest.

'Where's *my* money?' grumbled Mr Semenov.

Sherwood pursed his lips and skewed his eyebrows as he crossed the yacht's fourth-largest dining room. After a decade of service he was still viscerally repulsed by those whom his mandate dictated he serve.

'Speak, boy,' said Adipose Rhinegold.

'We're doing our best,' he said, holding back the contents of a retching stomach after glancing at her psoriatic scalp.

'And what's your best uncovered so far?'

'Muslims,' said Sherwood.

'What a-bloody-bout them?' said Semenov.

'They did this?' said Tempest. 'Why?'

'Terrorists!' said Rhinegold. 'We should deport the lot o' them.'

'We can't do that,' said Tempest.

'Why not?' said Rhinegold. 'We're rich.'

'Because they're the only ones who'll do the work that none of us want to do.'

'Oh yeah.'

'Wait,' said Semenov. 'How do you know it was Muslims?'

'They were dressed like Muslims,' said Sherwood.

'Ah.'

'And they stole a hundred and fourteen gold bars.'

'So?' said Rhinegold

'There are a hundred and fourteen chapters in the Koran. Indonesians we think. They looked Southeast Asian.'

'Bloody terrorists,' said Rhinegold. 'Just like Bali.'

'Muslims,' said Sherwood.

'That's what I said.'

'You said terrorists. I said Muslims.'

'Aren't they the same thing?'

'Regardless of whether or not they're the same fucking thing,' said Carbuncle Tempest. 'Find our fucking money.'

'Why would Muslims steal *our* money?' said Semenov. 'What have we done to them?'

'Yes, well… the United Nations thinks that at this point the robbery was probably a protest against what they call "Western corruption," *and* a fundraising operation.'

'Fundraising?' said Rhinegold.

'Fifty-seven million dollars,' said Semenov. 'How much baba ganoush can they eat?'

'Unfortunately, at the end of the day, there *is* only one thing that a group of criminal Muslims is going to use fifty-seven million dollars for.'

'Terrorists,' said Semenov.

'Terrorism,' Sherwood admitted.

'I told you!' said Rhinegold. 'They're the same bloody thing.'

'Dinner!' said Carbuncle Tempest as Michel and his sous-chefs reappeared.

They pushed three gurneys through the kitchen doors.

Upon each was prostrate a topless human. To Miss Rhinegold was conveyed a black-haired young man, chiselled of arm and thick of chest. Upon the ridges of his eight-pack a tenderloin of saola had been plated, encrusted in dried herbs, blood-pink among grilled brussel sprouts and gratin dauphinois. Streams of red-wine jus ran down the grooves of his pelvis and dripped onto the floor.

To Mr Tempest was wheeled a curvaceous brunette—his identical cut of meat kept afloat at her belly button by a tepid pool of red gravy. This ran down her groin and dribbled under her buttocks; cascaded over her waist when she jiggled from its tickling.

Mr Semenov received a gaunt and plastinated blonde. She lay on anterior implants, bulging over the gurney like squeezed water balloons. His tenderloin lay in the small of her back just above her posterior implants. There, Michel's translucent sauce distorted the wings of a butterfly tattoo.

The three plates turned their heads to smile and stare at the billionaires who were to eat off them. Not one flinched as forks were jabbed through saola into their torsos and knives scraped across their skin.

Sherwood darted his head from female to male, to female; male, female, male. He surveyed the shovelling in of food and the slurping up of gravy; the scratches given by serrated knives, the intermittent licking of chest and slapping of crotch—the drooling of unicorn blood onto naked human flesh. He forced himself for the third time that day not only to accept, but to love his employment. He wondered if the plates were being paid minimum wage. He hoped very much that they were. Then he shook his head and went to take another look at the scene of the war crime he was investigating.

3

Hector S. Grieve opened the passenger door and put one foot onto the driveway of his childhood home. 'Won't be long,' he said across to Elvis.

New laptop in hand, he was barked at by Foo Foo as he opened the front gate.

He found the house silent and the living room empty. He looked in the kitchen and called for his father at the bottom of the stairs.

John was in his bedroom—in his apparent uniform of white t-shirt and blue denim dungarees—curled in the centre of his toy-ridden floor almost to the foetal position and hugging a plush Ariel.

'Stand the fuck up.' John made no acknowledgment of the looming appearance of his brother. He put the tip of his thumb at his lips and deliberated upon inserting it into his mouth. Hector clenched his teeth. 'I said stand the fuck up.' He picked his brother up by the strap and denim leg of his outfit and set him on his bed. 'Where the fuck is Dad?' John pulled his Ariel closer to his chest and closed his eyes. Hector rose over him and raised his voice. 'Where's Dad, you peacock's superfluous nipple?' John rocked back and forth upon the edge of his mattress. 'I need his bank details, goddam it. Where the fuck is he?' Then Hector sensed a primeval anguish in his older brother. He stood back from him and said, 'What the fuck's the matter with you—someone steal your blanky?'

John was clearly holding back tears. 'Dad,' he seemed to say in a

283

feeble breath.

'Yes, Dad. Where is he?'

'Dead.'

'Yes, you fucking camel's anus. Where the fuck is Dad?'

'Dad's dead.'

'What?'

John squinted sadly and managed to raise his voice to speaking volume. 'Dad is dead.' Then he relented, and let recommence the sobbing that had after two days only just subsided.

'Dad's dead? What the fuck are you talking about?'

John said in a quiet stutter: 'Dad died.'

'Are you fucking serious?' John shut his eyes even tighter and nodded and drew his mouth wide. 'When?'

'Night before last!' John wailed.

'Why didn't you fucking call me?'

'We tried, in the ambulance. Your phone wouldn't even ring.'

'Are you fucking serious? What the fuck did you do to him?'

'Me?'

'Irrumator, did you suck a dick in front of him?'

'Fuck you.'

'Fuck me? I'm not responsible for this. You fucking killed him. Losing a son to tomorrow finally overgrew his spirit. And now look at you, crying like the two-day old mermaid's baby you really are. Look at me. … Look at me, goddam it!' John opened his eyes and obeyed his younger brother. 'I am the last Grieve. You do *not* call yourself by my name anymore. Come up with an Asian name, Donut. Call yourself whatever you want, you are not a Grieve. You're done. I am the last.'

John squinted and frowned, and blubbered and wailed as he ran out of his bedroom and went outside to seek consolation in Foo Foo.

Chapter Four

THE FVNERAL ORATION
OF HECTOR GRIEVE

1

For minutes he had been silently debating upon the dais as to whether his audience were worth the effort.

A coffin of walnut lay at his feet. He stood high over a yellowing lawn between a wreath and bouquet of flowers and a four-foot-high photograph of his father in the river valley of the monastery of Sanahin, Armenia.

He was in full battle dress, but held his garrison cap rather than his helmet. Over his tanker jacket he wore the collar of an ashen wool overcoat high to keep out the chill of constant wind. His bronze hair blew opposite to the side to which he combed it. Overhead a morose sky—the darkness of heavy blue-grey cloud broken only by occasional streaks of almost-white. Hector Grieve gripped tan gloves in one hand at the side of the lectern and squinted at the assembly beneath him.

His glare scanned as far to his left as it could before his head snapped to follow. His grandmother was at the centre of the front row, in black dress and long silken gloves. Beside her, Elvis; behind them, the enlisted men of the King Voar regiment each with a white lily for a buttonhole. On Margaret's other side was John J. Grieve, in a three-piece suit of azure and with his head downcast under a plum-coloured veil descending from a beret. Foo Foo was gleefully restless beside him, in a baby halter at Hansikoko's chest. Then an assembly of not more than thirty people, most of whose faces Hector recognised as schoolmates and associates of his father. Mike Isenhammer's parents were in the second-to-last row beside Helen and her son. He barely recognised his only uncle, a journalist on his mother's side.

At last Hector decided that the crowd was an unworthy one, that he should walk away and not deign to bow his instincts before low-minded ears. But he had things he knew his father would have wished him to say. Finally he decided to subordinate the shamefulness of its listeners to the greatness of his speech. He cleared his throat. His voice in the dull Melburnian wind sounded small and hollow.

'My father lived as the successor to a line of men who used their considerable talents and their meagre fortunes to do good in the world. Forgotten are all who accumulate riches. Remembered are they who use them for good. From Trajan to Cadbury to Patton—my father too, knew what could be done by the proper allocation of wealth, and he did it. Profit, in all ages the beginning and end of evil, William T. Grieve used only to push further the ox-cart of greatness, to draw everywhere he went the coveted rickshaw of freedom. In dispensing his magnanimous influence, my father was the very embodiment of the golden rule of this young nation—that greed no more shall those oppress who by the wayside fall.

'Twenty years ago William Grieve founded Selathoa Property Limited. Through this benevolent corporation he stood, like no other of his time, against the greed of the atheistic world. Against the gluttonous, the proud, against the wicked. Each time he stood his ground, and each time he rose from the fray with armour glistening. His whole life he worked not selfishness, but selflessness. He hoarded not his gold, but scattered it over the poor regions of the earth, to alleviate not material poverty but the spiritual degradation that is its chief result.

'Only, in the end, he forgot who he was and married a Turk. So he had his peace of mind, and his semen, stolen, by an insidious member of that heathen civilisation which is our sempiternal enemy.

'I, in my unworthy state, shall ever find it difficult to do my father's memory justice. Having spent so long out of Australia, so long absent from Dad's life and work, I can only relay to you that his life has hitherto, each and every day, served as exemplar to my own. On a much smaller scale I too have attempted to do some good, in protecting what is old and defenceless from what is dumb and insatiable.

'Now—my father gone, as for so long I was from him—now it not only falls to me alone, but falls to all of us here today, to take up the great task left unfinished by his early and entirely unnecessary death. With his younger son so long absent from him, he was forced to spend his final years in the company of his older; who worked not in his shadow but outside it; who attempted by the poison of false and prolific words to deepen the self-serving immorality of his own people rather than reform it; to widen the path of iniquity stridden by his degenerate compatriots, rather than nourish the budding virtues of the newly civilized.

'As Dad travelled the world he was kidnapped, shot, extorted, expelled. In response he liberated, healed, donated, gave shelter. Christ-like, Bill lived and suffered the ills of the world so that others might not have to. He travelled not to be tolerant, but to teach others courage. He did not wander in order to be friendly. *His* voyage sought to bring hope to the heathen. Yes, he respected—he respected the natural morality that can be just only when mankind has humbled himself before a planet and a universe unfathomably wiser and more powerful than ourselves. Kindness, I know, he thought dumber than a yachtful of yoga instructors.

'Surrounded by death, think today about the wealth that you each possess, the enormity of your bank accounts, the magnitude of your investments. And think about what pain and suffering, what iniquity and falsehood, what greed and what kindness you could by that wealth alleviate, reform, abolish. Cowardice, infidelity, pride, Russia—all would disappear overnight if only we worked for their abolition as hard as we work for our own vanity.

'We are now so accustomed to reading of the charitable works of others—nay not reading, dreaming, of others doing charitable works in our stead—that we have indeed lost the name of action. We speak, of wanting to do this, of hoping one day to be able to do that. My father did not want. To want is to be weak. Labradors want. My father acted. William T. Grieve hoped not; William T. Grieve did. If you want a hero, an uncommon want, look, as I do, to my father.

'The only great existence, and I know that until his illness my father agreed with me here, the only great existence, is that of a soldier fighting a war. Anybody who tells you otherwise is a coward. Whether it's a war against another nation, a barbaric religion, or a war against stupidity—find your war, and become a soldier. All devotion is heroic. Devote yourself to war, for war is the only place where a man really lives. The end is glorious, the striving cannot but be worth it. Do not take counsel of your fears. God favours the brave. Victory is to the audacious. *Our* dwelling is calm, above the clouds; the fields of *our* rest are pleasant. Thank you.'

Hector's conclusion was followed by a very confused and very protracted silence. Then there came some uncomfortable rearranging of crossed legs and folded arms. Thick paper was rubbed against itself as mourners rolled up their copies of the commemorative pamphlet printed by the funeral parlour. One woman worked herself up into a coughing fit. Few had understood quite what Hector was getting at. The third row had early spotted a possum and were still watching it play in the lower branches of an oak. The few who understood his assertions ached to denounce them.

The funeral director took the podium and announced that the coffin was to be taken to the crematorium. His employees raised the folding trolley on which it rested; locked its steel legs and wheeled it to the hearse and slowly it was driven away.

Hector and Margaret stood at the corner of the lawn nearest the car park and were given condolences as the guests filed out. Hector shook hands with Phil Isenhammer and was hugged by Karen, Mike's mother; then he was confronted by a grotesquely familiar face.

'Mr Grieve, we need to talk.' Carla—that young accountant whose appearance at Hector's Siem Reap breakfast table had marked precisely the commencement of his descent, had in black skirt and suit jacket watched the playing possum.

'You're fucking kidding me,' said Hector, withdrawing a hand mechanically offered as the previous funeral guest moved on. 'You stick of rancid goat butter, who the fuck let you in here? Doesn't consecrated ground catch fire when you walk on it?'

'Mr Grieve, you have to declare bankruptcy.'

'I don't,' said Hector, in an arrogant tone.

'Tasoli & Fafner have declared your family's account suspended until you can pay us at least the funeral costs plus the first instalment of the interest owed on your father's account.'

'I can pay it.'

'I don't see how, Mr Grieve. Even after the sale of your father's house, your legal and financial bills stand at precisely four hundred and thirteen thousand dollars and forty-three cents.'

'I can pay it.'

'You can *not*.'

'I can, you unitchable rash of somebody else's fucking donut.'

'How?'

'Hector S. Grieve,' said a smug voice from the asphalt behind him.

Hector turned to behold a young man crossing the car park in an ashen overcoat and tan gloves. He made condescendingly uneven his eyebrows and in contempt dropped one side of his mouth. He declined to shake the hand offered him. 'General, Hector S. Grieve,' said Hector.

'So I've read. A cavalry officer, in the Royal Cambodian Army.

And *not* a Muslim.'

'Ours is a crusading family.'

'But really just a cowboy. In 2010 you stole five million dollars in gold bullion from a Swiss antiquities dealer.'

'Who the fuck are you?'

'United Nations Special Detective Roger Sherwood.'

'That sounds like gibberish to me.'

'Ten gold bars that were to be used as payment for a frieze of devas taken from the temple of Ta Prohm in Siem Reap, Cambodia.'

'War booty rightfully belongs to the conquering army. That army just happened to be that of my commanding officer.'

'General Hun Monirith, who because you made him rich, allowed you for seven years to play cowboys and indians. Commanding officer of the King Voar regiment. Activated April 2010 under the royal patronage of King Norodom Sihamoni. A cavalry unit composed entirely of orphans, and every one of them here in Melbourne right now.'

'Are they just?'

'I do wonder what they're all doing here. They can't have *known* that your father was going to die when they arrived, all in the same week. Perhaps they're here to work for you, though that would be illegal, given they're Cambodian nationals on tourist visas.'

'Irrumator, what *is* your point?'

'Where were you at 11am last Monday?'

'In my room at the Hotel Bastogne.'

'Overlooking the Collins Street branch of the Commonwealth Bank.'

'Fucking the concierge.'

'Her former boss told me. Mr Grieve, you are a war criminal.'

'General Grieve.'

'According to Article 19, section 24, of the United Nations Declaration of the Rights of The Wealthy there's a world war going on, and I have reason to believe that you, according to paragraph three of that section, have committed an unlawful act in that war.'

'Which, dicksock, act would that be?'

'All in good time, Mr Grieve.'

'General.'

'Good day.' United Nations Special Detective Roger Sherwood bowed his head and withdrew.

As Hector and Elvis returned to their car Hector said, 'Where the *fuck* did he come from? And did he come to my father's funeral solely to inform me that I'm being investigated as a war criminal?'

'It is convenient for the narrative, sir.'

'I reckon so. Now was he a mental patient or is that shit for real? That's not possible is it?'

'I'll look into it, sir.'

'We need to get rid of this gold. And we need to get rid of this money.'

2

Hector and Elvis stepped from Bridge Road into Cupcakes' Jewellers & Pawn.

They said hello to Groucho's distant niece and Risotto's step-grandmother—the salesgirl leaning on an elbow halfway along a glass display case. Elvis said, 'Is Mikey in?'

She lifted her phone with her head—they seemed to be invisibly fixed to one another—towards the back of the store. The door to his office was open. A laptop played a song warning against the pursuit of waterfalls. Elvis knocked on the inside wall and Mikey stood from his laptop and paperwork and closed the door behind them.

With a slow and immediately unimpressed gaze Hector took in the clutter of the office as Elvis took a chair. There was an abundance of maroon memorabilia for what appeared to be an American football team; half a dozen posters of the same three barely-dressed women; a large photograph of a cheekily winking man who looked very much like the jeweler—and who was wearing precisely the same uniform, though without decorations, in which Hector now sat.

A watch with a band of silver mesh clanked at his wrist as Mikey sipped from a tumbler of orange fluid. 'I already know what this is about.'

'What's it about?' said Hector.

'The cop.'

'What cop?'

'He came by yesterday, United Nations. What the hummus have you guys done?'

'It's a mix up,' said Elvis. 'But Mikey, listen, we need to move more gold.'

'*More* gold? Not bullion. Elvis, tell me it's not bullion.'

'It's bullion,' said Elvis.

'How much more?'

'Twenty-eight million,' said Hector.

'Oh, frick off!' said Mikey.

'There's a million in it for you if you get it done,' said Hector.

'A million?' Mikey pulled a pink pocket square from the breast of his suit and wiped the sweat from his cheeks. He lifted the bottom of his glass high and finished all but its ice.

'What are you drinking? Is that Fanta?'

'With whipped vodka.'

'That's not a manly drink,' said Hector, repulsed.

'Well it's all I drink, so shut up. Here's how it goes down. I'll change the fifty-six million, on one condition. There's a million in it for me, but if I get extradited to the States, I get two. Deal?'

'We need it by the end of the week.'

'Oh, frick you, are you fricken serious? Elvis, is this psychopath for real?'

'I am fucking serious, Cupcakes. A million, and two if you get extradited. I'm not telling you how to do this, I'm telling you what needs to be done. Your genius figures out the how.' Hector rose and rebuttoned his jacket.

'All right,' said Mikey in a high-pitched exhalation. 'I'll get it done. Toy until then.'

'What?'

'Toy till then.' Mikey moved his waving hand from the pair of uniforms to the door of his office.

'What the fuck are you saying?'

'Until then. Toy.'

'What the fuck does toy mean?' said Hector, exhausted. 'Oh I don't give a millenial's foreskin of a fuck. None of you people speak English anymore.'

'Thinking of you. Toy, until then.'

Hector stopped at the doorway and slowly turned his head. He lifted his top lip toward his nose and began instantly to heave his breaths. He and Mikey locked stares. Hector was a foot taller than him. Mikey folded his arms and tapped a gold-ringed finger at his bicep and lifted his eyebrows.

'Get it done,' said Hector, looking down his nose.

Walking to their car Hector said, 'Assemble the men. Tomorrow, 1700 hours. Bopha Devi. I've found our war, Elvis. Greed no more shall those oppress who by the wayside fall. Soldiers again, one last time. Each of the King Voars is a finger, and when I close my hand they become a fist. Operation Nibelung. We're going to free this race of enslaved dwarves. We're doing good with this money.'

3

That night Hector went to Helen's for dinner.

They ate several courses of disguised potato and after a dessert made of sugar, cream, and potato, Hector sat with his laptop on his knees on the bench in her front yard. A Ford Falcon, deformed from its evening ram-raid, smouldered across the street

'Done.'

'What's done?'

'Check your bank account.'

Helen pulled out and tapped at her phone. Soon her head darted towards it, then up to Hector. 'Hector?' she said warily. 'What have you done?'

'What?' he grinned.

'How?' she said with more than a hint of sternness. 'And why?'

'Let's go.'

'Let's go where?'

'You're all set. We can go.'

'What do you mean, Go? Go where?'

'Anywhere. Like we talked about.'

'Hector,' she said, in the same disappointed tone she used when David was being obtuse. '*We* never talked about going anywhere. *You* talked about it, and all I said, again and again, was No.'

'Then say yes. You've got money.'

'You can't just throw money at a problem and expect it to be fixed.'

'I'm not throwing money at a problem, I'm throwing it at you. To throw money at the problem would be to reform all of Gladstone Park. For that I'd need an internment camp and a team of trigger-happy Navy SEALS. You've got the money, everything's solved. We can both get the fuck out of here.'

Helen closed her eyes and lifted her head to the cold and cloudy darkness of the evening sky. Gently she wiggled her head upon her neck. Hector had become to her a sadly irrational agent, a silly little boy who might as well have been asking her for a second date after having had the door slammed in his face on the first. For weeks now he had been by deluded increments losing the esteem in which she always held him. His intellect now seemed to her small, deluded—even pathetic.

'Hector, please listen to me. No. … OK? No. … I have a son. That son is in school, here. I have a grandmother. She lives here, in my house, with me, and I am caring for her. In my home, Hector. I have a home. I will not go away with you. That phrase doesn't even sound real when I say it. "Go away." It's a catchphrase, a fantasy. Something Peter Pan says to Wendy. "Let's go away",' she said in a high American accent. 'It has no—. Where, Hector? This isn't a James Bond movie. We can't just "go away for a while" and drink pina coladas on a beach. I have a child and a family and a home. I have a life.'

'I would never drink a pina colada. We go to Sicily, Helen. Have you been?'

'You need to listen to me. Please. *Have* you lost your mind? What is going on up there?' She put a fingertip to his forehead. 'Are you listening to the words that I am saying to you? Or are you hearing only what you desperately want to hear?'

'You said, that if you didn't have a mortgage you'd come away with me.'

When?!' said Helen, her voice raised by impatient disbelief. "When did I say that? Seriously! When did I say that?'

'You definitely said that.'

'I did not ever say that, Hector! To anybody!'

'If you never said it then why do I think that you said it? I'm not just making things up. Will you at least think about it? You have a million dollars in your bank account. A million. You know I'm in love with you, I always have been. And I know that you love me too.'

'I don't, Hector.'

He looked into her eyes. They seemed beadier than he remembered. 'Helen. You're angry because I *may* have misconstrued the exact precise nature of a few of our discussions. I admit that. But you have a million dollars in your bank account. Whatever you want, you can have. Whatever you want to do, you do. The world is yours. And I have many more times that. I'd even be willing to move back to Russia with you.'

Helen's pronunciation became biting. 'What the fuck are you talking about?!'

'I said, I'd even be willing to move back to Russia with you.'

'What do you meeaaan, move back to Russia!?' She stood and almost shouted. 'I've never been to Russia. I've never lived in Russia. I'm Lithuanian, and I was born here, you psychopath. We're not nineteenth century émigrés. "Move back to Russia?" What's going on in your head?!' She again tapped his forehead with her fingers. 'My home is here. This is my *home*. Do you understand that word? With David and my grandmother and with my job and my friends.'

'You call that gaggle of vulgar hairdressers your friends? The value of friendship depends on the quality of the people. Wouldn't you rather be alone with me in Russia than in Gladstone Park with those people for friends?'

Helen put the tips of her fingers to her own temples and looked at her feet. 'Alone with you in Russia?' she whimpered. 'Hector, I don't even—. *What* the fuck? Listen to me, OK? My one wish for you, is for you to find somebody who you *can* run away with. Somebody whose life is as sadly delusional as yours, so that you can both run away to Russia together and live happily ever after. In a cottage made of lilacs and rainbows. That's what I want for you.'

'You know I hate rainbows, that's mean.'

'Oh, I'm sorry, is it mean? Did I just tell you that your whole life is pathetic?'

'Yes.'

'And what have you told me every time we've hung out in the last month?'

'That there's a way out of your life. And I've just given it to you. We could move to America if you wanted. Or Italy. We could compromise. Croatia's half Russian, half civilised. You people love Croatia, the islands and the sailing.' Helen's hands moved from the sides of her head to its front. Into them she buried her face then shook it as though she was scrubbing it with a towel. 'Or not. You can pick where we go if you want. Not Sicily? Have you been, Helen? Oranges the size of your head.'

'Hhhhector,' said Helen, smiling at him in deranged disbelief. 'I'm sorry. I don't know what else to tell you. I don't know *how* else to tell you. You're not listening to me. No.'

'No?'

'No.'

'No to Croatia?'

'I will not come away with you,' she said, raising again her voice and her head to the sky. 'Ever. To *anywhere*!'

Helen's cheeks appeared to Hector to have grown chubby. Her

neck now seemed almost too thin for her head. The softness of her hair had definitely coarsened. 'You've become an uninspiring person.'

'Fuck you.'

'Fuck you too. Look around. Can you hear that? That's Arabic. This is a foreign country now. Arabic! It's the East, Helen. A Grecian Rome. It's Constantinople about to become Istanbul, 1452. Can you hear the burnouts? You live in literally the arsehole of the world's arsehole. This suburb is a cloaca. A chute into which falls the shit and the piss of humanity, and voluntarily you live here.'

Is it, lonely up there? In the towering clouds of delusion? Where the only people who share your weird ideas about running away to the nineteenth century are the six Cambodian orphans who *have* to do as you tell them because apparently they're your soldiers. I can't even imagine how sad that must be for you.'

'The King Voars *are* the last, but there'll be others. I'll have children. Sons. The men will have sons. We'll multiply.'

'You'll multiply? Like gremlins? You're going to repopulate the world are you? With what? Child soldiers, Hector? That's a war crime. You know that right?'

'Wouldn't it make you feel young to have dreams again?'

'No it wouldn't. But you *do* make me feel inadequate. You *do* make me feel small and pathetic and looked down on. You *are* mean, you *are* delusional, you come to my house for dinner and all you do is make fun of what we eat—'

'You only ever eat potatoes.'

'You're an arsehole, Hector Grieve. An enormous balding arsehole. It was endearing when you were a funny arsehole, and when I was an equal part of your funny little arsehole world, but—'

'I'm not balding am I?'

'But you don't see me on equal terms. You see me as something in need of curing, like I have a disease. And that's just mean.'

'Gladstone Park is the disease.'

'In need of rescuing? I'm not a princess in a tower, Hector, and it's condescending to be treated like one. It's cruel, and it's made you somebody I don't want to spend my time with. Please leave.'

'I'll go. But when I leave for good in a couple of weeks, you'll come with me, yes?'

For a few manic seconds Helen shook her head with frenzied eyes. Then she shouted: 'Are you even fucking kidding me?!'

Hector stood and made to put his hands on her shoulders. She broke for the front door and, still shaking her head, went inside.

Hector watched over his shoulder as she ascended the garden path. In the east a burst of AK-47 fire rattled into the night air; in the west, screams and a violent avowal in Turkish. He sat and crossed his legs and pouted his bottom lip and raised his eyebrows in a surprised shrug at how dramatically ungrateful had been her reaction to his gift. 'Angry.'

4

At 1655 the next day Hector and Elvis stood with gloved hands at their backs before the car park at the bottom of the laneway which rose to Bopha Devi, to Newquay Promenade, to *The Rhinegold.*

Hector Grieve's chin was raised, his eyes beneath the rim of his steel helmet scanning the traffic of passing cars beyond the empty lot. His two silver stars shone gold in the low sunlight.

Shortly an army-green Humvee tore off the street and came to a halt across two parking spaces. Out of it fumbled a tall and thin young woman in white fur. She held a pink-shirted chihuahua in one arm as she in stilettos went around to the rear of the car. Then its driver hopped out and took off very large sunglasses.

Somnang 'Groucho' Wales. The name he held at the orphanage; the name bestowed upon him by the regiment, the name he chose for himself upon passing King Voar training—a year-long ordeal of horsemanship, toughness, and elocution. Wales he selected after the exemplary outlaw, Josey. Groucho he was given partly because his disposition was grumpily un-Cambodian, partly because he was once caught painting onto his face in lieu of the facial hair which his people cannot grow, a moustache. His shoulder tattoo—which each successful recruit chose and was given at their induction banquet—was that of the screaming Eastwood poster, upon which when intoxicated beyond his waking brain's capacity the regiment always drew a thick line of greasepaint.

'What the fuck happened to your face?' said Hector when it was close enough for him to inspect. 'Did you rob a beehive?'

'We started botox yesterday,' Groucho mumbled.

Hector turned a confused ear. 'You what?'

'We started botox yesterday,' he seemed to repeat.

'I'm sorry. We started botox yesterday, *what?*'

'We started botox yesterday, sir.'

'That's right. Now are you trying to fucking tell me that you started botox yesterday?'

'Part of our youth regimen. Sir.'

Hector flicked his forehead at the girl. 'Who the fuck is she?'

'That's Yersinia. Yersinia, General Grieve.'

'Is she Russian?' said Hector, his ear still turned and lowered, his teeth ever-clenching.

'From Moscow.'

Hector glared at him. His breathing began to race. He darted his eyes between the young woman and Groucho's unmovable face. Her lips were like balloons swollen with sand; her thin hair fell in translucent noodles to the ermine of her collar. 'Groucho?'

'Sir?'

'Form rank.'

'Of course, sir.' Groucho saluted and put his hand in the woman's as he stepped to.

Hector's eyes bulged. 'Somnang!'

'Sir?'

'Not with the Mongol. This is a classified mission, soldier. Good fucking God, have you lost your mind? No whores. And definitely no fucking chihuahuas. Tell her to go shopping. Tell her to go and find a fucking baby to sacrifice.'

'Of course, sir.' Groucho mumbled quietly to the woman until she leaned down to kiss his bulbous lips. She was handed his sunglasses and squinted angrily at Hector as she left. Hector pointed his eyebrows in at the centre and bared at her his lower fangs. He looked across at his oldest soldier and glowered with an infuriated frown. Soon the low and disturbingly loud rumble of a car's engine returned his ire from Groucho to the car park.

A Lamborghini of light orange and unpolished grey seemed to hover across the asphalt as it came to rest beside Groucho's Humvee. Shortly its driver's side door was raised rather than opened.

Porn 'Risotto' Skywalker. Orphaned as a two-year old and interred by his village, having grown up on his own country's bland incarnation of rice he was in Grieve's mess hall so astounded by what the Italians did with it that within two months of his discovery his uniform would not fit and no horse could under him gallop. Newly chubby, the regiment pounced and the name stuck. Skywalker he selected because his resolution to lose the weight exactly coincided with his first viewing of *The Empire Strikes Back.* Luke's apprenticeship, and in particular his master's dictum, 'Do or do not. There is no try,' had seen him through both his diet and his training; his tattoo was of the exhausted padawan with Yoda in his backpack.

Risotto walked around to the passenger side and lifted its door and pulled from the car a wicker basket lined with a Hello Kitty blanket.

'That had better not be a fucking chihuahua,' said his commanding officer.

'Please,' said Risotto. 'What do you think of the car? What does it remind you of?' Hector Grieve was too busy seething at the machine to consider what it reminded him of. 'An X-wing!' Risotto enthused. 'See the doors? It's like an X-wing, right? I got it in republic orange. And look.' Risotto saluted with one hand and in the other presented to Hector the contents of the basket.

'What the fuck is it?' said Hector, impatiently

He moved aside a fold of the blanket and from it emerged a large yellow eye and a long ridged forehead and scaly snout. A tiny head rolled from side to side as a three-clawed hand appeared, then another. The creature opened its mouth and gave a sinister smile of tiny incisors before letting out a long squeal. 'What the fuck is that?'

'It's a velociraptor,' said Risotto.

'I don't understand. What the fuck is it?'

'What do you mean?'

'Well I *think* it's an animatronic toy.'

'It's a velociraptor.'

'A toy velociraptor?'

'No, it's real. A company in Sydney breeds them.' Hector leaned in to inspect the animal. He moved the blanket further aside. He promptly had his knuckle bitten. 'Careful!' said Risotto. 'They're very expensive.'

Hector stared at him and soon said, 'Did you learn nothing from Jurassic Park?'

'What do you mean?'

'Velociraptors are very fucking dangerous.'

'No!' Risotto scoffed. 'That was a movie! Look at how cute she is.'

'Why didn't you buy something harmless? Why didn't you get a brontosaurus?'

'Do you know how much a brontosaurus costs to feed? They're enormous.'

'This is going to turn into a killing machine. In six months it'll be stalking children through kitchens.'

'It won't! I'll train it!'

'Did you not see number four? They're prehistoric animals, Risotto, you can't train them.'

'Relax!'

'Relax?' said Hector, returning and relowering his furious ear.

'Sir. Sorry, sir.'

'Put it back in the car. We have work to do.'

'I can't leave it in the car, sir. It'll overheat.'

'It's a reptile, Porn. A prehistoric fucking reptile, it'll be fine in the car for an hour. Put it in the car and form rank.'

Reluctantly Risotto said, 'Yes, sir. I'll just crack the window.' He returned the basket to the passenger seat and cracked the window and lowered its door. He formed rank beside Groucho as the whirring thud of rotor blades sounded from over an apartment building behind them. All ignored their turning beat until it loudened and seemed to hover in the same position. First Groucho, then Risotto, then Elvis—at last a simmering Hector Grieve, looked up and beheld a helicopter slowly descending on the carpark. They turned their heads and shielded their eyes with their forearms as gravel and dust swept out in low plumes from its skids. It crunched against the asphalt as it touched down and the rotor mast's high pitch lowered to silence as its three blades drooped and the cockpit's glass door was pushed out.

Oudom 'KFC' Samcolt. The sisters at his orphanage had rescued the very young tuk-tuk driver from that uniquely Cambodian mafia by presenting to Hector Grieve a display of his uncanny driving abilities—pleaded that his skill as a driver would translate to riding prowess—and ambivalently he was accepted. He chose Samcolt because his favourite gun was the 1894 Winchester, which he thought was designed by Samuel Colt. At his induction banquet he mistook an image of Colonel Sanders for a likeness of the inventor and the erroneous tattoo was too good an opportunity for the regiment's wit to ignore. So he became KFC. Though determined in his reasoning, KFC was often mistaken in his nomenclature.

'Flying lessons, soldier?' said Hector. 'This is how you spend your fucking money?'

'Oh no,' said KFC as he took off his headset. 'She's all mine.'

Hector closed his eyes. 'Don't tell me you bought a helicopter.'

'And a vineyard!' KFC raised an unopened champagne bottle. 'We're importing grapes from Pol Roger. The first Cuvée Samuel

Colt will be ready to harvest in two years.'

'For fuck's fucking sake. Form rank, KFC. God damn it.' Hector took the corked bottle that was offered him and threw it into the car park. 'A week you've had money and you've already turned into a ffff…' But he broke off. He had no wish to insult the soldiers who had for so long served him with the utmost dedication to duty, and who had done so with such glorious success. He huffed out a breath through his nose and shook his head and resumed his wide stance and high chin.

Then there sounded, twice and long from the end of the laneway behind them, a high horn. A boat had stopped in view of their formation. Standing at the railing of its deck were two men, one skinny, one very fat.

Teng 'Pangolin' Tomhanks. Softly spoken at school and always kind to his carers, whether it was his widely set eyes or the curvature of his neck or his insistence on sporting a scaly-looking haircut—and probably a combination of all three—he just looked like a pangolin, that ancient and harmless creature by the world's stupidity endangered. He chose his last name because in training it had been pointed out to him that every one of his favourite movies starred the same actor. He was at first disbelieving. Only after the putting of two televisions side by side and the freeze-framing of two close-ups could Pangolin be convinced that the same man was both Viktor Navorski and Captain Miller. Pleasantly surprised and instantly adoring, his tattoo was of Woody from *Toy Story*, about whose voicing he still had his doubts.

Pangolin in fluorescent sunglasses raised both his arms and with one hand palmed from the other a shower of hundred dollar bills. Green strips of plastic rose and fluttered in the wind. When the entirety of his wad had been dispersed over the quay he jumped off the boat and landed on both feet. His fat companion attempted to do the same and fell forwards, somersaulting twice before recovering.

'Who the fuck is this?' said Hector when the pair had descended the laneway.

'This is Jonah Hill.'

'Who the fuck are you?' said Hector.

'Hi, I'm Jonah Hill,' he said in a husky voice. He took off a pair of large sunglasses and reached in to offer Hector his hand.

'He's met Tom Hanks. Isn't that awesome?'

'Yeah, I met Tom on SNL, we worked together. No big deal.

It's really cool to meet you guys too though.' He chewed gum with a widely opening mouth. 'Hector, right? Penguin's told me a lot about you. You sound like a cool dude, I'm looking forward to hanging out with y'all.' He gave a long and high and throaty laugh then took in the uniforms of the men arrayed before him. 'You guys shootin' Saving Private Penguin or somethin'?' He repeated his chortle and smiled and dusted a hand down over his Hawaiian shirt. 'Can I be like the jolly guy who dies kinda near the end, like three-quarters of the way through? Not the coward though. I always hated that guy. Upham. Am I right?'

Hector withdrew the longer of his Peacemakers and held it to the man's forehead. 'You can die now if you'd like.'

'Woah, woah, woah.' Mr Hill put his palms in the air. 'I'm only kiddin', man. All good. I'm good. You good? Are we good? 'Cos I'm cool. Are you cool? We're cool, right? Penguin, you wanna step in here? This is like a real situation, you told me your boys were cool.'

'Pangolin does not step in on any situation of which his superior officer is in command. Back the fuck up, fat boy. Get back on your boat.'

'My boat,' said Pangolin. Hector's head drooped instantly.

'Your boat?'

'My boat.'

'For fucking fuck me's fucking god damn *fucking* sake.'

'Jonah, maybe it's best if you go and wait on the boat.'

'Yeah man!' said Mr Hill. 'I'll wait on the boat. Don't wanna step on Walt Eastwood's grumpy button. Cool uniform, brah,' he said, pointing at the regiment as he backed away. He turned and put his hands in the pockets of his pink shorts and returned to the boat.

'Pangolin, form rank.' Hector shook his head as he turned and retook his position before the car park. His men reformed beside him and waited in the heat of latening day.

At last there strolled around the corner the youngest and greenest King Voar.

Leap 'Jerusalem' Dvarapala. Though the amputee uncles of the newest and youngest King Voar could not afford to take care of him, he had spent his weekends away from the orphanage riding—at first on water buffalo, then on an ageing mare which they inherited from another village—out into the fields to help his extended family plow and herd. In training he spent most of his free time studying the lives and campaigns of Godfrey de Bouillon and Guy de Lusignan and the various Tancreds of Hauteville. Free from any defects of vanity and apparently unmockable by the jest of his regiment, they bestowed upon him the nickname, Jerusalem. At graduation he chose Dvarapala, Khmer for 'Defender of Holy Places,' and his left arm was tattooed with the lotus-crowned guardian from the temple of Banteay Kdei with its broadsword pointed between its feet.

Jerusalem presented himself to Hector Grieve and saluted with his black cap—its shimmering argent shield and crossed sword—low over his eyes. Hector held the salute at his helmet and looked around for ostentatious displays of wealth or dishonourable wastes of money. Satisfied that there were none, he said, 'Thank you, soldier,' and lowered his hand.

Jerusalem completed the rank. Elvis called, 'Atteeen-hut!' Five boots sounded against the footpath as legs were brought together and the King Voar regiment came to attention. 'Right... turn!' And shortly they were in the main dining room at Bopha Devi.

'Operation Nibelung,' said Hector, standing before the blank wall again serving as projector screen.

He was twenty minutes explaining the strategies, tactics, and objectives of what would be their final mission in Australia. He explained at some length the dangers that they as men might face in this new mode of warfare and concluded with an outline of the sacrifices that might be needed in order to gain their objectives.

His men sat thereafter in uneasy silence.

'Sir?' said Groucho, eventually raising a doubtful hand.

'What?'

'Sir, I just umm...'

'You just what?'

'I don't know,' Groucho mumbled.

'You don't know what? I've just told you everything you need to know.'

'Yeah, I just... Well, I can't really leave the chihuahua with Yersinia for very long.'

'What?'

'I don't trust her, I think she beats the dog.'

'I can't leave Roxanne alone for longer than an hour,' said Risotto.

'Who the fuck is Roxanne?'

'The velociraptor.'

'You can't leave your pet velociraptor alone for longer than an hour?'

302

'She has to be hand fed every 90 minutes and *I* have to do it so that we form the bond that allows me to train her. Sir.'

'I have a mortgage,' said Pangolin. 'Sir. What if we get caught? How will I pay the mortgage on the boat if I go to prison? Legal costs as well? And if I get shot? Medical bills.'

'You have a mortgage?'

Pangolin nodded.

'Will we back by 2 o'clock?' said KFC.

'What?'

'On Thursday. Will we be back by 2 o'clock? I have a flying lesson Thursday afternoon.'

'Will we be back by 2 o'clock?' said Hector.

'If we're back by 2, I can do it no problem.'

'I don't know if we'll be back by two, Oudom. This is war.'

'It does all sound very risky, sir,' said Pangolin. 'Dangerous too.'

'And some of it actually sounds kind of mean,' said Groucho.

'Of course it's fucking dangerous, Teng. You can't make war safely. I hope to Christ you're all playing some kind of elaborate prank on me here.' Hector looked his men over and waited for them to smile, to betray a grin, to let slip a titter. None did. He looked to Elvis at the rear of the room. Elvis shook his head and shrugged his shoulders. 'Jerusalem?'

'With you a hundred percent, sir. The ancient ideals of manhood must be striven for. The end is glorious, the striving cannot but be worth it.'

'Are the rest of you fucking serious? You're not are you? Groucho, tell me you're joking. After six years?'

'Honestly I think she abuses the dog,' Groucho mumbled between barely flappable lips. 'She's hot but she *is* Russian. I came home from yoga yesterday and the dog was shaking in the corner. She said she didn't do anything, but I've seen her kick it before. I don't want to expose him to that, it's mean, he's only a puppy. God knows what psychological defects he'll suffer if he's exposed to violence while he's young.'

Hector snapped his unprecedentedly furious gaze to each of the four young men who were pleading for a reprieve from Operation Nibelung. None cracked so much as a corner of a smile. Hector scowled. The end of his nose turned downwards, the corners of his frown reached almost beyond his chin; his eyes bulged and the right corner of his right eyebrow shot all the way to his hairline. Groucho seemed to say, 'Jesus,' at just how infuriated his commanding officer's gaze was. 'Take a chill pill.'

Hector growled, then almost snarled. He heaved short deep breaths. Shortly he said softly, 'You all make me sick.' His voice rose as he erupted. 'You've had money for a week and not only have you wasted half of it on fucking bullshit—ridiculous fucking bullshit—but you've decided to abandon your duty as soldiers, and as men. You give up soldiering for what? For money? Money!? Of all things. The money with which you could all be doing nothing but good. But no. A helicopter. You sagging little salad tosser, a helicopter.'

'And a vineyard.'

'You shut the fuck up.'

'Free champagne, sir,' KFC pleaded.

'You shut the *fuck* up! You, a dinosaur. An actual real-life dinosaur. This is valuable to you? How much can that even have cost? And a boat, Teng, after all I've done for you. *And* you hire a court fucking jester to come and mock everything we stand for, all that we've achieved. Somnang Groucho Wales. My oldest soldier. Six years of campaigning at my side. And with the Grey Rider on your shoulder. "If you lose your head and give up, then you neither live nor win." And here you are, a part of the lunatic productivism of the day. With a fucking mail-order bride and a Chihuahua.'

'And a mortgage,' said Groucho. 'We bought a house. In Westmeadows! We'll be neighbours.'

'Like fucking fuck we will.'

'We're going to look at bathroom tiles on the weekend, you should come!'

Hector yelled in one rapid and gruff mumble: 'All of you shut the glitter-shitting fuck up. I cannot *wait* until your Velociraptor turns on you and bites your face in fucking half. And I hope to God you crash that helicopter into that goddam vineyard, and that you enjoy your little dick jamborees on your boat and that your fat friend leaves his herpes on the toilet seat. And you. My old guard. Your Cossack *will* steal your sperm and she *will* put a spell on it and she *will* steal your organs in your sleep and run you over with her car. And when that happens I hope the four of you remember this day. I hope you remember sitting here beneath the very towers of Angkor Wat.' Hector extended a hand to the painting beside them. 'The City Of The King Of The Angels. Which once counted a hundred and twenty kings under tribute, and put into the field an army of five million—I hope you all remember the day you ceased to be men.

From this day on you may no longer consider yourselves warriors. You are dismissed from the service of His Merciful Excellent Majesty Protector, King Norodom Sihamoni. You are discharged from the Royal Cambodian Army. You are relieved of your commission as soldiers of the King Voar regiment.'

Hector strode through the square beam of projected light and tore the triangular patch of red, yellow, and blue, from Groucho's shoulder. He tore their insignia from Pangolin's, from KFC's, from Risotto's—and flung them into the centre of the room and spat on the floor.

'Scatter yourselves, and be unremembered. May nothing grow that is by your hands sown. Get the fuck out of my site you bunch of she-hes, or I'll feed your livers to a monkey-eating eagle. All of you. Get the fuck out.'

Jerusalem and Elvis rose slowly from their seats. Their former brothers-in-arms looked at one another with wide eyes and eventually accepted that they had no choice but to obey their final order. They stood and slumped and filed out of the function room. Jerusalem and Elvis watched as the size of their regiment fell to three.

Hector stood to attention and raised his hand to salute. The remnants of his army did likewise. He snapped his hand back to his side and said, 'As long as I can raise my voice I will do so against the infatuated madness of the day.

'Chahik si chahiks. Men of men.

'Let's do this shit.'

Chapter Three

NIBELVNG

1

The whole festive intersection of Collins and Spencer Streets muggy with Christmas heat, Leap 'Jerusalem' Dvarapala strode up from King Street with his Thai police cap pulled down low over his eyes.

Trams dinged and taxis sounded impatient horns as beneath an afternoon sky bright with cloud Hector S. Grieve ascended north from the river and pulled his own cap down over his head. Pointed at its middle, with krabi sword and circular shield shimmering as whitest silk on darkest black, its sixteen royal akson letters—taken so long ago as a trophy of war—Hector had adopted the cap as the official uniform for the few taking part in Operation Nibelung. Elvis now descended from Batman's Hill with his head bowed, looking up under his own black brim.

All three King Voars lugged at their sides two blue duffle bags, fully stuffed. They looked up as they approached the intersection and saw by one another's arrival that the synchronisation of their watches had been precisely effective. They looked coldly back down at the pavement. When they each on the same step hit their marks they dropped the bags and turned left and hastened away.

The sight of two identical bags left unattended on a street corner set on edge those pedestrians who had witnessed their abandonment. All who had seen a drop froze and quickly found one another's frightened eyes. The spectacle of a behatted figure hastily fleeing the scene tipped a couple of them over. A montage of explosions from American movies flashed across their distrustful minds. They shrugged their shoulders, shook their heads, mouthed to one another, 'Really?' Two concerned citizens held out their arms and widened their stances and told everybody to stand back. Somebody used the phrase, 'suspicious package,' then someone the word, 'bomb.'

One woman screamed. Another shrieked, 'Terrorists!' and when another yelled, 'Run!' then instantly obeyed her own command she was followed by a panicked teenage boy, then a flock of young mothers pushing strollers at a sprint to get their babies out of harm's way. A stampede quickly worked itself up as each individual ran as fast as they could with laden arms, all hoping to save as much as possible of the Christmas shopping to which they had devoted their day.

The soldiers calmly reached their appointed markers and slid a hand into the pockets of their jackets. Without hesitation or backwards glance they hit their detonators.

Three loud bangs, the third slightly delayed, were followed by a chorus of terrified shrieks. Most dropped to the ground. Some in an instinctive gesture of self-preservation-through-sacrifice shielded the backs of their heads with their shopping bags.

When neither heat was felt nor blood spilled, the panicked and the fleeing eventually dared to slowly turn their heads. They beheld a fluttering shower of oversized rectangular confetti.

The moustachioed face of General Sir John Monash spun with Dame Nellie Melba's in falling leaf-clouds of green. The warm wind caught the higher reaches of the money and dispersed it over the open intersection. Slowly rose they who had hit the footpath; in disbelief turned they who had fled; in smiling glee did all who had bolted return to the scene of the atrocity.

Some jumped high to catch falling bills; others bent low to hurriedly gather what had already landed. Before the window of a franchised café two hands reached for, but only one obtained, a shred of vulgar shrapnel.

'I saw that first,' said the young woman who had failed to procure it.

'There's absolutely no way you can back that claim up,' said a young man, shuffling it into the bills already stacked between his fingers and opposable thumb.

'Give it to me.'

'I picked it up, it's mine.'

'But I saw it first.'

'Look… *you* have a handful of hundred dollar bills, *I* have a handful of hundred dollar bills. How can there possibly be an argument here?'

The woman stared at the young man—he gaunt with brown hair draped at his nipples beneath the almost-absent collar of a v-necked t-shirt—she dumpy with short hair and a grey moustache. Presently she snapped her hand at his wad and managed to snatch from it two banknotes.

'What the fuck, lady?'

'Don't you call me a lady,' said the woman. 'That's a sexist word, used to impose your bigoted ideas of femininity.'

'What?!'

'How would you like it if I called you a gentleman?'

'I'd like that a lot!' He snatched back to retrieve his money, then made an unsuccessful grab for the greater part of her haul.

Then a man in a suit, hitherto backing slowly towards the quarrel, turned and grabbed both their handfuls and sprinted off. 'Now look what you've done,' said the mammothy young woman.

'Look what *I've* done?!' said the petite young man.

And all of it but petty cash compared to the donations of Operation Nibelung, Phase 2.

2

On the pretext of meeting with a very wealthy potential new donor Elvis set a meeting with the Victorian Minister for Health.

Littleton van Herpen lunched at Hector's invitation in the wooden warmth of La Cacciatora. Beneath crossed and mounted Risorgimento muskets and paintings of Calabrese pheasant hunters they drank etna rosso and took square slices from a metre of pizza.

'Humilitotyn,' said Hector, when very shortly into the meeting he grew bored of the man's verbal dysentery.

'Expensive,' said van Herpen, a goatish-looking man who spoke and smiled as though he were constipated.

'Two hundred Australians die each year because they can't afford it.'

'Mm hm?'

'Should an Australian die because they can't afford medicine? Is that the Australian way, van Herpen? What kind of country lets its subjects die because they can't afford medicine? What *is* money to a nation of rich people?'

'A course of Humilitotyn costs ninety thousand dollars and has a twenty percent chance of remission. The average peripheral T-cell lymphoma patient is fifty-eight years old, with an APFEC of seven hundred and seventy thousand dollars.'

'A what?'

'Average potential future economic contribution. That's a cost-benefit factor of 0.117, Mr Grieve. Too low. We're an economy of incomes, not a commonwealth of people. A PFEC of 7.7k against a CBF of 0.117 is simply *not* a priority for the current government.'

Hector stared at the man with a brow whose furiousness could not by jagged wrinkles be adequately conveyed. Sitting opposite him, Hector thought, was the quintessence of immorality. Were he not integral to Operation Nibelung Hector might have shot him then and there, as he had often seen done in films. He calmed himself and thought of the mission and of his father. 'I want to subsidise Humilitotyn.'

'Impossible.'

'It's not impossible, you unshaven shitsack. Listen to me.' Van Herpen stopped chewing and raised his head to stare down Hector's insolence. 'I want to personally subsidise it. For a year. Two hundred patients at ninety thousand dollars a course. I'll donate half that, nine million, if you get the drug subsidised by Medicare.'

'Mmm?'

'What do you mean, Mmm?'

'Why should I?'

'Why should you what?' said Hector, by the question alarmed. 'Why should you save the lives of two hundred Australian subjects?'

'What's…' van Herpen began, then folded a crust and stuffed it into his mouth. '…in it for me?'

'You shamefully, *shamefully*, untrimmed labia. Have a fucking listen to you.'

'The clinical trials of Humilitotyn have been found by the ARGPM to be inconclusive.'

'Irrumator, do you know what is not inconclusive? My resolve to hold a gun to your head. And to tell you, that either your brains or your signature will end up on the bill that proposes the subsidisation of Humilitotyn. "What's in it for you?" Get it done. And you'll receive as a token of your country's immense gratitude, four hundred thousand dollars. You Pakistani dicksplash.'

'I'll see what I can do.'

Hector threw his napkin onto the table and rose to loom over the politician. 'You do that.' He grinned and shook his head before turning to walk out of the restaurant.

3

Next day, Hector was on the schoolside end of the four adjacent basketball courts of Gladstone Park Secondary College. A whole-school assembly had been called—its purpose the announcement to the student body of its largest ever private endowment. In battle dress and garrison cap Hector had his fists clenched at his knees upon a chair of hard green plastic. The principal, whose acquaintance Hector had made the afternoon before, took the rickety podium of gathered tables and announced the alumnus.

'Good morning teachers and students,' she, a crotchety-looking woman with a blonde-grey perm, beamed. 'Today's guest has asked that no introduction be given for him. But I would ask that a round of applause might be appropriate.'

To the sarcastic clapping of 1500 students Hector Grieve rose and stood in the wind before a black microphone and its stand. He waited until the congregation's palm-tapping quietened.

'This school was a piece of shit.' The 1454 children who were not paying attention now paid so. 'My chief reflection upon Gladstone Park Secondary College as an educational institution has always been, "What would my life have been like if I had have gone to *any other school?*" That tradition, of academic disappointment and intellectual damage, of de-inspiration and expectation lowering, ends with you.

'I think you'll all agree that little else compares in exhilaration to the galloping of a horse through open countryside. Naught compares in splendid intimacy to the timeless bond between rider and mount. No greater moulding of one's sense of discipline is known, than that of working up a warhorse to thrive in battle.

'As well, fewer human examples can be considered greater than those set by the heroes of the Greek and Roman Republics. No more moral instruction can be needed, than that given by the noble words and martial deeds of the unconscious founders of our own ancient civilization.

'So it is, yes as an ingrate, but also as somebody who would not wish his education upon even his own brother's adopted foreign hermaphrodites, that I announce the founding of this school's first ever Classics Department, and the opening of the Gladstone Park Secondary College Riding School For Young Ladies and Gentlemen.'

Elvis hit play on the PA system beside the stage. The *Kaiser Waltz* frolicked across the yard. Shoed hoof erupted onto asphalt as six gray stallions—their tails full and long and their riders in breeches and bicorn hats—cantered from the canteen out onto the basketball courts. They separated into two lines and sidepassed their way around the students, watched all in awed confusion.

One young lady rose instantly from being cross-legged on hard ground. She convulsed her way through the assembly and spun with flailing arms at its edge.

'Hazel King!' said the principal, stepping in front of Hector to screech into the microphone. 'Hazel King! Please sit down!'

But the girl could not by command nor warning be from dancing deterred.

The horses were ridden to the rear of the adolescent congregation and obediently and precisely they formed a guard between its last row and the water bubblers affixed to the gymnasium. Elvis faded the music to an indistinct frolic. On danced Miss Hazel King, to her own beat now, and with redoubled vigour.

'The traditions...' said Hector, loudly so as to redraw the crowd's attention, 'of the Spanish Riding School in Vienna reach as far back as Xenophon, the Athenian soldier-historian who wrote The Art of Horsemanship.'

And so Hector Grieve commenced a speech which surpassed by half the length of his funeral oration and by nine-tenths its incomprehension.

Then began Phase 3.

4

The Hume Islamic Youth Centre in Coolaroo—that iconic suburb, adjacent to Gladstone Park, in which Dale and Darryl Kerrigan are reputed to have lived and battled—from which had issued forth fatwas authorising demonstration killings and the beheading of atheists, whose premises had been for a decade of intense interest to state, federal, and international surveillance—counted among its attendees that Hashim al Katab who had grown up on Khartoum Crescent and who had once planned with four fellow Ethiopians to storm a Sydney military base and there kill as many soldiers as possible—and whose refugee sister had been in primary school taught to read by Hector S. Grieve—this cynosure of love and nucleus of joy, which counted among its speakers not only world-renowned advocates of rape, stoning, and jihad, had also very recently been proud host to an Englishman whose deportation followed the broadcasting of his smiling advocacy of the death-penalty for homosexuals.

So it was with an unsettled relish that Hector S. Grieve, Sros 'Elvis' Rath and Leap 'Jerusalem' Dvarapala watched from the

Turkish restaurant across the street as *Ta'zeer*—the pop-up gay bar launched and promoted by a creative agency very much in the employ of the King Voar regiment—prepared for its opening night.

Olivia Newton John was very loudly singing, *You're The One That I Want*. Purple neon pulsated from within and from without. Disco lights through the dusk whirled across the carpark in front of a halal butcher's shop, a hijab emporium, a hookah lounge. The first Ubers arrived. From them stepped the social media influencers whose attendance had been bribed by the promise of free and unlimited cocktails. As they in their straps and strips of leather crossed the grey concrete a procession of fecund mothers drew their several prams to a stop and watched over yashmaks the appearance of revelry. Under their breaths they to one another in Arabic cursed. This quickly rose to uncomprehended abuse. Soon one lifted her veil and spat on the ground. An influencer in policeman's hat and chaps meowed and said to his companion, 'Camels spit, darling.' Then at the cardboard palm trees which formed an archway over the bar's entrance he lowered his head and went inside.

'They're going to be *so* mad,' Hector smiled as he and his men sipped at coffee and ate baklava.

The bar filled up; the mob rose both in number and indignation. Enormous teenagers, emerging from their workouts in the adjacent gymnasium, joined with folded arms the crowd of moustachioed children and bearded cleric. Four men in lingerie and peacock feathers got out of a limousine and laughed with one another along the footpath. They stepped through the break in the low hedge which turned to the car park. Their laughter halted as their saunter broke and they stared back at a crowd of juvenile bicep, maternal monobrow, priestly hatred. The boyfriend of one of the influencers flapped a pinky in a gesture of kindly greeting. Several wads of mucus slapped the ground in response. The shortest of the men almost sang: 'A glittering evening to you all!' A shoe hit him in the face. 'Eww,' he said and rolled his eyes. 'That's *so rude*.'

Then four teenagers stepped forward from the assembled crescent and confronted as though in a mirror the befeathered men. Pectorals were tensed all around, shoulders put back, triceps by fists thrust forward. Something of a staring contest commenced. Then one of the men, in very little besides his boyfriend's underwear, reached out to tweak the half-showing nipples of his opposite. 'Lighten up, Aladdin,' he trilled, and was punched in the face. He shrieked and fled and was followed inside at a frolic to the relative safety of like-minded numbers.

'This is going to be a bloodbath,' said Hector. 'Let's get the fuck out of here.'

5

Hector sat with his ankles up on the iron windowsill of the vast living room of a rented high-rise penthouse. Its floor-to-ceiling windows looked out over the horrible city, down to the harbour and *The Rhinegold* at anchor below. His seven-and-a-half-inch Peacemaker was across his thighs. He clenched in his teeth an audibly smouldering Cohiba and read Clausewitz until Elvis crossed the carpeted floor and dropped a folded newspaper onto his pages.

The media had finally caught up. Public suspicions were mounting of a direct link between the Commonwealth Bank Raid and the avaricious brawl which for three hours had shut down the intersection of Spencer and Collins Street—the 'heinous display of economic terrorism which led immediately to mob violence and would in the long run only lead to inflation'—and which had cost the taxpayer three million dollars in policing.

John J. Grieve, despite the melodramatic mourning of his father's death and an increasingly obsessive attachment to his plush mermaid, had managed to keep up his linguistic diarrhea—that spurting of fluid-like opinion which had two years in a row made him Melbourne's most prolific journalist. He took for granted the connection between the theft of the billionaire's gold and the detonation of the cash.

Hector rolled his eyes and shook his head as he read.

'*A breakdown in civility. … No greater crime than a war crime. … The wealthy who make this country great. … Heroes to us all. … Attack on their enormous contribution to Australian prosperity. … Against the peaceful workings of a global democracy…*'

'Turn it over,' said Elvis, taking his morning coffee from a cup and saucer at Hector's shoulder.

Hashim al Katab, that person for whom Hector's brother had for months been broadcasting his fast and prayers of protest, had penned an article from his prison cell. He too was certain of the link.

Hector rolled his eyes and shook his head as he read.

'*A great service to humanity. … A profound act of charity. … In defiance of an amoral system of corruption. … No doubt performing zakat. … Closer to its spirit than to any Christian conception of goodness.'*

'God damn it, they think we're Muslims.' Hector turned to restless reflection. 'It's all just noise, Elvis. A high-pitched screeching and a low annoying drone, alternating without end. And none of it actually means anything. Not to anybody who reads it, and not to history. It's the stamp that free men give to destiny that makes history. The resolute individual who knows when and how to strike—not this shit. Not this noise. Noise, Elvis. Detrimental noise. I've got an idea for Nibelung's next phase. A new offensive. Bigger. Much bigger. You ready?'

6

A pair of headlights ascended the gentle rise on Western Avenue, moving at two kilometres above the speed limit. An adult son was steering his own car; his father his passenger.

'Watch the cops here,' said the father. 'They're dynamite.'

The son raised his eyebrows and smiled. Though he had for decades used as words of debilitating overcaution the same meaningless clichés, he knew his father to be a well meaning man. The car's tyres loudened against the asphalt; it passed; its tail-lights became a dwindling red before they made for St George's Drive.

Behind them glowed the blue lights of the torch-like sculpture, its plastic slats emblazoned with the white words *The Age*. A security guard leaned out of his booth's window and took the parking ticket from the last worker to leave for the night. He hit the button to raise the candy-striped boom, waved the driver goodbye, returned to his pornographical magazine. Beside him, beyond a car park, was the enormous blue-grey factory that printed each day's edition of the tabloid of which John J. Grieve was so babbling an employee.

At last the only human consideration in the manoeuvre, the security guard was watched through binoculars from the darkness across the street as he fell slowly to sleep. There was a window at his back that might shatter. Soon his eyes closed and his head fell against it. He began to snore. The vibrations of his throat became so intense that they closed it—his eyes shot open and he bolted to upright. He attempted to shake off the drowsiness that had already garnered him two written warnings. He stood up and stepped down out of the booth—at last away from the potentially fatal window—and put a cigarette in his mouth. Eventually he found the pocket in which he had last deposited his lighter. He ground its wheel once and was given only a spark. He put his left hand around his right and moved them to the end of his cigarette in order to shield it from any breeze. As he swiped his thumb a second time the enormous building at his back, that printing house behind the booth in which he was no longer sitting, very loudly exploded.

Hector Grieve's grinning squint, Elvis' glistening quiff of hair, the shimmering embroidery of Jerusalem's cap—were lit up all by enormous clouds of red inferno, risen over Westmeadows.

7

There Hector Grieve was again, his ankles on the windowsill, staring out at the thousands of golden- and yellow-lit windows of the high-rises, at the domestic insurance company logos, the Arabic kingdoms, the Communist corporations—at a dull blue sky. His larger Colt Single Action Army was on his knees, that gift given to him by Mel Gibson as gratitude for a week of partying, riding, and battle. A book was open at his thighs. The same creative agency that had masterminded the thirty minutes of partying which had been gotten in before Ta'zeer was set on fire had that morning placed a thousand copies of Plutarch's *Lives* in the branded newspaper bins which dotted the footpaths of the CBD. Hector was rereading Cato's life in his own new copy when Elvis came in from the study and said, 'Sir.'

'What now?'

'The television.' Hector turned his head and Elvis switched on the unnecessarily gigantic screen that had come with the penthouse. He changed channels until he found a press conference being given by Stephen Balqis, Federal Minister for Trade and Investment. The shutter and flash of journalist cameras flourished as he spoke.

'So we announce today the passing of the Ivory Levy, a one-off payment to be given by all Australians at the end of this financial year, to assist in repaying the money lost to terrorism and war crimes, and as a gesture of immense gratitude to the hard-working men and women who make and keep this country great. And rich.'

'Is he fucking serious?' Hector turned further his head to direct an astonished ear at the screen. 'He's making us pay for it? My fucking God.'

'There's something you should see.' Elvis stood at the window and handed Hector a pair of binoculars. Hector rose and looked down to the direction of Elvis' pointing finger. Hector could see on the deck of *The Rhinegold* the boat's owner in the sun with Carbuncle Tempest and Hiram Semenov. On the wooden table before which they were reclined, champagne and silver plates of helmeted honeyeater were arrayed. He recognised immediately United Nations Special Detective Roger Sherwood. Then he saw that all encircled the honourable Stephen Balqis, Federal Minister for Trade and Investment.

'Those little motherfuckers.'

'The levy's only half of it, sir.'

'What?'

'The levy's to pay the billionaires back for the money we stole. They're also reimbursing the insurance companies that have to pay out for the stolen gold. Balqis has arranged to do *that* by selling cattle runs in the Northern Territory to the Chinese government.'

'I'll kill him.'

'And it *does* get even worse.' Elvis' teeth were clenched. He knew the meagre limits of his old friend's temper. He looked around the penthouse for any laden plates that might be flung.

'What?'

Finding no culinary projectiles, Elvis handed Hector a copy of the newspaper whose printing factory they had not yesterday blown up. He pointed to a headline that read, 'Progress On Rare Cancer Drug.' Hector read aloud as he skimmed. '*Minister For Health... Seeking extra funding to continue subsidising Humilitotyn. ... Money so far raised by private benefactor... used on translating websites and information pamphlets into 150 languages.*

'That little motherfucker. A hundred and fifty languages? We speak English in this country. They can't pay for the fucking drug because they've spent all my money on a thousand scattered tongues? God fucking damn it.' Hector searched the room for a plate of food. 'What kind of world have I come home to? I want you to get the story out that van Herpen was bribed. Do that, then I've got another idea for Nibelung.'

'What is it?'

'Do you *see* that communist chubby chaser down there?'

'Which one, sir?'

'The politician.'

'What about him?'

'I'm going to assassinate him.'

'Sir,' said Elvis in a tone of deep warning.

'What?' Hector was surprised by his aide-de-campe's lack of instant enthusiasm.

'They won't tolerate violent crime.'

'Do you know why?'

'Why?'

'Because those in control want the only way that people can change things to be through the avenues that they themselves control. They can't control violence. They want things changed through politics, because they own the politicians. They want changes brought about through public discussion. Why? Because they control the channels of public discussion. They want things changed via "democracy",' he said, his fingers quoting in the air. 'Because they control the cowardly sloth-birthing elephant-poacher that is the democratic process.'

'Sir, if I may?'

'Please.'

'You're saying that the people dislike violence for the wrong reasons.'

'I am.'

'But you're admitting they don't like it. Regardless, sir, of *why* they won't accept something, that doesn't change the fact that they won't accept it.'

'Elvis my boy, this is war. A war that they have declared, on us. The ancient warriors, we the unconquered souls, transplanted into this feelgood Babylon of economics and foreigners' rights and all-out fucking cowardice. That politician is more than an enemy combatant. He is an enemy commander. He won't fight us in the open, so I'll get him in his mess hall.'

'Sir, it's a bad idea.'

'Maybe so. I am who I am. And people who are not themselves are nobody. We wrap up Nibelung with him. Then we lay low for a while. Sicily. New orders, Elvis. Him. Dead. I'll do it. You and Jerusalem track his movements and find out when he'll be on that boat again. Get me a sniper rifle. Then get the story written that he was a national traitor. Opinion pieces, on selling a country's soil to China being an act of treason. On how selling our uniquely delicate environment to a rice-loving soviet of queue-jumping earth-rapists is out-and-out treason. Get them written, and brief our journalists on when to print them. Make their editors offers they can't refuse. Then you and Jerusalem get yourselves out of Australia. I'll see you on the other side. They need to know that they can't get away with this shit. Not while I'm alive.

'But before I do this I need you both to do me a favour.'

8

Through the northern wing of Gladstone Park Shopping Centre—low-ceilinged and dimly lit and tiled in grimey taupe—Helen Gricius in yoga pants and hot pink shirt carried two handfuls of sagging plastic shopping bags. She passed the podiatrist's, the dentist's, the pharmacist, the superclinic. Automatic doors opened before her and she stepped into the Winfield-smoking huddle of cleft palette and foetal alcohol syndrome, of Ned Kelly tattoos and wheel-carted oxygen tank, heavy-booted plaster-flecked wife-beater and men's ponytails.

A white van sped to the kerb and jolted to a stop in front of her. Frightened by its sudden appearance and relieved that she had not a second earlier stepped onto the road, Helen stood frozen with wide eyes and tried to slow her panicked breath. The van's door slid open and from it sprung a black sack that was swiftly placed over her head. She was very abruptly hugged and she dropped her shopping bags as she was pulled into the van and driven away. Through her disturbing screams Jerusalem cable-tied her hands at her back. He slid off her hood and beheld terrified eyes. He was poised to place a strip of duct tape around her head when she instantly calmed and groaned and rolled her eyes.

'I should have fucking known,' she said, relieved by the familiar notion of green military uniform and Cambodian face.

'I'm sorry, ma'am. Orders.'

'Orders,' she said, tired. 'Don't gag me, I won't scream.'

Helen stormed into Bopha Devi and crossed the crowded restaurant with a pointed finger. 'You had me fucking kidnapped?! Have you lost your fucking mind?!' All diners turned to the confrontation.

'Calm down,' said Hector, standing to greet her. 'I know you're angry. But you weren't kidnapped, so please, calm down.'

'Then what the fuck just happened.'

'It was only so that you'd have dinner with me.'

'You couldn't have just invited me?'

'I didn't think you'd say yes.'

'I wouldn't have. But if I knew that the alternative was being kidnapped…'

'Well now you know.'

'What do you want?'

'Shall I order for us?'

'I'm not eating with you. What do you want?'

'Thirsty?'

'No,' she said, slowly and cruelly.

'OK. Sit down. Please. People are watching.'

'What do you want?'

'I'm going away for a while, next week. I love you. And I want you to come with me.'

'You're a fucking idiot.'

'Why?' said Hector in a high voice. 'Will you please sit?'

'How many times do I have to tell you? God damn it!' Helen turned and strode away from the low table.

Hector said, quickly and loudly: 'There's a guard outside with orders to shoot you! … If you walk out the door, before I do.'

Helen stopped her storming. Her shoulders dropped in a silent sigh. She turned about and sat on the footstool opposite him.

'I'm joking. There's not really anyone outside. Have a spring roll, they're delicious.'

Helen looked at Hector's redolent face. She saw her own youth, and his. He dipped a spring roll in soy sauce and bit half of it off. He smiled and urged her to join him.

'Thanks for sitting down. It means a lot.'

There, between a party of six enjoying several bottles of wine and a couple holding hands, Helen at last felt sorry for him. She smiled serenely. 'What do you want, Hector?'

'I want you to reconsider what we've discussed. Something's about to happen, something big, and I want you to come away with me afterwards.'

Helen pouted with indifference and shook her head. 'Nope.'

'Helen, please.'

'Nope,' she said, giving her head another nonchalant shake.

'You don't take existence seriously do you?'

'I'm not biting, Hector. You can say whatever you want, you are a delusional psychopath. You're not the boy I fell in love with,

319

you've changed. I'm not sure into what. But I don't like it. I don't love it, and I am absolutely never ever going to run away with it.'

'You have one life, Helen. *One* life. And look at what you're doing with it.'

'I have two, Hector. David is my other life. He's entirely my responsibility. No, I have three! My grandma's my responsibility as well. I have three lives, Hector, that I have to consider. *You* have one. *You're* the person who doesn't take existence seriously, because *you're* the person who lives only for yourself.'

'Come away with me.'

'You unhearing idiotic dicknose!'

'We can go to Sicily, I told you. I have to go away for a while.'

'Do you think you're The Godfather, Hector?'

'Whose godfather? David's? I will be if you want me to. Sicily'll do him good. Oranges the size of your head, Helen. Bays as blue as my eyes and mountains that lead to heaven. Twelfth century cathedrals, built by Frederick the second—stupor mundi, the wonder of the world. The Normans, Helen. The very embodiment of the name of action. You said you have three lives. Do this for them. Do this for David. What do you think he'll say in twenty years when he finds out his mother had the opportunity to take him anywhere in the world, anywhere, and she chose to keep him in Gladstone Park?'

'We're not staying in Gladstone Park, Hector.'

'You're not?'

'I bought a house in Westmeadows.'

'*Are* you fucking kidding me?! That's *not* what the money was to be used for. The money was so that you could arrange to look after your grandma so that we could run away together, Helen.'

'There. Is. No. We. Hector! Children, want to run away together. Children, and people who are in love. I am not a child, Hector Grieve, and I am not in love. Not with you, not with anybody. And I am not ever going to run away with you. Enjoy Sicily. I hope it exists. Because if it's in your head, there's a good chance it doesn't. Goodbye.'

9

A ginger-topped blob moved in towards a silver plate and mopped up with bread the last of its orangutan blood. An arm beneath a bald-headed blob extended to the centre of the round table and broke off the last peacock drumstick. The face beneath a blur of black curls—the only at the table in constant line of sight—rotated between a fork which conveyed to it beluga caviar and the thonged buttock at which a hand was squeezing.

Then beneath thin mats of brown-grey hair upon a long-engorged blob, two hands clapped twice.

At this signal three wheelchairs were pushed out from the second-level cabin that opened onto the forward deck. In them sat each a frail figure in green hospital gown. Each wore a plastic wristband and shower slippers and was entirely without hair. Servants conveyed the vehicles to halfway between the sliding doors and the dining table, where violently they lifted the handles to tip the occupants out. The invalids fell frailly onto their hands and knees, revealing to those high above a total lack of underwear beneath tied gown.

The gender of the three patients was in their identically emaciated state undiscernible. With pained effort they rose to their feet. That long-engorged blob now clapped a slow and slobbering beat towards them. The ginger-topped and bald-headed blobs quickly joined her. The blur of black curls removed his hand from the buttock and completed the cruel metronome.

One of the patients began to bounce their head up and down. Another raised their open hands from their sides and moved them in opposite circles. The third leaned gently onto one foot, then rocked gently to the other and back again. The patient bobbing its head soon added a turning of its shoulders. Shortly all moved their painstakingly lifted hands in opposite circles. The tempo of the clapping hastened; the barely-rhythmic movements of the infirm strained to keep pace.

The whole morbid dance was seen, not as through the glass of a sniper rifle, but literally through the glass of a sniper rifle. Hector S. Grieve was prostrate on a grimey concrete rooftop high above it all. He had had for half an hour a clear shot of Stephen Balqis, Federal Minister for Trade and Investment. The entertainments of those on the deck of *The Rhinegold* had been too enthrallingly grotesque to interrupt. Before lunch they had drooled over a performance given upon a turning bed of a tattooed and pot-bellied half-Asian man pounding from behind a kneeling blonde. From Hector's magnified distance of four hundred metres she had not appeared to very much enjoy it. Before that, a fatal bare-knuckle boxing match had taken place between a starving refugee and a middle-class voter. The ensuing arrest of the young Syrian girl had been met with frenzied howls of approval.

Hector watched an amplified Stephen Balqis smile dumbly and bob his gaping head to the enthusiastic beat of his own clapping. Every few seconds he broke rhythm to return to the topless woman whose grabbed arse had gotten him through a course each of peacock, Sumatran tiger, and two of pangolin.

Hector slowed his breathing and ran through the physical extensions and spiritual exercises which assured him that his rifle would by his left hand be accurate strength. He repositioned the butt against his shoulder and put his cheek to its stock and felt the warmth of the midday sun against his temple. The last time he held a sniper rifle he was reconnoitering the Tonle Sap from the stone-littered hilltop of Phnom Krom. The Dragunov he had that day held was the very gun that had shot him through the shoulder, taken with a snigger from the black-bloodied hands of the Russian who fired it. Now, after what seemed like a lifetime of Melburnian boredom he had once again ascended to the madness of action. He lifted his index finger from the trigger and pushed off the safety; relowered his finger and squinted through the scope.

Hiram Semenov and Carbuncle Tempest put their arms around the patients and kicked out their legs as they danced. A drop of sweat beaded at Hector's brow as he for the final time brought the crosshairs back to the table. Balqis laughed and slapped the nearby buttock. Hector waited for the sweat to finish crawling down his forehead.

'I won't let you kill him,' was called through the wind across the fenceless rooftop. In a single movement Hector stood and turned and pointed his rifle at United Nations Special Detective Roger Sherwood. Sherwood held his hands at his sides and said, 'I'm unarmed.'

Hector charged at him. 'Why would you come unarmed?'

'I don't want to kill you, Hector.'

'Then what the fuck are you doing here?'

'The land deal that Stephen Balqis just signed has a projected global worth of 650 million dollars, did you know that? An immediate cash value to Australia's economy of 300 million dollars and a long-term strategic regional value of anything upwards of a billion. He's an invaluable economic unit, Hector. The Ivory Levy he just passed—that man down there, who you're about to shoot—will single-handedly lead to a 0.005 percent rise in growth this quarter. A hero, Hector. An uncommon thing.'

'That all sounded like gibberish.'

'Heroes should be rewarded, don't you think? Not murdered. We speak the same language, you and I. You grew up in Westmeadows. I grew up in Tullamarine. We're from exactly the same place, Hector. And we're the same age.'

'And I can't understand a word of anything you say.'

'Of course you can. Tell me if you agree with this, General Grieve. The first step to greatness is the subordination of our own will to something greater than ourselves. You agree with that, I know you do.' Hector stared down the long barrel of his SR98. 'The greatest and most glorious thing on earth, Hector, *is* the global economy. It's creating wealth and freedom the likes of which the world has never seen. Happinesses we never even thought possible, and I'm telling you—submit to it and greatness will be yours. Embrace the social change demanded by an economy that holds that every person on earth has the right to do and act however she pleases. *Love* the obligation to subordinate that freedom to profit. And you shall, become the hero, Hector, that I know you want to be.

'I've studied your life and work, General. Impressive. I've read your novel, in the English. And I know that your head was in books from the age of sixteen, then you lived in the past for seven years. You missed that crucial period of every consumer's life, where we make it absolutely clear what your economy demands of you. Through no fault of your own you misunderstand the social contract in the modern economy. I understand this about you, Hector, and I sympathise. That's why I'm not here to kill you. I'm not even here to arrest you. I'm here to offer you a way out.

'Give up your ideals. Adopt our ideas. And we'll give you everything you want. You're under investigation for crimes against humanity. You know that, right?'

Hector smiled. 'I thought I was a lowly war criminal.'

'You've been upgraded. Serious stuff.' Sherwood counted out the charges on his fingers. 'Causing inflation by excessive charity. Investing in unproductive economic units—we know about the improvements to your grandmother's nursing home. Wilfully disobeying the free market. If the United Nations can invent sufficient evidence of these crimes you'll be arrested and flown to New York and put on trial for crimes against humanity. Do you know how serious that is? Life in Belgium, Hector.'

'You speak pretty good American,' said Hector, impersonating. 'For a Comanche. Someone teach you?'

'And I have incontrovertible evidence on you for the bank raid. I know it was you. Incredible that something like that could have been pulled off in today's day and age, but I know that only someone like you cold have done it. Victory is to the audacious, right, Hector? But the United Nations Department of Economic Crime knows you did it too.'

'You talk way too much, pee-snorkeller.'

'What's a pee-snorkeller?'

'Someone who snorkels in pee. Ya idiot.'

'We don't want you in prison. You have too much earning potential, we want you out there, in the business world. Think of what you can achieve! I'm *just* like you, Hector. I don't have friends either. Do you know why? Friendship costs the global economy 3 trillion dollars a year. And just like you, I refuse to love anybody but myself. Love *costs* the global economy 2.7 billion dollars a year, did you know that? It's lust. Lust makes the global economy turn. Floristry is now an 87-billion-dollar industry. Three years ago porn finally became a 100-billion-dollar industry. Lust defeats love, it always has—you should be a CEO by now, Hector.'

Hector herded Sherwood around the rooftop, his sniper rifle pointed delightfully at the detective's face. 'I'm a Commander of the Royal Order of Sahametrei.'

'It's you and I, General Grieve, the friendless, hard-working, self-absorbed egomaniac. We alone have the ability and the determination to reach our MEC.'

'A knight of the Guardians of Jayavarman the Seventh.'

'Your maximum earning capacity! I have a house. You could have a house too. Do you know how much *money* you could be earning right now? Today?'

'A Most Honourable Captain of Indra Protector of The East.'

'Three hundred thousand dollars a year!' said Sherwood, as though the figure were an astonishing one.

'A Dharmaraja of the Order of the Leper King and a Restorer of the Eternal Peace of Sangrama.'

'I've done your personality-based employment projection. According to the United Nations Framework on the Proper Education of Consumers you would have been a CEO by now, Hector, if you hadn't missed those all-important years, where you find out that there's nothing left to submit to *but* the global economy.'

'A Teahean of the Dynasty of the Seven Southern Lords.'

'And now, with your intellectual strength and your ability to command, you *will be* a CEO.'

Hector dropped the sniper rifle and kicked it to the ledge at which he had watched the depravations of *The Rhinegold*. 'I'm a Mahasena of the Most Exalted Order of the Lotus Pond. A two-star general in the Royal Cambodian Army.'

'An officer in a corporation, Hector. Not an officer in an imagined army from a thousand years ago, defending an empire that no longer exists.'

Hector unholstered his five-and-a-half-inch Colt Single Action Army and pointed and cocked it at the pretentiously dressed detective. He strode over the rooftop and closed the gap left by Sherwood's backstepping retreat. 'Amid the tempest let me die, you mathematical dick. Torn, in a cloud, by angry ghosts of men. Irrumator, arm, and prepare to acquit yourself like a man, for the day of your ordeal *is* at hand.'

His potential convert had come a little too close for Roger Sherwood's comfort. 'Hector Grieve…'

'General, Grieve. Commanding officer of The Royal King Voar Regiment.'

'As a legally authorised agent of the United Nations Department of Change, I am protected by international law from physical violence. I have the right to a safe and secure working environment. And an assault on an agent of the United Nations Department of Change is as good as an assault on the United Nations Department of Change itself.'

'Agreed,' and Hector punched him in the face.

Sherwood lifted his quivering chin. Blood seeping from his cheekbone, he said, 'You leave me with no choice.' He planted his feet and puffed out his chest. 'Hector Smith Grieve. Tax file number 437473052, bank balance nineteen dollars and forty-five cents, PFEC between thirteen and twenty million dollars. Under Article 19, Section 24 of the United Nations Charter on Crimes Against Humanity, I hereby place you under ar—'

With his ivory-handled Colt Single Action Army, that symbol of the freedom of the city of Siem Reap—Thailand Conquered—given to him by King Norodom Sihamoni of Cambodia, the Peacemaker handled with ivory from the royal hunting grounds,

Hector S. Grieve shot Roger Sherwood in the throat.

Sherwood gasped for air as blood gushed from his jugular. He clutched at his neck and his eyes bulged. His mouth widened as he went sideways to ground.

Hector reholstered the revolver and strode across the rooftop. He dropped to one knee and slammed the butt of the sniper rifle into his shoulder. He sighted Stephen Balqis through its scope. He slowed his breath. He went through the physical extensions and spiritual exercises which assured him his rifle would by his left hand be accurate strength and by his right establish.

With a squeeze of his finger and a single .50 calibre shot, Hector S. Grieve completed his mission.

Chapter Four

GRIEVES AT WAR

A goatherd limped along a ridge. The rusty bells of his flock jangled as it frolicked over pale dirt and russet shrub.

In brown shirtsleeves Hector S. Grieve raised the brim of his Jerusalem cap—its silver embroidery shimmering in Sicilian sun— and wiped with a white handkerchief the sweat streaming down his temples. Behind him the hills ascended like the spines of ancient giants, lying face down with their waists in the water. The taupe and terracotta roofs of the villages turned and twisted in knotted clusters about the hillsides and into the sky Etna rose long and gentle from the sea—her crater puffed with white smoke as though from a cigar, horizontal breaths blown out to the Straits of Messina.

Hector pulled down a strip of peel on an orange that was almost the size of his head. He threw the shred to the earth and worked at removing as much as possible of its pith. With finger and stabbing thumb he squeezed a segment out and slurped its juice as he breakfasted. He sucked the sticky sweetness from his hand and said, 'Salve,' to the goatherd. Ignored, he muttered, 'Irrumator,' as he passed.

The ridge steepened to the right; drab green succulents and straw cactus flowers burst improbably from rock and dirt. He came at last to the purple creeper and the olive trees which almost concealed the narrow stairway rising to the lowest street of Castelmola.

Hector stepped onto the terrace outside the Caffè San Giorgio and caught Aretusa—almond-eyed, full-bodied, black-haired; exquisite in a flowing shoulderless gypsy-blouse of white cotton— crossing from a table upon which she was waiting.

'Ciao, Hector!'

'Principess'! Buongiorno! We a-swim-a this afternoon-a?'

'You are such an idiot,' she laughed. Inside she called out the table's order to the barista. 'Always you are talking like this.'

'But why I am-a idiot-a? This is how-a you talk-a.'

'Hector, this is not how I talk-a, come on!'

'No?'

'No,' she said, then stepped into him and lowered her voice. 'But sometimes is how you make-a me scream-a.'

'Ho!' cried Hector, and closed his eyes and threw his head back with his hands over his heart. 'Turiddu! Ciao!' He shook the hand of the large grey-haired man in shirt and apron behind the coffee machine. 'You believe this woman, T?' Hector handed him an envelope; Turiddu inserted it into the wide pocket of his apron. Anyway-a, Aretusa, we swim-a this afternoon-a?'

'I finish at 3.'

'Isola bella?'

'I see you there.'

'I-a see-a you-a there-a.'

As he did every morning he stood at the terrace's cast-iron balustrade and looked out over the eastward vista—to the cypress trees rising from Taormina, the Greek and Roman amphitheatre high to the north, the Saracen castle taken by Roger I in ruins atop a distant hill.

He had been here before, Hector thought. He recalled fighting Octavian in the name of the extinct Republic; taking a Muslim arrow through the eye as he stormed the castle walls beside Stupor Mundi, Roger II. Hector S. Grieve's warrior soul had returned again to Sicily, here to continue its madness for action.

He wandered up the cobblestone street beside the single-towered Church of St George and came to the piazza which ran under the widely pointed arches of the monastery, now a guesthouse, where Hector's newest operation was to today take place.

Today.

Today was the day.

He had decided upon it the evening before and had risen with undiminished resolve. He had taken his morning walk with no thought but that of the immediate commencement of the task ahead. 'The end is glorious, the striving cannot but be worth it,' he had repeated to himself as he turned in his bed. 'When talent is paired with resolve triumph is inevitable,' he said aloud as he first came into sight of the smoke of Mt Etna—that Monte Bello whose eruptions were said to be caused by Typhon, progenitor of lawless monsters, buried within after Victory implored Zeus to stand up as champion of his own children and so with thunderbolts cut off his innumerable heads; that Mountain Of Vulcan, Placater of Fire, in whose furnaces Hephaestus hammered ore into molten rivers when Venus, his wife, was unfaithful.

At last, as he lowered his head at the stuccoed façade and crossed the monastic threshold there returned to him his father's vocational trinity.

'Do not take counsel of your fears…'

That triumvirate of aphorisms which taken together had not ever failed him.

'God favours the brave…'

Hector said it once as he passed the vacant reception then again as he sat down at the desk at the dining room window which overlooked the ocean—

'Do not take counsel of your fears. God favours the brave. Victory is to the audacious.'

He had been procrastinating for weeks and he knew it. Though he had written every day since arriving he truly was daunted by the task ahead of him. So he had thus far only composed treatises—one proposing a new Reconquista, one on the virtue of anger, and one—by far his favourite—called 'On The Environment', a 10,000-word essay arguing that horses are the solution to man's environmental problems. 'If every man rode a horse instead of driving a car,' he wrote in longhand, 'we'd have no choice but to turn the world back into pasture.'

But today.

Today came the glorious end. The striving could not but be worth it.

He had convinced himself that the recovery of a true and glorious memoir fit indisputably into his fervour for a life of sensation. He was to take up the pen and restore *Grieves At War*, that paean to the noblest pursuit of man by his own brother's hand adulterated. Hector would recover from between the insidious whimpers of a cowardly journalist his grandfather's reverent voice. So would Hector regain the name of action.

From Mildura to Puckapunyal, to Britain to Libya; from Egypt to Tunisia, New Guinea to Borneo—his grandfather's odyssey through war, and the voyages of his brothers, would be expunged of malignant cowardice and repaired to the shining throne from which Hector knew they loudly heralded war, the only place where a man really lives.

He would add to it an account of his father's financial exploits—two decades of fighting monetary oppression from Nigeria to Burma to Nicaragua; of being kidnapped, shot, expelled; and in response liberating, healing, giving shelter.

And he would append to it an account of his own martial service. Seven years of soldiering, protecting on horseback things ancient and dead though still persisting; encircled and overrun, defeated, and ignored. The necessary and lamentable difference between a writer and a man of action troubled Hector Grieve no longer. For a decade he had sought life and had lived it at a thunderous charge. He had striven to exist, even though in pain; risked dying tomorrow if today he could be great; had acted, that he might become king.

He was to today commence the new operation.

He stared down at the urine-stained manuscript. Its title page still read, GRIEVES AT WAR. He uncapped his pen and inserted its end into the lid. He put the title page's bottom corner between his thumb and finger and prepared to peel it off.

Today. Was the day.

In editing, amending, and rewriting the patrimonial words before him Hector had once again found his war. It was to be the work by which he would return the world's head to the direction in which it ought to face.

He had resolved, in the name of lost causes, forsaken beliefs, unpopular names, forbidden loyalties—in the name of exalted human values and the virtue of suffering—in the name of action, of audacity, and in the name of all that in mankind is noblest—to put pen to paper.

He peeled back the title page and put it beside the stacked manuscript.

He had resolved to do so.

And he did.

THE END

Printed in Poland
by Amazon Fulfillment
Poland Sp. z o.o., Wrocław

53617358R00195